VIRAGO

MODERN CLASSICS

492

*Daphne du Maurier*

DAPHNE DU MAURIER (1907–89) was born in London, the daughter of the famous actor-manager Sir Gerald du Maurier and granddaughter of George du Maurier, the author and artist. A voracious reader, she was from an early age fascinated by imaginary worlds and even created a male alter ego for herself. Educated at home with her sisters and later in Paris, she began writing short stories and articles in 1928, and in 1931 her first novel, *The Loving Spirit*, was published. A biography of her father and three other novels followed, but it was the novel *Rebecca* that launched her into the literary strato-sphere and made her one of the most popular authors of her day. In 1932, du Maurier married Major Frederick Browning, with whom she had three children.

Besides novels, du Maurier published short stories, plays and biographies. Many of her bestselling novels became award-winning films, and in 1969 du Maurier was herself awarded a DBE. She lived most of her life in Cornwall, the setting for many of her books, and when she died in 1989, Margaret Forster wrote in tribute: 'No other popular writer has so triumphantly defied classification . . . She satisfied all the questionable criteria of popular fiction, and yet satisfied too the exacting requirements of "real literature", something very few novelists ever do.'

# REBECCA

*Daphne du Maurier*

with an afterword
by Sally Beauman

virago

VIRAGO

Published by Virago Press in 2003

33 35 37 39 40 38 36 34 32

First published in 1938 by Victor Gollancz Ltd

Copyright © The Estate of Daphne du Maurier 1938
Introduction copyright © Sally Beauman 2003

Sally Beauman asserts the right to be identified as the author
of the Introduction to the Work in accordance with
the Copyright, Designs and Patents Act 1988.

A CIP catalogue record for this book
is available from the British Library.

ISBN 978-1-84408-038-0

Typeset by Palimpsest Book Production Limited,
Grangemouth, Stirlingshire
Printed and bound in Great Britain by
Clays Ltd, St Ives plc

Papers used by Virago are from well-managed forests
and other responsible sources.

MIX
Paper from
responsible sources
FSC  FSC® C104740
www.fsc.org

Virago Press
An imprint of
Little, Brown Book Group
100 Victoria Embankment
London EC4Y 0DY

An Hachette UK Company
www.hachette.co.uk

www.virago.co.uk

# 1

Last night I dreamt I went to Manderley again. It seemed to me I stood by the iron gate leading to the drive, and for a while I could not enter, for the way was barred to me. There was a padlock and a chain upon the gate. I called in my dream to the lodge-keeper, and had no answer, and peering closer through the rusted spokes of the gate I saw that the lodge was uninhabited.

No smoke came from the chimney, and the little lattice windows gaped forlorn. Then, like all dreamers, I was possessed of a sudden with supernatural powers and passed like a spirit through the barrier before me. The drive wound away in front of me, twisting and turning as it had always done, but as I advanced I was aware that a change had come upon it; it was narrow and unkept, not the drive that we had known. At first I was puzzled and did not understand, and it was only when I bent my head to avoid the low swinging branch of a tree that I realized what had happened. Nature had come into her own again and, little by little, in her stealthy, insidious way had encroached upon the drive with long, tenacious fingers. The woods, always a menace even in the past, had triumphed in the end. They crowded, dark and uncontrolled, to the borders of the drive. The beeches with white, naked limbs leant close to one another, their branches intermingled in a strange embrace, making a vault above my head like the archway of a church. And there were other trees as well, trees that I did not recognize, squat oaks and tortured elms that straggled cheek by jowl with the beeches, and had thrust themselves out of the quiet earth, along with monster shrubs and plants, none of which I remembered.

The drive was a ribbon now, a thread of its former self, with gravel surface gone, and choked with grass and moss. The trees had thrown out low branches, making an impediment to progress; the gnarled roots looked like skeleton claws. Scattered here and again amongst this jungle growth I would recognize shrubs that had been landmarks in our time, things of culture and grace, hydrangeas whose blue heads had been famous. No hand had checked their progress, and they had gone native now, rearing to monster height without a bloom, black and ugly as the nameless parasites that grew beside them.

On and on, now east now west, wound the poor thread that once had been our drive. Sometimes I thought it lost, but it appeared again, beneath a fallen tree perhaps, or struggling on the other side of a muddied ditch created by the winter rains. I had not thought the way so long. Surely the miles had multiplied, even as the trees had done, and this path led but to a labyrinth, some choked wilderness, and not to the house at all. I came upon it suddenly; the approach masked by the unnatural growth of a vast shrub that spread in all directions, and I stood, my heart thumping in my breast, the strange prick of tears behind my eyes.

There was Manderley, our Manderley, secretive and silent as it had always been, the grey stone shining in the moonlight of my dream, the mullioned windows reflecting the green lawns and the terrace. Time could not wreck the perfect symmetry of those walls, nor the site itself, a jewel in the hollow of a hand.

The terrace sloped to the lawns, and the lawns stretched to the sea, and turning I could see the sheet of silver placid under the moon, like a lake undisturbed by wind or storm. No waves would come to ruffle this dream water, and no bulk of cloud, wind-driven from the west, obscure the clarity of this pale sky. I turned again to the house, and though it stood inviolate, untouched, as though we ourselves had left but yesterday, I saw that the garden had obeyed the jungle law, even as the woods had done. The rhododendrons stood fifty feet high, twisted and entwined with bracken, and they had entered into alien marriage with a host of nameless shrubs, poor, bastard things that clung

2

about their roots as though conscious of their spurious origin. A lilac had mated with a copper beech, and to bind them yet more closely to one another the malevolent ivy, always an enemy to grace, had thrown her tendrils about the pair and made them prisoners. Ivy held prior place in this lost garden, the long strands crept across the lawns, and soon would encroach upon the house itself. There was another plant too, some half-breed from the woods, whose seed had been scattered long ago beneath the trees and then forgotten, and now, marching in unison with the ivy, thrust its ugly form like a giant rhubarb towards the soft grass where the daffodils had blown.

Nettles were everywhere, the vanguard of the army. They choked the terrace, they sprawled about the paths, they leant, vulgar and lanky, against the very windows of the house. They made indifferent sentinels, for in many places their ranks had been broken by the rhubarb plant, and they lay with crumpled heads and listless stems, making a pathway for the rabbits. I left the drive and went on to the terrace, for the nettles were no barrier to me, a dreamer. I walked enchanted, and nothing held me back.

Moonlight can play odd tricks upon the fancy, even upon a dreamer's fancy. As I stood there, hushed and still, I could swear that the house was not an empty shell but lived and breathed as it had lived before.

Light came from the windows, the curtains blew softly in the night air, and there, in the library, the door would stand half open as we had left it, with my handkerchief on the table beside the bowl of autumn roses.

The room would bear witness to our presence. The little heap of library books marked ready to return, and the discarded copy of *The Times*. Ash-trays, with the stub of a cigarette; cushions, with the imprint of our heads upon them, lolling in the chairs; the charred embers of our log fire still smouldering against the morning. And Jasper, dear Jasper, with his soulful eyes and great, sagging jowl, would be stretched upon the floor, his tail a-thump when he heard his master's footsteps.

3

A cloud, hitherto unseen, came upon the moon, and hovered an instant like a dark hand before a face. The illusion went with it, and the lights in the windows were extinguished. I looked upon a desolate shell, soulless at last, unhaunted, with no whisper of the past about its staring walls.

The house was a sepulchre, our fear and suffering lay buried in the ruins. There would be no resurrection. When I thought of Manderley in my waking hours I would not be bitter. I should think of it as it might have been, could I have lived there without fear. I should remember the rose-garden in summer, and the birds that sang at dawn. Tea under the chestnut tree, and the murmur of the sea coming up to us from the lawns below.

I would think of the blown lilac, and the Happy Valley. These things were permanent, they could not be dissolved. They were memories that cannot hurt. All this I resolved in my dream, while the clouds lay across the face of the moon, for like most sleepers I knew that I dreamed. In reality I lay many hundred miles away in an alien land, and would wake, before many seconds had passed, in the bare little hotel bedroom, comforting in its very lack of atmosphere. I would sigh a moment, stretch myself and turn, and opening my eyes, be bewildered at that glittering sun, that hard, clean sky, so different from the soft moonlight of my dream. The day would lie before us both, long no doubt, and uneventful, but fraught with a certain stillness, a dear tranquillity we had not known before. We would not talk of Manderley, I would not tell my dream. For Manderley was ours no longer. Manderley was no more.

# 2

We can never go back again, that much is certain. The past is still too close to us. The things we have tried to forget and put behind us would stir again, and that sense of fear, of furtive unrest, struggling at length to blind unreasoning panic – now mercifully stilled, thank God – might in some manner unforeseen become a living companion, as it had been before.

He is wonderfully patient and never complains, not even when he remembers . . . which happens, I think, rather more often than he would have me know.

I can tell by the way he will look lost and puzzled suddenly, all expression dying away from his dear face as though swept clean by an unseen hand, and in its place a mask will form, a sculptured thing, formal and cold, beautiful still but lifeless. He will fall to smoking cigarette after cigarette, not bothering to extinguish them, and the glowing stubs will lie around on the ground like petals. He will talk quickly and eagerly about nothing at all, snatching at any subject as a panacea to pain. I believe there is a theory that men and women emerge finer and stronger after suffering, and that to advance in this or any world we must endure ordeal by fire. This we have done in full measure, ironic though it seems. We have both known fear, and loneliness, and very great distress. I suppose sooner or later in the life of everyone comes a moment of trial. We all of us have our particular devil who rides us and torments us, and we must give battle in the end. We have conquered ours, or so we believe.

The devil does not ride us any more. We have come through our crisis, not unscathed of course. His premonition of disaster was correct from the beginning; and like a ranting actress in an

5

indifferent play, I might say that we have paid for freedom. But I have had enough melodrama in this life, and would willingly give my five senses if they could ensure us our present peace and security. Happiness is not a possession to be prized, it is a quality of thought, a state of mind. Of course we have our moments of depression; but there are other moments too, when time, unmeasured by the clock, runs on into eternity and, catching his smile, I know we are together, we march in unison, no clash of thought or of opinion makes a barrier between us.

We have no secrets now from one another. All things are shared. Granted that our little hotel is dull, and the food indifferent, and that day after day dawns very much the same, yet we would not have it otherwise. We should meet too many of the people he knows in any of the big hotels. We both appreciate simplicity, and we are sometimes bored – well, boredom is a pleasing antidote to fear. We live very much by routine, and I – I have developed a genius for reading aloud. The only time I have known him show impatience is when the postman lags, for it means we must wait another day before the arrival of our English mail. We have tried wireless, but the noise is such an irritant, and we prefer to store up our excitement; the result of a cricket match played many days ago means much to us.

Oh, the Test matches that have saved us from ennui, the boxing bouts, even the billiard scores. Finals of schoolboy sports, dog racing, strange little competitions in the remoter counties, all these are grist to our hungry mill. Sometimes old copies of the *Field* come my way, and I am transported from this indifferent island to the realities of an English spring. I read of chalk streams, of the mayfly, of sorrel growing in green meadows, of rooks circling above the woods as they used to do at Manderley. The smell of wet earth comes to me from those thumbed and tattered pages, the sour tang of moorland peat, the feel of soggy moss spattered white in places by a heron's droppings.

Once there was an article on wood pigeons, and as I read it aloud it seemed to me that once again I was in the deep woods at Manderley, with pigeons fluttering above my head. I heard their soft, complacent call, so comfortable and cool on a hot summer's afternoon, and there would be no disturbing of their peace until Jasper came loping through the undergrowth to find me, his damp muzzle questing the ground. Like old ladies caught at their ablutions, the pigeons would flutter from their hiding-place, shocked into silly agitation, and, making a monstrous to-do with their wings, streak away from us above the tree-tops, and so out of sight and sound. When they were gone a new silence would come upon the place, and I – uneasy for no known reason – would realize that the sun no longer wove a pattern on the rustling leaves, that the branches had grown darker, the shadows longer; and back at the house there would be fresh raspberries for tea. I would rise from my bed of bracken then, shaking the feathery dust of last year's leaves from my skirt and whistling to Jasper, set off towards the house, despising myself even as I walked for my hurrying feet, my one swift glance behind.

How strange that an article on wood pigeons could so recall the past and make me falter as I read aloud. It was the grey look on his face that made me stop abruptly, and turn the pages until I found a paragraph on cricket, very practical and dull – Middlesex batting on a dry wicket at the Oval and piling up interminable dreary runs. How I blessed those solid, flannelled figures, for in a few minutes his face had settled back into repose, the colour had returned, and he was deriding the Surrey bowling in healthy irritation.

We were saved a retreat into the past, and I had learnt my lesson. Read English news, yes, and English sport, politics, and pomposity, but in future keep the things that hurt to myself alone. They can be my secret indulgence. Colour and scent and sound, rain and the lapping of water, even the mists of autumn and the smell of the flood tide, these are memories of Manderley that will not be denied. Some people have a vice of reading Bradshaws. They plan innumerable journeys across country for the fun of linking up impossible connexions. My hobby is less tedious, if as strange. I am a mine of information on the English countryside. I know the name of every owner of every British moor, yes – and their tenants too. I know how many grouse are killed, how many partridge, how many head of deer. I know where trout are rising, and where the salmon leap. I attend all meets, I follow every run. Even the names of those who walk hound puppies are familiar to me. The state of the crops, the price of fat cattle, the mysterious ailments of swine, I relish them all. A poor pastime, perhaps, and not a very intellectual one, but I breathe the air of England as I read, and can face this glittering sky with greater courage.

The scrubby vineyards and the crumbling stones become things of no account, for if I wish I can give rein to my imagination, and pick foxgloves and pale campions from a wet, streaking hedge.

Poor whims of fancy, tender and un-harsh. They are the enemy to bitterness and regret, and sweeten this exile we have brought upon ourselves.

Because of them I can enjoy my afternoon, and return, smiling and refreshed, to face the little ritual of our tea. The order never varies. Two slices of bread and butter each, and China tea. What a hide-bound couple we must seem, clinging to custom because we did so in England. Here, on this clean balcony, white and impersonal with centuries of sun, I think of half past four at Manderley, and the table drawn before the library fire. The door flung open, punctual to the minute, and the performance, never-varying, of the laying of the tea, the silver tray, the kettle, the snowy cloth. While Jasper, his spaniel ears a-droop, feigns indifference to the arrival of the cakes. That feast was laid before us always, and yet we ate so little.

Those dripping crumpets, I can see them now. Tiny crisp wedges of toast, and piping-hot, floury scones. Sandwiches of unknown nature, mysteriously flavoured and quite delectable, and that very special gingerbread. Angel cake, that melted in the mouth, and his rather stodgier companion, bursting with peel and raisins. There was enough food there to keep a starving family for a week. I never knew what happened to it all, and the waste used to worry me sometimes.

8

But I never dared ask Mrs Danvers what she did about it. She would have looked at me in scorn, smiling that freezing, superior smile of hers, and I can imagine her saying: 'There were never any complaints when Mrs de Winter was alive.' Mrs Danvers. I wonder what she is doing now. She and Favell. I think it was the expression on her face that gave me my first feeling of unrest. Instinctively I thought, 'She is comparing me to Rebecca'; and sharp as a sword the shadow came between us . . .

Well, it is over now, finished and done with. I ride no more tormented, and both of us are free. Even my faithful Jasper has gone to the happy hunting grounds, and Manderley is no more. It lies like an empty shell amidst the tangle of the deep woods, even as I saw it in my dream. A multitude of weeds, a colony of birds. Sometimes perhaps a tramp will wander there, seeking shelter from a sudden shower of rain and, if he is stout-hearted, he may walk there with impunity. But your timid fellow, your nervous poacher – the woods of Manderley are not for him. He might stumble upon the little cottage in the cove and he would not be happy beneath its tumbled roof, the thin rain beating a tattoo. There might linger there still a certain atmosphere of stress . . . That corner in the drive, too, where the trees encroach upon the gravel, is not a place in which to pause, not after the sun has set. When the leaves rustle, they sound very much like the stealthy movement of a woman in evening dress, and when they shiver suddenly, and fall, and scatter away along the ground, they might be the patter, patter, of a woman's hurrying footstep, and the mark in the gravel the imprint of a high-heeled satin shoe.

It is when I remember these things that I return with relief to the prospect from our balcony. No shadows steal upon this hard glare, the stony vineyards shimmer in the sun and the bougainvillaea is white with dust. I may one day look upon it with affection. At the moment it inspires me, if not with love, at least with confidence. And confidence is a quality I prize, although it has come to me a little late in the day. I suppose it is his dependence upon me that has made me bold at last. At any rate I have lost my diffidence, my timidity, my shyness with strangers. I am very different from that self who drove to Manderley for the first time, hopeful and eager, handicapped by a rather desperate gaucherie and filled with an intense desire to please. It was my lack of poise of course that made such a bad impression on people like Mrs Danvers. What must I have seemed like after Rebecca? I can see myself now, memory spanning the years like a bridge, with straight, bobbed hair and youthful, unpowdered face, dressed in an ill-fitting coat and skirt and a jumper of my own creation, trailing in the wake of Mrs Van Hopper like a shy, uneasy colt. She would precede me in to lunch, her short body ill-balanced upon tottering, high heels, her fussy, frilly blouse a compliment to her large bosom and swinging hips, her new hat pierced with a monster quill aslant upon her head, exposing a wide expanse of forehead bare as a schoolboy's knee. One hand carried a gigantic bag, the kind that holds passports, engagement diaries, and bridge scores, while the other hand toyed with that inevitable lorgnette, the enemy to other people's privacy.

She would make for her usual table in the corner of the restaurant, close to the window, and lifting her lorgnette to her small pig's eyes survey the scene to right and left of her, then she would let the lorgnette fall at length upon its black ribbon and utter a little exclamation of disgust: 'Not a single well-known personality, I shall tell the management they must make a reduction on my bill. What do they think I come here for? To look at the page boys?' And she would summon the waiter to her side, her voice sharp and staccato, cutting the air like a saw.

How different the little restaurant where we are today to that vast dining-room, ornate and ostentatious, the Hôtel Côte d'Azur at Monte Carlo; and how different my present companion, his steady, well-shaped hands peeling a mandarin in quiet, methodical fashion, looking up now and again from his task to smile at me, compared to Mrs Van Hopper, her fat, bejewelled fingers questing a plate heaped high with ravioli, her eyes darting suspiciously from her plate to mine for fear I should have made the better choice. She need not have disturbed herself, for the waiter, with the uncanny swiftness of his kind, had long sensed my position as inferior and subservient to hers, and had placed before me a plate of ham and tongue that somebody had sent back to the cold buffet half an hour before as badly carved. Odd, that resentment of servants, and their obvious impatience. I remember staying once with Mrs Van Hopper in a country house, and the maid never answered my timid bell, or brought up my shoes, and early morning tea, stone cold, was dumped outside my bedroom door. It was the same at the Côte d'Azur, though to a lesser degree, and sometimes the studied indifference turned to familiarity, smirking and offensive, which made buying stamps from the reception clerk an ordeal I would avoid. How young and inexperienced I must have seemed, and how I felt it, too. One was too sensitive, too raw, there were thorns and pin-pricks in so many words that in reality fell lightly on the air.

I remember well that plate of ham and tongue. It was dry, unappetizing, cut in a wedge from the outside, but I had not the courage to refuse it. We ate in silence, for Mrs Van Hopper liked to concentrate on food, and I could tell by the way the sauce ran down her chin that her dish of ravioli pleased her.

It was not a sight that engendered into me great appetite for my own cold choice, and looking away from her I saw that the table next to ours, left vacant for three days, was to be occupied once more. The *maître d'hôtel*, with the particular bow reserved for his more special patrons, was ushering the new arrival to his place.

Mrs Van Hopper put down her fork, and reached for her lorgnette. I blushed for her while she stared, and the newcomer, unconscious of her interest, cast a wandering eye over the menu. Then Mrs Van Hopper folded her lorgnette with a snap, and leant across the table to me, her small eyes bright with excitement, her voice a shade too loud.

'It's Max de Winter,' she said, 'the man who owns Manderley. You've heard of it, of course. He looks ill, doesn't he? They say he can't get over his wife's death . . .'

11

# 3

I wonder what my life would be today, if Mrs Van Hopper had not been a snob.

Funny to think that the course of my existence hung like a thread upon that quality of hers. Her curiosity was a disease, almost a mania. At first I had been shocked, wretchedly embarrassed; I would feel like a whipping boy who must bear his master's pains when I watched people laugh behind her back, leave a room hurriedly upon her entrance, or even vanish behind a Service door on the corridor upstairs. For many years now she had come to the Hôtel Côte d'Azur, and, apart from bridge, her one pastime which was notorious by now in Monte Carlo, was to claim visitors of distinction as her friends had she but seen them once at the other end of the post-office. Somehow she would manage to introduce herself, and before her victim had scented danger she had proffered an invitation to her suite. Her method of attack was so downright and sudden that there was seldom opportunity to escape. At the Côte d'Azur she staked a claim upon a certain sofa in the lounge, midway between the reception hall and the passage to the restaurant, and she would have her coffee there after luncheon and dinner, and all who came and went must pass her by. Sometimes she would employ me as a bait to draw her prey, and, hating my errand, I would be sent across the lounge with a verbal message, the loan of a book or paper, the address of some shop or other, the sudden discovery of a mutual friend. It seemed as though notables must be fed to her, much as invalids are spooned their jelly; and though titles were preferred by her, any face once seen in a social paper served as well. Names scattered in a gossip column, authors, artists, actors, and their kind, even the mediocre ones, as long as she had learnt of them in print.

I can see her as though it were but yesterday, on that unforgettable afternoon – never mind how many years ago – when she sat at her favourite sofa in the lounge, debating her method of attack. I could tell by her abrupt manner, and the way she tapped her lorgnette against her teeth, that she was questing possibilities. I knew, too, when she had missed the sweet and rushed through dessert, that she had wished to finish luncheon before the new arrival and so install herself where he must pass. Suddenly she turned to me, her small eyes alight.

'Go upstairs quickly and find that letter from my nephew. You remember, the one written on his honeymoon, with the snapshot. Bring it down to me right away.'

I saw then that her plans were formed, and the nephew was to be the means of introduction. Not for the first time I resented the part that I must play in her schemes. Like a juggler's assistant I produced the props, then silent and attentive I waited on my cue. This newcomer would not welcome intrusion, I felt certain of that. In the little I had learnt of him at luncheon, a smattering of hearsay garnered by her ten months ago from the daily papers and stored in her memory for future use, I could imagine, in spite of my youth and inexperience of the world, that he would resent this sudden bursting in upon his solitude. Why he should have chosen to come to the Côte d'Azur at Monte Carlo was not our concern, his problems were his own, and anyone but Mrs Van Hopper would have understood. Tact was a quality unknown to her, discretion too, and because gossip was the breath of life to her this stranger must be served for her dissection. I found the letter in a pigeon-hole in her desk, and hesitated a moment before going down again to the lounge. It seemed to me, rather senselessly, that I was allowing him a few more moments of seclusion.

I wished I had the courage to go by the Service staircase and so by roundabout way to the restaurant, and there warn him of the ambush. Convention was too strong for me though, nor did I know how I should frame my sentence. There was nothing for it but to sit in my usual place beside Mrs Van Hopper while she,

13

like a large, complacent spider, spun her wide net of tedium about the stranger's person.

I had been longer than I thought, for when I returned to the lounge I saw he had already left the dining-room, and she, fearful of losing him, had not waited for the letter, but had risked a bare-faced introduction on her own. He was even now sitting beside her on the sofa. I walked across to them, and gave her the letter without a word. He rose to his feet at once, while Mrs Van Hopper, flushed with her success, waved a vague hand in my direction and mumbled my name.

'Mr de Winter is having coffee with us, go and ask the waiter for another cup,' she said, her tone just casual enough to warn him of my footing. It meant I was a youthful thing and unimportant, and that there was no need to include me in the conversation. She always spoke in that tone when she wished to be impressive, and her method of introduction was a form of self-protection, for once I had been taken for her daughter, an acute embarrassment for us both. This abruptness showed that I could safely be ignored, and women would give me a brief nod which served as a greeting and a dismissal in one, while men, with large relief, would realize they could sink back into a comfortable chair without offending courtesy.

It was a surprise, therefore, to find that this newcomer remained standing on his feet, and it was he who made a signal to the waiter.

'I'm afraid I must contradict you,' he said to her, 'you are both having coffee with me'; and before I knew what had happened he was sitting in my usual hard chair, and I was on the sofa beside Mrs Van Hopper.

For a moment she looked annoyed – this was not what she had intended – but she soon composed her face, and thrusting her large self between me and the table she leant forward to his chair, talking eagerly and loudly, fluttering the letter in her hand.

'You know I recognized you just as soon as you walked into the restaurant,' she said, 'and I thought, "Why, there's Mr de Winter, Billy's friend, I simply must show him those snaps of

Billy and his bride taken on their honeymoon", and here they are. There's Dora. Isn't she just adorable? That little, slim waist, those great big eyes. Here they are sun-bathing at Palm Beach. Billy is crazy about her, you can imagine. He had not met her of course when he gave that party at Claridge's, and where I saw you first. But I dare say you don't remember an old woman like me?'

This with a provocative glance and a gleam of teeth.

'On the contrary I remember you very well,' he said, and before she could trap him into a resurrection of their first meeting he had handed her his cigarette case, and the business of lighting-up stalled her for the moment. 'I don't think I should care for Palm Beach,' he said, blowing the match, and glancing at him I thought how unreal he would look against a Florida background. He belonged to a walled city of the fifteenth century, a city of narrow, cobbled streets, and thin spires, where the inhabitants wore pointed shoes and worsted hose. His face was arresting, sensitive, medieval in some strange inexplicable way, and I was reminded of a portrait seen in a gallery, I had forgotten where, of a certain Gentleman Unknown. Could one but rob him of his English tweeds, and put him in black, with lace at his throat and wrists, he would stare down at us in our new world from a long-distant past – a past where men walked cloaked at night, and stood in the shadow of old doorways, a past of narrow stairways and dim dungeons, a past of whispers in the dark, of shimmering rapier blades, of silent, exquisite courtesy.

I wished I could remember the Old Master who had painted that portrait. It stood in a corner of the gallery, and the eyes followed one from the dusky frame . . .

They were talking though, and I had lost the thread of conversation. 'No, not even twenty years ago,' he was saying. 'That sort of thing has never amused me.'

I heard Mrs Van Hopper give her fat, complacent laugh. 'If Billy had a home like Manderley he would not want to play around in Palm Beach,' she said. 'I'm told it's like fairyland, there's no other word for it.'

15

She paused, expecting him to smile, but he went on smoking his cigarette, and I noticed, faint as gossamer, the line between his brows.

'I've seen pictures of it, of course,' she persisted, 'and it looks perfectly enchanting. I remember Billy telling me it had all those big places beat for beauty. I wonder you can ever bear to leave it.'

His silence now was painful, and would have been patent to anyone else, but she ran on like a clumsy goat, trampling and trespassing on land that was preserved, and I felt the colour flood my face, dragged with her as I was into humiliation.

'Of course you Englishmen are all the same about your homes,' she said, her voice becoming louder and louder, 'you depreciate them so as not to seem proud. Isn't there a minstrels' gallery at Manderley, and some very valuable portraits?' She turned to me by way of explanation. 'Mr de Winter is so modest he won't admit to it, but I believe that lovely home of his has been in his family's possession since the Conquest. They say that minstrels' gallery is a gem. I suppose your ancestors often entertained royalty at Manderley, Mr de Winter?'

This was more than I had hitherto endured, even from her, but the swift lash of his reply was unexpected. 'Not since Ethelred,' he said, 'the one who was called Unready. In fact, it was while staying with my family that the name was given him. He was invariably late for dinner.'

She deserved it, of course, and I waited for her change of face, but incredible as it may seem his words were lost on her, and I was left to writhe in her stead, feeling like a child that had been smacked.

'Is that really so?' she blundered. 'I'd no idea. My history is very shaky and the kings of England always muddled me. How interesting, though. I must write and tell my daughter; she's a great scholar.'

There was a pause, and I felt the colour flood into my face. I was too young, that was the trouble. Had I been older I would have caught his eye and smiled, her unbelievable behaviour

16

making a bond between us; but as it was I was stricken into shame, and endured one of the frequent agonies of youth.

I think he realized my distress, for he leant forward in his chair and spoke to me, his voice gentle, asking if I would have more coffee, and when I refused and shook my head I felt his eyes were still on me, puzzled, reflective. He was pondering my exact relationship to her, and wondering whether he must bracket us together in futility.

'What do you think of Monte Carlo, or don't you think of it at all?' he said. This including of me in the conversation found me at my worst, the raw ex-schoolgirl, red-elbowed and lanky-haired, and I said something obvious and idiotic about the place being artificial, but before I could finish my halting sentence Mrs Van Hopper interrupted.

'She's spoilt, Mr de Winter, that's her trouble. Most girls would give their eyes for the chance of seeing Monte.'

'Wouldn't that rather defeat the purpose?' he said, smiling.

She shrugged her shoulders, blowing a great cloud of cigarette smoke into the air. I don't think she understood him for a moment. 'I'm faithful to Monte,' she told him; 'the English winter gets me down, and my constitution just won't stand it. What brings you here? You're not one of the regulars. Are you going to play "Chemy", or have you brought your golfclubs?'

'I have not made up my mind,' he said; 'I came away in rather a hurry.'

His own words must have jolted a memory, for his face clouded again and he frowned very slightly. She babbled on, impervious. 'Of course you miss the fogs at Manderley; it's quite another matter; the west country must be delightful in the spring.' He reached for the ash-tray, squashing his cigarette, and I noticed the subtle change in his eyes, the indefinable something that lingered there, momentarily, and I felt I had looked upon something personal to himself with which I had no concern.

'Yes,' he said shortly, 'Manderley was looking its best.'

A silence fell upon us during a moment or two, a silence that brought something of discomfort in its train, and stealing a glance at him I was reminded more than ever of my Gentleman Unknown who, cloaked and secret, walked a corridor by night. Mrs Van Hopper's voice pierced my dream like an electric bell.

'I suppose you know a crowd of people here, though I must say Monte is very dull this winter. One sees so few well-known faces. The Duke of Middlesex is here in his yacht, but I haven't been aboard yet.' She never had, to my knowledge. 'You know Nell Middlesex of course,' she went on. 'What a charmer she is. They always say that second child isn't his, but I don't believe it. People will say anything, won't they, when a woman is attractive? And she is so very lovely. Tell me, is it true the Caxton-Hyslop marriage is not a success?' She ran on, through a tangled fringe of gossip, never seeing that these names were alien to him, they meant nothing, and that as she prattled unaware he grew colder and more silent. Never for a moment did he interrupt or glance at his watch; it was as though he had set himself a standard of behaviour, since the original lapse when he had made a fool of her in front of me, and clung to it grimly rather than offend again. It was a page-boy in the end who released him, with the news that a dress-maker awaited Mrs Van Hopper in the suite.

He got up at once, pushing back his chair. 'Don't let me keep you,' he said. 'Fashions change so quickly nowadays they may even have altered by the time you get upstairs.'

The sting did not touch her, she accepted it as a pleasantry. 'It's so delightful to have run into you like this, Mr de Winter,' she said, as we went towards the lift; 'now I've been brave enough to break the ice I hope I shall see something of you. You must come and have a drink some time in the suite. I may have one or two people coming in tomorrow evening. Why not join us?' I turned away so that I should not watch him search for an excuse.

'I'm so sorry,' he said, 'tomorrow I am probably driving to Sospel, I'm not sure when I shall get back.'

Reluctantly she left it, but we still hovered at the entrance to the lift.

'I hope they've given you a good room; the place is half empty, so if you are uncomfortable mind you make a fuss. Your valet has unpacked for you, I suppose?' This familiarity was excessive, even for her, and I caught a glimpse of his expression.

'I don't possess one,' he said quietly; 'perhaps you would like to do it for me?'

This time his shaft had found its mark, for she reddened, and laughed a little awkwardly.

'Why, I hardly think . . .' she began, and then suddenly, and unbelievably, she turned upon me, 'Perhaps you could make yourself useful to Mr de Winter, if he wants anything done. You're a capable child in many ways.'

There was a momentary pause, while I stood stricken, waiting for his answer. He looked down at us, mocking, faintly sardonic, a ghost of a smile on his lips.

'A charming suggestion,' he said, 'but I cling to the family motto. He travels the fastest who travels alone. Perhaps you have not heard of it.'

And without waiting for her answer he turned and left us.

'What a funny thing,' said Mrs Van Hopper, as we went upstairs in the lift. 'Do you suppose that sudden departure was a form of humour? Men do such extraordinary things. I remember a well-known writer once who used to dart down the Service staircase whenever he saw me coming. I suppose he had a penchant for me and wasn't sure of himself. However, I was younger then.'

The lift stopped with a jerk. We arrived at our floor. The page-boy flung open the gates. 'By the way, dear,' she said, as we walked along the corridor, 'don't think I mean to be unkind, but you put yourself just a teeny bit forward this afternoon. Your efforts to monopolize the conversation quite embarrassed me, and I'm sure it did him. Men loathe that sort of thing.'

I said nothing. There seemed no possible reply. 'Oh, come, don't sulk,' she laughed, and shrugged her shoulders; 'after all, I am responsible for your behaviour here, and surely you can accept advice from a woman old enough to be your mother. *Eh bien,*

*Blaize, je viens . . .'* and humming a tune she went into the bedroom where the dressmaker was waiting for her.

I knelt on the window-seat and looked out upon the afternoon. The sun shone very brightly still, and there was a gay high wind. In half an hour we should be sitting to our bridge, the windows tightly closed, the central heating turned to the full. I thought of the ash-trays I would have to clear, and how the squashed stubs, stained with lip-stick, would sprawl in company with discarded chocolate creams. Bridge does not come easily to a mind brought up on Snap and Happy Families; besides, it bored her friends to play with me.

I felt my youthful presence put a curb upon their conversation, much as a parlour-maid does until the arrival of dessert, and they could not fling themselves so easily into the melting pot of scandal and insinuation. Her men-friends would assume a sort of forced heartiness and ask me jocular questions about history or painting, guessing I had not long left school and that this would be my only form of conversation.

I sighed, and turned away from the window. The sun was so full of promise, and the sea was whipped white with a merry wind. I thought of that corner of Monaco which I had passed a day or two ago, and where a crooked house leant to a cobbled square. High up in the tumbled roof there was a window, narrow as a slit. It might have held a presence medieval; and, reaching to the desk for pencil and paper, I sketched in fancy with an absent mind a profile, pale and aquiline. A sombre eye, a high-bridged nose, a scornful upper lip. And I added a pointed beard and lace at the throat, as the painter had done, long ago in a different time.

Someone knocked at the door, and the lift-boy came in with a note in his hand. 'Madame is in the bedroom,' I told him but he shook his head and said it was for me. I opened it, and found a single sheet of note-paper inside, with a few words written in an unfamiliar hand.

'Forgive me. I was very rude this afternoon.' That was all. No signature, and no beginning. But my name was on the envelope, and spelt correctly, an unusual thing.

20

'Is there an answer?' asked the boy.

I looked up from the scrawled words. 'No,' I said. 'No, there isn't any answer.'

When he had gone I put the note away in my pocket, and turned once more to my pencil drawing, but for no known reason it did not please me any more; the face was stiff and lifeless, and the lace collar and the beard were like props in a charade.

# 4

The morning after the bridge party Mrs Van Hopper woke with a sore throat and a temperature of a hundred and two. I rang up her doctor, who came round at once and diagnosed the usual influenza. 'You are to stay in bed until I allow you to get up,' he told her; 'I don't like the sound of that heart of yours, and it won't get better unless you keep perfectly quiet and still. I should prefer', he went on, turning to me, 'that Mrs Van Hopper had a trained nurse. You can't possibly lift her. It will only be for a fortnight or so.'

I thought this rather absurd, and protested, but to my surprise she agreed with him. I think she enjoyed the fuss it would create, the sympathy of people, the visits and messages from friends, and the arrival of flowers. Monte Carlo had begun to bore her, and this little illness would make a distraction.

The nurse would give her injections, and a light massage, and she would have a diet. I left her quite happy after the arrival of the nurse, propped up on pillows with a falling temperature, her best bed-jacket round her shoulders and be-ribboned boudoir cap upon her head. Rather ashamed of my light heart, I telephoned her friends, putting off the small party she had arranged for the evening, and went down to the restaurant for lunch, a good half hour before our usual time. I expected the room to be empty – nobody lunched generally before one o'clock. It was empty, except for the table next to ours. This was a contingency for which I was unprepared. I thought he had gone to Sospel. No doubt he was lunching early because he hoped to avoid us at one o'clock. I was already half-way across the room and could not go back. I had not seen him since we disappeared in the lift the day before, for wisely he had avoided dinner in the restaurant, possibly for the same reason that he lunched early now.

It was a situation for which I was ill-trained. I wished I was older, different. I went to our table, looking straight before me, and immediately paid the penalty of gaucherie by knocking over the vase of stiff anemones as I unfolded my napkin. The water soaked the cloth, and ran down on to my lap. The waiter was at the other end of the room, nor had he seen. In a second though my neighbour was by my side, dry napkin in hand.

'You can't sit at a wet tablecloth,' he said brusquely; 'it will put you off your food. Get out of the way.'

He began to mop the cloth, while the waiter, seeing the disturbance, came swiftly to the rescue.

'I don't mind,' I said, 'it doesn't matter a bit. I'm all alone.'

He said nothing, and then the waiter arrived and whipped away the vase and the sprawling flowers.

'Leave that,' he said suddenly, 'and lay another place at my table. Mademoiselle will have luncheon with me.'

I looked up in confusion. 'Oh, no,' I said, 'I couldn't possibly.'

'Why not?' he said.

I tried to think of an excuse. I knew he did not want to lunch with me. It was his form of courtesy. I should ruin his meal. I determined to be bold and speak the truth.

'Please,' I begged, 'don't be polite. It's very kind of you but I shall be quite all right if the waiter just wipes the cloth.'

'But I'm not being polite,' he insisted. 'I would like you to have luncheon with me. Even if you had not knocked over that vase so clumsily I should have asked you.' I suppose my face told him my doubt, for he smiled. 'You don't believe me,' he said; 'never mind, come and sit down. We needn't talk to each other unless we feel like it.'

We sat down, and he gave me the menu, leaving me to choose, and went on with his *hors d'œuvre* as though nothing had happened.

His quality of detachment was peculiar to himself, and I knew that we might continue thus, without speaking, throughout the meal and it would not matter. There would be no sense of strain. He would not ask me questions on history.

'What's happened to your friend?' he said. I told him about the influenza. 'I'm so sorry,' he said, and then, after pausing a moment, 'you got my note, I suppose. I felt very much ashamed of myself. My manners were atrocious. The only excuse I can make is that I've become boorish through living alone. That's why it's so kind of you to lunch with me today.'

'You weren't rude,' I said, 'at least, not the sort of rudeness she would understand. That curiosity of hers – she does not mean to be offensive, but she does it to everyone. That is, everyone of importance.'

'I ought to be flattered then,' he said; 'why should she consider me of any importance?'

I hesitated a moment before replying.

'I think because of Manderley,' I said.

He did not answer, and I was aware again of that feeling of discomfort, as though I had trespassed on forbidden ground. I wondered why it was that this home of his, known to so many people by hearsay, even to me, should so inevitably silence him, making as it were a barrier between him and others.

We ate for a while without talking, and I thought of a picture postcard I had bought once at a village shop, when on holiday as a child in the west country. It was the painting of a house, crudely done of course and highly coloured, but even those faults could not destroy the symmetry of the building, the wide stone steps before the terrace, the green lawns stretching to the sea. I paid twopence for the painting – half my weekly pocket money – and then asked the wrinkled shop woman what it was meant to be. She looked astonished at my ignorance.

'That's Manderley,' she said, and I remember coming out of the shop feeling rebuffed, yet hardly wiser than before.

Perhaps it was the memory of this postcard, lost long ago in some forgotten book, that made me sympathize with his defensive attitude. He resented Mrs Van Hopper and her like with their intruding questions. Maybe there was something inviolate about Manderley that made it a place apart; it would not bear discussion. I could imagine her tramping through the rooms, perhaps paying sixpence for admission, ripping the quietude with her sharp, staccato laugh. Our minds must have run in the same channel, for he began to talk about her.

'Your friend,' he began, 'she is very much older than you. Is she a relation? Have you known her long?' I saw he was still puzzled by us.

'She's not really a friend,' I told him, 'she's an employer. She's training me to be a thing called a companion, and she pays me ninety pounds a year.'

'I did not know one could buy companionship,' he said; 'it sounds a primitive idea. Rather like the Eastern slave market.'

'I looked up the word "companion" once in the dictionary,' I admitted, 'and it said "a companion is a friend of the bosom."'

'You haven't much in common with her,' he said.

He laughed, looking quite different, younger somehow and less detached. 'What do you do it for?' he asked me.

'Ninety pounds is a lot of money to me,' I said.

'Haven't you any family?'

'No – they're dead.'

'You have a very lovely and unusual name.'

'My father was a lovely and unusual person.'

'Tell me about him,' he said.

I looked at him over my glass of citronade. It was not easy to explain my father and usually I never talked about him. He was my secret property. Preserved for me alone, much as Manderley was preserved for my neighbour. I had no wish to introduce him casually over a table in a Monte Carlo restaurant.

There was a strange air of unreality about that luncheon, and looking back upon it now it is invested for me with a curious glamour. There was I, so much of a schoolgirl still, who only the day before had sat with Mrs Van Hopper, prim, silent, and subdued, and twenty-four hours afterwards my family history was mine no longer, I shared it with a man I did not know. For some reason I felt impelled to speak, because his eyes followed me in sympathy like the Gentleman Unknown.

My shyness fell away from me, loosening as it did so my reluctant tongue, and out they all came, the little secrets of childhood, the pleasures and the pains. It seemed to me as though he understood, from my poor description, something of the vibrant personality that had been my father's, and something too of the love my mother had for him, making it a vital, living force, with a spark of divinity about it, so much that when he died that desperate winter, struck down by pneumonia, she lingered behind him for five short weeks and stayed no more. I remember pausing, a little breathless, a little dazed. The restaurant was filled now with people who chatted and laughed to an orchestral background and a clatter of plates, and glancing at the clock above the door I saw that it was two o'clock. We had been sitting there an hour and a half, and the conversation had been mine alone.

I tumbled down into reality, hot-handed and self-conscious, with my face aflame, and began to stammer my apologies. He would not listen to me.

'I told you at the beginning of lunch you had a lovely and unusual name,' he said. 'I shall go further, if you will forgive me, and say that it becomes you as well as it became your father. I've enjoyed this hour with you more than I have enjoyed anything for a very long time. You've taken me out of myself, out of despondency and introspection, both of which have been my devils for a year.'

I looked at him, and believed he spoke the truth; he seemed less fettered than he had been before, more modern, more human; he was not hemmed in by shadows.

'You know,' he said, 'we've got a bond in common, you and I. We are both alone in the world. Oh, I've got a sister, though we don't see much of each other, and an ancient grandmother whom I pay duty visits to three times a year, but neither of them make for companionship. I shall have to congratulate Mrs Van Hopper. You're cheap at ninety pounds a year.'

'You forget', I said, 'you have a home and I have none.'

The moment I spoke I regretted my words, for the secret, inscrutable look came back in his eyes again, and once again I suffered the intolerable discomfort that floods one after lack of tact. He bent his head to light a cigarette, and did not reply immediately.

'An empty house can be as lonely as a full hotel,' he said at length. 'The trouble is that it is less impersonal.' He hesitated, and for a moment I thought he was going to talk of Manderley at last, but something held him back, some phobia that struggled to the surface of his mind and won supremacy, for he blew out his match and his flash of confidence at the same time.

'So the friend of the bosom has a holiday?' he said, on a level plane again, an easy camaraderie between us. 'What does she propose to do with it?'

I thought of the cobbled square in Monaco and the house with the narrow window. I could be off there by three o'clock with my sketchbook and pencil, and I told him as much, a little shyly perhaps, like all untalented persons with a pet hobby.

'I'll drive you there in the car,' he said, and would not listen to protests.

I remembered Mrs Van Hopper's warning of the night before about putting myself forward and was embarrassed that he might think my talk of Monaco was a subterfuge to win a lift. It was so blatantly the type of thing that she would do herself, and I did not want him to bracket us together. I had already risen in importance from my lunch with him, for as we got up from the table the little *maître d'hôtel* rushed forward to pull away my chair. He bowed and smiled – a total change from his usual attitude of indifference – picked up my handkerchief that had fallen on the floor, and hoped 'mademoiselle had enjoyed her lunch'. Even the page-boy by the swing doors glanced at me with respect. My companion accepted it as natural, of course; he knew nothing of the ill-carved ham of yesterday. I found the change depressing, it made me despise myself. I remembered my father and his scorn of superficial snobbery.

'What are you thinking about?' We were walking along the

27

corridor to the lounge, and looking up I saw his eyes fixed on me in curiosity.

'Has something annoyed you?' he said.

The attentions of the *maître d'hôtel* had opened up a train of thought, and as we drank coffee I told him about Blaize, the dressmaker. She had been so pleased when Mrs Van Hopper had bought three frocks, and I, taking her to the lift afterwards, had pictured her working upon them in her own small salon, behind the stuffy little shop, with a consumptive son wasting upon her sofa. I could see her, with tired eyes, threading needles, and the floor covered with snippets of material.

'Well?' he said smiling, 'wasn't your picture true?'

'I don't know,' I said, 'I never found out.' And I told him how I had rung the bell for the lift, and as I had done so she had fumbled in her bag and gave me a note for a hundred francs. 'Here,' she had whispered, her tone intimate and unpleasant, 'I want you to accept this small commission in return for bringing your patron to my shop.' When I had refused, scarlet with embarrassment, she had shrugged her shoulders disagreeably. 'Just as you like,' she had said, 'but I assure you it's quite usual. Perhaps you would rather have a frock. Come along to the shop some time without Madame and I will fix you up without charging you a sou.' Somehow, I don't know why, I had been aware of that sick, unhealthy feeling I had experienced as a child when turning the pages of a forbidden book. The vision of the consumptive son faded, and in its stead arose the picture of myself had I been different, pocketing that greasy note with an understanding smile, and perhaps slipping round to Blaize's shop on this my free afternoon and coming away with a frock I had not paid for.

I expected him to laugh, it was a stupid story, I don't know why I told him, but he looked at me thoughtfully as he stirred his coffee.

'I think you've made a big mistake,' he said, after a moment.

'In refusing that hundred francs?' I asked, revolted.

'No – good heavens, what do you take me for? I think you've

made a mistake in coming here, in joining forces with Mrs Van Hopper. You are not made for that sort of job. You're too young, for one thing, and too soft. Blaize and her commission, that's nothing. The first of many similar incidents from other Blaizes. You will either have to give in, and become a sort of Blaize yourself, or stay as you are and be broken. Who suggested you took on this thing in the first place?' It seemed natural for him to question me, nor did I mind. It was as though we had known one another for a long time, and had met again after a lapse of years.

'Have you ever thought about the future?' he asked me, 'and what this sort of thing will lead to? Supposing Mrs Van Hopper gets tired of her "friend of the bosom", what then?'

I smiled, and told him that I did not mind very much. There would be other Mrs Van Hoppers, and I was young, and confident, and strong. But even as he spoke I remembered those advertisements seen often in good class magazines where a friendly society demands succour for young women in reduced circumstances; I thought of the type of boarding-house that answers the advertisement and gives temporary shelter, and then I saw myself, useless sketch-book in hand, without qualifications of any kind, stammering replies to stern employment agents. Perhaps I should have accepted Blaize's ten per cent.

'How old are you?' he said, and when I told him he laughed, and got up from his chair. 'I know that age, it's a particularly obstinate one, and a thousand bogies won't make you fear the future. A pity we can't change over. Go upstairs and put your hat on, and I'll have the car brought round.'

As he watched me into the lift I thought of yesterday, Mrs Van Hopper's chattering tongue, and his cold courtesy. I had ill-judged him, he was neither hard nor sardonic, he was already my friend of many years, the brother I had never possessed. Mine was a happy mood that afternoon, and I remember it well. I can see the rippled sky, fluffy with cloud, and the white whipped sea. I can feel again the wind on my face, and hear my laugh, and his that echoed it. It was not the Monte Carlo I had known, or perhaps the truth was that it pleased me better. There was a glamour about it that had not been before. I must have looked upon it before with dull eyes. The harbour was a dancing thing, with fluttering paper boats, and the sailors on the quay were jovial, smiling fellows, merry as the wind. We passed the yacht, beloved of Mrs Van Hopper because of its ducal owner, and snapped our fingers at the glistening brass, and looked at one another and laughed again. I can remember as though I wore it still my comfortable, ill-fitting flannel suit, and how the skirt was lighter than the coat through harder wear. My shabby hat, too broad about the brim, and my low-heeled shoes, fastened with a single strap. A pair of gauntlet gloves clutched in a grubby hand. I had never looked more youthful, I had never felt so old. Mrs Van Hopper and her influenza did not exist for me. The bridge and the cocktail parties were forgotten, and with them my own humble status.

I was a person of importance, I was grown up at last. That girl who, tortured by shyness, would stand outside the sitting-room door twisting a handkerchief in her hands, while from within came that babble of confused chatter so unnerving to the intruder – she had gone with the wind that afternoon. She was a poor creature, and I thought of her with scorn if I considered her at all.

The wind was too high for sketching, it tore in cheerful gusts around the corner of my cobbled square, and back to the car we went and drove I know not where. The long road climbed the hills, and the car climbed with it, and we circled in the heights like a bird in the air. How different his car to Mrs Van Hopper's hireling for the season, a square old-fashioned Daimler that took us to Mentone on placid afternoons, when I, sitting on the little seat with my back to the driver, must crane my neck to see the view. This car had the wings of Mercury, I thought, for higher yet we climbed, and dangerously fast, and the danger pleased me because it was new to me, because I was young.

I remember laughing aloud, and the laugh being carried by

the wind away from me; and looking at him, I realized he laughed no longer, he was once more silent and detached, the man of yesterday wrapped in his secret self.

I realized, too, that the car could climb no more, we had reached the summit, and below us stretched the way that we had come, precipitous and hollow. He stopped the car, and I could see that the edge of the road bordered a vertical slope that crumbled into vacancy, a fall of perhaps two thousand feet. We got out of the car and looked beneath us. This sobered me at last. I knew that but half the car's length had lain between us and the fall. The sea, like a crinkled chart, spread to the horizon, and lapped the sharp outline of the coast, while the houses were white shells in a rounded grotto, pricked here and there by a great orange sun. We knew another sunlight on our hill, and the silence made it harder, more austere. A change had come upon our afternoon; it was not the thing of gossamer it had been. The wind dropped, and it suddenly grew cold.

When I spoke my voice was far too casual, the silly, nervous voice of someone ill at ease. 'Do you know this place?' I said. 'Have you been here before?' He looked down at me without recognition, and I realized with a little stab of anxiety that he must have forgotten all about me, perhaps for some considerable time, and that he himself was so lost in the labyrinth of his own unquiet thoughts that I did not exist. He had the face of one who walks in his sleep, and for a wild moment the idea came to me that perhaps he was not normal, not altogether sane. There were people who had trances, I had surely heard of them, and they followed strange laws of which we could know nothing, they obeyed the tangled orders of their own subconscious minds. Perhaps he was one of them, and here we were within six feet of death.

'It's getting late, shall we go home?' I said, and my careless tone, my little ineffectual smile would scarcely have deceived a child.

I had misjudged him, of course, there was nothing wrong after all, for as soon as I spoke this second time he came clear

31

of his dream and began to apologize. I had gone white, I suppose, and he had noticed it.

'That was an unforgivable thing for me to do,' he said, and taking my arm he pushed me back towards the car, and we climbed in again, and he slammed the door. 'Don't be frightened, the turn is far easier than it looks,' he said, and while I, sick and giddy, clung to the seat with both hands, he manoeuvred the car gently, very gently, until it faced the sloping road once more.

'Then you have been here before?' I said to him, my sense of strain departing, as the car crept away down the twisting narrow road.

'Yes,' he said, and then, after pausing a moment, 'but not for many years. I wanted to see if it had changed.'

'And has it?' I asked him.

'No,' he said. 'No, it has not changed.'

I wondered what had driven him to this retreat into the past, with me an unconscious witness of his mood. What gulf of years stretched between him and that other time, what deed of thought and action, what difference in temperament? I did not want to know. I wished I had not come.

Down the twisting road we went without a check, without a word, a great ridge of cloud stretched above the setting sun, and the air was cold and clean. Suddenly he began to talk about Manderley. He said nothing of his life there, no word about himself, but he told me how the sun set there, on a spring afternoon, leaving a glow upon the headland. The sea would look like slate, cold still from the long winter, and from the terrace you could hear the ripple of the coming tide washing in the little bay. The daffodils were in bloom, stirring in the evening breeze, golden heads cupped upon lean stalks, and however many you might pick there would be no thinning of the ranks, they were massed like an army, shoulder to shoulder. On a bank below the lawns, crocuses were planted, golden, pink, and mauve, but by this time they would be past their best, dropping and fading, like pallid snowdrops. The primrose was more vulgar, a homely pleasant creature who appeared in every cranny like a weed. Too early yet for bluebells, their heads were still hidden beneath last year's leaves, but when they came, dwarfing the more humble violet, they choked the very bracken in the woods, and with their colour made a challenge to the sky.

He never would have them in the house, he said. Thrust into vases they became dank and listless, and to see them at their best you must walk in the woods in the morning, about twelve o'clock, when the sun was overhead. They had a smoky, rather bitter smell, as though a wild sap ran in their stalks, pungent and juicy. People who plucked bluebells from the woods were vandals; he had forbidden it at Manderley. Sometimes, driving in the country, he had seen bicyclists with huge bunches strapped before them on the handles, the bloom already fading from the dying heads, the ravaged stalks straggling naked and unclean.

The primrose did not mind it quite so much; although a creature of the wilds it had a leaning towards civilization, and preened and smiled in a jam-jar in some cottage window without resentment, living quite a week if given water. No wild flowers came in the house at Manderley. He had special cultivated flowers, grown for the house alone, in the walled garden. A rose was one of the few flowers, he said, that looked better picked than growing. A bowl of roses in a drawing-room had a depth of colour and scent they had not possessed in the open. There was something rather blowzy about roses in full bloom, something shallow and raucous, like women with untidy hair. In the house they became mysterious and subtle. He had roses in the house at Manderley for eight months in the year. Did I like syringa, he asked me? There was a tree on the edge of the lawn he could smell from his bedroom window. His sister, who was a hard, rather practical person, used to complain that there were too many scents at Manderley, they made her drunk. Perhaps she was right. He did not care. It was the only form of intoxication that appealed to him. His earliest recollection was of great branches of lilac, standing in white jars, and they filled the house with a wistful, poignant smell.

33

The little pathway down the valley to the bay had clumps of azalea and rhododendron planted to the left of it, and if you wandered down it on a May evening after dinner it was just as though the shrubs had sweated in the air. You could stoop down and pick a fallen petal, crush it between your fingers, and you had there, in the hollow of your hand, the essence of a thousand scents, unbearable and sweet. All from a curled and crumpled petal. And you came out of the valley, heady and rather dazed, to the hard white shingle of the beach and the still water. A curious, perhaps too sudden contrast . . .

As he spoke the car became one of many once again, dusk had fallen without my noticing it, and we were in the midst of light and sound in the streets of Monte Carlo. The clatter jagged on my nerves, and the lights were far too brilliant, far too yellow. It was a swift, unwelcome anticlimax.

Soon we would come to the hotel, and I felt for my gloves in the pocket of the car. I found them, and my fingers closed upon a book as well, whose slim covers told of poetry. I peered to read the title as the car slowed down before the door of the hotel. 'You can take it and read it if you like,' he said, his voice casual and indifferent now that the drive was over, and we were back again, and Manderley was many hundreds of miles distant.

I was glad, and held it tightly with my gloves. I felt I wanted some possession of his, now that the day was finished.

'Hop out,' he said. 'I must go and put the car away. I shan't see you in the restaurant this evening as I'm dining out. But thank you for today.'

I went up the hotel steps alone, with all the despondency of a child whose treat is over. My afternoon had spoilt me for the hours that still remained, and I thought how long they would seem until my bed-time, how empty too my supper all alone. Somehow I could not face the bright inquiries of the nurse upstairs, or the possibilities of Mrs Van Hopper's husky interrogation, so I sat down in the corner of the lounge behind a pillar and ordered tea.

The waiter appeared bored; seeing me alone there was no

need for him to press, and anyway it was that dragging time of day, a few minutes after half past five, when the normal tea is finished and the hour for drinks remote.

Rather forlorn, more than a little dissatisfied, I leant back in my chair and took up the book of poems. The volume was well worn, well thumbed, falling open automatically at what must be a much-frequented page.

> I fled Him, down the nights and down the days;
> I fled Him, down the arches of the years;
> I fled Him, down the labyrinthine ways
> Of my own mind; and in the midst of tears
> I hid from Him, and under running laughter.
> Up vistaed slopes I sped
> And shot, precipited
> Adown Titanic glooms of chasmed fears,
> From those strong feet that followed, followed after.

I felt rather like someone peering through the keyhole of a locked door, and a little furtively I laid the book aside. What hound of heaven had driven him to the high hills this afternoon? I thought of his car, with half a length between it and that drop of two thousand feet, and the blank expression on his face. What footsteps echoed in his mind, what whispers, and what memories, and why, of all poems, must he keep this one in the pocket of his car? I wished he were less remote; and I anything but the creature that I was in my shabby coat and skirt, my broad-brimmed school-girl hat.

The sulky waiter brought my tea, and while I ate bread-and-butter dull as sawdust I thought of the pathway through the valley he had described to me this afternoon, the smell of the azaleas, and the white shingle of the bay. If he loved it all so much why did he seek the superficial froth of Monte Carlo? He had told Mrs Van Hopper he had made no plans, he came away in rather a hurry. And I pictured him running down that pathway in the valley with his own hound of heaven at his heels.

I picked up the book again, and this time it opened at the title-page, and I read the dedication. 'Max – from Rebecca. 17 May', written in a curious slanting hand. A little blob of ink marred the white page opposite, as though the writer, in impatience, had shaken her pen to make the ink flow freely. And then as it bubbled through the nib, it came a little thick, so that the name Rebecca stood out black and strong, the tall and sloping R dwarfing the other letters.

I shut the book with a snap, and put it away under my gloves; and stretching to a nearby chair, I took up an old copy of *L'Illustration* and turned the pages. There were some fine photographs of the chateaux of the Loire, and an article as well. I read it carefully, referring to the photographs, but when I finished I knew I had not understood a word. It was not Blois with its thin turrets and its spires that stared up at me from the printed page. It was the face of Mrs Van Hopper in the restaurant the day before, her small pig's eyes darting to the neighbouring table, her fork, heaped high with ravioli, pausing in mid-air.

'An appalling tragedy,' she was saying, 'the papers were full of it of course. They say he never talks about it, never mentions her name. She was drowned you know, in the bay near Manderley . . .'

# 5

I am glad it cannot happen twice, the fever of first love. For it is a fever, and a burden, too, whatever the poets may say. They are not brave, the days when we are twenty-one. They are full of little cowardices, little fears without foundation, and one is so easily bruised, so swiftly wounded, one falls to the first barbed word. Today, wrapped in the complacent armour of approaching middle age, the infinitesimal pricks of day by day brush one lightly and are soon forgotten, but then − how a careless word would linger, becoming a fiery stigma, and how a look, a glance over a shoulder, branded themselves as things eternal. A denial heralded the thrice crowing of a cock, and an insincerity was like the kiss of Judas. The adult mind can lie with untroubled conscience and a gay composure, but in those days even a small deception scoured the tongue, lashing one against the stake itself.

'What have you been doing this morning?' I can hear her now, propped against her pillows, with all the small irritability of the patient who is not really ill, who has lain in bed too long, and I, reaching to the bedside drawer for the pack of cards, would feel the guilty flush form patches on my neck.

'I've been playing tennis with the professional,' I told her, the false words bringing me to panic, even as I spoke, for what if the professional himself should come up to the suite, then, that very afternoon, and bursting in upon her complain that I had missed my lesson now for many days?

'The trouble is with me laid up like this you haven't got enough to do,' she said, mashing her cigarette in a jar of cleansing cream, and taking the cards in her hand she mixed them in the deft, irritating shuffle of the inveterate player, shaking them in threes, snapping the backs.

'I don't know what you find to do with yourself all day,' she went on; 'you never have any sketches to show me, and when I do ask you to do some shopping for me you forget to buy my Taxol. All I can say is that I hope your tennis will improve; it will be useful to you later on. A poor player is a great bore. Do you still serve underhand?' She flipped the Queen of Spades into the pool, and the dark face stared up at me like Jezebel.

'Yes,' I said, stung by her question, thinking how just and appropriate her word. It described me well. I was underhand. I had not played tennis with the professional at all. I had not once played since she had lain in bed, and that was a little over a fortnight now. I wondered why it was I clung to this reserve, and why it was I did not tell her that every morning I drove with de Winter in his car, and lunched with him, too, at his table in the restaurant.

'You must come up to the net more; you will never play a good game until you do,' she continued, and I agreed, flinching at my own hypocrisy, covering the Queen with the weak-chinned Knave of Hearts.

I have forgotten much of Monte Carlo, of those morning drives, of where we went, even our conversation; but I have not forgotten how my fingers trembled, cramming on my hat, and how I ran along the corridor and down the stairs, too impatient to wait for the slow whining of the lift, and so outside, brushing the swing doors before the commissionaire could help me.

He would be there, in the driver's seat, reading a paper while he waited, and when he saw me he would smile, and toss it behind him in the back seat, and open the door, saying, 'Well, how is the friend-of-the-bosom this morning, and where does she want to go?' If he had driven round in circles it would not have mattered to me, for I was in that first flushed stage when to climb into the seat beside him, and lean forward to the windscreen hugging my knees, was almost too much to bear. I was like a little scrubby schoolboy with a passion for a sixth-form prefect, and he kinder, and far more inaccessible.

'There's a cold wind this morning, you had better put on my coat.'

I remember that, for I was young enough to win happiness in the wearing of his clothes, playing the schoolboy again who carries his hero's sweater and ties it about his throat choking with pride, and this borrowing of his coat, wearing it around my shoulders for even a few minutes at a time, was a triumph in itself, and made a glow about my morning.

Not for me the languor and the subtlety I had read about in books. The challenge and the chase. The sword-play, the swift glance, the stimulating smile. The art of provocation was unknown to me, and I would sit with his map upon my lap, the wind blowing my dull, lanky hair, happy in his silence yet eager for his words. Whether he talked or not made little difference to my mood. My only enemy was the clock on the dashboard, whose hands would move relentlessly to one o'clock. We drove east, we drove west, amidst the myriad villages that cling like limpets to the Mediterranean shore, and today I remember none of them.

All I remember is the feel of the leather seats, the texture of the map upon my knee, its frayed edges, its worn seams, and how one day, looking at the clock, I thought to myself, 'This moment now, at twenty past eleven, this must never be lost,' and I shut my eyes to make the experience more lasting. When I opened my eyes we were by a bend in the road, and a peasant girl in a black shawl waved to us; I can see her now, her dusty skirt, her gleaming, friendly smile, and in a second we had passed the bend and could see her no more. Already she belonged to the past, she was only a memory.

I wanted to go back again, to recapture the moment that had gone, and then it came to me that if we did it would not be the same, even the sun would be changed in the sky, casting another shadow, and the peasant girl would trudge past us along the road in a different way, not waving this time, perhaps not even seeing us. There was something chilling in the thought, something a little melancholy, and looking at the clock I saw that five more minutes had gone by. Soon we would have reached our time limit, and must return to the hotel.

'If only there could be an invention', I said impulsively, 'that bottled up a memory, like scent. And it never faded, and it never got stale. And then, when one wanted it, the bottle could be uncorked, and it would be like living the moment all over again.' I looked up at him, to see what he would say. He did not turn to me, he went on watching the road ahead.

'What particular moments in your young life do you wish uncorked?' he said. I could not tell from his voice whether he was teasing me or not. 'I'm not sure,' I began, and then blundered on, rather foolishly, not thinking of my words, 'I'd like to keep this moment and never forget it.'

'Is that meant to be a compliment to the day, or to my driving?' he said, and as he laughed, like a mocking brother, I became silent, overwhelmed suddenly by the great gulf between us, and how his very kindness to me widened it.

I knew then that I would never tell Mrs Van Hopper about these morning expeditions, for her smile would hurt me as his laugh had done. She would not be angry, nor would she be shocked; she would raise her eyebrows very faintly as though she did not altogether believe my story, and then with a tolerant shrug of the shoulder she would say, 'My dear child, it's extremely sweet and kind of him to take you driving; the only thing is – are you sure it does not bore him dreadfully?' And then she would send me out to buy Taxol, patting me on the shoulder. What degradation lay in being young, I thought, and fell to tearing my nails.

'I wish,' I said savagely, still mindful of his laugh and throwing discretion to the wind, 'I wish I was a woman of about thirty-six dressed in black satin with a string of pearls.'

'You would not be in this car with me if you were,' he said; 'and stop biting those nails, they are ugly enough already.'

'You'll think me impertinent and rude I dare say,' I went on, 'but I would like to know why you ask me to come out in the car, day after day. You are being kind, that's obvious, but why do you choose me for your charity?'

I sat up stiff and straight in my seat and with all the poor pomposity of youth.

'I ask you,' he said gravely, 'because you are not dressed in black satin, with a string of pearls, nor are you thirty-six.' His face was without expression, I could not tell whether he laughed inwardly or not.

'It's all very well,' I said; 'you know everything there is to know about me. There's not much, I admit, because I have not been alive for very long, and nothing much has happened to me, except people dying, but you – I know nothing more about you than I did the first day we met.'

'And what did you know then?' he asked.

'Why, that you lived at Manderley and – and that you had lost your wife.' There, I had said it at last, the word that had hovered on my tongue for days. Your wife. It came out with ease, without reluctance, as though the mere mention of her must be the most casual thing in all the world. Your wife. The word lingered in the air once I had uttered it, dancing before me, and because he received it silently, making no comment, the word magnified itself into something heinous and appalling, a forbidden word, unnatural to the tongue. And I could not call it back, it could never be unsaid. Once again I saw the inscription on the fly-leaf of that book of poems, and the curious slanting R. I felt sick at heart and cold. He would never forgive me, and this would be the end of our friendship.

I remember staring straight in front of me at the windscreen, seeing nothing of the flying road, my ears still tingling with that spoken word. The silence became minutes, and the minutes became miles, and everything is over now, I thought, I shall never drive with him again. Tomorrow he will go away. And Mrs Van Hopper will be up again. She and I will walk along the terrace as we did before. The porter will bring down his trunks, I shall catch a glimpse of them in the luggage lift, with new-plastered

41

labels. The bustle and finality of departure. The sound of the car changing gear as it turned the corner, and then even that sound merging into the common traffic, and being lost, and so absorbed for ever.

I was so deep in my picture, I even saw the porter pocketing his tip and going back through the swing-door of the hotel, saying something over his shoulder to the commissionaire, that I did not notice the slowing-down of the car, and it was only when we stopped, drawing up by the side of the road, that I brought myself back to the present once again. He sat motionless, looking without his hat and with his white scarf round his neck, more than ever like someone medieval who lived within a frame. He did not belong to the bright landscape, he should be standing on the steps of a gaunt cathedral, his cloak flung back, while a beggar at his feet scrambled for gold coins.

The friend had gone, with his kindliness and his easy *camaraderie*, and the brother too, who had mocked me for nibbling at my nails. This man was a stranger. I wondered why I was sitting beside him in the car.

Then he turned to me and spoke. 'A little while ago you talked about an invention,' he said, 'some scheme for capturing a memory. You would like, you told me, at a chosen moment to live the past again. I'm afraid I think rather differently from you. All memories are bitter, and I prefer to ignore them. Something happened a year ago that altered my whole life, and I want to forget every phase in my existence up to that time. Those days are finished. They are blotted out. I must begin living all over again. The first day we met, your Mrs Van Hopper asked me why I came to Monte Carlo. It put a stopper on those memories you would like to resurrect. It does not always work, of course; sometimes the scent is too strong for the bottle, and too strong for me. And then the devil in one, like a furtive peeping Tom, tries to draw the cork. I did that in the first drive we took together. When we climbed the hills and looked down over the precipice. I was there some years ago, with my wife. You asked me if it was still the same, if it had changed at all. It was just the same, but – I was thankful to realize – oddly impersonal. There was no suggestion of the other time. She and I had left no record. It may have been because you were with me. You have blotted out the past for me, you know, far more effectively than all the bright lights of Monte Carlo. But for you I should have left long ago, gone on to Italy, and Greece, and further still perhaps. You have spared me all those wanderings. Damn your puritanical little tight-lipped speech to me. Damn your idea of my kindness and my charity. I ask you to come with me because I want you and your company, and if you don't believe me you can leave the car now and find your own way home. Go on, open the door, and get out.'

I sat still, my hands in my lap, not knowing whether he meant it or not.

'Well,' he said, 'what are you going to do about it?'

Had I been a year or two younger I think I should have cried. Children's tears are very near the surface, and come at the first crisis. As it was I felt them prick behind my eyes, felt the ready colour flood my face, and catching a sudden glimpse of myself in the glass above the windscreen saw in full the sorry spectacle that I made, with troubled eyes and scarlet cheeks, lank hair flopping under broad felt hat.

'I want to go home,' I said, my voice perilously near to trembling, and without a word he started up the engine, let in the clutch, and turned the car round the way that we had come.

Swiftly we covered the ground, far too swiftly, I thought, far too easily, and the callous countryside watched us with indifference. We came to the bend in the road that I had wished to imprison as a memory, and the peasant girl was gone, and the colour was flat, and it was no more after all than any bend in any road passed by a hundred motorists. The glamour of it had gone with my happy mood, and at the thought of it my frozen face quivered into feeling, my adult pride was lost, and those despicable tears rejoicing at their conquest welled into my eyes and strayed upon my cheeks.

43

I could not check them, for they came unbidden, and had I reached in my pocket for a handkerchief he would have seen I must let them fall untouched, and suffer the bitter salt upon my lips, plumbing the depths of humiliation. Whether he had turned his head to look at me I do not know, for I watched the road ahead with blurred and steady stare, but suddenly he put out his hand and took hold of mine, and kissed it, still saying nothing, and then he threw his handkerchief on my lap, which I was too ashamed to touch.

I thought of all those heroines of fiction who looked pretty when they cried, and what a contrast I must make with blotched and swollen face, and red rims to my eyes. It was a dismal finish to my morning, and the day that stretched ahead of me was long. I had to lunch with Mrs Van Hopper in her room because the nurse was going out, and afterwards she would make me play bezique with all the tireless energy of the convalescent. I knew I should stifle in that room. There was something sordid about the tumbled sheets, the sprawling blankets, and the thumped pillows, and that bedside table dusty with powder, spilt scent, and melting liquid rouge. Her bed would be littered with the separated sheets of the daily papers folded anyhow, while French novels with curling edges and the covers torn kept company with American magazines. The mashed stubs of cigarettes lay everywhere – in cleansing cream, in a dish of grapes, and on the floor beneath the bed. Visitors were lavish with their flowers, and the vases stood cheek-by-jowl in any fashion, hot-house exotics crammed beside mimosa, while a great beribboned casket crowned them all, with tier upon tier of crystallized fruit. Later her friends would come in for a drink, which I must mix for them, hating my task, shy and ill-at-ease in my corner hemmed in by their parrot chatter, and I would be a whipping-boy again, blushing for her when, excited by her little crowd, she must sit up in bed and talk too loudly, laugh too long, reach to the portable gramophone and start a record, shrugging her large shoulders to the tune. I preferred her irritable and snappy, her hair done up in pins, scolding me for forgetting her Taxol. All this awaited me in the suite, while he, once he had left me at the hotel, would go away somewhere alone, towards the sea perhaps, feel the wind on his cheek, follow the sun; and it might happen that he would lose himself in those memories that I knew nothing of, that I could not share, he would wander down the years that were gone.

The gulf that lay between us was wider now than it had ever been, and he stood away from me, with his back turned, on the further shore. I felt young and small and very much alone, and now, in spite of my pride, I found his handkerchief and blew my nose, throwing my drab appearance to the winds. It could never matter.

'To hell with this,' he said suddenly, as though angry, as though bored, and he pulled me beside him, and put his arm round my shoulder, still looking straight ahead of him, his right hand on the wheel. He drove, I remember, even faster than before. 'I suppose you are young enough to be my daughter, and I don't know how to deal with you,' he said. The road narrowed then to a corner, and he had to swerve to avoid a dog. I thought he would release me, but he went on holding me beside him, and when the corner was passed, and the road came straight again he did not let me go. 'You can forget all I said to you this morning,' he said; 'that's all finished and done with. Don't let's ever think of it again. My family always call me Maxim, I'd like you to do the same. You've been formal with me long enough.' He felt for the brim of my hat, and took hold of it, throwing it over his shoulder to the back seat, and then bent down and kissed the top of my head. 'Promise me you will never wear black satin,' he said. I smiled then, and he laughed back at me, and the morning was gay again, the morning was a shining thing. Mrs Van Hopper and the afternoon did not matter a flip of the finger. It would pass so quickly, and there would be tonight, and another day tomorrow. I was cocksure, jubilant; at that moment I almost had the courage to claim equality. I saw myself strolling into Mrs Van Hopper's bedroom rather late for my bezique, and when questioned by her, yawning carelessly, saying, 'I forgot the time. I've been lunching with Maxim.'

I was still child enough to consider a Christian name like a plume in the hat, though from the very first he had called me by mine. The morning, for all its shadowed moments, had promoted me to a new level of friendship, I did not lag so far behind as I had thought. He had kissed me too, a natural business, comforting and quiet. Not dramatic as in books. Not embarrassing. It seemed to bring about an ease in our relationship, it made everything more simple. The gulf between us had been bridged after all. I was to call him Maxim. And that afternoon playing bezique with Mrs Van Hopper was not so tedious as it might have been, though my courage failed me and I said nothing of my morning. For when, gathering her cards together at the end, and reaching for the box, she said casually, 'Tell me, is Max de Winter still in the hotel?' I hesitated a moment, like a diver on the brink, then lost my nerve and my tutored self-possession, saying, 'Yes, I believe so – he comes into the restaurant for his meals.'

Someone has told her, I thought, someone has seen us together, the tennis professional has complained, the manager has sent a note, and I waited for her attack. But she went on putting the cards back into the box, yawning a little, while I straightened the tumbled bed. I gave her the bowl of powder, the rouge compact, and the lip-stick, and she put away the cards and took up the hands glass from the table by her side. 'Attractive creature,' she said, 'but queer-tempered I should think, difficult to know. I thought he might have made some gesture of asking one to Manderley that day in the lounge, but he was very close.'

I said nothing. I watched her pick up the lip-stick and outline a bow upon her hard mouth. 'I never saw her,' she said, holding the glass away to see the effect, 'but I believe she was very lovely. Exquisitely turned out, and brilliant in every way. They used to give tremendous parties at Manderley. It was all very sudden and tragic, and I believe he adored her. I need the darker shade of powder with this brilliant red, my dear: fetch it, will you, and put this box back in the drawer?'

And we were busy then with powder, scent, and rouge, until the bell rang and her visitors came in. I handed them their drinks, dully, saying little; I changed the records on the gramophone, I threw away the stubs of cigarettes.

'Been doing any sketching lately, little lady?' The forced heartiness of an old banker, his monocle dangling on a string, and my bright smile of insincerity: 'No, not very lately; will you have another cigarette?'

It was not I that answered, I was not there at all. I was following a phantom in my mind, whose shadowy form had taken shape at last. Her features were blurred, her colouring indistinct, the setting of her eyes and the texture of her hair was still uncertain, still to be revealed.

She had beauty that endured, and a smile that was not forgotten. Somewhere her voice still lingered, and the memory of her words. There were places she had visited, and things that she had touched. Perhaps in cupboards there were clothes that she had worn, with the scent about them still. In my bedroom, under my pillow, I had a book that she had taken in her hands, and I could see her turning to that first white page, smiling as she wrote, and shaking the bent nib. Max from Rebecca. It must have been his birthday, and she had put it amongst her other presents on the breakfast table. And they had laughed together as he tore off the paper and string. She leant, perhaps, over his shoulder, while he read. Max. She called him Max. It was familiar, gay, and easy on the tongue. The family could call him Maxim if they liked. Grandmothers and aunts. And people like myself, quiet and dull and youthful, who did not matter. Max was her choice, the word was her possession; she had written it with so great a confidence on the fly-leaf of that book. That bold, slanting hand, stabbing the white paper, the symbol of herself, so certain, so assured.

How many times she must have written to him thus, in how many varied moods.

Little notes, scrawled on half-sheets of paper, and letters, when he was away, page after page, intimate, *their* news. Her voice, echoing through the house, and down the garden, careless and familiar like the writing in the book.

And I had to call him Maxim.

# 6

Packing up. The nagging worry of departure. Lost keys, unwritten labels, tissue paper lying on the floor. I hate it all. Even now, when I have done so much of it, when I live, as the saying goes, in my boxes. Even today, when shutting drawers and flinging wide an hotel wardrobe, or the impersonal shelves of a furnished villa, is a methodical matter of routine, I am aware of sadness, of a sense of loss. Here, I say, we have lived, we have been happy. This has been ours, however brief the time. Though two nights only have been spent beneath a roof, yet we leave something of ourselves behind. Nothing material, not a hair-pin on a dressing-table, not an empty bottle of Aspirin tablets, not a handkerchief beneath a pillow, but something indefinable, a moment of our lives, a thought, a mood.

This house sheltered us, we spoke, we loved within those walls. That was yesterday. Today we pass on, we see it no more, and we are different, changed in some infinitesimal way. We can never be quite the same again. Even stopping for luncheon at a wayside inn, and going to a dark, unfamiliar room to wash my hands, the handle of the door unknown to me, the wallpaper peeling in strips, a funny little cracked mirror above the basin; for this moment, it is mine, it belongs to me. We know one another. This is the present. There is no past and no future. Here I am washing my hands, and the cracked mirror shows me to myself, suspended as it were, in time; this is me, this moment will not pass.

And then I open the door and go to the dining-room, where he is sitting waiting for me at a table, and I think how in that moment I have aged, passed on, how I have advanced one step towards an unknown destiny.

We smile, we choose our lunch, we speak of this and that, but — I say to myself — I am not she who left him five minutes ago. She stayed behind. I am another woman, older, more mature . . .

I saw in a paper the other day that the Hôtel Côte d'Azur at Monte Carlo had gone to new management, and had a different name. The rooms have been redecorated, and the whole interior changed. Perhaps Mrs Van Hopper's suite on the first floor exists no more. Perhaps there is no trace of the small bedroom that was mine. I knew I should never go back, that day I knelt on the floor and fumbled with the awkward catch of her trunk.

The episode was finished, with the snapping of the lock. I glanced out of the window, and it was like turning the page of a photograph album. Those roof-tops and that sea were mine no more. They belonged to yesterday, to the past. The rooms already wore an empty air, stripped of our possessions, and there was something hungry about the suite, as though it wished us gone, and the new arrivals, who would come tomorrow, in our place. The heavy luggage stood ready strapped and locked in the corridor outside. The smaller stuff would be finished later. Waste-paper baskets groaned under litter. All her half empty medicine bottles and discarded face-cream jars, with torn-up bills and letters. Drawers in tables gaped, the bureau was stripped bare.

She had flung a letter at me the morning before, as I poured out her coffee at breakfast. 'Helen is sailing for New York on Saturday. Little Nancy has a threatened appendix, and they've cabled her to go home. That's decided me. We're going too. I'm tired to death of Europe, and we can come back in the early fall. How d'you like the idea of seeing New York?'

The thought was worse than prison. Something of my misery must have shown in my face, for at first she looked astonished, then annoyed.

'What an odd, unsatisfactory child you are. I can't make you out. Don't you realize that at home girls in your position without any money can have the grandest fun? Plenty of boys and excitement. All in your own class. You can have your own little set of friends, and needn't be at my beck and call as much as you are here. I thought you didn't care for Monte?'

'I've got used to it,' I said lamely, wretchedly, my mind a conflict.

'Well, you'll just have to get used to New York, that's all. We're going to catch that boat of Helen's, and it means seeing about our passage at once. Go down to the reception office right away, and make that young clerk show some sign of efficiency. Your day will be so full that you won't have time to have any pangs about leaving Monte!' She laughed disagreeably, squashing her cigarette in the butter, and went to the telephone to ring up all her friends.

I could not face the office right away. I went into the bathroom and locked the door, and sat down on the cork mat, my head in my hands. It had happened at last, the business of going away. It was all over. Tomorrow evening I should be in the train, holding her jewel case and her rug, like a maid, and she in that monstrous new hat with the single quill, dwarfed in her fur-coat, sitting opposite me in the wagon-lit. We would wash and clean our teeth in that stuffy little compartment with the rattling doors, the splashed basin, the damp towel, the soap with a single hair on it, the carafe half-filled with water, the inevitable notice on the wall 'Sous le lavabo se trouve une vase', while every rattle, every throb and jerk of the screaming train would tell me that the miles carried me away from him, sitting alone in the restaurant of the hotel, at the table I had known, reading a book, not minding, not thinking.

I should say good-bye to him in the lounge, perhaps, before we left. A furtive, scrambled farewell, because of her, and there would be a pause, and a smile, and words like 'Yes, of course, do write', and 'I've never thanked you properly for being so kind', and 'You must forward those snapshots', 'What about your address?' 'Well, I'll have to let you know.' And he would light a cigarette casually, asking a passing waiter for a light, while I thought, 'Four and a half more minutes to go. I shall never see him again.'

51

Because I was going, because it was over, there would suddenly be nothing more to say, we would be strangers, meeting for the last and only time, while my mind clamoured painfully, crying 'I love you so much. I'm terribly unhappy. This has never come to me before, and never will again.' My face would be set in a prim, conventional smile, my voice would be saying, 'Look at that funny old man over there; I wonder who he is; he must be new here.' And we would waste the last moments laughing at a stranger, because we were already strangers to one another. 'I hope the snapshots come out well,' repeating oneself in desperation, and he 'Yes, that one of the square ought to be good; the light was just right.' Having both of us gone into all that at the time, having agreed upon it, and anyway I would not care if the result was fogged and black, because this was the last moment, the final good-bye had been attained.

'Well,' my dreadful smile stretching across my face, 'thanks most awfully once again, it's been so ripping . . .' using words I had never used before. Ripping: what did it mean? – God knows, I did not care; it was the sort of word that schoolgirls had for hockey, wildly inappropriate to those past weeks of misery and exultation. Then the doors of the lift would open upon Mrs Van Hopper and I would cross the lounge to meet her, and he would stroll back again to his corner and pick up a paper.

Sitting there, ridiculously, on the cork mat of the bathroom floor, I lived it all, and our journey too, and our arrival in New York. The shrill voice of Helen, a narrower edition of her mother, and Nancy, her horrid little child. The college boys that Mrs Van Hopper would have me know, and the young bank clerks, suitable to my station. 'Let's make Wednesday night a date.' 'D'you like Hot music?' Snub-nosed boys, with shiny faces. Having to be polite. And wanting to be alone with my own thoughts as I was now, locked behind the bathroom door . . .

She came and rattled on the door. 'What are you doing?'

'All right – I'm sorry, I'm coming now,' and I made a pretence of turning on the tap, of bustling about and folding a towel on a rail.

She glanced at me curiously as I opened the door. 'What a time you've been. You can't afford to dream this morning, you know, there's too much to be done.'

He would go back to Manderley, of course, in a few weeks; I felt certain of that. There would be a great pile of letters waiting for him in the hall, and mine amongst them, scribbled on the boat. A forced letter, trying to amuse, describing my fellow passengers. It would lie about inside his blotter, and he would answer it weeks later, one Sunday morning in a hurry, before lunch, having come across it when he paid some bills. And then no more. Nothing until the final degradation of the Christmas card. Manderley itself perhaps, against a frosted background. The message printed, saying 'A happy Christmas and a prosperous New Year from Maximilian de Winter.' Gold lettering. But to be kind he would have run his pen through the printed name and written in ink underneath 'from Maxim', as a sort of sop, and if there was space, a message, 'I hope you are enjoying New York.' A lick of the envelope, a stamp, and tossed in a pile of a hundred others.

'It's too bad you are leaving tomorrow,' said the reception clerk, telephone in hand; 'the Ballet starts next week, you know. Does Mrs Van Hopper know?' I dragged myself back from Christmas at Manderley to the realities of the wagon-lit.

Mrs Van Hopper lunched in the restaurant for the first time since her influenza, and I had a pain in the pit of my stomach as I followed her into the room. He had gone to Cannes for the day, that much I knew, for he had warned me the day before, but I kept thinking the waiter might commit an indiscretion and say: 'Will Mademoiselle be dining with Monsieur tonight as usual?' I felt a little sick whenever he came near the table, but he said nothing.

The day was spent in packing, and in the evening people came to say good-bye. We dined in the sitting-room, and she went to bed directly afterwards. Still I had not seen him. I went down to the lounge about half past nine on the pretext of getting luggage labels and he was not there. The odious reception clerk smiled when he saw me. 'If you are looking for Mr de Winter we had a message from Cannes to say he would not be back before midnight.'

'I want a packet of luggage labels,' I said, but I saw by his eye that he was not deceived. So there would be no last evening after all. The hour I had looked forward to all day must be spent by myself alone, in my own bedroom, gazing at my Revelation suit-case and the stout hold-all. Perhaps it was just as well, for I should have made a poor companion, and he must have read my face.

I know I cried that night, bitter youthful tears that could not come from me today. That kind of crying, deep into a pillow, does not happen after we are twenty-one. The throbbing head, the swollen eyes, the tight, contracted throat. And the wild anxiety in the morning to hide all traces from the world, sponging with cold water, dabbing eau-de-Cologne, the furtive dash of powder that is significant in itself. The panic, too, that one might cry again, the tears swelling without control, and a fatal trembling of the mouth lead one to disaster. I remember opening wide my window and leaning out, hoping the fresh morning air would blow away the tell-tale pink under the powder, and the sun had never seemed so bright, nor the day so full of promise. Monte Carlo was suddenly full of kindliness and charm, the one place in the world that held sincerity. I loved it. Affection overwhelmed me. I wanted to live there all my life. And I was leaving it today. This is the last time I brush my hair before the looking-glass, the last time I shall clean my teeth into the basin. Never again sleep in that bed. Never more turn off the switch of that electric light. There I was, padding about in a dressing-gown, making a slough of sentiment out of a commonplace hotel bedroom.

'You haven't started a cold, have you?' she said at breakfast.

'No,' I told her, 'I don't think so,' clutching at a straw, for this might serve as an excuse later, if I was over-pink about the eyes.

'I hate hanging about once everything is packed,' she grumbled; 'we ought to have decided on the earlier train. We could get it if we made the effort, and then have longer in Paris. Wire

Helen not to meet us, but arrange another *rendezvous*. I wonder' – she glanced at her watch – 'I suppose they could change the reservations. Anyway it's worth trying. Go down to the office and see.'

'Yes,' I said, a dummy to her moods going into my bedroom and flinging off my dressing-gown, fastening my inevitable flannel skirt and stretching my home-made jumper over my head. My indifference to her turned to hatred. This was the end then, even my morning must be taken from me. No last half-hour on the terrace, not even ten minutes perhaps to say good-bye. Because she had finished breakfast earlier than she expected, because she was bored. Well then, I would fling away restraint and modesty, I would not be proud any more. I slammed the door of the sitting-room and ran along the passage. I did not wait for the lift, I climbed the stairs, three at a time, up to the third floor. I knew the number of his room, 148, and I hammered at the door, very flushed in the face and breathless.

'Come in,' he shouted, and I opened the door, repenting already, my nerve failing me; for perhaps he had only just woken up, having been late last night, and would be still in bed, tousled in the head and irritable.

He was shaving by the open window, a camel-hair jacket over his pyjamas, and I in my flannel suit and heavy shoes felt clumsy and over dressed. I was merely foolish, when I had felt myself dramatic.

'What do you want?' he said. 'Is something the matter?'

'I've come to say good-bye,' I said, 'we're going this morning.'

He stared at me, then put his razor down on the washstand. 'Shut the door,' he said.

I closed it behind me, and stood there, rather self-conscious, my hands hanging by my side. 'What on earth are you talking about?' he asked.

'It's true, we're leaving today. We were going by the later train, and now she wants to catch the earlier one, and I was afraid I shouldn't see you again. I felt I must see you before I left, to thank you.'

55

They tumbled out, the idiotic words, just as I had imagined them. I was stiff and awkward; in a moment I should say he had been ripping.

'Why didn't you tell me about this before?' he said.

'She only decided yesterday. It was all done in a hurry. Her daughter sails for New York on Saturday, and we are going with her. We're joining her in Paris, and going through to Cherbourg.'

'She's taking you with her to New York?'

'Yes, and I don't want to go. I shall hate it; I shall be miserable.'

'Why in heaven's name go with her then?'

'I have to, you know that. I work for a salary. I can't afford to leave her.' He picked up his razor again, and took the soap off his face. 'Sit down,' he said. 'I shan't be long. I'll dress in the bathroom, and be ready in five minutes.'

He took his clothes off the chair and threw them on the bathroom floor, and went inside, slamming the door. I sat down on the bed and began biting my nails. The situation was unreal, and I felt like a lay-figure. I wondered what he was thinking, what he was going to do. I glanced round the room, it was the room of any man, untidy and impersonal. Lots of shoes, more than ever were needed, and strings of ties. The dressing-table was bare, except for a large bottle of hair-wash and a pair of ivory hair-brushes. No photographs. No snapshots. Nothing like that. Instinctively I had looked for them, thinking there would be one photograph at least beside his bed, or in the middle of the mantelpiece. One large one, in a leather frame. There were only books though, and a box of cigarettes.

He was ready, as he had promised, in five minutes. 'Come down to the terrace while I eat my breakfast,' he said.

I looked at my watch. 'I haven't time,' I told him. 'I ought to be in the office now, changing the reservations.'

'Never mind about that, I've got to talk to you,' he said.

We walked down the corridor and he rang for the lift. He can't realize, I thought, that the early train leaves in about an hour and a half. Mrs Van Hopper will ring up the office, in a moment, and ask if I am there. We went down in the lift, not talking, and so out to the terrace, where the tables were laid for breakfast.

'What are you going to have?' he said.

'I've had mine already,' I told him, 'and I can only stay four minutes anyway.'

'Bring me coffee, a boiled egg, toast, marmalade, and a tangerine,' he said to the waiter. And he took an emery board out of his pocket and began filing his nails.

'So Mrs Van Hopper has had enough of Monte Carlo,' he said, 'and now she wants to go home. So do I. She to New York and I to Manderley. Which would you prefer? You can take your choice.'

'Don't make a joke about it; it's unfair,' I said; 'and I think I had better see about those tickets, and say good-bye now.'

'If you think I'm one of the people who try to be funny at breakfast you're wrong,' he said. 'I'm invariably ill-tempered in the early morning. I repeat to you, the choice is open to you. Either you go to America with Mrs Van Hopper or you come home to Manderley with me.'

'Do you mean you want a secretary or something?'

'No, I'm asking you to marry me, you little fool.'

The waiter came with the breakfast, and I sat with my hands in my lap, watching while he put down the pot of coffee and the jug of milk.

'You don't understand,' I said, when the waiter had gone; 'I'm not the sort of person men marry.'

'What the devil do you mean?' he said, staring at me, laying down his spoon.

I watched a fly settle on the marmalade, and he brushed it away impatiently.

'I'm not sure,' I said slowly. 'I don't think I know how to explain. I don't belong to your sort of world for one thing.'

'What is my world?'

'Well – Manderley. You know what I mean.'

He picked up his spoon again and helped himself to marmalade.

'You are almost as ignorant as Mrs Van Hopper, and just as unintelligent. What do you know of Manderley? I'm the person to judge that, whether you would belong there or not. You think I ask you this on the spur of the moment, don't you? Because you say you don't want to go to New York. You think I ask you to marry me for the same reason you believed I drove you about in the car, yes, and gave you dinner that first evening. To be kind. Don't you?'

'Yes,' I said.

'One day,' he went on, spreading his toast thick, 'you may realize that philanthropy is not my strongest quality. At the moment I don't think you realize anything at all. You haven't answered my question. Are you going to marry me?'

I don't believe, even in my fiercest moments, I had considered this possibility. I had once, when driving with him and we had been silent for many miles, started a rambling story in my head about him being very ill, delirious I think, and sending for me and I having to nurse him. I had reached the point in my story where I was putting eau-de-Cologne on his head when we arrived at the hotel, and so it finished there. And another time I had imagined living in a lodge in the grounds of Manderley, and how he would visit me sometimes, and sit in front of the fire. This sudden talk of marriage bewildered me, even shocked me I think. It was as though the King asked one. It did not ring true. And he went on eating his marmalade as though everything were natural. In books men knelt to women, and it would be moonlight. Not at breakfast, not like this.

'My suggestion doesn't seem to have gone too well,' he said. 'I'm sorry. I rather thought you loved me. A fine blow to my conceit.'

'I do love you,' I said. 'I love you dreadfully. You've made me very unhappy and I've been crying all night because I thought I should never see you again.'

When I said this I remember he laughed, and stretched his hand to me across the breakfast table. 'Bless you for that,' he said; 'one day, when you reach that exalted age of thirty-six which

58

you told me was your ambition, I'll remind you of this moment. And you won't believe me. It's a pity you have to grow up.'

I was ashamed already, and angry with him for laughing. So women did not make those confessions to men. I had a lot to learn.

'So that's settled, isn't it?' he said, going on with his toast and marmalade; 'instead of being companion to Mrs Van Hopper you become mine, and your duties will be almost exactly the same. I also like new library books, and flowers in the drawing-room, and bezique after dinner. And someone to pour out my tea. The only difference is that I don't take Taxol, I prefer Eno's, and you must never let me run out of my particular brand of tooth-paste.'

I drummed with my fingers on the table, uncertain of myself and of him. Was he still laughing at me, was it all a joke? He looked up, and saw the anxiety on my face. 'I'm being rather a brute to you, aren't I?' he said; 'this isn't your idea of a proposal. We ought to be in a conservatory, you in a white frock with a rose in your hand, and a violin playing a waltz in the distance. And I should make violent love to you behind a palm tree. You would feel then you were getting your money's worth. Poor darling, what a shame. Never mind, I'll take you to Venice for our honeymoon and we'll hold hands in the gondola. But we won't stay too long, because I want to show you Manderley.'

He wanted to show me Manderley . . . And suddenly I realized that it would all happen; I would be his wife, we would walk in the garden together, we would stroll down that path in the valley to the shingle beach. I knew how I would stand on the steps after breakfast, looking at the day, throwing crumbs to the birds, and later wander out in a shady hat with long scissors in my hand, and cut flowers for the house. I knew now why I had bought that picture post-card as a child; it was a premonition, a blank step into the future.

He wanted to show me Manderley . . . My mind ran riot then, figures came before me and picture after picture – and all the while he ate his tangerine, giving me a piece now and then, and watching me. We would be in a crowd of people, and he would say, 'I don't think you have met my wife.' Mrs de Winter. I would be Mrs de Winter. I considered my name, and the signature on cheques, to tradesmen, and in letters asking people to dinner. I heard myself talking on the telephone: 'Why not come down to Manderley next week-end?' People, always a throng of people. 'Oh, but she's simply charming, you must meet her—' This about me, a whisper on the fringe of a crowd, and I would turn away, pretending I had not heard.

Going down to the lodge with a basket on my arm, grapes and peaches for the old lady who was sick. Her hands stretched out to me, 'The Lord bless you, Madam, for being so good,' and my saying, 'Just send up to the house for anything you want.' Mrs de Winter. I would be Mrs de Winter. I saw the polished table in the dining-room, and the long candles. Maxim sitting at the end. A party of twenty-four. I had a flower in my hair. Everyone looked towards me, holding up his glass. 'We must drink the health of the bride,' and Maxim saying afterwards, 'I have never seen you look so lovely.' Great cool rooms, filled with flowers. My bedroom, with a fire in the winter, someone knocking at the door. And a woman comes in, smiling; she is Maxim's sister, and she is saying, 'It's really wonderful how happy you have made him; everyone is so pleased, you are such a success.' Mrs de Winter. I would be Mrs de Winter.

'The rest of the tangerine is sour, I shouldn't eat it,' he said, and I stared at him, the words going slowly to my head, then looked down at the fruit on my plate. The quarter was hard and pale. He was right. The tangerine was very sour. I had a sharp, bitter taste in my mouth, and I had only just noticed it.

'Am I going to break the news to Mrs Van Hopper or are you?' he said.

He was folding up his napkin, pushing back his plate, and I wondered how it was he spoke so casually, as though the matter was of little consequence, a mere adjustment of plans. Whereas to me it was a bomb-shell, exploding in a thousand fragments.

'You tell her,' I said; 'she'll be so angry.'

We got up from the table, I excited and flushed, trembling already in anticipation. I wondered if he would tell the waiter, take my arm smilingly and say, 'You must congratulate us, Mademoiselle and I are going to be married.' And all the other waiters would hear, would bow to us, would smile, and we would pass into the lounge, a wave of excitement following us, a flutter of expectation. But he said nothing. He left the terrace without a word, and I followed him to the lift. We passed the reception desk and no one even looked at us. The clerk was busy with a sheaf of papers, he was talking over his shoulder to his junior. He does not know, I thought, that I am going to be Mrs de Winter. I am going to live at Manderley. Manderley will belong to me. We went up in the lift to the first floor, and so along the passage. He took my hand and swung it as we went along. 'Does forty-two seem very old to you?' he said.

'Oh, no,' I told him, quickly, too eagerly perhaps. 'I don't like young men.'

'You've never known any,' he said.

We came to the door of the suite. 'I think I had better deal with this alone,' he said; 'tell me something – do you mind how soon you marry me? You don't want a trousseau, do you, or any of that nonsense? Because the whole thing can be so easily arranged in a few days. Over a desk, with a licence, and then off in the car to Venice or anywhere you fancy.'

'Not in a church?' I asked. 'Not in white, with bridesmaids, and bells, and choir boys? What about your relations, and all your friends?'

'You forget,' he said, 'I had that sort of wedding before.'

We went on standing in front of the door of the suite, and I noticed that the daily paper was still thrust through the letter-box. We had been too busy to read it at breakfast.

'Well?' he said, 'what about it?'

'Of course,' I answered, 'I was thinking for the moment we would be married at home. Naturally I don't expect a church, or people, or anything like that.'

And I smiled at him. I made a cheerful face. 'Won't it be fun?' I said.

He had turned to the door though, and opened it, and we were inside the suite in the little entrance passage.

'Is that you?' called Mrs Van Hopper from the sitting-room. 'What in the name of Mike have you been doing? I've rung the office three times and they said they hadn't seen you.'

I was seized with a sudden desire to laugh, to cry, to do both, and I had a pain, too, at the pit of my stomach. I wished, for one wild moment, that none of this had happened, that I was alone somewhere, going for a walk, and whistling.

'I'm afraid it's all my fault,' he said, going into the sitting-room, shutting the door behind him, and I heard her exclamation of surprise.

Then I went into my bedroom and sat down by the open window. It was like waiting in the ante-room at a doctor's. I ought to turn over the pages of a magazine, look at photographs that did not matter and read articles I should never remember, until the nurse came, bright and efficient, all humanity washed away by years of disinfectant: 'It's all right, the operation was quite successful. There is no need to worry at all. I should go home and have some sleep.'

The walls of the suite were thick, I could hear no hum of voices. I wondered what he was saying to her, how he phrased his words. Perhaps he said, I fell in love with her, you know, the very first time we met. We've been seeing one another every day.' And she in answer, 'Why, Mr de Winter, it's quite the most romantic thing I've ever heard.' Romantic, that was the word I had tried to remember coming up in the lift. Yes, of course. Romantic. That was what people would say. It was all very sudden and romantic. They suddenly decided to get married and there it was. Such an adventure. I smiled to myself as I hugged my knees on the window seat, thinking how wonderful it was, how happy I was going to be. I was to marry the man I loved. I was to be Mrs de Winter. It was foolish to go on having that pain in the pit of my stomach when I was so happy. Nerves of course.

Waiting like this; the doctor's ante-room. It would have been better, after all, more natural surely to have gone into the sitting-room hand in hand, laughing, smiling at one another and for him to say 'We're going to be married, we're very much in love.'

In love. He had not said anything yet about being in love. No time perhaps. It was all so hurried at the breakfast table. Marmalade, and coffee, and that tangerine. No time. The tangerine was very bitter. No, he had not said anything about being in love. Just that we would be married. Short and definite, very original. Original proposals were much better. More genuine. Not like other people. Not like younger men who talked nonsense probably, not meaning half they said. Not like younger men being very incoherent, very passionate, swearing impossibilities. Not like him the first time, asking Rebecca . . . I must not think of that. Put it away. A thought forbidden, prompted by demons. Get thee behind me, Satan. I must never think about that, never, never, never. He loves me, he wants to show me Manderley. Would they ever have done with their talking, would they ever call me into the room?

There was the book of poems lying beside my bed. He had forgotten he had ever lent them to me. They could not mean much to him then. 'Go on,' whispered the demon, 'open the title-page; that's what you want to do, isn't it? Open the title-page.' Nonsense, I said, I'm only going to put the book with the rest of the things. I yawned. I wandered to the table beside the bed. I picked up the book. I caught my foot in the flex of the bedside lamp, and stumbled, the book falling from my hands on to the floor. It fell open, at the title-page. 'Max from Rebecca.' She was dead, and one must not have thoughts about the dead. They slept in peace, the grass blew over their graves. How alive was her writing though, how full of force. Those curious, sloping letters. The blob of ink. Done yesterday. It was just as if it had been written yesterday. I took my nail scissors from the dressing-case and cut the page, looking over my shoulder like a criminal.

I cut the page right out of the book. I left no jagged edges, and the book looked white and clean when the page was gone.

A new book, that had not been touched. I tore the page up in many little fragments and threw them into the waste-paper basket. Then I went and sat on the window seat again. But I kept thinking of the torn scraps in the basket, and after a moment I had to get up and look in the basket once more. Even now the ink stood up on the fragments thick and black, the writing was not destroyed. I took a box of matches and set fire to the fragments. The flame had a lovely light, staining the paper, curling the edges, making the slanting writing impossible to distinguish. The fragments fluttered to grey ashes. The letter R was the last to go, it twisted in the flame, it curled outwards for a moment, becoming larger than ever. Then it crumpled too; the flame destroyed it. It was not ashes even, it was feathery dust . . . I went and washed my hands in the basin. I felt better, much better. I had the clean new feeling that one has when the calendar is hung on the wall at the beginning of the year. January the 1st. I was aware of the same freshness, the same gay confidence. The door opened and he came into the room.

'All's well,' he said; 'shock made her speechless at first, but she's beginning to recover, so I'm going downstairs to the office, to make certain she will catch the first train. For a moment she wavered; I think she had hopes of acting witness at the wedding, but I was very firm. Go and talk to her.'

He said nothing about being glad, about being happy. He did not take my arm and go into the sitting-room with me. He smiled, and waved his hand, and went off down the corridor alone. I went to Mrs Van Hopper, uncertain, rather self-conscious, like a maid who has handed in her notice through a friend.

She was standing by the window, smoking a cigarette, an odd, dumpy little figure I should not see again, her coat stretched tight over her large breasts, her ridiculous hat perched sideways on her head.

'Well,' she said, her voice dry and hard, not the voice she would have used to him. 'I suppose I've got to hand it to you for a double-time worker. Still waters certainly run deep in your case. How did you manage it?'

I did not know what to answer. I did not like her smile. 'It was a lucky thing for you I had the influenza,' she said. 'I realize now how you spent your days, and why you were so forgetful. Tennis lessons my eye. You might have told me, you know.'

'I'm sorry,' I said.

She looked at me curiously, she ran her eyes over my figure. 'And he tells me he wants to marry you in a few days. Lucky again for you that you haven't a family to ask questions. Well, it's nothing to do with me any more, I wash my hands of the whole affair. I rather wonder what his friends will think, but I suppose that's up to him. You realize he's years older than you?'

'He's only forty-two,' I said, 'and I'm old for my age.'

She laughed, she dropped cigarette ash on the floor. 'You certainly are,' she said. She went on looking at me in a way she had never done before. Appraising me, running her eyes over my points like a judge at a cattle show. There was something inquisitive about her eyes, something unpleasant.

'Tell me,' she said, intimate, a friend to a friend, 'have you been doing anything you shouldn't?'

She was like Blaize, the dressmaker, who had offered me that ten per cent.

'I don't know what you mean,' I said.

She laughed, she shrugged her shoulders. 'Oh, well . . . never mind. But I always said English girls were dark horses, for all their hockey-playing attitude. So I'm supposed to travel to Paris alone, and leave you here while your beau gets a marriage licence? I notice he doesn't ask me to the wedding.'

'I don't think he wants anyone, and anyway you would have sailed,' I said.

'H'm, h'm,' she said. She took out her vanity case and began powdering her nose. 'I suppose you really do know your own mind,' she went on; 'after all, the whole thing has been very hurried, hasn't it? A matter of a few weeks. I don't suppose he's too easy, and you'll have to adapt yourself to his ways. You've led an extremely sheltered life up to now, you know, and you can't say that I've run you off your feet. You will have your work cut out as mistress of Manderley. To be perfectly frank, my dear, I simply can't see you doing it.'

Her words sounded like the echo of my own an hour before.

'You haven't the experience,' she continued, 'you don't know that milieu. You can scarcely string two sentences together at my bridge teas, what are you going to say to all his friends? The Manderley parties were famous when she was alive. Of course he's told you all about them?'

I hesitated, but she went on, thank heaven, not waiting for my answer.

'Naturally one wants you to be happy, and I grant you he's a very attractive creature but – well, I'm sorry; and personally I think you are making a big mistake – one you will bitterly regret.'

She put down the box of powder, and looked at me over her shoulder. Perhaps she was being sincere at last, but I did not want that sort of honesty. I did not say anything. I looked sullen, perhaps, for she shrugged her shoulders and wandered to the looking-glass, straightening her little mushroom hat. I was glad she was going, glad I should not see her again. I grudged the months I had spent with her, employed by her, taking her money, trotting in her wake like a shadow, drab and dumb. Of course I was inexperienced, of course I was idiotic, shy, and young. I knew all that. She did not have to tell me. I suppose her attitude was deliberate, and for some odd feminine reason she resented this marriage; her scale of values had received a shock.

Well, I would not care, I would forget her and her barbed words. A new confidence had been born in me when I burnt that page and scattered the fragments. The past would not exist for either of us; we were starting afresh, he and I. The past had blown away like the ashes in the waste-paper basket. I was going to be Mrs de Winter. I was going to live at Manderley.

Soon she would be gone, rattling alone in the wagon-lit without me, and he and I would be together in the dining-room of the hotel, lunching at the same table, planning the future. The brink of a big adventure. Perhaps, once she had gone, he would talk to me at last, about loving me, about being happy. Up to now there had been no time, and anyway those things are not easily said, they must wait their moment. I looked up, and caught her reflection in the looking-glass. She was watching me, a little tolerant smile on her lips. I thought she was going to be generous after all, hold out her hand and wish me luck, give me encouragement and tell me that everything was going to be all right. But she went on smiling, twisting a stray hair into place beneath her hat.

'Of course,' she said, 'you know why he is marrying you, don't you? You haven't flattered yourself he's in love with you? The fact is that empty house got on his nerves to such an extent he nearly went off his head. He admitted as much before you came into the room. He just can't go on living there alone . . .'

# 7

We came to Manderley in early May, arriving, so Maxim said, with the first swallows and the bluebells. It would be the best moment, before the full flush of summer, and in the valley the azaleas would be prodigal of scent, and the blood-red rhododendrons in bloom. We motored, I remember, leaving London in the morning in a heavy shower of rain, coming to Manderley about five o'clock, in time for tea. I can see myself now, unsuitably dressed as usual, although a bride of seven weeks, in a tan-coloured stockinette frock, a small fur known as a stone marten round my neck, and over all a shapeless mackintosh, far too big for me and dragging to my ankles. It was, I thought, a gesture to the weather, and the length added inches to my height. I clutched a pair of gauntlet gloves in my hands, and carried a large leather handbag.

'This is London rain,' said Maxim when we left, 'you wait, the sun will be shining for you when we come to Manderley'; and he was right, for the clouds left us at Exeter, they rolled away behind us, leaving a great blue sky above our heads and a white road in front of us.

I was glad to see the sun, for in superstitious fashion I looked upon rain as an omen of ill-will, and the leaden skies of London had made me silent.

'Feeling better?' said Maxim, and I smiled at him, taking his hand, thinking how easy it was for him, going to his own home, wandering into the hall, picking up letters, ringing a bell for tea, and I wondered how much he guessed of my nervousness, and whether his question 'Feeling better?' meant that he understood. 'Never mind, we'll soon be there. I expect you want your tea,' he said, and he let go my hand because we had reached a bend in the road, and must slow down.

I knew then that he had mistaken my silence for fatigue, and it had not occurred to him I dreaded this arrival at Manderley as much as I had longed for it in theory. Now the moment was upon me I wished it delayed. I wanted to draw up at some wayside inn and stay there, in a coffee-room, by an impersonal fire. I wanted to be a traveller on the road, a bride in love with her husband. Not myself coming to Manderley for the first time, the wife of Maxim de Winter. We passed many friendly villages where the cottage windows had a kindly air. A woman, holding a baby in her arms, smiled at me from a doorway, while a man clanked across a road to a well, carrying a pail.

I wished we could have been one with them, perhaps their neighbours, and that Maxim could lean over a cottage gate in the evenings, smoking a pipe, proud of a very tall hollyhock he had grown himself, while I bustled in my kitchen, clean as a pin, laying the table for supper. There would be an alarm clock on the dresser ticking loudly, and a row of shining plates, while after supper Maxim would read his paper, boots on the fender, and I reach for a great pile of mending in the dresser drawer. Surely it would be peaceful and steady, that way of living, and easier, too, demanding no set standard?

'Only two miles further,' said Maxim; 'you see that great belt of trees on the brow of the hill there, sloping to the valley, with a scrap of sea beyond? That's Manderley, in there. Those are the woods.'

I forced a smile, and did not answer him, aware now of a stab of panic, an uneasy sickness that could not be controlled. Gone was my glad excitement, vanished my happy pride. I was like a child brought to her first school, or a little untrained maid who has never left home before, seeking a situation. Any measure of self-possession I had gained hitherto during the brief seven weeks of marriage, was like a rag now, fluttering before the wind; it seemed to me that even the most elementary knowledge of behaviour was unknown to me now, I should not know my right hand from my left, whether to stand or sit, what spoons and forks to use at dinner.

'I should shed that mackintosh,' he said, glancing down at me, 'it has not rained down here at all, and put your funny little fur straight. Poor lamb, I've bustled you down here like this, and you probably ought to have bought a lot of clothes in London.'

'It doesn't matter to me, as long as you don't mind,' I said.

'Most women think of nothing but clothes,' he said absently, and turning a corner we came to a cross-road, and the beginning of a high wall.

'Here we are,' he said, a new note of excitement in his voice, and I gripped the leather seat of the car with my two hands.

The road curved, and before us, on the left, were two high iron gates beside a lodge, open wide to the long drive beyond. As we drove through I saw faces peering through the dark window of the lodge, and a child ran round from the back, staring curiously. I shrank back against the seat, my heart beating quickly, knowing why the faces were at the window, and why the child stared.

They wanted to see what I was like. I could imagine them now, talking excitedly, laughing in the little kitchen. 'Only caught sight of the top of her hat,' they would say, 'she wouldn't show her face. Oh, well, we'll know by tomorrow. Word will come from the house.' Perhaps he guessed something of my shyness at last, for he took my hand, and kissed it, and laughed a little, even as he spoke.

'You mustn't mind if there's a certain amount of curiosity,' he said; 'everyone will want to know what you are like. They have probably talked of nothing else for weeks. You've only got to be yourself and they will all adore you. And you don't have to worry about the house, Mrs Danvers does everything. Just leave it all to her. She'll be stiff with you at first, I dare say, she's an extraordinary character, but you mustn't let it worry you. It's just her manner. See those shrubs? It's like a blue wall along here when the hydrangeas are in bloom.'

I did not answer him, for I was thinking of that self who long

70

ago bought a picture post-card in a village shop, and came out into the bright sunlight twisting it in her hands, pleased with her purchase, thinking 'This will do for my album. "Manderley", what a lovely name.' And now I belonged here, this was my home. I would write letters to people saying, 'We shall be down at Manderley all the summer, you must come and see us,' and I would walk along this drive, strange and unfamiliar to me now, with perfect knowledge, conscious of every twist and turn, marking and approving where the gardeners had worked, here a cutting back of the shrubs, there a lopping of a branch, calling at the lodge by the iron gates on some friendly errand, saying, 'Well, how's the leg today?' while the old woman, curious no longer, bade me welcome to her kitchen. I envied Maxim, careless and at ease, and the little smile on his lips which meant he was happy to be coming home.

It seemed remote to me, and far too distant, the time when I too should smile and be at ease, and I wished it could come quickly; that I could be old even, with grey hair and slow of step, having lived here many years – anything but the timid, foolish creature I felt myself to be.

The gates had shut to with a crash behind us, the dusty high-road was out of sight, and I became aware that this was not the drive I had imagined would be Manderley's, this was not a broad and spacious thing of gravel, flanked with neat turf at either side, kept smooth with rake and brush.

This drive twisted and turned as a serpent, scarce wider in places than a path, and above our heads was a great colonnade of trees, whose branches nodded and intermingled with one another, making an archway for us, like the roof of a church. Even the midday sun would not penetrate the interlacing of those green leaves, they were too thickly entwined, one with another, and only little flickering patches of warm light would come in intermittent waves to dapple the drive with gold. It was very silent, very still. On the high-road there had been a gay west wind blowing in my face, making the grass on the hedges dance in unison, but here there was no wind. Even the engine of the car had taken a new note, throbbing low, quieter than before. As the drive descended to the valley so the trees came in upon us, great beeches with lovely smooth white stems, lifting their myriad branches to one another, and other trees, trees I could not name, coming close, so close that I could touch them with my hands. On we went, over a little bridge that spanned a narrow stream, and still this drive that was no drive twisted and turned like an enchanted ribbon through the dark and silent woods, penetrating even deeper to the very heart surely of the forest itself, and still there was no clearing, no space to hold a house.

The length of it began to nag at my nerves; it must be this turn, I thought, or round that further bend; but as I leant forward in my seat I was for ever disappointed, there was no house, no field, no broad and friendly garden, nothing but the silence and deep woods. The lodge gates were a memory, and the high-road something belonging to another time, another world.

Suddenly I saw a clearing in the dark drive ahead, and a patch of sky, and in a moment the dark trees had thinned, the nameless shrubs had disappeared, and on either side of us was a wall of colour, blood-red, reaching far above our heads. We were amongst the rhododendrons. There was something bewildering, even shocking, about the suddenness of their discovery. The woods had not prepared me for them. They startled me with their crimson faces, massed one upon the other in incredible profusion, showing no leaf, no twig, nothing but the slaughterous red, luscious and fantastic, unlike any rhododendron plant I had seen before.

I glanced at Maxim. He was smiling. 'Like them?' he said.

I told him 'Yes,' a little breathlessly, uncertain whether I was speaking the truth or not, for to me a rhododendron was a homely, domestic thing, strictly conventional, mauve or pink in colour, standing one beside the other in a neat round bed. And these were monsters, rearing to the sky, massed like a battalion, too beautiful I thought, too powerful; they were not plants at all.

We were not far from the house now, I saw the drive broaden to the sweep I had expected, and with the blood-red wall still flanking us on either side, we turned the last corner, and so came to Manderley. Yes, there it was, the Manderley I had expected, the Manderley of my picture post-card long ago. A thing of grace and beauty, exquisite and faultless, lovelier even than I had ever dreamed, built in its hollow of smooth grassland and mossy lawns, the terraces sloping to the gardens, and the gardens to the sea. As we drove up to the wide stone steps and stopped before the open door, I saw through one of the mullioned windows that the hall was full of people, and I heard Maxim swear under his breath. 'Damn that woman,' he said; 'she knows perfectly well I did not want this sort of thing,' and he put on the brakes with a jerk.

'What's the matter?' I said. 'Who are all those people?'

'I'm afraid you will have to face it now,' he said, in irritation. 'Mrs Danvers has collected the whole damned staff in the house and on the estate to welcome us. It's all right, you won't have to say anything, I'll do it all.'

I fumbled for the handle of the door, feeling slightly sick, and cold now too from the long drive, and as I fumbled with the catch the butler came down the steps, followed by a footman, and he opened the door for me.

He was old, he had a kind face, and I smiled up at him, holding out my hand, but I don't think he could have seen, for he took the rug instead, and my small dressing-case, and turned to Maxim, helping me from the car at the same time.

'Well, here we are, Frith,' said Maxim, taking off his gloves. 'It was raining when we left London. You don't seem to have had it here. Everyone well?'

'Yes, sir, thank you, sir. No, we have had a dry month on the whole. Glad to see you home, and hope you have been keeping well. And Madam too.'

'Yes, we are both well, thank you, Frith. Rather tired from the drive, and wanting our tea. I didn't expect this business.' He jerked his head to the hall.

'Mrs Danvers' orders, sir,' said the man, his face expression-less.

'I might have guessed it,' said Maxim abruptly. 'Come on' – he turned to me – 'it won't take long, and then you shall have your tea.'

We went together up the flight of steps, Frith and the footman following with the rug and my mackintosh, and I was aware of a little pain at the pit of my stomach, and a nervous contraction in my throat.

I can close my eyes now, and look back on it, and see myself as I must have been, standing on the threshold of the house, a slim, awkward figure in my stockinette dress, clutching in my sticky hands a pair of gauntlet gloves. I can see the great stone hall, the wide doors open to the library, the Peter Lelys and the Vandykes on the walls, the exquisite staircase leading to the minstrels' gallery, and there, ranged one behind the other in the hall, overflowing to the stone passages beyond, and to the dining-room, a sea of faces, open-mouthed and curious, gazing at me as though they were the watching crowd about the block, and I the victim with my hands behind my back. Someone advanced from the sea of faces, someone tall and gaunt, dressed in deep black, whose prominent cheek-bones and great, hollow eyes gave her a skull's face, parchment-white, set on a skeleton's frame.

She came towards me, and I held out my hand, envying her for her dignity and her composure; but when she took my hand hers was limp and heavy, deathly cold, and it lay in mine like a lifeless thing.

'This is Mrs Danvers,' said Maxim, and she began to speak, still leaving that dead hand in mine, her hollow eyes never leaving my eyes, so that my own wavered and would not meet hers, and as they did so her hand moved in mine, the life returned to it, and I was aware of a sensation of discomfort and of shame.

I cannot remember her words now, but I know that she bade me welcome to Manderley, in the name of herself and the staff, a stiff, conventional speech rehearsed for the occasion, spoken in a voice as cold and lifeless as her hands had been. When she had finished she waited, as though for a reply, and I remember blushing scarlet, stammering some sort of thanks in return, and dropping both my gloves in my confusion. She stooped to pick them up, and as she handed them to me I saw a little smile of scorn upon her lips, and I guessed at once she considered me ill-bred. Something, in the expression of her face, gave me a feeling of unrest, and even when she had stepped back, and taken her place amongst the rest, I could see that black figure standing out alone, individual and apart, and for all her silence I knew her eye to be upon me. Maxim took my arm and made a little speech of thanks, perfectly easy and free from embarrassment, as though the making of it was no effort to him at all, and then he bore me off to the library to tea, closing the doors behind us, and we were alone again.

Two cocker spaniels came from the fireside to greet us. They pawed at Maxim, their long, silken ears strained back with affection, their noses questing his hands, and then they left him and came to me, sniffing at my heels, rather uncertain, rather suspicious. One was the mother, blind in one eye, and soon she had enough of me, and took herself with a grunt to the fire again, but Jasper, the younger, put his nose into my hand, and laid a chin upon my knee, his eyes deep with meaning, his tail a-thump when I stroked his silken ears.

I felt better when I had taken my hat off, and my wretched little fur, and thrown them both beside my gloves and my bag on to the window seat. It was a deep, comfortable room, with books lining the walls to the ceiling, the sort of room a man would move from never, did he live alone, solid chairs beside a great open fireplace, baskets for the two dogs in which I felt they never sat, for the hollows in the chairs had tell-tale marks. The long windows looked out upon the lawns, and beyond the lawns to the distant shimmer of the sea.

There was an old quiet smell about the room, as though the air in it was little changed, for all the sweet lilac scent and the roses brought to it throughout the early summer. Whatever air came to this room, whether from the garden or from the sea, would lose its first freshness, becoming part of the unchanging room itself, one with the books, musty and never read, one with the scrolled ceiling, the dark panelling, the heavy curtains.

It was an ancient mossy smell, the smell of a silent church where services are seldom held, where rusty lichen grows upon the stones and ivy tendrils creep to the very windows. A room for peace, a room for meditation.

Soon tea was brought to us, a stately little performance enacted by Frith and the young footman, in which I played no part until they had gone, and while Maxim glanced through his great pile of letters I played with two dripping crumpets, crumbled cake with my hands, and swallowed my scalding tea.

Now and again he looked up at me and smiled, and then returned to his letters, the accumulation of the last months I supposed, and I thought how little I knew of his life here at Manderley, of how it went day by day, of the people he knew, of his friends, men and women, of what bills he paid, what orders he gave about his household. The last weeks had gone so swiftly, and I – driving by his side through France and Italy – thought only of how I loved him, seeing Venice with his eyes, echoing his words, asking no questions of the past and future, content with the little glory of the living present.

For he was gayer than I had thought, more tender than I had dreamed, youthful and ardent in a hundred happy ways, not the Maxim I had first met, not the stranger who sat alone at the table in the restaurant, staring before him, wrapped in his secret self. My Maxim laughed and sang, threw stones into the water, took my hand, wore no frown between his eyes, carried no burden on his shoulder. I knew him as a lover, as a friend, and during those weeks I had forgotten that he had a life, orderly, methodical, a life which must be taken up again, continued as before, making vanished weeks a brief discarded holiday.

I watched him read his letters, saw him frown at one, smile at another, dismiss the next with no expression, and but for the grace of God I thought, my letter would be lying there, written from New York, and he would read it in the same indifferent fashion, puzzled at first perhaps by the signature, and then tossing it with a yawn to the pile of others in the basket, reaching for his cup of tea. The knowledge of this chilled me; how narrow a chance had stood between me and what might-have-been, for he would have sat here to his tea, as he sat now, continuing his home life as he would in any case, and perhaps he would not have thought of me much, not with regret anyway, while I, in New York, playing bridge with Mrs Van Hopper, would wait day after day for a letter that never came.

I leant back in my chair, glancing about the room, trying to instil into myself some measure of confidence, some genuine realization that I was here, at Manderley, the house of the picture post-card, the Manderley that was famous. I had to teach myself that all this was mine now, mine as much as his, the deep chair I was sitting in, that mass of books stretching to the ceiling, the pictures on the walls, the gardens, the woods, the Manderley I had read about, all of this was mine now because I was married to Maxim.

We should grow old here together, we should sit like this to our tea as old people, Maxim and I, with other dogs, the successors of these, and the library would wear the same ancient musty smell that it did now. It would know a period of glorious shabbiness and wear when the boys were young – our boys – for I saw them sprawling on the sofa with muddy boots, bringing with them always a litter of rods, and cricket bats, great clasp-knives, bows-and-arrows.

On the table there, polished now and plain, an ugly case would stand containing butterflies and moths, and another one with birds' eggs, wrapped in cotton wool. 'Not all this junk in here,' I would say, 'take them to the schoolroom, darlings,' and they would run off, shouting, calling to one another, but the little one staying behind, pottering on his own, quieter than the others.

My vision was disturbed by the opening of the door, and Frith came in with the footman to clear the tea. 'Mrs Danvers wondered, Madam, whether you would like to see your room,' he said to me, when the tea had been taken away.

Maxim glanced up from his letters. 'What sort of job have they made of the east wing?' he said.

'Very nice indeed, sir, it seems to me; the men made a mess when they were working, of course, and for a time Mrs Danvers was rather afraid it would not be finished by your return. But they cleared out last Monday. I should imagine you would be very comfortable there, sir; it's a lot lighter of course on that side of the house.'

'Have you been making alterations?' I asked.

'Oh, nothing much,' said Maxim briefly, 'only redecorating and painting the suite in the east wing, which I thought we would use for ours. As Frith says, it's much more cheerful on that side of the house, and it has a lovely view of the rose-garden. It was the visitors' wing when my mother was alive. I'll just finish these letters and then I'll come up and join you. Run along and make friends with Mrs Danvers; it's a good opportunity.'

I got up slowly, my old nervousness returning, and went out into the hall. I wished I could have waited for him, and then, taking his arm, seen the rooms together. I did not want to go alone, with Mrs Danvers. How vast the great hall looked now that it was empty. My feet rang on the flagged stones, echoing to the ceiling, and I felt guilty at the sound, as one does in church, self-conscious, aware of the same constraint. My feet made a stupid pitter-patter as I walked, and I thought that Frith, with his felt soles, must have thought me foolish.

'It's very big, isn't it?' I said, too brightly, too forced, a school-girl still, but he answered me in all solemnity.

'Yes, Madam, Manderley is a big place. Not so big as some, of course, but big enough. This was the old banqueting hall, in old days. It is used still on great occasions, such as a big dinner, or a ball. And the public are admitted here, you know, once a week.'

'Yes,' I said, still aware of my loud footsteps, feeling, as I followed him, that he considered me as he would one of the public visitors, and I behaved like a visitor too, glancing politely to right and left, taking in the weapons on the wall, and the pictures, touching the carved staircase with my hands.

A black figure stood waiting for me at the head of the stairs, the hollow eyes watching me intently from the white skull's face. I looked round for the solid Frith, but he had passed along the hall and into the further corridor.

I was alone now with Mrs Danvers. I went up the great stairs towards her, and she waited motionless, her hands folded before her, her eyes never leaving my face. I summoned a smile, which was not returned, nor did I blame her, for there was no purpose to the smile, it was a silly thing, bright and artificial. 'I hope I haven't kept you waiting,' I said.

'It's for you to make your own time, Madam,' she answered, 'I'm here to carry out your orders,' and then she turned, through the archway of the gallery, to the corridor beyond. We went along a broad, carpeted passage, and then turned left, through an oak door, and down a narrow flight of stairs and up a corresponding flight, and so to another door. This she flung open, standing aside to let me pass, and I came to a little ante-room, or boudoir, furnished with a sofa, chairs, and writing-desk, which opened out to a large double bedroom with wide windows and a bathroom beyond. I went at once to the window, and looked out. The rose-garden lay below, and the eastern part of the terrace, while beyond the rose-garden rose a smooth grass bank, stretching to the near woods.

'You can't see the sea from here, then,' I said, turning to Mrs Danvers.

'No, not from this wing,' she answered; 'you can't even hear it, either. You would not know the sea was anywhere near, from this wing.'

She spoke in a peculiar way, as though something lay behind her words, and she laid an emphasis on the words 'this wing', as if suggesting that the suite where we stood now held some inferiority.

'I'm sorry about that; I like the sea,' I said.

She did not answer; she just went on staring at me, her hands folded before her.

'However, it's a very charming room,' I said, 'and I'm sure I shall be comfortable. I understand that it's been done up for our return.'

'Yes,' she said.

'What was it like before?' I asked.

'It had a mauve paper, and different hangings; Mr de Winter did not think it very cheerful. It was never much used, except for occasional visitors. But Mr de Winter gave special orders in his letters that you would have this room.'

'Then this was not his bedroom originally?' I said.

'No, Madam, he's never used the room in this wing before.'

'Oh,' I said, 'he didn't tell me that,' and I wandered to the dressing-table and began combing my hair. My things were already unpacked, my brushes and comb upon the tray. I was glad Maxim had given me a set of brushes, and that they were laid out there, upon the dressing-table, for Mrs Danvers to see. They were new, they had cost money, I need not be ashamed of them.

'Alice has unpacked for you and will look after you until your maid arrives,' said Mrs Danvers. I smiled at her again. I put down the brush upon the dressing-table.

'I don't have a maid,' I said awkwardly; 'I'm sure Alice, if she is the housemaid, will look after me all right.'

She wore the same expression that she had done on our first meeting, when I dropped my gloves so gauchely on the floor.

'I'm afraid that would not do for very long,' she said; 'it's usual, you know, for ladies in your position to have a personal maid.'

I flushed, and reached for my brush again. There was a sting in her words I understood too well. 'If you think it necessary perhaps you would see about it for me,' I said, avoiding her eyes; 'some young girl perhaps, wanting to train.'

'If you wish,' she said. 'It's for you to say.'

There was silence between us. I wished she would go away. I wondered why she must go on standing there, watching me, her hands folded on her black dress.

'I suppose you have been at Manderley for many years,' I said, making a fresh effort, 'longer than anyone else?'

'Not so long as Frith,' she said, and I thought how lifeless her voice was, and cold, like her hand when it had lain in mine; 'Frith was here when the old gentleman was living, when Mr de Winter was a boy.'

'I see,' I said; 'so you did not come till after that?'

'No,' she said, 'not till after that.'

Once more, I glanced up at her and once more I met her eyes, dark and sombre, in that white face of hers, instilling into me, I knew not why, a strange feeling of disquiet, of foreboding. I tried to smile, and could not; I found myself held by those eyes, that had no light, no flicker of sympathy towards me.

'I came here when the first Mrs de Winter was a bride,' she said, and her voice, which had hitherto, as I said, been dull and toneless, was harsh now with unexpected animation, with life and meaning, and there was a spot of colour on the gaunt cheekbones.

The change was so sudden that I was shocked, and a little scared. I did not know what to do, or what to say. It was as though she had spoken words that were forbidden, words that she had hidden within herself for a long time and now would be repressed no longer. Still her eyes never left my face; they looked upon me with a curious mixture of pity and of scorn, until I felt myself to be even younger and more untutored to the ways of life than I had believed.

I could see she despised me, marking with all the snobbery of her class that I was no great lady, that I was humble, shy, and diffident. Yet there was something beside scorn in those eyes of hers, something surely of positive dislike, or actual malice?

I had to say something, I could not go on sitting there, playing with my hair-brush, letting her see how much I feared and mistrusted her.

'Mrs Danvers,' I heard myself saying, 'I hope we shall be friends and come to understand one another. You must have patience with me, you know, because this sort of life is new to me, I've lived rather differently. And I do want to make a success of it, and above all to make Mr de Winter happy. I know I can leave all household arrangements to you, Mr de Winter said so, and you must just run things as they have always been run; I shan't want to make any changes.'

I stopped, a little breathless, still uncertain of myself and whether I was saying the right thing, and when I looked up again I saw that she had moved, and was standing with her hand on the handle of the door.

'Very good,' she said; 'I hope I shall do everything to your satisfaction. The house has been in my charge now for more than a year, and Mr de Winter has never complained. It was very different of course when the late Mrs de Winter was alive; there was a lot of entertaining then, a lot of parties, and though I managed for her, she liked to supervise things herself.'

Once again I had the impression that she chose her words with care, that she was feeling her way, as it were, into my mind, and watching for the effect upon my face.

'I would rather leave it to you,' I repeated, 'much rather,' and into her face came the same expression I had noticed before, when first I had shaken hands with her in the hall, a look surely of derision, of definite contempt. She knew that I would never withstand her, and that I feared her too.

'Can I do anything more for you?' she said, and pretended to glance round the room. 'No,' I said. 'No, I think I have everything. I shall be very comfortable here. You have made the room so charming' – this last a final crawling sop to win her approval. She shrugged her shoulders, and still she did not smile. 'I only followed out Mr de Winter's instructions,' she said.

She hesitated by the doorway, her hand on the handle of the open door. It was as though she still had something to say to me, and could not decide upon the words, yet waited there, for me to give her opportunity.

I wished she would go; she was like a shadow standing there, watching me, appraising me with her hollow eyes, set in that dead skull's face.

82

'If you find anything not to your liking you will tell me at once?' she asked.

'Yes,' I said. 'Yes, of course, Mrs Danvers,' but I knew this was not what she had meant to say, and silence fell between us once again.

'If Mr de Winter asks for his big wardrobe,' she said suddenly, 'you must tell him it was impossible to move. We tried, but we could not get it through these narrow doorways. These are smaller rooms than those in the west wing. If he doesn't like the arrangement of this suite he must tell me. It was difficult to know how to furnish these rooms.'

'Please don't worry, Mrs Danvers,' I said. 'I'm sure he will be pleased with everything. But I'm sorry it's given you so much trouble. I had no idea he was having rooms redecorated and furnished. He shouldn't have bothered. I'm sure I should have been just as happy and comfortable in the west wing.'

She looked at me curiously, and began twisting the handle of the door. 'Mr de Winter said you would prefer to be on this side,' she said, 'the rooms in the west wing are very old. The bedroom in the big suite is twice as large as this; a very beautiful room too, with a scrolled ceiling. The tapestry chairs are very valuable, and so is the carved mantelpiece. It's the most beautiful room in the house. And the windows look down across the lawns to the sea.'

I felt uncomfortable, a little shy. I did not know why she must speak with such an undercurrent of resentment, implying as she did at the same time that this room, where I found myself to be installed, was something inferior, not up to Manderley standard, a second-rate room, as it were, for a second-rate person.

'I suppose Mr de Winter keeps the most beautiful room to show to the public,' I said. She went on twisting the handle of the door, and then looked up at me again, watching my eyes, hesitating before replying, and when she spoke her voice was quieter even, and more toneless, than it had been before.

'The bedrooms are never shown to the public,' she said, 'only the hall and the gallery, and the room below.' She paused an instant, feeling me with her eyes. 'They used to live in the west wing and use those rooms when Mrs de Winter was alive. That big room, I was telling you about, that looked down to the sea, was Mrs de Winter's bedroom.'

Then I saw a shadow flit across her face, and she drew back against the wall, effacing herself, as a step sounded outside and Maxim came into the room.

'How is it?' he said to me. 'All right? Do you think you'll like it?'

He looked round with enthusiasm, pleased as a schoolboy. 'I always thought this a most attractive room,' he said. 'It was wasted all those years as a guest-room, but I always thought it had possibilities. You've made a great success of it, Mrs Danvers: I give you full marks.'

'Thank you, sir,' she said, her face expressionless, and then she turned, and went out of the room, closing the door softly behind her.

Maxim went and leant out of the window. 'I love the rose-garden,' he said; 'one of the first things I remember is walking after my mother, on very small, unsteady legs, while she picked off the dead heads of the roses. There's something peaceful and happy about this room, and it's quiet too. You could never tell you were within five minutes of the sea, from this room.'

'That's what Mrs Danvers said,' I told him.

He came away from the window, he prowled about the room, touching things, looking at the pictures, opening wardrobes, fingering my clothes, already unpacked.

'How did you get on with old Danvers?' he said abruptly.

I turned away, and began combing my hair again before the looking-glass. 'She seems just a little bit stiff,' I said, after a moment or two; 'perhaps she thought I was going to interfere with the running of the house.'

'I don't think she would mind your doing that,' he said. I looked up and saw him watching my reflection in the looking-glass, and then he turned away and went over to the window again, whistling quietly, under his breath, rocking backwards and forwards on his heels.

'Don't mind her,' he said; 'she's an extraordinary character in many ways, and possibly not very easy for another woman to get on with. You mustn't worry about it. If she really makes herself a nuisance we'll get rid of her. But she's efficient, you know, and will take all housekeeping worries off your hands. I dare say she's a bit of a bully to the staff. She doesn't dare bully me though. I'd have given her the sack long ago if she had tried.'

'I expect we shall get on very well when she knows me better,' I said quickly; 'after all, it's natural enough that she should resent me a bit at first.'

'Resent you? Why resent you? What the devil do you mean?' he said.

He turned from the window, frowning, an odd, half angry expression on his face. I wondered why he should mind, and wished I had said something else.

'I mean, it must be much easier for a housekeeper to look after a man alone,' I said. 'I dare say she had got into the way of doing it, and perhaps she was afraid I should be very over-bearing.'

'Overbearing, my God . . .' he began, 'if you think . . .' and then he stopped, and came across to me, and kissed me on the top of my head.

'Let's forget about Mrs Danvers,' he said; 'she doesn't interest me very much, I'm afraid. Come along, and let me show you something of Manderley.'

I did not see Mrs Danvers again that evening, and we did not talk about her any more. I felt happier when I had dismissed her from my thoughts, less of an interloper, and as we wandered about the rooms downstairs, and looked at the pictures, and Maxim put his arm around my shoulder, I began to feel more like the self I wanted to become, the self I had pictured in my dreams, who made Manderley her home.

My footsteps no longer sounded foolish on the stone flags of the hall, for Maxim's nailed shoes made far more noise than mine, and the pattering feet of the two dogs was a comfortable, pleasing note.

I was glad, too, because it was the first evening and we had only been back a little while and the showing of the pictures had taken time, when Maxim, looking at the clock, said it was too late to change for dinner, so that I was spared the embarrassment of Alice, the maid, asking what I should wear, and of her helping me to dress, and myself walking down that long flight of stairs to the hall, cold, with bare shoulders, in a dress that Mrs Van Hopper had given me because it did not suit her daughter. I had dreaded the formality of dinner in that austere dining-room, and now, because of the little fact that we had not changed, it was quite all right, quite easy, just the same as when we had dined together in restaurants. I was comfortable in my stockinette dress, I laughed and talked about things we had seen in Italy and France, we even had the snapshots on the table, and Frith and the footman were impersonal people, as the waiters had been; they did not stare at me as Mrs Danvers had done.

We sat in the library after dinner, and presently the curtains were drawn, and more logs thrown on the fire; it was cool for May, I was thankful for the warmth that came from the steady burning logs.

It was new for us to sit together like this, after dinner, for in Italy we had wandered about, walked or driven, gone into little cafés, leant over bridges. Maxim made instinctively now for the chair on the left of the open fireplace, and stretched out his hand for the papers. He settled one of the broad cushions behind his head, and lit a cigarette. 'This is his routine,' I thought, 'this is what he always does: this has been his custom now for years.'

He did not look at me, he went on reading his paper, contented, comfortable, having assumed his way of living, the master of his house. And as I sat there, brooding, my chin in my hands, fondling the soft ears of one of the spaniels, it came to me that I was not the first one to lounge there in possession of the chair; someone had been before me, and surely left an imprint of her person on the cushions, and on the arm where her hand had rested. Another one had poured the coffee from that same silver coffee pot, had placed the cup to her lips, had bent down to the dog, even as I was doing.

Unconsciously, I shivered as though someone had opened the door behind me and let a draught into the room. I was sitting in Rebecca's chair, I was leaning against Rebecca's cushion, and the dog had come to me and laid his head upon my knee because that had been his custom, and he remembered, in the past, she had given sugar to him there.

# 8

I had never realized, of course, that life at Manderley would be so orderly and planned. I remember now, looking back, how on that first morning Maxim was up and dressed and writing letters, even before breakfast, and when I got downstairs, rather after nine o'clock, a little flurried by the booming summons of the gong, I found he had nearly finished, he was already peeling his fruit.

He looked up at me and smiled. 'You mustn't mind,' he said; 'this is something you will have to get used to. I've no time to hang about at this hour of the day. Running a place like Manderley, you know, is a full-time job. The coffee and the hot dishes are on the sideboard. We always help ourselves at breakfast.' I said something about my clock being slow, about having been too long in the bath, but he did not listen, he was looking down at a letter, frowning at something.

How impressed I was, I remember well; impressed and a little overawed by the magnificence of the breakfast offered to us. There was tea, in a great silver urn, and coffee too, and on the heater, piping hot, dishes of scrambled eggs, of bacon, and another of fish. There was a little clutch of boiled eggs as well, in their own special heater, and porridge, in a silver porringer. On another sideboard was a ham, and a great piece of cold bacon. There were scones too, on the table, and toast, and various pots of jam, marmalade, and honey, while dessert dishes, piled high with fruit, stood at either end. It seemed strange to me that Maxim, who in Italy and France had eaten a *croissant* and fruit only, and drunk a cup of coffee, should sit down to this breakfast at home, enough for a dozen people, day after day probably, year after year, seeing nothing ridiculous about it, nothing wasteful.

I noticed he had eaten a small piece of fish. I took a boiled egg. And I wondered what happened to the rest, all those scrambled eggs, that crisp bacon, the porridge, the remains of the fish. Were there menials, I wondered, whom I should never know, never see, waiting behind kitchen doors for the gift of our breakfast? Or was it all thrown away, shovelled into dustbins? I would never know, of course, I would never dare to ask.

'Thank the Lord I haven't a great crowd of relations to inflict upon you,' said Maxim, 'a sister I very rarely see, and a grandmother who is nearly blind. Beatrice, by the way, asks herself over to lunch. I half expected she would. I suppose she wants to have a look at you.'

'Today?' I said, my spirits sinking to zero.

'Yes, according to the letter I got this morning. She won't stay long. You'll like her, I think. She's very direct, believes in speaking her mind. No humbug at all. If she doesn't like you she'll tell you so, to your face.'

I found this hardly comforting, and wondered if there was not some virtue in the quality of insincerity. Maxim got up from his chair, and lit a cigarette. 'I've a mass of things to see to this morning, do you think you can amuse yourself?' he said. 'I'd like to have taken you round the garden, but I must see Crawley, my agent. I've been away from things too long. He'll be in to lunch, too, by the way. You don't mind, do you? You will be all right?'

'Of course,' I said, 'I shall be quite happy.'

Then he picked up his letters, and went out of the room, and I remember thinking this was not how I imagined my first morning; I had seen us walking together, arms linked, to the sea, coming back rather late and tired and happy to a cold lunch, alone, and sitting afterwards under that chestnut tree I could see from the library window.

I lingered long over my first breakfast, spinning out the time, and it was not until I saw Frith come in and look at me, from behind the service screen, that I realized it was after ten o'clock. I sprang to my feet at once, feeling guilty, and apologized for sitting there so late, and he bowed, saying nothing, very polite, very correct, and I caught a flicker of surprise in his eyes. I wondered if I had said the wrong thing. Perhaps it did not do to apologize. Perhaps it lowered me in his estimation. I wished I knew what to say, what to do. I wondered if he suspected, as Mrs Danvers had done, that poise, and grace, and assurance were not qualities inbred in me, but were things to be acquired, painfully perhaps, and slowly, costing me many bitter moments.

As it was, leaving the room, I stumbled, not looking where I was going, catching my foot on the step by the door, and Frith came forward to help me, picking up my handkerchief, while Robert, the young footman, who was standing behind the screen, turned away to hide his smile.

I heard the murmur of their voices as I crossed the hall, and one of them laughed – Robert, I supposed. Perhaps they were laughing about me. I went upstairs again, to the privacy of my bedroom, but when I opened the door I found the housemaids in there doing the room; one was sweeping the floor, the other dusting the dressing-table. They looked at me in surprise. I quickly went out again. It could not be right, then, for me to go to my room at that hour in the morning. It was not expected of me. It broke the household routine. I crept downstairs once more, silently, thankful of my slippers that made no sound on the stone flags, and so into the library, which was chilly, the windows flung wide open, the fire laid but not lit.

I shut the windows, and looked round for a box of matches. I could not find one. I wondered what I should do. I did not like to ring. But the library, so snug and warm last night with the burning logs, was like an ice-house now, in the early morning. There were matches upstairs in the bedroom, but I did not like to go for them because it would mean disturbing the house-maids at their work. I could not bear their moon faces staring at me again. I decided that when Frith and Robert had left the dining-room I would fetch the matches from the sideboard. I tiptoed out into the hall and listened. They were still clearing, I could hear the sound of voices, and the movement of trays.

Presently all was silent, they must have gone through the service doors into the kitchen quarters, so I went across the hall and into the dining-room once more. Yes, there was a box of matches on the sideboard, as I expected. I crossed the room quickly and picked them up, and as I did so Frith came back into the room. I tried to cram the box furtively into my pocket, but I saw him glance at my hand in surprise.

'Did you require anything, Madam?' he said.

'Oh, Frith,' I said awkwardly, 'I could not find any matches.' He at once proffered me another box, handing me the cigarettes too, at the same time. This was another embarrassment, for I did not smoke.

'No, the fact is,' I said, 'I felt rather cool in the library, I suppose the weather seems chilly to me, after being abroad and I thought perhaps I would just put a match to the fire.'

'The fire in the library is not usually lit until the afternoon, Madam,' he said. 'Mrs de Winter always used the morning-room. There is a good fire in there. Of course if you should wish to have the fire in the library as well I will give orders for it to be lit.'

'Oh, no,' I said, 'I would not dream of it. I will go into the morning-room. Thank you, Frith.'

'You will find writing-paper, and pens, and ink, in there, Madam,' he said. 'Mrs de Winter always did all her correspondence and telephoning in the morning-room, after breakfast. The house telephone is also there, should you wish to speak to Mrs Danvers.'

'Thank you, Frith,' I said.

I turned away into the hall again, humming a little tune to give me an air of confidence. I could not tell him that I had never seen the morning-room, that Maxim had not shown it to me the night before. I knew he was standing in the entrance to the dining-room, watching me, as I went across the hall, and that I must make some show of knowing my way. There was a door to the left of the great staircase, and I went recklessly towards it, praying in my heart that it would take me to my goal, but when I came to it and opened it I saw that it was a garden room, a place for odds and ends: there was a table where flowers were done, there were basket chairs stacked against the wall, and a couple of mackintoshes too, hanging on a peg. I came out, a little defiantly, glancing across the hall, and saw Frith still standing there. I had not deceived him, though, not for a moment.

'You go through the drawing-room to the morning-room, Madam,' he said, 'through the door there, on your right, this side of the staircase. You go straight through the double drawing-room, and turn to your left.'

'Thank you, Frith,' I said humbly, pretending no longer.

I went through the long drawing-room, as he had directed; a lovely room this, beautifully proportioned, looking out upon the lawns down to the sea. The public would see this room, I supposed, and Frith, if he showed them round, would know the history of the pictures on the wall, and the period of the furniture. It was beautiful of course, I knew that, and those chairs and tables probably without price, but for all that I had no wish to linger there; I could not see myself sitting ever in those chairs, standing before that carved mantelpiece, throwing books down on to the tables. It had all the formality of a room in a museum, where alcoves were roped off, and a guardian, in cloak and hat like the guides in the French châteaux, sat in a chair beside the door. I went through then, and turned to the left, and so on to the little morning-room I had not seen before.

I was glad to see the dogs there, sitting before the fire, and Jasper, the younger, came over to me at once, his tail wagging, and thrust his nose into my hand. The old one lifted her muzzle at my approach, and gazed in my direction with her blind eyes, but when she had sniffed the air a moment, and found I was not the one she sought, she turned her head away with a grunt, and looked steadily into the fire again. Then Jasper left me, too, and settled himself by the side of his companion, licking his side. This was their routine. They knew, even as Frith had known, that the library fire was not lit until the afternoon. They came to the morning-room from long custom. Somehow I guessed, before going to the window, that the room looked out upon the rhododendrons. Yes, there they were, blood-red and luscious, as I had seen them the evening before, great bushes of them, massed beneath the open window, encroaching on to the sweep of the drive itself. There was a little clearing too, between the bushes, like a miniature lawn, the grass a smooth carpet of moss, and in the centre of this, the tiny statue of a naked faun, his pipes to his lips.

The crimson rhododendrons made his background, and the clearing itself was like a little stage, where he would dance, and play his part. There was no musty smell about this room, as there had been in the library. There were no old well-worn chairs, no tables littered with magazines and papers, seldom if ever read, but left there from long custom, because Maxim's father, or even his grandfather perhaps, had wished it so.

This was a woman's room, graceful, fragile, the room of someone who had chosen every particle of furniture with great care, so that each chair, each vase, each small, infinitesimal thing should be in harmony with one another, and with her own personality. It was as though she who had arranged this room had said: 'This I will have, and this, and this,' taking piece by piece from the treasures in Manderley each object that pleased her best, ignoring the second-rate, the mediocre, laying her hand with sure certain instinct only upon the best. There was no inter-mingling of style, no confusing of period, and the result was perfection in a strange and startling way, not coldly formal like the drawing-room shown to the public, but vividly alive, having something of the same glow and brilliance that the rhododen-drons had, massed there, beneath the window. And I noticed then that the rhododendrons, not content with forming their theatre on the little lawn outside the window, had been permitted to the room itself. Their great warm faces looked down upon me from the mantelpiece, they floated in a bowl upon the table by the sofa, they stood, lean and graceful, on the writing-desk beside the golden candlesticks.

The room was filled with them, even the walls took colour

from them, becoming rich and glowing in the morning sun. They were the only flowers in the room, and I wondered if there was some purpose in it, whether the room had been arranged originally with this one end in view, for nowhere else in the house did the rhododendrons obtrude. There were flowers in the dining-room, flowers in the library, but orderly and trim, rather in the background, not like this, not in profusion. I went and sat down at the writing-desk, and I thought how strange it was that this room, so lovely and so rich in colour, should be, at the same time, so business-like and purposeful. Somehow I should have expected that a room furnished as this was in such exquisite taste, for all the exaggeration of the flowers, would be a place of decoration only, languorous and intimate.

But this writing-table, beautiful as it was, was no pretty toy where a woman would scribble little notes, nibbling the end of a pen, leaving it, day after day, in carelessness, the blotter a little askew. The pigeon-holes were docketed, 'letters unanswered', 'letters-to-keep', 'household', 'estate', 'menus', 'miscellaneous', 'addresses'; each ticket written in that same scrawling pointed hand that I knew already. And it shocked me, even startled me, to recognize it again, for I had not seen it since I had destroyed the page from the book of poems, and I had not thought to see it again.

I opened a drawer at hazard, and there was the writing once more, this time in an open leather book, whose heading 'Guests at Manderley' showed at once, divided into weeks and months, what visitors had come and gone, the rooms they had used, the food they had eaten. I turned over the pages and saw that the book was a complete record of a year, so that the hostess, glancing back, would know to the day, almost to the hour, what guest had passed what night under her roof, and where he had slept, and what she had given him to eat. There was notepaper also in the drawer, thick white sheets, for rough writing, and the notepaper of the house, with the crest, and the address, and visiting cards, ivory white, in little boxes.

I took one out and looked at it, unwrapped it from its thin

tissue of paper. 'Mrs M. de Winter' it said, and in the corner 'Manderley'. I put it back in the box again, and shut the drawer, feeling guilty suddenly, and deceitful, as though I were staying in somebody else's house and my hostess had said to me, 'Yes, of course, write letters at my desk,' and I had unforgivably, in a stealthy manner, peeped at her correspondence. At any moment she might come back into the room and she would see me there, sitting before her open drawer, which I had no right to touch.

And when the telephone rang, suddenly, alarmingly, on the desk in front of me, my heart leapt and I started up in terror, thinking I had been discovered. I took the receiver off with trembling hands, and 'Who is it?' I said, 'who do you want?' There was a strange buzzing at the end of the line, and then a voice came, low and rather harsh, whether that of a woman or a man I could not tell, and 'Mrs de Winter?' it said, 'Mrs de Winter?'

'I'm afraid you have made a mistake,' I said; 'Mrs de Winter has been dead for over a year.' I sat there, waiting, staring stupidly into the mouthpiece, and it was not until the name was repeated again, the voice incredulous, slightly raised, that I became aware, with a rush of colour to my face, that I had blundered irretrievably, and could not take back my words. 'It's Mrs Danvers, Madam,' said the voice. 'I'm speaking to you on the house telephone.' My *faux pas* was so palpably obvious, so idiotic and unpardonable, that to ignore it would show me to be an even greater fool, if possible, than I was already.

'I'm sorry, Mrs Danvers,' I said, stammering, my words tumbling over one another; 'the telephone startled me, I didn't know what I was saying, I didn't realize the call was for me, and I never noticed I was speaking on the house telephone.'

'I'm sorry to have disturbed you, Madam,' she said; and she knows, I thought, she guesses I have been looking through the desk. 'I only wondered whether you wished to see me, and whether you approved of the menus for today.'

'Oh,' I said. 'Oh, I'm sure I do; that is, I'm sure I approve of the menus. Just order what you like, Mrs Danvers, you needn't bother to ask me.'

'It would be better, I think, if you read the list,' continued the voice; 'you will find the menu of the day on the blotter, beside you.'

I searched feverishly about me on the desk, and found at last a sheet of paper I had not noticed before. I glanced hurriedly through it: curried prawns, roast veal, asparagus, cold chocolate mousse – was this lunch or dinner? I could not see; lunch, I suppose.

'Yes, Mrs Danvers,' I said, 'very suitable, very nice indeed.'

'If you wish anything changed please say so,' she answered, 'and I will give orders at once. You will notice I have left a blank space beside the sauce, for you to mark your preference. I was not sure what sauce you are used to having served with the roast veal. Mrs de Winter was most particular about her sauces, and I always had to refer to her.'

'Oh,' I said. 'Oh, well . . . let me see, Mrs Danvers, I hardly know; I think we had better have what you usually have, whatever you think Mrs de Winter would have ordered.'

'You have no preference, Madam?'

'No,' I said. 'No, really, Mrs Danvers.'

'I rather think Mrs de Winter would have ordered a wine sauce, Madam.'

'We will have the same then, of course,' I said.

'I'm very sorry I disturbed you while you were writing, Madam.'

'You didn't disturb me at all,' I said; 'please don't apologize.'

'The post leaves at midday, and Robert will come for your letters, and stamp them himself,' she said; 'all you have to do is ring through to him, on the telephone, if you have anything urgent to be sent, and he will give orders for them to be taken in to the post-office immediately.'

'Thank you, Mrs Danvers,' I said. I listened for a moment, but she said no more, and then I heard a little click at the end of the telephone, which meant she had replaced the receiver. I did the same. Then I looked down again at the desk, and the notepaper, ready for use, upon the blotter. In front of me stared the ticketed pigeon-holes, and the words upon them 'letters unanswered', 'estate', 'miscellaneous', were like a reproach to me for my idleness. She who sat here before me had not wasted her time, as I was doing. She had reached out for the house telephone and given her orders for the day, swiftly, efficiently, and run her pencil perhaps through an item in the menu that had not pleased her. She had not said 'Yes, Mrs Danvers,' and 'Of course, Mrs Danvers,' as I had done. And then, when she had finished, she began her letters, five, six, seven perhaps to be answered, all written in that same curious, slanting hand I knew so well. She would tear off sheet after sheet of that smooth white paper, using it extravagantly, because of the long strokes she made when she wrote, and at the end of each of her personal letters she put her signature, 'Rebecca', that tall sloping R dwarfing its fellows.

I drummed with my fingers on the desk. The pigeon-holes were empty now. There were no 'letters unanswered' waiting to be dealt with, no bills to pay that I knew anything about. If I had anything urgent, Mrs Danvers said, I must telephone through to Robert and he would give orders for it to be taken to the post. I wondered how many urgent letters Rebecca used to write, and who they were written to. Dressmakers perhaps – 'I must have the white satin on Tuesday, without fail,' or to her hair-dresser – 'I shall be coming up next Friday, and want an appointment at three o'clock with Monsieur Antoine himself. Shampoo, massage, set, and manicure.' No, letters of that type would be a waste of time. She would have a call put through to London. Frith would do it. Frith would say 'I am speaking for Mrs de Winter.' I went on drumming with my fingers on the desk. I could think of nobody to write to. Only Mrs Van Hopper. And there was something foolish, rather ironical, in the realization that here I was sitting at my own desk in my own home with nothing better to do than to write a letter to Mrs Van Hopper, a woman I disliked, whom I should never see again. I pulled a sheet of notepaper towards me. I took up the narrow, slender pen, with the bright pointed nib. 'Dear Mrs Van Hopper,' I began. And as I wrote, in halting, laboured fashion, saying I hoped the voyage had been good, that she had found her daughter better, that the weather in New York was fine and warm, I noticed for the first time how cramped and unformed was my own handwriting; without individuality, without style, uneducated even, the writing of an indifferent pupil taught in a second-rate school.

# 9

When I heard the sound of the car in the drive I got up in sudden panic, glancing at the clock, for I knew that it meant Beatrice and her husband had arrived. It was only just gone twelve; they were much earlier than I expected. And Maxim was not yet back. I wondered if it would be possible to hide, to get out of the window, into the garden so that Frith, bringing them to the morning-room, would say, 'Madam must have gone out,' and it would seem quite natural, they would take it as a matter of course. The dogs looked up inquiringly as I ran to the window, and Jasper followed me, wagging his tail.

The window opened out on to the terrace and the little grass clearing beyond, but as I prepared to brush past the rhododendrons the sound of voices came close, and I backed again into the room. They were coming to the house by way of the garden, Frith having told them doubtless that I was in the morning-room. I went quickly into the big drawing-room, and made for a door near me on the left. It led into a long stone passage, and I ran along it, fully aware of my stupidity, despising myself for this sudden attack of nerves, but I knew I could not face these people, not for a moment anyway. The passage seemed to be taking me to the back regions, and as I turned a corner, coming upon another staircase, I met a servant I had not seen before, a scullery-maid perhaps; she carried a mop and pail in her hands. She stared at me in wonder, as though I were a vision, unexpected in this part of the house, and 'Good morning,' I said, in great confusion, making for the stairway, and 'Good morning, Madam,' she returned, her mouth open, her round eyes inquisitive as I climbed the stairs.

They would lead me, I supposed, to the bedrooms, and I could find my suite in the east wing, and sit up there a little while, until I judged it nearly time for lunch, when good manners would compel me to come down again.

I must have lost my bearings, for passing through a door at the head of the stairs I came to a long corridor that I had not seen before, similar in some ways to the one in the east wing, but broader and darker – dark owing to the panelling of the walls.

I hesitated, then turned left, coming upon a broad landing and another staircase. It was very quiet and dark. No one was about. If there had been housemaids here, during the morning, they had finished their work by now and gone downstairs. There was no trace of their presence, no lingering dust smell of carpets lately swept, and I thought, as I stood there, wondering which way to turn, that the silence was unusual, holding something of the same oppression as an empty house does, when the owners have gone away.

I opened a door at hazard, and found a room in total darkness, no chink of light coming through the closed shutters, while I could see dimly, in the centre of the room, the outline of furniture swathed in white dust-sheets. The room smelt close and stale, the smell of a room seldom if ever used, whose ornaments are herded together in the centre of a bed and left there, covered with a sheet. It might be too that the curtain had not been drawn from the window since some preceding summer, and if one crossed there now and pulled them aside, opening the creaking shutters, a dead moth who had been imprisoned behind them for many months would fall to the carpet and lie there, beside a forgotten pin, and a dried leaf blown there before the windows were closed for the last time. I shut the door softly, and went uncertainly along the corridor, flanked on either side by doors, all of them closed, until I came to a little alcove, set in an outside wall, where a broad window gave me light at last. I looked out, and I saw below me the smooth grass lawns stretching to the sea, and the sea itself, bright green with white-tipped crests, whipped by a westerly wind and scudding from the shore.

It was closer than I had thought, much closer; it ran, surely, beneath that little knot of trees below the lawns, barely five minutes away, and if I listened now, my ear to the window, I could hear the surf breaking on the shores of some little bay I could not see. I knew then I had made the circuit of the house, and was standing in the corridor of the west wing. Yes, Mrs Danvers was right. You could hear the sea from here. You might imagine, in the winter, it would creep up on to those green lawns and threaten the house itself, for even now, because of the high wind, there was a mist upon the window-glass, as though someone had breathed upon it. A mist salt-laden, borne upwards from the sea. A hurrying cloud hid the sun for a moment as I watched, and the sea changed colour instantly, becoming black, and the white crests with them very pitiless suddenly, and cruel, not the gay sparkling sea I had looked on first.

Somehow I was glad my rooms were in the east wing. I preferred the rose-garden, after all, to the sound of the sea. I went back to the landing then, at the head of the stairs, and as I prepared to go down, one hand upon the banister, I heard the door behind me open, and it was Mrs Danvers. We stared at one another for a moment without speaking, and I could not be certain whether it was anger I read in her eyes or curiosity, for her face became a mask directly she saw me. Although she said nothing I felt guilty and ashamed, as though I had been caught trespassing, and I felt the tell-tale colour come up into my face.

'I lost my way,' I said, 'I was trying to find my room.'

'You have come to the opposite side of the house,' she said; 'this is the west wing.'

'Yes, I know,' I said.

'Did you go into any of the rooms?' she asked me.

'No,' I said. 'No, I just opened a door, I did not go in. Everything was dark, covered up in dust-sheets. I'm sorry. I did not mean to disturb anything. I expect you like to keep all this shut up.'

'If you wish to open up the rooms I will have it done,' she

said; 'you have only to tell me. The rooms are all furnished, and can be used.'

'Oh, no,' I said. 'No. I did not mean you to think that.'

'Perhaps you would like me to show you all over the west wing?' she said.

I shook my head. 'No, I'd rather not,' I said. 'No, I must go downstairs.' I began to walk down the stairs, and she came with me, by my side, as though she were a warder, and I in custody.

'Any time, when you have nothing to do, you have only to ask me, and I will show you the rooms in the west wing,' she persisted, making me vaguely uncomfortable. I knew not why. Her insistence struck a chord in my memory, reminding me of a visit to a friend's house, as a child, when the daughter of the house, older than me, took my arm and whispered in my ear, 'I know where there is a book, locked in a cupboard, in my mother's bedroom. Shall we go and look at it?' I remembered her white, excited face, and her small, beady eyes, and the way she kept pinching my arm.

'I will have the dust-sheets removed, and then you can see the rooms as they looked when they were used,' said Mrs Danvers. 'I would have shown you this morning, but I believed you to be writing letters in the morning-room. You have only to telephone through to my room, you know, when you want me. It would only take a short while to have the rooms in readiness.'

We had come down the short flight of stairs, and she opened another door, standing aside for me to pass through, her dark eyes questing my face.

'It's very kind of you, Mrs Danvers,' I said. 'I will let you know some time.'

We passed out together on to the landing beyond, and I saw we were at the head of the main staircase now, behind the minstrel's gallery.

'I wonder how you came to miss your way?' she said, 'the door through the west wing is very different to this.'

'I did not come this way,' I said.

102

'Then you must have come up the back way, from the stone passage?' she said.

'Yes,' I said, not meeting her eyes. 'Yes, I came through a stone passage.'

She went on looking at me, as though she expected me to tell her why I left the morning-room in sudden panic, going through the back regions, and I felt suddenly that she knew, that she must have watched me, that she had seen me wandering perhaps in that west wing from the first, her eye to a crack in the door. 'Mrs Lacy, and Major Lacy, have been here some time,' she said. 'I heard their car drive up shortly after twelve.'

'Oh!' I said. 'I had not realized that.'

'Frith will have taken them to the morning-room,' she said: 'it must be getting on for half past twelve. You know your way now, don't you?'

'Yes, Mrs Danvers,' I said. And I went down the big stairway into the hall, knowing she was standing there above me, her eyes watching me.

I knew I must go back now, to the morning-room, and meet Maxim's sister and her husband. I could not hide in my bedroom now. As I went into the drawing-room I glanced back, over my shoulder, and I saw Mrs Danvers still standing there at the head of the stairs, like a black sentinel.

I stood for a moment outside the morning-room, with my hand on the door, listening to the hum of voices. Maxim had returned, then, while I had been upstairs, bringing his agent with him I supposed, for it sounded to me as if the room was full of people. I was aware of the same feeling of sick uncertainty I had experienced so often as a child, when summoned to shake hands with visitors, and turning the handle of the door I blundered in, to be met at once, it seemed, with a sea of faces and a general silence.

'Here she is at last,' said Maxim. 'Where have you been hiding? We were thinking of sending out a search party. Here is Beatrice, and this is Giles, and this is Frank Crawley. Look out, you nearly trod on the dog.'

Beatrice was tall, broad-shouldered, very handsome, very much like Maxim about the eyes and jaw, but not as smart as I had expected, much tweedier; the sort of person who would nurse dogs through distemper, know about horses, shoot well. She did not kiss me. She shook hands very firmly, looking me straight in the eyes, and then turned to Maxim. 'Quite different from what I expected. Doesn't answer to your description at all.'

Everyone laughed, and I joined in, not quite certain if the laugh was against me or not, wondering secretly what it was she had expected, and what had been Maxim's description.

And 'This is Giles,' said Maxim, prodding my arm, and Giles stretched out an enormous paw and wrung my hand, squeezing the fingers limp, genial eyes smiling from behind horn-rimmed glasses.

'Frank Crawley,' said Maxim, and I turned to the agent, a colourless, rather thin man with a prominent Adam's apple, in whose eyes I read relief as he looked upon me. I wondered why, but I had no time to think of that, because Frith had come in, and was offering me sherry, and Beatrice was talking to me again. 'Maxim tells me you only got back last night. I had not realized that, or of course we would never have thrust ourselves upon you so soon. Well, what do you think of Manderley?'

'I've scarcely seen anything of it yet,' I answered; 'it's beautiful, of course.'

She was looking me up and down, as I had expected, but in a direct, straightforward fashion, not maliciously like Mrs Danvers, not with unfriendliness. She had a right to judge me, she was Maxim's sister, and Maxim himself came to my side now, putting his arm through mine, giving me confidence.

'You're looking better, old man,' she said to him, her head on one side, considering him; 'you've lost that fine-drawn look, thank goodness. I suppose we've got you to thank for that?' nodding at me.

'I'm always very fit,' said Maxim shortly, 'never had anything wrong with me in my life. You imagine everyone ill who doesn't look as fat as Giles.'

'Bosh,' said Beatrice; 'you know perfectly well you were a perfect wreck six months ago. Gave me the fright of my life when I came and saw you. I thought you were in for a breakdown. Giles, bear me out. Didn't Maxim look perfectly ghastly last time we came over, and didn't I say he was heading for a breakdown?'

'Well, I must say, old chap, you're looking a different person,' said Giles. 'Very good thing you went away. Doesn't he look well, Crawley?'

I could tell by the tightening of Maxim's muscles under my arm that he was trying to keep his temper. For some reason this talk about his health was not welcome to him, angered him even, and I thought it tactless of Beatrice to harp upon it in this way, making so big a point of it.

'Maxim's very sunburnt,' I said shyly; 'it hides a multitude of sins. You should have seen him in Venice having breakfast on the balcony, trying to get brown on purpose. He thinks it makes him better-looking.'

Everyone laughed, and Mr Crawley said, 'It must have been wonderful in Venice, Mrs de Winter, this time of year,' and 'Yes,' I said, 'we had really wonderful weather. Only one bad day, wasn't it, Maxim?' the conversation drawing away happily from his health, and so to Italy, safest of subjects, and the blessed topic of fine weather. Conversation was easy now, no longer an effort. Maxim and Giles and Beatrice were discussing the running of Maxim's car, and Mr Crawley was asking if it were true that there were no more gondolas in the canals now, only motorboats. I don't think he would have cared at all had there been steamers at anchor in the Grand Canal, he was saying this to help me, it was his contribution to the little effort of steering the talk away from Maxim's health, and I was grateful to him, feeling him an ally, for all his dull appearance.

'Jasper wants exercise,' said Beatrice, stirring the dog with her foot; 'he's getting much too fat, and he's barely two years old. What do you feed him on, Maxim?'

'My dear Beatrice, he has exactly the same routine as your

dogs,' said Maxim. 'Don't show off and make out you know more about animals than I do.'

'Dear old boy, how can you pretend to know what Jasper has been fed on when you've been away for a couple of months? Don't tell me Frith walks to the lodge gates with him twice a day. This dog hasn't had a run for weeks. I can tell by the condition of his coat.'

'I'd rather he looked colossal than half-starved like that half-wit dog of yours,' said Maxim.

'Not a very intelligent remark when Lion won two firsts at Cruft's last February,' said Beatrice.

The atmosphere was becoming rather strained again, I could tell by the narrow lines of Maxim's mouth, and I wondered if brothers and sisters always sparred like this, making it uncomfortable for those who listened. I wished that Frith would come in and announce lunch. Or would we be summoned by a booming gong? I did not know what happened at Manderley.

'How far away from us are you?' I asked, sitting down by Beatrice; 'did you have to make a very early start?'

'We're fifty miles away, my dear, in the next county, the other side of Trowchester. The hunting is so much better with us. You must come over and stay, when Maxim can spare you. Giles will mount you.'

'I'm afraid I don't hunt,' I confessed. 'I learnt to ride, as a child, but very feebly; I don't remember much about it.'

'You must take it up again,' she said. 'You can't possibly live in the country and not ride: you wouldn't know what to do with yourself. Maxim says you paint. That's very nice, of course, but there's no exercise in it, is there? All very well on a wet day when there's nothing better to do.'

'My dear Beatrice, we are not all such fresh-air fiends as you,' said Maxim.

'I wasn't talking to you, old boy. We all know you are perfectly happy slopping about the Manderley gardens and never breaking out of a slow walk.'

'I'm very fond of walking too,' I said swiftly. 'I'm sure I shall

106

never get tired of rambling about Manderley. And I can bathe too, when it's warmer.'

'My dear, you are an optimist,' said Beatrice. 'I can hardly ever remember bathing here. The water is far too cold, and the beach is shingle.'

'I don't mind that,' I said. 'I love bathing. As long as the currents are not too strong. Is the bathing safe in the bay?'

Nobody answered, and I realized suddenly what I had said. My heart thumped, and I felt my cheeks go flaming red. I bent down to stroke Jasper's ear, in an agony of confusion. 'Jasper could do with a swim, and get some of that fat off,' said Beatrice, breaking the pause, 'but he'd find it a bit too much for him in the bay, wouldn't you, Jasper? Good old Jasper. Nice old man.' We patted the dog together, not looking at one another.

'I say, I'm getting infernally hungry. What on earth is happening to lunch?' said Maxim.

'It's only just on one now,' said Mr Crawley, 'according to the clock on the mantelpiece.'

'That clock was always fast,' said Beatrice.

'It's kept perfect time now for months,' said Maxim.

At that moment the door opened and Frith announced that luncheon was served.

'I say, I must have a wash,' said Giles, looking at his hands.

We all got up and wandered through the drawing-room to the hall in great relief, Beatrice and I a little ahead of the men, she taking my arm.

'Dear old Frith,' she said, 'he always looks exactly the same, and makes me feel like a girl again. You know, don't mind me saying so, but you are even younger than I expected. Maxim told me your age, but you're an absolute child. Tell me, are you very much in love with him?'

I was not prepared for this question, and she must have seen the surprise in my face, for she laughed lightly, and squeezed my arm.

'Don't answer,' she said. 'I can see what you feel. I'm an interfering bore, aren't I? You mustn't mind me. I'm devoted to Maxim, you know, though we always bicker like cat and dog when we meet. I congratulate you again on his looks. We were all very worried about him this time last year, but of course you know the whole story.' We had come to the dining-room by now, and she said no more, for the servants were there and the others had joined us, but as I sat down, and unfolded my napkin, I wondered what Beatrice would say did she realize that I knew nothing of that preceding year, no details of the tragedy that had happened down there, in the bay, that Maxim kept these things to himself, that I questioned him never.

Lunch passed off better than I had dared to hope. There were few arguments, or perhaps Beatrice was exercising tact at last; at any rate she and Maxim chatted about matters concerning Manderley, her horses, the garden, mutual friends, and Frank Crawley, on my left, kept up an easy patter with me for which I was grateful, as it required no effort. Giles was more concerned with food than with the conversation, though now and again he remembered my existence and flung me a remark at hazard.

'Same cook I suppose, Maxim?' he said, when Robert had offered him the cold soufflé for the second time. 'I always tell Bee, Manderley's the only place left in England where one can get decent cooking. I remember this soufflé of old.'

'I think we change cooks periodically,' said Maxim, 'but the standard of cooking remains the same. Mrs Danvers has all the recipes, she tells them what to do.'

'Amazing woman, that Mrs Danvers,' said Giles, turning to me; 'don't you think so?'

'Oh, yes,' I said. 'Mrs Danvers seems to be a wonderful person.'

'She's no oil painting though, is she?' said Giles, and he roared with laughter. Frank Crawley said nothing, and looking up I saw Beatrice was watching me. She turned away then, and began talking to Maxim.

'Do you play golf at all, Mrs de Winter?' said Mr Crawley.

'No, I'm afraid I don't,' I answered, glad that the subject had been changed again, that Mrs Danvers was forgotten, and even though I was no player, knew nothing of the game, I was prepared to listen to him as long as he pleased; there was something solid and safe and dull about golf, it could not bring us into any difficulties. We had cheese, and coffee, and I wondered whether I was supposed to make a move. I kept looking at Maxim, but he gave no sign, and then Giles embarked upon a story, rather difficult to follow, about digging a car out of a snow-drift – what had started the train of thought I could not tell – and I listened to him politely, nodding my head now and again and smiling, aware of Maxim becoming restive at his end of the table. At last he paused, and I caught Maxim's eye. He frowned very slightly and jerked his head towards the door.

I got up at once, shaking the table clumsily as I moved my chair, and upsetting Giles's glass of port. 'Oh, dear,' I said, hovering, wondering what to do, reaching ineffectively for my napkin, but 'All right, Frith will deal with it,' said Maxim, 'don't add to the confusion. Beatrice, take her out in the garden; she's scarcely seen the place yet.'

He looked tired, rather jaded. I began to wish none of them had come. They had spoilt our day anyway. It was too much of an effort, just as we returned. I felt tired too, tired and depressed. Maxim had seemed almost irritable when he suggested we should go into the garden. What a fool I had been, upsetting that glass of port.

We went out on to the terrace and walked down on to the smooth green lawns.

'I think it's a pity you came back to Manderley so soon,' said Beatrice, 'it would have been far better to potter about in Italy for three or four months, and then come back in the middle of the summer. Done Maxim a power of good too, besides being easier from your point of view. I can't help feeling it's going to be rather a strain here for you at first.'

'Oh, I don't think so,' I said. 'I know I shall come to love Manderley.'

She did not answer, and we strolled backwards and forwards on the lawns.

'Tell me a bit about yourself,' she said at last; 'what was it you were doing in the south of France? Living with some appalling American woman, Maxim said.'

I explained about Mrs Van Hopper, and what had led to it, and she seemed sympathetic but a little vague, as though she was thinking of something else.

'Yes,' she said, when I paused, 'it all happened very suddenly, as you say. But of course we were all delighted, my dear, and I do hope you will be happy.'

'Thank you, Beatrice,' I said, 'thank you very much.'

I wondered why she said she hoped we would be happy, instead of saying she knew we would be so. She was kind, she was sincere, I liked her very much, but there was a tiny doubt in her voice that made me afraid.

'When Maxim wrote and told me,' she went on, taking my arm, 'and said he had discovered you in the south of France, and you were very young, very pretty, I must admit it gave me a bit of a shock. Of course we all expected a social butterfly, very modern and plastered with paint, the sort of girl you expected to meet in those sort of places. When you came into the morning-room before lunch you could have knocked me down with a feather.'

She laughed, and I laughed with her. But she did not say whether or not she was disappointed in my appearance or relieved.

'Poor Maxim,' she said: 'he went through a ghastly time, and let's hope you have made him forget about it. Of course he adores Manderley.'

Part of me wanted her to continue her train of thought, to tell me more of the past, naturally and easily like this, and something else, way back in my mind, did not want to know, did not want to hear.

'We are not a bit alike, you know,' she said, 'our characters are poles apart. I show everything on my face: whether I like people or not, whether I am angry or pleased. There's no reserve about me. Maxim is entirely different. Very quiet, very reserved. You never know what's going on in that funny mind of his. I

110

lose my temper on the slightest provocation, flare up, and then it's all over. Maxim loses his temper once or twice in a year, and when he does – my God – he *does* lose it. I don't suppose he ever will with you, I should think you are a placid little thing.'

She smiled, and pinched my arm, and I thought about being placid, how quiet and comfortable it sounded, someone with knitting on her lap, with calm unruffled brow. Someone who was never anxious, never tortured by doubt and indecision, someone who never stood as I did, hopeful, eager, frightened, tearing at bitten nails, uncertain which way to go, what star to follow.

'You won't mind me saying so, will you?' she went on, 'but I think you ought to do something to your hair. Why don't you have it waved? It's so very lanky, isn't it, like that? Must look awful under a hat. Why don't you sweep it back behind your ears?'

I did so obediently, and waited for her approval. She looked at me critically, her head on one side. 'No,' she said. 'No, I think that's worse. It's too severe, and doesn't suit you. No, all you need is a wave, just to pinch it up. I never have cared for that Joan of Arc business or whatever they call it. What does Maxim say? Does he think it suits you?'

'I don't know,' I said, 'he's never mentioned it.'

'Oh well,' she said, 'perhaps he likes it. Don't go by me. Tell me, did you get any clothes in London or Paris?'

'No,' I said, 'we had no time. Maxim was anxious to get home. And I can always send for catalogues.'

'I can tell by the way you dress that you don't care a hoot what you wear,' she said. I glanced at my flannel skirt apologetically.

'I do,' I said. 'I'm very fond of nice things. I've never had much money to spend on clothes up to now.'

'I wonder Maxim did not stay a week or so in London and get you something decent to wear,' she said. 'I must say, I think it's rather selfish of him. So unlike him too. He's generally so particular.'

'Is he?' I said; 'he's never seemed particular to me. I don't think he notices what I wear at all. I don't think he minds.'

'Oh,' she said. 'Oh, well, he must have changed then.'

She looked away from me, and whistled to Jasper, her hands in her pockets, and then stared up at the house above us.

'You're not using the west wing then,' she said.

'No,' I said. 'No, we have the suite in the east wing. It's all been done up.'

'Has it?' she said. 'I didn't know that. I wonder why.'

'It was Maxim's idea,' I said, 'he seems to prefer it.'

She said nothing, she went on looking at the windows, and whistling. 'How do you get on with Mrs Danvers?' she said suddenly.

I bent down, and began patting Jasper's head, and stroking his ears. 'I have not seen very much of her,' I said; 'she scares me a little. I've never seen anyone quite like her before.'

'I don't suppose you have,' said Beatrice.

Jasper looked up at me with great eyes, humble, rather self-conscious. I kissed the top of his silken head, and put my hand over his black nose.

'There's no need to be frightened of her,' said Beatrice; 'and don't let her see it, whatever you do. Of course I've never had anything to do with her, and I don't think I ever want to either. However, she's always been very civil to me.'

I went on patting Jasper's head.

'Did she seem friendly?' said Beatrice.

'No,' I said. 'No, not very.'

Beatrice began whistling again, and she rubbed Jasper's head with her foot. 'I shouldn't have more to do with her than you can help,' she said.

'No,' I said. 'She runs the house very efficiently, there's no need for me to interfere.'

'Oh, I don't suppose she'd mind that,' said Beatrice. That was what Maxim had said, the evening before, and I thought it odd that they should both have the same opinion. I should have imagined that interference was the one thing Mrs Danvers did not want.

112

'I dare say she will get over it in time,' said Beatrice, 'but it may make things rather unpleasant for you at first. Of course she's insanely jealous. I was afraid she would be.'

'Why?' I asked, looking up at her, 'why should she be jealous? Maxim does not seem to be particularly fond of her.'

'My dear child, it's not Maxim she's thinking of,' said Beatrice; 'I think she respects him and all that, but nothing more very much.

'No, you see,' – she paused, frowning a little, looking at me uncertainly – 'she resents your being here at all, that's the trouble.'

'Why?' I said, 'why should she resent me?'

'I thought you knew,' said Beatrice; 'I thought Maxim would have told you. She simply adored Rebecca.'

'Oh,' I said. 'Oh, I see.'

We both went on patting and stroking Jasper, who, unaccustomed to such attention, rolled over on his back in ecstasy.

'Here are the men,' said Beatrice, 'let's have some chairs out and sit under the chestnut. How fat Giles is getting, he looks quite repulsive beside Maxim. I suppose Frank will go back to the office. What a dull creature he is, never has anything interesting to say. Well, all of you. What have you been discussing? Pulling the world to bits, I suppose.' She laughed, and the others strolled towards us, and we stood about. Giles threw a twig for Jasper to retrieve. We all looked at Jasper. Mr Crawley looked at his watch. 'I must be off,' he said; 'thank you very much for lunch, Mrs de Winter.'

'You must come often,' I said, shaking hands.

I wondered if the others would go too. I was not sure whether they had just come over for lunch or to spend the day. I hoped they would go. I wanted to be alone with Maxim again, and that it would be like we were in Italy. We all went and sat down under the chestnut tree. Robert brought out chairs and rugs. Giles lay down on his back and tipped his hat over his eyes. After a while he began to snore, his mouth open.

'Shut up, Giles,' said Beatrice. 'I'm not asleep,' he muttered, opening his eyes, and shutting them again. I thought him unattractive. I wondered why Beatrice had married him. She could never have been in love with him. Perhaps that was what she was thinking about me. I caught her eye upon me now and again, puzzled, reflective, as though she was saying to herself 'What on earth does Maxim see in her?' but kind at the same time, not unfriendly. They were talking about their grandmother.

'We must go over and see the old lady,' Maxim was saying, and 'She's getting gaga,' said Beatrice, 'drops food all down her chin, poor darling.'

I listened to them both, leaning against Maxim's arm, rubbing my chin on his sleeve. He stroked my hand absently, not thinking, talking to Beatrice.

'That's what I do to Jasper,' I thought. 'I'm being like Jasper now, leaning against him. He pats me now and again, when he remembers, and I'm pleased, I get closer to him for a moment. He likes me in the way I like Jasper.'

The wind had dropped. The afternoon was drowsy, peaceful. The grass had been new-mown; it smelt sweet and rich, like summer. A bee droned above Giles's head, and he flicked at it with his hat. Jasper sloped in to join us, too warm in the sun, his tongue lolling from his mouth. He flopped beside me, and began licking his side, his large eyes apologetic. The sun shone on the mullioned windows of the house, and I could see the green lawns and the terrace reflected in them. Smoke curled thinly from one of the near chimneys, and I wondered if the library fire had been lit, according to routine.

A thrush flew across the lawn to the magnolia tree outside the dining-room window. I could smell the faint, soft magnolia scent as I sat here, on the lawn. Everything was quiet and still. Very distant now came the washing of the sea in the bay below. The tide must have gone out. The bee droned over us again, pausing to taste the chestnut blossom above our heads. 'This is what I always imagined,' I thought, 'this is how I hoped it would be, living at Manderley.'

I wanted to go on sitting there, not talking, not listening to the others, keeping the moment precious for all time, because we were peaceful, all of us, we were content and drowsy even as the bee who droned above our heads. In a little while it would be different, there would come tomorrow, and the next day, and another year. And we would be changed perhaps, never sitting quite like this again. Some of us would go away, or suffer, or die; the future stretched away in front of us, unknown, unseen, not perhaps what we wanted, not what we planned. This moment was safe though, this could not be touched. Here we sat together, Maxim and I, hand-in-hand, and the past and the future mattered not at all. This was secure, this funny fragment of time he would never remember, never think about again. He would not hold it sacred; he was talking about cutting away some of the undergrowth in the drive, and Beatrice agreed, interrupting with some suggestion of her own, and throwing a piece of grass at Giles at the same time. For them it was just after lunch, quarter past three on a haphazard afternoon, like any hour, like any day. They did not want to hold it close, imprisoned and secure, as I did. They were not afraid.

'Well, I suppose we ought to be off,' said Beatrice, brushing the grass from her skirt; 'I don't want to be late, we've got the Cartrights dining.'

'How is old Vera?' asked Maxim.

'Oh, same as ever, always talking about her health. He's getting very old. They're sure to ask all about you both.'

'Give them my love,' said Maxim.

We got up. Giles shook the dust off his hat. Maxim yawned and stretched. The sun went in. I looked up at the sky. It had changed already, a mackerel sky. Little clouds scurrying in formation, line upon line.

'Wind's backing,' said Maxim.

'I hope we don't run into rain,' said Giles.

'I'm afraid we've had the best of the day,' said Beatrice.

We wandered slowly towards the drive and the waiting car.

'You haven't seen what's been done to the east wing,' said Maxim.

'Come upstairs,' I suggested; 'it won't take a minute.'

We went into the hall, and up the big staircase, the men following behind.

It seemed strange that Beatrice had lived here for so many years. She had run down these same stairs as a little girl, with her nurse. She had been born here, bred here; she knew it all, she belonged here more than I should ever do. She must have many memories locked inside her heart. I wondered if she ever thought about the days that were gone, ever remembered the lanky pig-tailed child that she had been once, so different from the woman she had become, forty-five now, vigorous and settled in her ways, another person . . .

We came to the rooms, and Giles, stooping under the low doorway, said, 'How very jolly; this is a great improvement, isn't it, Bee?' and 'I say, old boy, you have spread yourself,' said Beatrice: 'new curtains, new beds, new everything. You remember, Giles, we had this room that time you were laid up with your leg? It was very dingy then. Of course Mother never had much idea of comfort. And then, you never put people here, did you, Maxim? Except when there was an overflow. The bachelors were always dumped here. Well, it's charming, I must say. Looks over the rose-garden too, which was always an advantage. May I powder my nose?'

The men went downstairs, and Beatrice peered in the mirror.

'Did old Danvers do all this for you?' she said.

'Yes,' I said. 'I think she's done it very well.'

'So she should, with her training,' said Beatrice. 'I wonder what on earth it cost. A pretty packet, I bet. Did you ask?'

'No, I'm afraid I did not,' I said.

'I don't suppose it worried Mrs Danvers,' said Beatrice. 'Do you mind if I use your comb? These are nice brushes. Wedding present?'

'Maxim gave them to me.'

'H'm. I like them. We must give you something of course. What do you want?'

'Oh, I don't really know. You mustn't bother,' I said.

116

'My dear, don't be absurd. I'm not one to grudge you a present, even though we weren't asked to your wedding!'

'I hope you did not mind about that. Maxim wanted it to be abroad.'

'Of course not. Very sensible of you both. After all, it wasn't as though . . .' she stopped in the middle of her sentence, and dropped her bag. 'Damn, have I broken the catch? No, all is well. What was I saying? I can't remember. Oh, yes, wedding presents. We must think of something. You probably don't care for jewellery.'

I did not answer. 'It's so different from the ordinary young couple,' she said. 'The daughter of a friend of mine got married the other day, and of course they were started off in the usual way, with linen, and coffee sets, and dining-room chairs, and all that. I gave rather a nice standard lamp. Cost me a fiver at Harrods. If you do go up to London to buy clothes mind you go to my woman, Madame Carroux. She has damn good taste, and she doesn't rook you.'

She got up from the dressing-table, and pulled at her skirt.

'Do you suppose you will have a lot of people down?' she said.

'I don't know. Maxim hasn't said.'

'Funny old boy, one never quite knows with him. At one time one could not get a bed in the house, the place would be chock-a-block. I can't somehow see you . . .' she stopped abruptly, and patted my arm. 'Oh, well,' she said, 'we'll see. It's a pity you don't ride or shoot, you miss such a lot. You don't sail by any chance, do you?'

'No,' I said.

'Thank God for that,' she said.

She went to the door, and I followed her down the corridor.

'Come and see us if you feel like it,' she said. 'I always expect people to ask themselves. Life is too short to send out invitations.'

'Thank you very much,' I said.

We came to the head of the stairs looking down upon the

117

hall. The men were standing on the steps outside. 'Come on, Bee,' shouted Giles. 'I felt a spot of rain, so we've put on the cover. Maxim says the glass is falling.'

Beatrice took my hand, and bending down gave me a swift peck on my cheek. 'Good-bye,' she said; 'forgive me if I've asked you a lot of rude questions, my dear, and said all sorts of things I shouldn't. Tact never was my strong point, as Maxim will tell you. And, as I told you before, you're not a bit what I expected.' She looked at me direct, her lips pursed in a whistle, and then took a cigarette from her bag, and flashed her lighter.

'You see,' she said, snapping the top, and walking down the stairs, 'you are so very different from Rebecca.'

And we came out on to the steps and found the sun had gone behind a bank of cloud, a little thin rain was falling, and Robert was hurrying across the lawn to bring in the chairs.

# 10

We watched the car disappear round the sweep of the drive, and then Maxim took my arm and said, 'Thank God that's that. Get a coat quickly, and come out. Damn the rain, I want a walk. I can't stand this sitting about.' He looked white and strained, and I wondered why the entertaining of Beatrice and Giles, his own sister and brother-in-law, should have tired him so.

'Wait while I run upstairs for my coat,' I said.

'There's a heap of mackintoshes in the flower room, get one of them,' he said impatiently, 'women are always half an hour when they go to their bedrooms. Robert, fetch a coat from the flower room, will you, for Mrs de Winter? There must be half a dozen raincoats hanging there left by people at one time or another.' He was already standing in the drive, and calling to Jasper, 'Come on, you lazy little beggar, and take some of that fat off.' Jasper ran round in circles, barking hysterically at the prospect of his walk. 'Shut up, you idiot,' said Maxim. 'What on earth is Robert doing?'

Robert came running out of the hall carrying a raincoat, and I struggled into it hurriedly, fumbling with the collar. It was too big, of course, and too long, but there was no time to change it, and we set off together across the lawn to the woods, Jasper running in front.

'I find a little of my family goes a very long way,' said Maxim. 'Beatrice is one of the best people in the world, but she invariably puts her foot in it.'

I was not sure where Beatrice had blundered, and thought it better not to ask. Perhaps he still resented the chat about his health before lunch.

'What did you think of her?' he went on.

'I liked her very much,' I said; 'she was very nice to me.'

'What did she talk to you about out here, after lunch?'

'Oh, I don't know. I think I did most of the talking. I was telling her about Mrs Van Hopper, and how you and I met, and all that. She said I was quite different from what she expected.'

'What the devil did she expect?'

'Someone much smarter, more sophisticated, I imagine. A social butterfly, she said.'

Maxim did not answer for a moment; he bent down, and threw a stick for Jasper. 'Beatrice can sometimes be infernally unintelligent,' he said.

We climbed the grass bank above the lawns, and plunged into the woods. The trees grew very close together, and it was dark. We trod upon broken twigs, and last year's leaves, and here and there the fresh green stubble of the young bracken, and the shoots of the bluebells soon to blossom. Jasper was silent now, his nose to the ground. I took Maxim's arm.

'Do you like my hair?' I said.

He stared down at me in astonishment. 'Your hair?' he said. 'Why on earth do you ask? Of course I like it. What's the matter with it?'

'Oh, nothing,' I said, 'I just wondered.'

'How funny you are,' he said.

We came to a clearing in the woods, and there were two paths, going in opposite directions. Jasper took the right-hand path without hesitation.

'Not that way,' called Maxim; 'come on, old chap.'

The dog looked back at us and stood there, wagging his tail, but did not return. 'Why does he want to go that way?' I asked.

'I suppose he's used to it,' said Maxim briefly; 'it leads to a small cove, where we used to keep a boat. Come on, Jasper, old man.'

We turned into the left-hand path, not saying anything, and presently I looked over my shoulder and saw that Jasper was following us.

'This brings us to the valley I told you about,' said Maxim, 'and you shall smell the azaleas. Never mind the rain, it will bring out the scent.'

He seemed all right again now, happy and cheerful, the Maxim I knew and loved, and he began talking about Frank Crawley and what a good fellow he was, so thorough and reliable, and devoted to Manderley.

'This is better,' I thought; 'this is like it was in Italy', and I smiled up at him, squeezing his arm, relieved that the odd strained look on his face had passed away, and while I said 'Yes,' and 'Really?' and 'Fancy, darling,' my thoughts wandered back to Beatrice, wondering why her presence should have disturbed him, what she had done; and I thought too of all she had said about his temper, how he lost it, she told me, about once or twice a year.

She must know him, of course; she was his sister. But it was not what I had thought; it was not my idea of Maxim. I could see him moody, difficult, irritable perhaps, but not angry as she had inferred, not passionate. Perhaps she had exaggerated; people very often were wrong about their relatives.

'There,' said Maxim suddenly, 'take a look at that.'

We stood on a slope of a wooded hill, and the path wound away before us to a valley, by the side of a running stream. There were no dark trees here, no tangled undergrowth, but on either side of the narrow path stood azaleas and rhododendrons, not blood-coloured like the giants in the drive, but salmon, white, and gold, things of beauty and of grace, drooping their lovely, delicate heads in the soft summer rain.

The air was full of their scent, sweet and heady, and it seemed to me as though their very essence had mingled with the running waters of the stream, and become one with the falling rain and the dank rich moss beneath our feet. There was no sound here but the tumbling of the little stream, and the quiet rain. When Maxim spoke, his voice was hushed too, gentle and low, as if he had no wish to break upon the silence.

'We call it the Happy Valley,' he said.

We stood quite still, not speaking, looking down upon the

clear white faces of the flowers closest to us, and Maxim stooped, and picked up a fallen petal and gave it to me. It was crushed and bruised, and turning brown at the curled edge, but as I rubbed it across my hand the scent rose to me, sweet and strong, vivid as the living tree from which it came.

Then the birds began. First a blackbird, his note clear and cool above the running stream, and after a moment he had answer from his fellow hidden in the woods behind us, and soon the still air about us was made turbulent with song, pursuing us as we wandered down into the valley, and the fragrance of the white petals followed us too. It was disturbing, like an enchanted place. I had not thought it could be as beautiful as this.

The sky, now overcast and sullen, so changed from the early afternoon, and the steady insistent rain could not disturb the soft quietude of the valley; the rain and the rivulet mingled with one another, and the liquid note of the black bird fell upon the damp air in harmony with them both. I brushed the dripping heads of azaleas as I passed, so close they grew together, bordering the path. Little drops of water fell on to my hands from the soaked petals. There were petals at my feet too, brown and sodden, bearing their scent upon them still, and a richer, older scent as well, the smell of deep moss and bitter earth, the stems of bracken, and the twisted buried roots of trees. I held Maxim's hand and I had not spoken. The spell of the Happy Valley was upon me. This at last was the core of Manderley, the Manderley I would know and learn to love. The first drive was forgotten, the black, herded woods, the glaring rhododendrons, luscious and over-proud. And the vast house too, the silence of that echoing hall, the uneasy stillness of the west wing, wrapped in dust-sheets. There I was an interloper, wandering in rooms that did not know me, sitting at a desk and in a chair that were not mine. Here it was different. The Happy Valley knew no trespassers. We came to the end of the path, and the flowers formed an archway above our heads. We bent down, passing underneath, and when I stood straight again, brushing the raindrops from my hair, I saw that the valley was behind us, and the azaleas, and the trees, and, as Maxim had described to me that afternoon many weeks ago in Monte Carlo, we were standing in a little narrow cove, the shingle hard and white under our feet, and the sea was breaking on the shore beyond us.

Maxim smiled down at me, watching the bewilderment on my face.

'It's a shock, isn't it?' he said; 'no one ever expects it. The contrast is too sudden; it almost hurts.' He picked up a stone and flung it across the beach for Jasper. 'Fetch it, good man,' and Jasper streaked away in search of the stone, his long black ears flapping in the wind.

The enchantment was no more, the spell was broken. We were mortal again, two people playing on a beach. We threw more stones, went to the water's edge, flung ducks and drakes, and fished for driftwood. The tide had turned, and came lapping in the bay. The small rocks were covered, the seaweed washed on the stones. We rescued a big floating plank and carried it up the beach above high-water mark. Maxim turned to me, laughing, wiping the hair out of his eyes, and I unrolled the sleeves of my mackintosh caught by the sea spray. And then we looked round, and saw that Jasper had disappeared. We called and whistled, and he did not come. I looked anxiously towards the mouth of the cove where the waves were breaking upon the rocks.

'No,' said Maxim, 'we should have seen him, he can't have fallen. Jasper, you idiot, where are you? Jasper, Jasper?'

'Perhaps he's gone back to the Happy Valley?' I said.

'He was by that rock a minute ago, sniffing a dead sea-gull,' said Maxim.

We walked up the beach towards the valley once again. 'Jasper, Jasper?' called Maxim.

In the distance, beyond the rocks to the right of the beach, I heard a short, sharp bark. 'Hear that?' I said. 'He's climbed over this way.' I began to scramble up the slippery rocks in the direction of the bark.

'Come back,' said Maxim sharply; 'we don't want to go that way. The fool of a dog must look after himself.'

I hesitated, looked down from my rock. 'Perhaps he's fallen,' I said, 'poor little chap. Let me fetch him.' Jasper barked again, further away this time. 'Oh, listen,' I said, 'I must get him. It's quite safe, isn't it? The tide won't have cut him off?'

'He's all right,' said Maxim irritably; 'why not leave him? He knows his own way back.'

I pretended not to hear, and began scrambling over the rocks towards Jasper. Great jagged boulders screened the view, and I slipped and stumbled on the wet rocks, making my way as best I could in Jasper's direction. It was heartless of Maxim to leave Jasper, I thought, and I could not understand it. Besides, the tide was coming in. I came up beside the big boulder that had hidden the view, and looked beyond it. And I saw, to my surprise, that I was looking down into another cove, similar to the one I had left, but wider and more rounded. A small stone breakwater had been thrown out across the cove for shelter, and behind it the bay formed a tiny natural harbour. There was a buoy anchored there, but no boat. The beach in the cove was white shingle, like the one behind me, but steeper, shelving suddenly to the sea. The woods came right down to the tangle of seaweed marking high water, encroaching almost to the rocks themselves, and at the fringe of the woods was a long low building, half cottage, half boat-house, built of the same stone as the breakwater.

There was a man on the beach, a fisherman perhaps, in long boots and a sou'wester, and Jasper was barking at him, running round him in circles, darting at his boots. The man took no notice; he was bending down, and scraping in the shingle. 'Jasper,' I shouted, 'Jasper, come here.'

The dog looked up, wagging his tail, but he did not obey me. He went on baiting the solitary figure on the beach.

I looked over my shoulder. There was still no sign of Maxim. I climbed down over the rocks to the beach below. My feet made a crunching noise across the shingle, and the man looked up at the sound. I saw then that he had the small slit eyes of an idiot, and the red, wet mouth. He smiled at me, showing toothless gums.

124

'G'day,' he said. 'Dirty, ain't it?'

'Good afternoon,' I said. 'No. I'm afraid it's not very nice weather.'

He watched me with interest, smiling all the while. 'Diggin' for shell,' he said. 'No shell here. Been diggin' since forenoon.'

'Oh,' I said, 'I'm sorry you can't find any.'

'That's right,' he said, 'no shell here.'

'Come on, Jasper,' I said, 'it's getting late. Come on, old boy.'

But Jasper was in an infuriating mood. Perhaps the wind and the sea had gone to his head, for he backed away from me, barking stupidly, and began racing round the beach after nothing at all. I saw he would never follow me, and I had no lead. I turned to the man, who had bent down again to his futile digging.

'Have you got any string?' I said.

'Eh?' he said.

'Have you got any string?' I repeated.

'No shell here,' he said, shaking his head. 'Been diggin' since forenoon.' He nodded his head at me, and wiped his pale blue watery eyes.

'I want something to tie the dog,' I said. 'He won't follow me.'

'Eh?' he said. And he smiled his poor idiot's smile.

'All right,' I said; 'it doesn't matter.'

He looked at me uncertainly, and then leant forward, and poked me in the chest.

'I know that dog,' he said; 'he comes fro' the house.'

'Yes,' I said. 'I want him to come back with me now.'

'He's not yourn,' he said.

'He's Mr de Winter's dog,' I said gently. 'I want to take him back to the house.'

'Eh?' he said.

I called Jasper once more, but he was chasing a feather blown by the wind. I wondered if there was any string in the boathouse, and I walked up the beach towards it. There must have been a garden once, but now the grass was long and overgrown, crowded with nettles. The windows were boarded up. No doubt

125

the door was locked, and I lifted the latch without much hope. To my surprise it opened after the first stiffness, and I went inside, bending my head because of the low door. I expected to find the usual boat store, dirty and dusty with disuse, ropes and blocks and oars upon the floor. The dust was there, and the dirt too in places, but there were no ropes or blocks. The room was furnished, and ran the whole length of the cottage. There was a desk in the corner, a table, and chairs, and a bed-sofa pushed against the wall. There was a dresser too, with cups and plates. Bookshelves, the books inside them, and models of ships standing on the top of the shelves. For a moment I thought it must be inhabited – perhaps the poor man on the beach lived here – but I looked around me again and saw no sign of recent occupation. That rusted grate knew no fire, this dusty floor no footsteps, and the china there on the dresser was blue-spotted with the damp. There was a queer musty smell about the place. Cobwebs spun threads upon the ships' models, making their own ghostly rigging. No one lived here. No one came here. The door had creaked on its hinges when I opened it. The rain pattered on the roof with a hollow sound, and tapped upon the boarded windows. The fabric of the sofa-bed had been nibbled by mice or rats. I could see the jagged holes, and the frayed edges. It was damp in the cottage, damp and chill. Dark, and oppressive. I did not like it. I had no wish to stay there. I hated the hollow sound of the rain pattering on the roof. It seemed to echo in the room itself, and I heard the water dripping too into the rusted grate.

I looked about me for some string. There was nothing that would serve my purpose, nothing at all. There was another door at the end of the room, and I went to it, and opened it, a little fearful now, a little afraid, for I had the odd, uneasy feeling that I might come upon something unawares, that I had no wish to see. Something that might harm me, that might be horrible.

It was nonsense of course, and I opened the door. It was only a boat store after all. Here were the ropes and blocks I had expected, two or three sails, fenders, a small punt, pots of paints, all the litter and junk that goes with the using of boats. A ball of twine lay on a shelf, a rusted clasp knife beside it. This would be all I needed for Jasper. I opened the knife, and cut a length of twine, and came back into the room again. The rain still fell upon the roof, and into the grate. I came out of the cottage hurriedly, not looking behind me, trying not to see the torn sofa and the mildewed china, the spun cobwebs on the model ships, and so through the creaking gate and on to the white beach.

The man was not digging any more; he was watching me, Jasper at his side.

'Come along, Jasper,' I said; 'come on, good dog.' I bent down and this time he allowed me to touch him and pull hold of his collar. 'I found some string in the cottage,' I said to the man.

He did not answer, and I tied the string loosely round Jasper's collar.

'Good afternoon,' I said, tugging at Jasper.

The man nodded, staring at me with his narrow idiot's eyes. 'I saw'ee go in yonder,' he said.

'Yes,' I said; 'it's all right, Mr de Winter won't mind.'

'She don't go in there now,' he said.

'No,' I said, 'not now.'

'She's gone in the sea, ain't she?' he said; 'she won't come back no more?'

'No,' I said, 'she'll not come back.'

'I never said nothing, did I?' he said.

'No, of course not; don't worry,' I said.

He bent down again to his digging, muttering to himself. I went across the shingle and I saw Maxim waiting for me by the rocks, his hands in his pockets.

'I'm sorry,' I said. 'Jasper would not come. I had to get some string.'

He turned abruptly on his heel, and made towards the woods.

'Aren't we going back over the rocks?' I said.

'What's the point? We're here now,' he said briefly.

We went up past the cottage and struck into a path through the woods. 'I'm sorry I was such a time; it was Jasper's fault,' I said, 'he kept barking at the man. Who was he?'

'Only Ben,' said Maxim; 'he's quite harmless, poor devil. His old father used to be one of the keepers; they live near the home farm. Where did you get that piece of twine?'

'I found it in the cottage on the beach,' I said.

'Was the door open?' he asked.

'Yes, I pushed it open. I found the string in the other room, where the sails were, and a small boat.'

'Oh,' he said shortly. 'Oh, I see,' and then he added, after a moment or two: 'That cottage is supposed to be locked, the door has no business to be open.'

I said nothing; it was not my affair.

'Did Ben tell you the door was open?'

'No,' I said, 'he did not seem to understand anything I asked him.'

'He makes out he's worse than he is,' said Maxim. 'He can talk quite intelligibly if he wants to. He's probably been in and out of the cottage dozens of times, and did not want you to know.'

'I don't think so,' I answered; 'the place looked deserted, quite untouched. There was dust everywhere, and no footmarks. It was terribly damp. I'm afraid those books will be quite spoilt, and the chairs, and that sofa. There are rats there, too; they have eaten away some of the covers.'

Maxim did not reply. He walked at a tremendous pace, and the climb up from the beach was steep. It was very different from the Happy Valley. The trees were dark here and close together, there were no azaleas brushing the path. The rain dripped heavily from the thick branches. It splashed on my collar and trickled down my neck. I shivered; it was unpleasant, like a cold finger. My legs ached, after the unaccustomed scramble over the rocks. And Jasper lagged behind, weary from his wild scamper, his tongue hanging from his mouth.

'Come on, Jasper, for God's sake,' said Maxim. 'Make him walk up, pull at the twine or something, can't you? Beatrice was right. The dog is much too fat.'

'It's your fault,' I said, 'you walk so fast. We can't keep up with you.'

'If you had listened to me instead of rushing wildly over those rocks we would have been home by now,' said Maxim. 'Jasper knew his way back perfectly. I can't think what you wanted to go after him for.'

'I thought he might have fallen, and I was afraid of the tide,' I said.

'Is it likely I should have left the dog had there been any question of the tide?' said Maxim. 'I told you not to go on those rocks, and now you are grumbling because you are tired.'

'I'm not grumbling,' I said. 'Anyone, even if they had legs of iron, would be tired walking at this pace. I thought you would come with me when I went after Jasper anyway, instead of staying behind.'

'Why should I exhaust myself careering after the damn dog?' he said.

'It was no more exhausting careering after Jasper on the rocks than it was careering after the driftwood on the beach,' I answered. 'You just say that because you have not any other excuse.'

'My good child, what am I supposed to excuse myself about?'

'Oh, I don't know,' I said wearily; 'let's stop this.'

'Not at all, you began it. What do you mean by saying I was trying to find an excuse? Excuse for what?'

'Excuse for not having come with me over the rocks, I suppose,' I said.

'Well, and why do you think I did not want to cross to the other beach?'

'Oh, Maxim, how should I know? I'm not a thought-reader. I know you did not want to, that's all. I could see it in your face.'

'See what in my face?'

'I've already told you. I could see you did not want to go. Oh, do let's have an end to it. I'm sick to death of the subject.'

'All women say that when they've lost an argument. All right, I did not want to go to the other beach. Will that please you? I never go near the bloody place, or that God-damned cottage.

And if you had my memories you would not want to go there either, or talk about it, or even think about it. There. You can digest that if you like, and I hope it satisfies you.'

His face was white, and his eyes strained and wretched with that dark lost look they had had when I first met him. I put out my hand to him, I took hold of his, holding it tight.

'Please, Maxim, please,' I said.

'What's the matter?' he said roughly.

'I don't want you to look like that,' I said. 'It hurts too much. Please, Maxim. Let's forget all we said. A futile silly argument. I'm sorry, darling. I'm sorry. Please let everything be all right.'

'We ought to have stayed in Italy,' he said. 'We ought never to have come back to Manderley. Oh, God, what a fool I was to come back.'

He brushed through the trees impatiently, striding even faster than before, and I had to run to keep pace with him, catching at my breath, tears very near the surface, dragging poor Jasper after me on the end of his string.

At last we came to the top of the path, and I saw its fellow branching left to the Happy Valley. We had climbed the path then that Jasper had wished to take at the beginning of the afternoon. I knew now why Jasper had turned to it. It led to the beach he knew best, and the cottage. It was his old routine.

We came out on to the lawns, and went across them to the house without a word. Maxim's face was hard, with no expression. He went straight into the hall and on to the library without looking at me. Frith was in the hall.

'We want tea at once,' said Maxim, and he shut the library door.

I fought to keep back my tears. Frith must not see them. He would think we had been quarrelling, and he would go to the servants' hall and say to them all, 'Mrs de Winter was crying in the hall just now. It looks as though things are not going very well.' I turned away, so that Frith should not see my face. He came towards me though, he began to help me off with my mackintosh.

'I'll put your raincoat away for you in the flower-room, Madam,' he said.

'Thank you, Frith,' I replied, my face still away from him.

'Not a very pleasant afternoon for a walk, I fear, Madam.'

'No,' I said. 'No, it was not very nice.'

'Your handkerchief, Madam?' he said, picking up something that had fallen on the floor. 'Thank you,' I said, putting it in my pocket.

I was wondering whether to go upstairs or whether to follow Maxim to the library. Frith took the coat to the flower-room. I stood there, hesitating, biting my nails. Frith came back again. He looked surprised to see me still there.

'There is a good fire in the library now, Madam.'

'Thank you, Frith,' I said.

I walked slowly across the hall to the library. I opened the door and went in. Maxim was sitting in his chair, Jasper at his feet, the old dog in her basket. Maxim was not reading the paper, though it lay on the arm of the chair beside him. I went and knelt down by his side and put my face close to his.

'Don't be angry with me any more,' I whispered.

He took my face in his hands, and looked down at me with his tired, strained eyes. 'I'm not angry with you,' he said.

'Yes,' I said. 'I've made you unhappy. It's the same as making you angry. You're all wounded and hurt and torn inside. I can't bear to see you like this. I love you so much.'

'Do you?' he said. 'Do you?' He held me very tight, and his eyes questioned me, dark and uncertain, the eyes of a child in pain, a child in fear.

'What is it, darling?' I said. 'Why do you look like that?'

I heard the door open before he could answer, and I sank back on my heels, pretending to reach for a log to throw on the fire, while Frith came into the room followed by Robert, and the ritual of our tea began.

The performance of the day before was repeated, the placing of the table, the laying of the snow-white cloth, the putting down of cakes and crumpets, the silver kettle of hot water placed on its little flame, while Jasper, wagging his tail, his ears stretched back in anticipation, watched my face. Five minutes must have passed before we were alone again, and when I looked at Maxim I saw the colour had come back into his face, the tired, lost look was gone, and he was reaching for a sandwich.

'Having all that crowd to lunch was the trouble,' he said. 'Poor old Beatrice always does rub me up the wrong way. We used to scrap like dogs as children. I'm so fond of her too, bless her. Such a relief though that they don't live too near. Which reminds me, we'll have to go over and see Granny some time. Pour out my tea, sweetheart, and forgive me for being a bear to you.'

It was over then. The episode was finished. We must not speak of it again. He smiled at me over his cup of tea, and then reached for the newspaper on the arm of his chair. The smile was my reward. Like a pat on the head to Jasper. Good dog then, lie down, don't worry me any more. I was Jasper again. I was back where I had been before. I took a piece of crumpet and divided it between the two dogs. I did not want it myself, I was not hungry. I felt very weary now, very tired in a dull, spent way. I looked at Maxim but he was reading his paper, he had folded it over to another page. My fingers were messy with the butter from the crumpet, and I felt in my pocket for a handkerchief. I drew it out, a tiny scrap of a thing, lace-edged. I stared at it, frowning, for it was not mine. I remembered then that Frith had picked it up from the stone floor of the hall. It must have fallen out of the pocket in the mackintosh. I turned it over in my hand. It was grubby; little bits of fluff from the pocket clung to it. It must have been in the mackintosh pocket for a long time. There was a monogram in the corner. A tall sloping R, with the letters de W interlaced. The R dwarfed the other letters, the tail of it ran down into the cambric, away from the laced edge. It was only a small handkerchief, quite a scrap of a thing. It had been rolled in a ball and put away in the pocket and forgotten.

I must have been the first person to put on that mackintosh since the handkerchief was used. She who had worn the coat then was tall, slim, broader than me about the shoulders, for I had found it big and overlong, and the sleeves had come below my wrist. Some of the buttons were missing. She had not bothered then to do it up. She had thrown it over her shoulders like a cape, or worn it loose, hanging open, her hands deep in the pockets.

There was a pink mark upon the handkerchief. The mark of lip-stick. She had rubbed her lips with the handkerchief, and then rolled it in a ball, and left it in the pocket. I wiped my fingers with the handkerchief, and as I did so I noticed that a dull scent clung about it still. A scent I recognized, a scent I knew. I shut my eyes and tried to remember. It was something elusive, something faint and fragrant that I could not name. I had breathed it before, touched it surely, that very afternoon.

And then I knew that the vanished scent upon the handkerchief was the same as the crushed white petals of the azaleas in the Happy Valley.

# 11

The weather was wet and cold for quite a week, as it often can be in the west country in the early summer, and we did not go down to the beach again. I could see the sea from the terrace, and the lawns. It looked grey and uninviting, great rollers sweeping in to the bay past the beacon on the headland. I pictured them surging into the little cove and breaking with a roar upon the rocks, then running swift and strong to the shelving beach. If I stood on the terrace and listened I could hear the murmur of the sea below me, low and sullen. A dull, persistent sound that never ceased. And the gulls flew inland too, driven by the weather. They hovered above the house in circles, wheeling and crying, flapping their spread wings. I began to understand why some people could not bear the clamour of the sea. It has a mournful harping note sometimes, and the very persistence of it, that eternal roll and thunder and hiss, plays a jagged tune upon the nerves. I was glad our rooms were in the east wing and I could lean out of my window and look down upon the rose-garden. For sometimes I could not sleep, and getting softly out of bed in the quiet night I would wander to the window, and lean there, my arms upon the sill, and the air would be very peaceful, very still.

I could not hear the restless sea, and because I could not hear it my thoughts would be peaceful too. They would not carry me down that steep path through the woods to the grey cove and the deserted cottage. I did not want to think about the cottage. I remembered it too often in the day. The memory of it nagged at me whenever I saw the sea from the terrace. For I would see once more the blue spots on the china, the spun webs on the little masts of those model ships, and the rat holes on the sofa bed. I would remember the pattering of the rain on the roof. And I thought of Ben, too, with his narrow watery blue eyes, his sly idiot's smile. These things disturbed me, I was not happy about them. I wanted to forget them but at the same time I wanted to know why they disturbed me, why they made me uneasy and unhappy. Somewhere, at the back of my mind, there was a frightened furtive seed of curiosity that grew slowly and stealthily, for all my denial of it, and I knew all the doubt and anxiety of the child who has been told, 'these things are not discussed, they are forbidden.'

I could not forget the white, lost look in Maxim's eyes when we came up the path through the woods, and I could not forget his words. 'Oh, God, what a fool I was to come back.' It was all my fault, because I had gone down into the bay. I had opened up a road into the past again. And although Maxim had recovered, and was himself again, and we lived our lives together, sleeping, eating, walking, writing letters, driving to the village, working hour by hour through our day, I knew there was a barrier between us because of it.

He walked alone, on the other side, and I must not come to him. And I became nervous and fearful that some heedless word, some turn in a careless conversation should bring that expression back to his eyes again. I began to dread any mention of the sea, for the sea might lead to boats, to accidents, to drowning . . . Even Frank Crawley, who came to lunch one day, put me in a little fever of fear when he said something about the sailing races in Kerrith harbour, three miles away. I looked steadily at my plate, a stab of sickness in my heart at once, but Maxim went on talking quite naturally, he did not seem to mind, while I sat in a sweat of uncertainty wondering what would happen and where the conversation would lead us.

It was during cheese, Frith had left the room, and I remember getting up and going to the sideboard, and taking some more cheese, not wanting it, so as not to be at the table with them, listening; humming a little tune to myself so I could not hear.

135

I was wrong of course, morbid, stupid; this was the hypersensitive behaviour of a neurotic, not the normal happy self I knew myself to be. But I could not help it. I did not know what to do. My shyness and gaucherie became worse, too, making me stolid and dumb when people came to the house. For we were called upon, I remember, during those first weeks, by people who lived near us in the county, and the receiving of them, and the shaking hands, and the spinning out of the formal half-hour became a worse ordeal than I first anticipated, because of this new fear of mine that they would talk about something that must not be discussed. The agony of those wheels on the drive, of that pealing bell, of my own first wild rush for flight to my own room. The scrambled dab of powder on my nose, the hasty comb through my hair, and then the inevitable knock on the door and the entrance of the cards on a silver salver.

'All right. I'll be down immediately.' The clap of my heels on the stairs and across the hall, the opening of the library door or, worse still, that long, cold, lifeless drawing-room, and the strange woman waiting there, or two of them perhaps, or a husband and a wife.

'How do you do? I'm sorry; Maxim is in the garden somewhere, Frith has gone to find him.'

'We felt we must come and pay our respects to the bride.'

A little laughter, a little flurry of chat, a pause, a glance round the room.

'Manderley is looking as charming as ever. Don't you love it?'

'Oh, yes, rather . . .' And in my shyness and anxiety to please, those schoolgirls' phrases would escape from me again, those words I never used except in moments like these, 'Oh, ripping'; and 'Oh, topping'; and 'absolutely'; and 'priceless'; even, I think, to one dowager who had carried a lorgnette 'cheerio'. My relief at Maxim's arrival would be tempered by the fear they might say something indiscreet, and I became dumb at once, a set smile on my lips, my hands in my lap. They would turn to Maxim then, talking of people and places I had not met or did not know, and now and again I would find their eyes upon me, doubtful, rather bewildered.

I could picture them saying to one another as they drove away, 'My dear, what a dull girl. She scarcely opened her mouth,' and then the sentence I had first heard upon Beatrice's lips, haunting me ever since, a sentence I read in every eye, on every tongue – 'She's so different from Rebecca.'

Sometimes I would glean little snatches of information to add to my secret store. A word dropped here at random, a question, a passing phrase. And, if Maxim was not with me, the hearing of them would be a furtive, rather painful pleasure, guilty knowledge learnt in the dark.

I would return a call perhaps, for Maxim was punctilious in these matters and would not spare me, and if he did not come with me I must brave the formality alone, and there would be a pause in the conversation while I searched for something to say. 'Will you be entertaining much at Manderley, Mrs de Winter?' they would say, and my answer would come, 'I don't know, Maxim has not said much about it up to the present.' 'No, of course not, it's early yet. I believe the house was generally full of people in the old days.' Another pause. 'People from London, you know. There used to be tremendous parties.' 'Yes,' I would say. 'Yes, so I have heard.' A further pause, and then the lowered voice that is always used about the dead or in a place of worship, 'She was so tremendously popular, you know. Such a personality.' 'Yes,' I would say. 'Yes, of course.' And after a moment or so I would glance at my watch under cover of my glove, and say, 'I'm afraid I ought to be going; it must be after four.'

'Won't you stay for tea? We always have it at quarter past.'

'No – No, really, thanks most awfully. I promised Maxim . . .' my sentence would go trailing off into nothing, but the meaning would be understood. We would both rise to our feet, both of us knowing I was not deceived about her offer to tea nor she in my mention of a promise to Maxim. I had sometimes wondered what would happen if convention were denied, if, having got into the car and waved a hand to my hostess on the doorstep,

I suddenly opened it again, and said, 'I don't think I'll go back after all. Let's go to your drawing-room again and sit down. I'll stay to dinner if you like, or stop the night.'

I used to wonder if convention and good county manners would brave the surprise, and whether a smile of welcome would be summoned to the frozen face, 'But of course! How very delightful of you to suggest it.' I used to wish I had the courage to try. But instead the door would slam, the car would go bowling away down the smooth gravel drive, and my late hostess would wander back to her room with a sigh of relief and become herself again. It was the wife of the bishop in the neighbouring cathedral town who said to me, 'Will your husband revive the Manderley Fancy Dress ball, do you suppose? Such a lovely sight always; I shall never forget it.'

I had to smile as though I knew all about it and say, 'We have not decided. There have been so many things to do and to discuss.'

'Yes, I suppose so. But I do hope it won't be dropped. You must use your influence with him. There was not one last year of course. But I remember two years ago, the bishop and I went, and it was quite enchanting. Manderley so lends itself to anything like that. The hall looked wonderful. They danced there, and had the music in the gallery; it was all so in keeping. A tremendous thing to organize, but everybody appreciated it so.'

'Yes,' I said. 'Yes, I must ask Maxim about it.'

I thought of the docketed pigeon-hole in the desk in the morning room, I pictured the stack upon stack of invitation cards, the long list of names, the addresses, and I could see a woman sitting there at the desk and putting a V beside the names she wanted, and reaching for the invitation cards, dipping her pen in the ink, writing upon them swift and sure in that long, slanting hand.

'There was a garden party, too, we went to one summer,' said the bishop's wife. 'Everything always so beautifully done. The flowers at their best. A glorious day, I remember. Tea was served at little tables in the rose-garden; such an attractive original idea. Of course, she was so clever . . .'

She stopped, turning a little pink, fearing a loss of tact; but I agreed with her at once to save embarrassment, and I heard myself saying boldly, brazenly, 'Rebecca must have been a wonderful person.'

I could not believe that I had said the name at last. I waited, wondering what would happen. I had said the name. I had said the word Rebecca aloud. It was a tremendous relief. It was as though I had taken a purge and rid myself of an intolerable pain. Rebecca. I had said it aloud.

I wondered if the bishop's wife saw the flush on my face, but she went on smoothly with the conversation, and I listened to her greedily, like an eavesdropper at a shuttered window.

'You never met her then?' she asked, and when I shook my head she hesitated a moment, a little uncertain of her ground. 'We never knew her well personally, you know: the bishop was only inducted here four years ago, but of course she received us when we went to the ball and the garden party. We dined there, too, one winter. Yes, she was a very lovely creature. So full of life.'

'She seems to have been so good at everything too,' I said, my voice just careless enough to show I did not mind, while I played with the fringe of my glove. 'It's not often you get some-one who is clever and beautiful and fond of sport.'

'No, I suppose you don't,' said the bishop's wife. 'She was certainly very gifted. I can see her now, standing at the foot of the stairs on the night of the ball, shaking hands with every-body, that cloud of dark hair against the very white skin, and her costume suited her so. Yes, she was very beautiful.'

'She ran the house herself, too,' I said, smiling, as if to say, 'I am quite at my ease, I often discuss her.' 'It must have taken a lot of time and thought. I'm afraid I leave it to the housekeeper.'

'Oh, well, we can't all do everything. And you are very young, aren't you? No doubt in time, when you have settled down. Besides, you have your own hobby, haven't you? Someone told me you were fond of sketching.'

139

'Oh, that,' I said. 'I don't know that I can count it for much.'

'It's a nice little talent to have,' said the bishop's wife; 'it's not everyone that can sketch. You must not drop it. Manderley must be full of pretty spots to sketch.'

'Yes,' I said. 'Yes, I suppose so,' depressed by her words, having a sudden vision of myself wandering across the lawns with a camp-stool and a box of pencils under one arm, and my 'little talent' as she described it, under the other. It sounded like a pet disease.

'Do you play any games? Do you ride, or shoot?' she asked.

'No,' I said, 'I don't do anything like that. I'm fond of walking,' I added, as a wretched anticlimax.

'The best exercise in the world,' she said briskly; 'the bishop and I walk a lot.' I wondered if he went round and round the cathedral, in his shovel hat and his gaiters, with her on his arm. She began to talk about a walking holiday they had taken once, years ago, in the Pennines, how they had done an average of twenty miles a day, and I nodded my head, smiling politely, wondering about the Pennines, thinking they were something like the Andes, remembering, afterwards, they were that chain of hills marked with a furry line in the middle of a pink England on my school atlas. And he all the time in his hat and gaiters.

The inevitable pause, the glance at the watch unnecessary, as her drawing-room clock chimed four in shrill tones, and my rise from the chair. 'I'm so glad I found you in. I hope you will come and see us.'

'We should love to. The bishop is always so busy, alas. Please remember me to your husband, and be sure to ask him to revive the ball.'

'Yes, indeed I will.' Lying, pretending I knew all about it; and in the car going home I sat in my corner, biting my thumb nail, seeing the great hall at Manderley thronged with people in fancy dress, the chatter, hum, and laughter of the moving crowd, the musicians in the gallery, supper in the drawing-room probably, long buffet tables against the wall, and I could see Maxim standing at the front of the stairs, laughing, shaking hands, turning to someone who stood by his side, tall and slim, with dark hair, said the bishop's wife, dark hair against a white face, someone whose quick eyes saw to the comfort of her guests, who gave an order over her shoulder to a servant, someone who was never awkward, never without grace, who when she danced left a stab of perfume in the air like a white azalea.

'Will you be entertaining much at Manderley, Mrs de Winter?' I heard the voice again, suggestive, rather inquisitive, in the voice of that woman I had called upon who lived the other side of Kerrith, and I saw her eye too, dubious, considering, taking in my clothes from top to toe, wondering, with that swift down- ward glance given to all brides, if I was going to have a baby.

I did not want to see her again. I did not want to see any of them again. They only came to call at Manderley because they were curious and prying. They liked to criticize my looks, my manners, my figure, they liked to watch how Maxim and I behaved to each other, whether we seemed fond of one another, so that they could go back afterwards and discuss us, saying, 'Very different from the old days.' They came because they wanted to compare me to Rebecca . . . I would not return these calls any more, I decided. I should tell Maxim so. I did not mind if they thought me rude and ungracious. It would give them more to criticize, more to discuss. They could say I was ill-bred. 'I'm not surprised,' they would say; 'after all, who was she?' And then a laugh and a shrug of the shoulder. 'My dear, don't you know? He picked her up in Monte Carlo or somewhere; she hadn't a penny. She was a companion to some old woman.' More laughter, more lifting of the eyebrows. 'Nonsense, not really? How extra- ordinary men are. Maxim, of all people, who was so fastidious. How could he, after Rebecca?'

I did not mind. I did not care. They could say what they liked. As the car turned in at the lodge gates I leant forward in my seat to smile at the woman who lived there. She was bending down, picking flowers in the front garden. She straightened up as she heard the car, but she did not see me smile. I waved, and she stared at me blankly. I don't think she knew who I was. I leant back in my seat again. The car went on down the drive.

When we turned at one of the narrow bends I saw a man walking along the drive a little distance ahead. It was the agent, Frank Crawley. He stopped when he heard the car, and the chauffeur slowed down. Frank Crawley took off his hat and smiled when he saw me in the car. He seemed glad to see me. I smiled back at him. It was nice of him to be glad to see me. I liked Frank Crawley. I did not find him dull or uninteresting as Beatrice had done. Perhaps it was because I was dull myself. We were both dull. We neither of us had a word to say for ourselves. Like to like.

I tapped on the glass and told the chauffeur to stop.

'I think I'll get out and walk with Mr Crawley,' I said.

He opened the door for me. 'Been paying calls, Mrs de Winter?' he said.

'Yes, Frank,' I said. I called him Frank because Maxim did, but he would always call me Mrs de Winter. He was that sort of person. Even if we had been thrown on a desert island together and lived there in intimacy for the rest of our lives, I should have been Mrs de Winter.

'I've been calling on the bishop,' I said, 'and I found the bishop out, but the bishop's lady was at home. She and the bishop are very fond of walking. Sometimes they do twenty miles a day, in the Pennines.'

'I don't know that part of the world,' said Frank Crawley; 'they say the country round is very fine. An uncle of mine used to live there.'

It was the sort of remark Frank Crawley always made. Safe, conventional, very correct.

'The bishop's wife wants to know when we are going to give a Fancy Dress ball at Manderley,' I said, watching him out of the tail of my eye. 'She came to the last one, she said, and enjoyed it very much. I did not know you have Fancy Dress dances here, Frank.'

He hesitated a moment before replying. He looked a little troubled. 'Oh, yes,' he said after a moment, 'the Manderley ball was generally an annual affair. Everyone in the county came. A lot of people from London too. Quite a big show.'

'It must have taken a lot of organization,' I said.

'Yes,' he said.

'I suppose', I said carelessly, 'Rebecca did most of it?'

I looked straight ahead of me along the drive, but I could see his face was turned towards me, as though he wished to read my expression.

'We all of us worked pretty hard,' he said quietly.

There was a funny reserve in his manner as he said this, a certain shyness that reminded me of my own. I wondered suddenly if he had been in love with Rebecca. His voice was the sort of voice I should have used in his circumstances, had this been so. The idea opened up a new field of possibilities. Frank Crawley being so shy, so dull, he would never have told anyone, least of all Rebecca.

'I'm afraid I should not be much use if we have a dance,' I said, 'I'm no earthly use at organizing anything.'

'There would be no need for you to do anything,' he said, 'you would just be your self and look decorative.'

'That's very polite of you, Frank,' I said, 'but I'm afraid I should not be able to do that very well either.'

'I think you would do it excellently,' he said. Dear Frank Crawley, how tactful he was and considerate. I almost believed him. But he did not deceive me really.

'Will you ask Maxim about the ball?' I said.

'Why don't you ask him?' he answered.

'No,' I said. 'No, I don't like to.'

We were silent then. We went on walking along the drive. Now that I had broken down my reluctance at saying Rebecca's name, first with the bishop's wife and now with Frank Crawley, the urge to continue was strong within me. It gave me a curious satisfaction, it acted upon me like a stimulant. I knew that in a moment or two I should have to say it again. 'I was down on one of the beaches the other day,' I said, 'the one with the breakwater. Jasper was being infuriating,

143

he kept barking at the poor man with the idiot's eyes.'

'You must mean Ben,' said Frank, his voice quite easy now; 'he always potters about on the shore. He's quite a nice fellow, you need never be frightened of him. He would not hurt a fly.'

'Oh, I wasn't frightened,' I said. I waited a moment, humming a tune to give me confidence. 'I'm afraid that cottage place is going to rack and ruin,' I said lightly. 'I had to go in, to find a piece of string or something to tie up Jasper. The china is mouldy and the books are being ruined. Why isn't something done about it? It seems such a pity.'

I knew he would not answer at once. He bent down to tie up his shoe lace.

I pretended to examine a leaf on one of the shrubs. 'I think if Maxim wanted anything done he would tell me,' he said, still fumbling with his shoe.

'Are they all Rebecca's things?' I asked.

'Yes,' he said.

I threw the leaf away and picked another, turning it over in my hands.

'What did she use the cottage for?' I asked; 'it looked quite furnished. I thought from the outside it was just a boat-house.'

'It was a boat-house originally,' he said, his voice constrained again, difficult, the voice of someone who is uncomfortable about his subject. 'Then – then she converted it like that, had furniture put in, and china.'

I thought it funny the way he called her 'she'. He did not say Rebecca or Mrs de Winter, as I expected him to do.

'Did she use it a great deal?' I asked.

'Yes,' he said. 'Yes, she did. Moonlight picnics, and – and one thing and another.'

We were walking again side by side, I still humming my little tune. 'How jolly,' I said brightly. 'Moonlight picnics must be great fun. Did you ever go to them?'

'Once or twice,' he said. I pretended not to notice his manner, how quiet it had become, how reluctant to speak about these things.

'Why is the buoy there in the little harbour place?' I said.

'The boat used to be moored there,' he said.

'What boat?' I asked.

'Her boat,' he said.

A strange sort of excitement was upon me. I had to go on with my questions. He did not want to talk about it. I knew that, but although I was sorry for him and shocked at my own self I had to continue, I could not be silent.

'What happened to it?' I said. 'Was that the boat she was sailing when she was drowned?'

'Yes,' he said quietly, 'it capsized and sank. She was washed overboard.'

'What sort of size boat was it?' I asked.

'About three tons. It had a little cabin.'

'What made it capsize?' I said.

'It can be very squally in the bay,' he said.

I thought of that green sea, foam-flecked, that ran down channel beyond the headland. Did the wind come suddenly, I wondered, in a funnel from the beacon on the hill, and did the little boat heel to it, shivering, the white sail flat against a breaking sea?

'Could not someone have got out to her?' I said.

'Nobody saw the accident, nobody knew she had gone,' he said.

I was very careful not to look at him. He might have seen the surprise in my face. I had always thought it happened in a sailing race, that other boats were there, the boats from Kerrith, and that people were watching from the cliffs. I did not know she had been alone, quite alone, out there in the bay.

'They must have known up at the house!' I said.

'No,' he said. 'She often went out alone like that. She would come back any time of the night, and sleep at the cottage on the beach.'

'Was not she nervous?'

'Nervous?' he said; 'no, she was not nervous of anything.'

'Did – did Maxim mind her going off alone like that?'

145

He waited a minute, and then 'I don't know,' he said shortly. I had the impression he was being loyal to someone. Either to Maxim or to Rebecca, or perhaps even to himself. He was odd. I did not know what to make of it.

'She must have been drowned, then, trying to swim to shore, after the boat sank?' I said.

'Yes,' he said.

I knew how the little boat would quiver and plunge, the water gushing into the steering well, and how the sails would press her down, suddenly, horribly, in that gust of wind. It must have been very dark out there in the bay. The shore must have seemed very far away to anyone swimming there, in the water.

'How long afterwards was it that they found her?' I said.

'About two months,' he said.

Two months. I thought drowned people were found after two days. I thought they would be washed up close to the shore when the tide came.

'Where did they find her?' I asked.

'Near Edgecoombe, about forty miles up channel,' he said.

I had spent a holiday at Edgecoombe once, when I was seven. It was a big place, with a pier, and donkeys. I remembered riding a donkey along the sands.

'How did they know it was her – after two months, how could they tell?' I said. I wondered why he paused before each sentence, as though he weighed his words. Had he cared for her, then, had he minded so much?

'Maxim went up to Edgecoombe to identify her,' he said.

Suddenly I did not want to ask him any more. I felt sick at myself, sick and disgusted. I was like a curious sightseer standing on the fringe of a crowd after someone had been knocked down. I was like a poor person in a tenement building, when someone had died, asking if I might see the body. I hated myself. My questions had been degrading, shameful. Frank Crawley must despise me.

'It was a terrible time for all of you,' I said rapidly. 'I don't suppose you like being reminded about it. I just wondered if there was anything one could do to the cottage, that's all. It seems such a pity, all the furniture being spoilt by the damp.'

He did not say anything. I felt hot and uncomfortable. He must have sensed that it was not concern for the empty cottage that had prompted me to all these questions, and now he was silent because he was shocked at me. Ours had been a comfortable, steady sort of friendship. I had felt him an ally. Perhaps I had destroyed all this, and he would never feel the same about me again.

'What a long drive this is,' I said; 'it always reminds me of the path in the forest in a Grimm's fairy tale, where the prince gets lost, you know. It's always longer than one expects, and the trees are so dark, and close.'

'Yes, it is rather exceptional,' he said.

I could tell by his manner he was still on his guard, as though waiting for a further question from me. There was an awkwardness between us that could not be ignored. Something had to be done about it, even if it covered me with shame.

'Frank,' I said desperately, 'I know what you are thinking. You can't understand why I asked all those questions just now. You think I'm morbid, and curious, in a rather beastly way. It's not that, I promise you. It's only that — that sometimes I feel myself at such a disadvantage. It's all very strange to me, living here at Manderley. Not the sort of life I've been brought up to. When I go returning these calls, as I did this afternoon, I know people are looking me up and down, wondering what sort of success I'm going to make of it. I can imagine them saying, "What on earth does Maxim see in her?" And then, Frank, I begin to wonder myself, and I begin to doubt, and I have a fearful haunting feeling that I should never have married Maxim, that we are not going to be happy. You see, I know that all the time, whenever I meet anyone new, they are all thinking the same thing — How different she is to Rebecca.'

I stopped breathless, already a little ashamed of my outburst, feeling that now at any rate I had burnt my boats for all time. He turned to me looking very concerned and troubled.

'Mrs de Winter, please don't think that,' he said. 'For my part I can't tell you how delighted I am that you have married Maxim. It will make all the difference to his life. I am positive that you will make a great success of it. From my point of view it's – it's very refreshing and charming to find someone like yourself who is not entirely – er—' he blushed, searching for a word 'not entirely *au fait*, shall we say, with ways at Manderley. And if people around here give you the impression that they are criticizing you, it's – well – it's most damnably offensive of them, that's all. I've never heard a word of criticism, and if I did I should take great care that it was never uttered again.'

'That's very sweet of you, Frank,' I said, 'and what you say helps enormously. I dare say I've been very stupid. I'm not good at meeting people, I've never had to do it, and all the time I keep remembering how – how it must have been at Manderley before, when there was someone there who was born and bred to it, did it all naturally and without effort. And I realize, every day, that things I lack, confidence, grace, beauty, intelligence, wit – Oh, all the qualities that mean most in a woman – she possessed. It doesn't help, Frank, it doesn't help.'

He said nothing. He went on looking anxious, and distressed. He pulled out his handkerchief and blew his nose. 'You must not say that,' he said.

'Why not? It's true,' I said.

'You have qualities that are just as important, far more so, in fact. It's perhaps cheek of me to say so, I don't know you very well. I'm a bachelor, I don't know very much about women, I lead a quiet sort of life down here at Manderley as you know, but I should say that kindness, and sincerity, and – if I may say so – modesty are worth far more to a man, to a husband, than all the wit and beauty in the world.'

He looked very agitated, and blew his nose again. I saw that I had upset him far more than I had upset myself, and the realization of this calmed me and gave me a feeling of superiority. I wondered why he was making such a fuss. After all, I had not said very much. I had only confessed my sense of insecurity,

148

following as I did upon Rebecca. And she must have had these qualities that he presented to me as mine. She must have been kind and sincere, with all her friends, her boundless popularity. I was not sure what he meant by modesty. It was a word I had never understood. I always imagined it had something to do with minding meeting people in a passage on the way to the bathroom. . . Poor Frank. And Beatrice had called him a dull man, with never a word to say for himself.

'Well,' I said, rather embarrassed, 'well, I don't know about all that. I don't think I'm very kind, or particularly sincere, and as for being modest, I don't think I've ever had much of a chance to be anything else. It was not very modest, of course, being married hurriedly like that, down in Monte Carlo, and being alone there in that hotel, beforehand, but perhaps you don't count that?'

'My dear Mrs de Winter, you don't think I imagine for one moment that your meeting down there was not entirely above board?' he said in a low voice.

'No, of course not,' I said gravely. Dear Frank. I think I had shocked him. What a Frank-ish expression, too, 'above board'. It made one think immediately of the sort of things that would happen below board.

'I'm sure,' he began, and hesitated, his expression still troubled, 'I'm sure that Maxim would be very worried, very distressed, if he knew how you felt. I don't think he can have any idea of it.'

'You won't tell him?' I said hastily.

'No, naturally not, what do you take me for? But you see, Mrs de Winter, I know Maxim pretty well, and I've seen him through many . . . moods. If he thought you were worrying about – well – about the past, it would distress him more than anything on earth. I can promise you that. He's looking very well, very fit, but Mrs Lacy was quite right the other day when she said he had been on the verge of a breakdown last year, though it was tactless of her to say so in front of him. That's why you are so good for him. You are fresh and young and – and sensible, you have nothing to do with all that time that has gone. Forget it, Mrs de Winter, forget it, as he has done, thank heaven, and the rest of us. We none of us want to bring back the past. Maxim least of all. And it's up to you, you know, to lead us away from it. Not to take us back there again.'

He was right, of course he was right. Dear good Frank, my friend, my ally. I had been selfish and hypersensitive, a martyr to my own inferiority complex. 'I ought to have told you all this before,' I said.

'I wish you had,' he said. 'I might have spared you some worry.'

'I feel happier,' I said, 'much happier. And I've got you for my friend whatever happens, haven't I, Frank?'

'Yes, indeed,' he said.

We were out of the dark wooded drive and into the light again. The rhododendrons were upon us. Their hour would soon be over. Already they looked a little overblown, a little faded. Next month the petals would fall one by one from the great faces, and the gardeners would come and sweep them away. Theirs was a brief beauty. Not lasting very long.

'Frank,' I said, 'before we put an end to this conversation, for ever let's say, will you promise to answer me one thing, quite truthfully?'

He paused, looking at me a little suspiciously. 'That's not quite fair,' he said, 'you might ask me something that I should not be able to answer, something quite impossible.'

'No,' I said, 'it's not that sort of question. It's not intimate or personal, or anything like that.'

'Very well, I'll do my best,' he said.

We came round the sweep of the drive and Manderley was before us, serene and peaceful in the hollow of the lawns, surprising me as it always did, with its perfect symmetry and grace, its great simplicity.

The sunlight flickered on the mullioned windows, and there was a soft rusted glow about the stone walls where the lichen clung. A thin column of smoke curled from the library chimney. I bit my thumb nail, watching Frank out of the tail of my eye.

'Tell me,' I said, my voice casual, not caring a bit, 'tell me, was Rebecca very beautiful?'

Frank waited a moment. I could not see his face. He was looking away from me towards the house. 'Yes,' he said slowly, 'yes, I suppose she was the most beautiful creature I ever saw in my life.'

We went up the steps then to the hall, and I rang the bell for tea.

# 12

I did not see much of Mrs Danvers. She kept very much to herself. She still rang the house telephone to the morning-room every day and submitted the menu to me as a matter of form, but that was the limit of our intercourse. She had engaged a maid for me, Clarice, the daughter of somebody on the estate, a nice quiet well-mannered girl, who, thank heaven, had never been in service before and had no alarming standards. I think she was the only person in the house who stood in awe of me. To her I was the mistress: I was Mrs de Winter. The possible gossip of the others could not affect her. She had been away for some time, brought up by an aunt fifteen miles away, and in a sense she was as new to Manderley as I was. I felt at ease with her. I did not mind saying 'Oh, Clarice, would you mend my stocking?'

The housemaid Alice had been so superior. I used to sneak my chemise and nightgowns out of my drawer and mend them myself rather than ask her to do them. I had seen her once, with one of my chemises over her arm, examining the plain material with its small edging of lace. I shall never forget her expression. She looked almost shocked, as though her own personal pride had received a blow. I had never thought about my underclothes before. As long as they were clean and neat I had not thought the material or the existence of lace mattered. Brides one read about had trousseaux, dozens of sets at a time, and I had never bothered. Alice's face taught me a lesson. I wrote quickly to a shop in London and asked for a catalogue of under-linen. By the time I had made my choice Alice was looking after me no longer and Clarice was installed instead. It seemed such a waste buying new underclothes for Clarice that

I put the catalogue away in a drawer and never wrote to the shop after all.

I often wondered whether Alice told the others, and if my underclothes became a topic of conversation in the servants' hall, something rather dreadful, to be discussed in low tones when the men were nowhere about. She was too superior for it to be made a joking question. Phrases like 'Chemise to you' would never be bandied between her and Frith, for instance.

No, my underclothes were more serious than that. More like a divorce case heard *in camera* . . . At any rate I was glad when Alice surrendered me to Clarice. Clarice would never know real lace from false. It was considerate of Mrs Danvers to have engaged her. She must have thought we would be fit company, one for the other. Now that I knew the reason for Mrs Danvers' dislike and resentment it made things a little easier. I knew it was not just me personally she hated, but what I represented. She would have felt the same towards anyone who had taken Rebecca's place. At least that was what I understood from Beatrice the day she came to lunch.

'Did not you know?' she had said; 'she simply adored Rebecca.'

The words had shocked me at the time. Somehow I had not expected them. But when I thought it over I began to lose my first fear of Mrs Danvers. I began to be sorry for her. I could imagine what she must feel. It must hurt her every time she heard me called 'Mrs de Winter'. Every morning when she took up the house telephone and spoke to me, and I answered 'Yes, Mrs Danvers,' she must be thinking of another voice. When she passed through the rooms and saw traces of me about the place, a beret on a window-seat, a bag of knitting on a chair, she must think of another one, who had done these things before. Even as I did. I, who had never known Rebecca. Mrs Danvers knew how she walked and how she spoke. Mrs Danvers knew the colour of her eyes, her smile, the texture of her hair. I knew none of these things, I had never asked about them, but sometimes I felt Rebecca was as real to me as she was to Mrs Danvers.

Frank had told me to forget the past, and I wanted to forget it. But Frank did not have to sit in the morning-room as I did, every day, and touch the pen she had held between her fingers. He did not have to rest his hands on the blotter, and stare in front of him at her writing on the pigeon-holes. He did not have to look at the candlesticks on the mantelpiece, the clock, the vase in which the flowers stood, the pictures on the walls and remember, every day, that they belonged to her, she had chosen them, they were not mine at all. Frank did not have to sit at her place in the dining-room, hold the knife and fork that she had held, drink from her glass. He did not throw a coat over his shoulders which had been hers, nor find her handkerchief in the pocket. He did not notice, every day, as I did, the blind gaze of the old dog in its basket in the library, who lifted its head when it heard my footstep, the footstep of a woman, and sniffing the air drooped its head again, because I was not the one she sought.

Little things, meaningless and stupid in themselves, but they were there for me to see, for me to hear, for me to feel. Dear God, I did not want to think about Rebecca. I wanted to be happy, to make Maxim happy, and I wanted us to be together. There was no other wish in my heart but that. I could not help it if she came to me in thoughts, in dreams. I could not help it if I felt like a guest in Manderley, my home, walking where she had trodden, resting where she had lain. I was like a guest, biding my time, waiting for the return of the hostess. Little sentences, little reproofs reminding me every hour, every day.

'Frith,' I said, coming into the library on a summer morning, my arms full of lilac, 'Frith, where can I find a tall vase for these? They are all too small in the flower-room.'

'The white alabaster vase in the drawing-room was always used for the lilac, Madam.'

'Oh, wouldn't it be spoilt? It might get broken.'

'Mrs de Winter always used the alabaster vase, Madam.'

'Oh, oh, I see.'

Then the alabaster vase was brought for me, already filled with water, and as I put the sweet lilac in the vase and arranged the

154

sprigs, one by one, the mauve warm scent filling the room, mingling with the smell of the new-mown lawn outside coming from the open window, I thought: 'Rebecca did this. She took the lilac, as I am doing, and put the sprigs one by one in the white vase. I'm not the first to do it. This is Rebecca's vase, this is Rebecca's lilac.' She must have wandered out into the garden as I did, in that floppy garden hat that I had seen once at the back of the cupboard in the flower-room, hidden under some old cushions, and crossed the lawn to the lilac bushes, whistling perhaps, humming a tune, calling to the dogs to follow her, carrying in her hands the scissors that I carried now.

'Frith, could you move that book-stand from the table in the window, and I will put the lilac there?'

'Mrs de Winter always had the alabaster vase on the table behind the sofa, Madam.'

'Oh, well . . .' I hesitated, the vase in my hands, Frith's face impassive. He would obey me of course if I said I preferred to put the vase on the smaller table by the window. He would move the book-stand at once.

'All right,' I said, 'perhaps it would look better on the larger table.' And the alabaster vase stood, as it had always done, on the table behind the sofa . . .

Beatrice remembered her promise of a wedding present. A large parcel arrived one morning, almost too large for Robert to carry. I was sitting in the morning-room, having just read the menu for the day. I have always had a childish love of parcels. I snipped the string excitedly, and tore off the dark brown paper. It looked like books. I was right. It was books. Four big volumes. *A History of Painting.* And a sheet of notepaper in the first volume saying 'I hope this is the sort of thing you like,' and signed 'Love from Beatrice.' I could see her going into the shop in Wigmore Street and buying them. Looking about her in her abrupt, rather masculine way. 'I want a set of books for someone who is keen on Art,' she would say, and the attendant would answer, 'Yes, Madam, will you come this way.' She would finger the volumes a little suspiciously. 'Yes, that's about the price. It's for a wedding present. I want them to look good. Are these all about Art?' 'Yes, this is the standard work on the subject,' the assistant would say. And then Beatrice must have written her note, and paid her cheque, and given the address 'Mrs de Winter, Manderley.'

It was nice of Beatrice. There was something rather sincere and pathetic about her going off to a shop in London and buying me these books because she knew I was fond of painting. She imagined me, I expect, sitting down on a wet day and looking solemnly at the illustrations, and perhaps getting a sheet of drawing-paper and a paint-box and copying one of the pictures. Dear Beatrice. I had a sudden, stupid desire to cry. I gathered up the heavy volumes and looked round the morning-room for somewhere to put them. They were out of place in that fragile delicate room. Never mind, it was my room now, after all. I arranged them in a row on the top of the desk. They swayed dangerously, leaning one against the other. I stood back a bit, to watch the effect. Perhaps I moved too quickly, and it disturbed them. At any rate the foremost one fell, and the others slid after him. They upset a little china cupid who had hitherto stood alone on the desk except for the candle-sticks. He fell to the ground, hitting the waste-paper basket as he did so, and broke into fragments. I glanced hurriedly at the door, like a guilty child. I knelt on the floor and swept up the pieces into my hand. I found an envelope to put them in. I hid the envelope at the back of one of the drawers in the desk. Then I took the books off to the library and found room for them on the shelves.

Maxim laughed when I showed them to him with pride.

'Dear old Bee,' he said, 'you must have had a success with her. She never opens a book if she can help it.'

'Did she say anything about – well – what she thought of me?' I asked.

'The day she came to lunch? No, I don't think so.'

'I thought she might have written or something.'

'Beatrice and I don't correspond unless there's a major event in the family. Writing letters is a waste of time,' said Maxim.

156

I supposed I was not a major event. Yet if I had been Beatrice, and had a brother, and the brother married, surely one would have said something, expressed an opinion, written two words? Unless of course one had taken a dislike to the wife, or thought her unsuitable. Then of course it would be different. Still, Beatrice had taken the trouble to go up to London and to buy the books for me. She would not have done that if she disliked me.

It was the following day I remember, when Frith, who had brought in the coffee after lunch to the library, waited a moment, hovering behind Maxim, and said,

'Could I speak to you, sir?' Maxim glanced up from his paper.

'Yes, Frith, what is it?' he said, rather surprised. Frith wore a stiff solemn expression, his lips pursed. I thought at once his wife had died.

'It's about Robert, sir. There has been a slight unpleasantness between him and Mrs Danvers. Robert is very upset.'

'Oh, Lord,' said Maxim, making a face at me. I bent down to fondle Jasper, my unfailing habit in moments of embarrassment.

'Yes, sir. It appears Mrs Danvers has accused Robert of secreting a valuable ornament from the morning-room. It is Robert's business to bring in the fresh flowers to the morning-room and place the vases. Mrs Danvers went in this morning after the flowers had been done, and noticed one of the ornaments was missing. It was there yesterday, she said. She accused Robert of either taking the ornament or breaking it and concealing the breakage. Robert denied both accusations most emphatically, and came to me nearly in tears, sir. You may have noticed he was not himself at lunch.'

'I wondered why he handed me the cutlets without giving me a plate,' murmured Maxim. 'I did not know Robert was so sensitive. Well, I suppose someone else did it. One of the maids.'

'No, sir. Mrs Danvers went into the room before the girl had done the room. Nobody had been there since Madam yesterday, and Robert first thing with the flowers. It makes it very unpleasant for Robert and myself, sir.'

'Yes, of course it does. Well you had better ask Mrs Danvers

157

to come here and we'll get to the bottom of it. What ornament was it, anyway?'

'The china cupid, sir, that stands on the writing-table.'

'Oh! Oh, Lord. That's one of our treasures, isn't it? It will have to be found. Get hold of Mrs Danvers at once.'

'Very good, sir.'

Frith left the room and we were alone again. 'What a confounded nuisance,' said Maxim; 'that cupid is worth a hell of a lot. How I loathe servants' rows too. I wonder why they come to me about it. That's your job, sweetheart.'

I looked up from Jasper, my face red as fire. 'Darling,' I said, 'I meant to tell you before, but — but I forgot. The fact is I broke that cupid when I was in the morning-room yesterday.'

'You broke it? Well, why the devil didn't you say so when Frith was here?'

'I don't know. I didn't like to. I was afraid he would think me a fool.'

'He'll think you much more of a fool now. You'll have to explain to him and Mrs Danvers.'

'Oh, no, please, Maxim, you tell them. Let me go upstairs.'

'Don't be a little idiot. Anyone would think you were afraid of them.'

'I am afraid of them. At least, not afraid, but . . .'

The door opened, and Frith ushered Mrs Danvers into the room. I looked nervously at Maxim. He shrugged his shoulders, half amused, half angry.

'It's all a mistake, Mrs Danvers. Apparently Mrs de Winter broke the cupid herself and forgot to say anything,' said Maxim.

They all looked at me. It was like being a child again. I was still aware of my guilty flush. 'I'm so sorry,' I said, watching Mrs Danvers, 'I never thought Robert would get into trouble.'

'Is it possible to repair the ornament, Madam?' said Mrs Danvers. She did not seem to be surprised that I was the culprit. She looked at me with her white skull's face and her dark eyes. I felt she had known it was me all along and had accused Robert to see if I would have the courage to confess.

'I'm afraid not,' I said, 'it's smashed in little pieces.'

'What did you do with the pieces?' said Maxim.

It was like being a prisoner, giving evidence. How paltry and mean my actions sounded, even to myself. 'I put them all into an envelope,' I said.

'Well, what did you do with the envelope?' said Maxim, lighting a cigarette, his tone a mixture of amusement and exasperation.

'I put it at the back of one of the drawers in the writing-desk,' I said.

'It looks as though Mrs de Winter thought you would put her in prison, doesn't it, Mrs Danvers?' said Maxim. 'Perhaps you would find the envelope and send the pieces up to London. If they are too far gone to mend it can't be helped. All right, Frith. Tell Robert to dry his tears.'

Mrs Danvers lingered when Frith had gone. 'I will apologize to Robert of course,' she said, 'but the evidence pointed so strongly to him. It did not occur to me that Mrs de Winter had broken the ornament herself. Perhaps, if such a thing should happen again, Mrs de Winter will tell me personally, and I will have the matter attended to? It would save everybody a lot of unpleasantness.'

'Naturally,' said Maxim impatiently, 'I can't think why she didn't do so yesterday. I was just going to tell her when you came into the room.'

'Perhaps Mrs de Winter was not aware of the value of the ornament?' said Mrs Danvers, turning her eyes upon me.

'Yes,' I said wretchedly. 'Yes, I was afraid it was valuable. That's why I swept the pieces up so carefully.'

'And hid them at the back of a drawer where no one would find them, eh?' said Maxim, with a laugh, and a shrug of the shoulders. 'Is not that the sort of thing the between-maid is supposed to do, Mrs Danvers?'

'The between-maid at Manderley would never be allowed to touch the valuable things in the morning-room, sir,' said Mrs Danvers.

'No, I can't see you letting her,' said Maxim.

'It's very unfortunate,' said Mrs Danvers, 'I don't think we have ever had any breakages in the morning-room before. We were always so particular. I've done the dusting in there myself since – last year. There was no one I could trust. When Mrs de Winter was alive we used to do the valuables together.'

'Yes, well – it can't be helped,' said Maxim. 'All right, Mrs Danvers.'

She went out of the room, and I sat on the window-seat, looking out of the window. Maxim picked up his paper again. Neither of us spoke.

'I'm awfully sorry, darling,' I said, after a moment, 'it was very careless of me. I can't think how it happened. I was just arranging those books on the desk, to see if they would stand, and the cupid slipped.'

'My sweet child, forget it. What does it matter?'

'It does matter. I ought to have been more careful. Mrs Danvers must be furious with me.'

'What the devil has she got to be furious about? It's not her bit of china.'

'No, but she takes such a pride in it all. It's so awful to think nothing in there has ever been broken before. It had to be me.'

'Better you than the luckless Robert.'

'I wish it had been Robert. Mrs Danvers will never forgive me.'

'Damn Mrs Danvers,' said Maxim, 'she's not God Almighty, is she? I can't understand you. What do you mean by saying you are afraid of her?'

'I did not mean afraid exactly. I don't see much of her. It's not that. I can't really explain.'

'You do such extraordinary things,' said Maxim; 'fancy not getting hold of her when you broke the thing and saying, "Here, Mrs Danvers, get this mended." She'd understand that. Instead of which you scrape up the remains in an envelope and hide 'em at the back of a drawer. Just like a between-maid, as I said, and not the mistress of a house.'

'I am like a between-maid,' I said slowly, 'I know I am, in lots of ways. That's why I have so much in common with Clarice. We are on the same sort of footing. And that's why she likes me. I went and saw her mother the other day. And do you know what she said? I asked her if she thought Clarice was happy with us, and she said, "Oh, yes, Mrs de Winter. Clarice seems quite happy. She says, 'It's not like being with a lady, Mum, it's like being with one of ourselves.'" Do you suppose she meant it as a compliment or not?'

'God knows,' said Maxim; 'remembering Clarice's mother, I should take it as a direct insult. Her cottage is generally a shambles and smells of boiled cabbage. At one time she had nine children under eleven, and she herself used to patter about in that patch of garden with no shoes and a stocking round her head. We nearly gave her notice to quit. Why Clarice looks as neat and clean as she does I can't imagine.'

'She's been living with an aunt,' I said, feeling rather subdued. 'I know my flannel skirt has a dirty mark down the front, but I've never walked barefoot with a stocking round my head.' I knew now why Clarice did not disdain my underclothes as Alice had done. 'Perhaps that's why I prefer calling on Clarice's mother to calling on people like the bishop's wife?' I went on. 'The bishop's wife never said I was like one of themselves.'

'If you wear that grubby skirt when you call on her I don't suppose she does,' said Maxim.

'Of course I didn't call on her in my old skirt, I wore a frock,' I said, 'and anyway I don't think much of people who just judge one by one's clothes.'

'I hardly think the bishop's wife cares twopence about clothes,' said Maxim, 'but she may have been rather surprised if you sat on the extreme edge of the chair and answered "Yes" and "No" like someone after a new job, which you did the only time we returned a call together.'

'I can't help being shy.'

'I know you can't, sweetheart. But you don't make an effort to conquer it.'

'I think that's very unfair,' I said. 'I try every day, every time I go out or meet anyone new. I'm always making efforts. You don't understand. It's all very well for you, you're used to that sort of thing. I've not been brought up to it.'

'Rot,' said Maxim; 'it's not a question of bringing up, as you put it. It's a matter of application. You don't think I like calling on people, do you? It bores me stiff. But it has to be done, in this part of the world.'

'We're not talking about boredom,' I said; 'there's nothing to be afraid of in being bored. If I was just bored it would be different. I hate people looking me up and down as though I were a prize cow.'

'Who looks you up and down?'

'All the people down here. Everybody.'

'What does it matter if they do? It gives them some interest in life.'

'Why must I be the one to supply the interest, and have all the criticism?'

'Because life at Manderley is the only thing that ever interests anybody down here.'

'What a slap in the eye I must be to them then.'

Maxim did not answer. He went on looking at his paper.

'What a slap in the eye I must be to them,' I repeated. And then, 'I suppose that's why you married me,' I said; 'you knew I was dull and quiet and inexperienced, so that there would never be any gossip about me.'

Maxim threw his paper on the ground and got up from his chair. 'What do you mean?' he said.

His face was dark and queer, and his voice was rough, not his voice at all.

'I – I don't know,' I said, leaning back against the window, 'I don't mean anything. Why do you look like that?'

'What do you know about any gossip down here?' he said.

'I don't,' I said, scared by the way he looked at me. 'I only said it because – because of something to say. Don't look at me like that. Maxim, what have I said? what's the matter?'

162

'Who's been talking to you,' he said slowly.

'No one. No one at all.'

'Why did you say what you did?'

'I tell you, I don't know. It just came to my head. I was angry, cross. I do hate calling on these people. I can't help it. And you criticized me for being shy. I didn't mean it. Really, Maxim, I didn't. Please believe me.'

'It was not a particularly attractive thing to say, was it?' he said.

'No,' I said. 'No, it was rude, hateful.'

He stared at me moodily, his hands in his pockets, rocking backwards and forwards on his heels. 'I wonder if I did a very selfish thing in marrying you,' he said. He spoke slowly, thoughtfully.

I felt very cold, rather sick. 'How do you mean?' I said.

'I'm not much of a companion to you, am I?' he said. 'There are too many years between us. You ought to have waited, and then married a boy of your own age. Not someone like myself, with half his life behind him.'

'That's ridiculous,' I said hurriedly, 'you know age doesn't mean anything in marriage. Of course we are companions.'

'Are we? I don't know,' he said.

I knelt up on the window-seat and put my arms round his shoulders. 'Why do you say these things to me?' I said; 'you know I love you more than anything in the world. There has never been anyone but you. You are my father and my brother and my son. All those things.'

'It was my fault,' he said, not listening. 'I rushed you into it. I never gave you a chance to think it over.'

'I did not want to think it over,' I said, 'there was no other choice. You don't understand, Maxim. When one loves a person . . .'

'Are you happy here?' he said, looking away from me, out of the window, 'I wonder sometimes. You've got thinner. Lost your colour.'

'Of course I'm happy,' I said, 'I love Manderley. I love the garden, I love everything. I don't mind calling on people. I just said that to be tiresome. I'll call on people every day, if you want me to. I don't mind what I do. I've never for one moment regretted marrying you, surely you must know that?'

He patted my cheek in his terrible absent way, and bent down, and kissed the top of my head. 'Poor lamb, you don't have much fun, do you? I'm afraid I'm very difficult to live with.'

'You're not difficult,' I said eagerly, 'you are easy, very easy. Much easier than I thought you would be. I used to think it would be dreadful to be married, that one's husband would drink, or use awful language, or grumble if the toast was soft at breakfast, and be rather unattractive altogether, smell possibly. You don't do any of those things.'

'Good God, I hope not,' said Maxim, and he smiled.

I seized advantage of his smile, I smiled too, and took his hands and kissed them. 'How absurd to say we are not companions,' I said; 'why look how we sit here every evening, you with a book or a paper, and me with my knitting. Just like cups of tea. Just like old people, married for years and years. Of course we are companions. Of course we are happy. You talk as though you thought we had made a mistake? You don't mean it like that, do you, Maxim? You know our marriage is a success, a wonderful success?'

'If you say so, then it's all right,' he said.

'No, but you think it too, don't you, darling? It's not just me? We are happy, aren't we? Terribly happy?'

He did not answer. He went on staring out of the window while I held his hands. My throat felt dry and tight, and my eyes were burning. Oh, God, I thought, this is like two people in a play, in a moment the curtain will come down, we shall bow to the audience, and go off to our dressing-rooms. This can't be a real moment in the lives of Maxim and myself. I sat down on the window-seat, and let go of his hands. I heard myself speaking in a hard cool voice. 'If you don't think we are happy it would be much better if you would admit it. I don't want you to pretend anything. I'd much rather go away. Not live with you any more.' It was not really happening of course. It was the girl in the play talking, not me to Maxim. I pictured the type of girl who would play the part. Tall and slim, rather nervy.

'Well, why don't you answer me?' I said.

He took my face in his hands and looked at me, just as he had before, when Frith had come into the room with tea, the day we went to the beach.

'How can I answer you?' he said. 'I don't know the answer myself. If you say we are happy, let's leave it at that. It's something I know nothing about. I take your word for it. We are happy. All right then, that's agreed!' He kissed me again, and then walked away across the room. I went on sitting by the window, stiff and straight, my hands in my lap.

'You say all this because you are disappointed in me,' I said. 'I'm gauche and awkward, I dress badly, I'm shy with people. I warned you in Monte Carlo how it would be. You think I'm not right for Manderley.'

'Don't talk nonsense,' he said. 'I've never said you dressed badly or were gauche. It's your imagination. As for being shy, you'll get over that. I've told you so before.'

'We've argued in a circle,' I said, 'we've come right back to where we started. This all began because I broke the cupid in the morning-room. If I hadn't broken the cupid none of this would have happened. We'd have drunk our coffee, and gone out into the garden.'

'Oh, damn that infernal cupid,' said Maxim wearily. 'Do you really think I care whether it's in ten thousand pieces or not?'

'Was it very valuable?'

'Heaven knows. I suppose so. I've really forgotten.'

'Are all those things in the morning-room valuable?'

'Yes, I believe so.'

'Why were all the most valuable things put in the morning-room?'

'I don't know. I suppose because they looked well there.'

'Were they always there? When your mother was alive?'

'No. No, I don't think they were. They were scattered about the house. The chairs were in a lumber room I believe.'

'When was the morning-room furnished as it is now?'

'When I was married.'

'I suppose the cupid was put there then?'

'I suppose so.'

'Was that found in a lumber room?'

'No. No, I don't think it was. As a matter of fact I believe it was a wedding-present. Rebecca knew a lot about china.'

I did not look at him. I began to polish my nails. He had said the word quite naturally, quite calmly. It had been no effort to him. After a minute I glanced at him swiftly. He was standing by the mantelpiece, his hands in his pockets. He was staring straight in front of him. He is thinking about Rebecca, I said to myself. He is thinking how strange it was that a wedding present to me should have been the cause of destroying a wedding present to Rebecca. He is thinking about the cupid. He is remembering who gave it to Rebecca. He is going over in his mind how the parcel came and how pleased she was. Rebecca knew a lot about china. Perhaps he came into the room, and she was kneeling on the floor, wrenching open the little crate in which the cupid was packed. She must have glanced up at him, and smiled. 'Look, Max,' she would have said, 'look what we've been sent.' And she then would have plunged her hand down into the shavings and brought out the cupid who stood on one foot, his bow in his hand. 'We'll have it in the morning-room,' she must have said, and he must have knelt down beside her, and they must have looked at the cupid together.

I went on polishing my nails. They were scrubby, like a schoolboy's nails. The cuticles grew up over the half moons. The thumb was bitten nearly to the quick. I looked at Maxim again. He was still standing in front of the fireplace.

'What are you thinking about?' I said.

My voice was steady and cool. Not like my heart, thumping inside me. Not like my mind, bitter and resentful. He lit a cigarette, surely the twenty-fifth that day, and we had only just finished lunch; he threw the match into the empty grate, he picked up the paper.

'Nothing very much, why?' he said.

'Oh, I don't know,' I said, 'you looked so serious, so far away.'

He whistled a tune absently, the cigarette twisting in his fingers. 'As a matter of fact I was wondering if they had chosen the Surrey side to play Middlesex at the Oval,' he said.

He sat down in the chair again and folded the paper. I looked out of the window. Presently Jasper came to me and climbed on my lap.

# 13

M axim had to go up to London at the end of June to some public dinner. A man's dinner. Something to do with the county. He was away for two days and I was left alone. I dreaded his going. When I saw the car disappear round the sweep in the drive I felt exactly as though it were to be a final parting and I should never see him again. There would be an accident of course and later on in the afternoon, when I came back from my walk, I should find Frith white and frightened waiting for me with a message. The doctor would have rung up from some cottage hospital. 'You must be very brave,' he would say, 'I'm afraid you must be prepared for a great shock.'

And Frank would come, and we would go to the hospital together. Maxim would not recognize me. I went through the whole thing as I was sitting at lunch, I could see the crowd of local people clustering round the churchyard at the funeral, and myself leaning on Frank's arm. It was so real to me that I could scarcely eat any lunch, and I kept straining my ears to hear the telephone should it ring.

I sat out in the garden under the chestnut tree in the afternoon, with a book on my lap, but I scarcely read at all. When I saw Robert come across the lawn I knew it was the telephone and I felt physically sick. 'A message from the club, Madam, to say Mr de Winter arrived ten minutes ago.'

I shut up my book. 'Thank you, Robert. How quickly he got up.'

'Yes, Madam. A very good run.'

'Did he ask to speak to me, or leave any special message?'

'No, Madam. Just that he had arrived safely. It was the porter speaking.'

'All right, Robert. Thanks very much.'

The relief was tremendous. I did not feel sick any more. The pain had gone. It was like coming ashore after a channel crossing. I began to feel rather hungry, and when Robert had gone back into the house I crept into the dining-room through the long window and stole some biscuits from the sideboard. I had six of them. Bath Olivers. And then an apple as well. I had no idea I was so empty. I went and ate them in the woods, in case one of the servants should see me on the lawn from the windows, and then go and tell the cook that they did not think Mrs de Winter cared for the food prepared in the kitchen, as they had just seen her filling herself with fruit and biscuits. The cook would be offended, and perhaps go to Mrs Danvers.

Now that Maxim was safe in London, and I had eaten my biscuits, I felt very well and curiously happy. I was aware of a sense of freedom, as though I had no responsibilities at all. It was rather like a Saturday when one was a child. No lessons, and no prep. One could do as one liked. One put on an old skirt and a pair of sand-shoes and played Hares and Hounds on the common with the children who lived next door.

I had just the same feeling. I had not felt like this all the time I had been at Manderley. It must be because Maxim had gone to London.

I was rather shocked at myself. I could not understand it at all. I had not wanted him to go. And now this lightness of heart, this spring in my step, this childish feeling that I wanted to run across the lawn, and roll down the bank. I wiped the biscuit crumbs from my mouth and called to Jasper. Perhaps I was just feeling like this because it was a lovely day . . .

We went through the Happy Valley to the little cove. The azaleas were finished now, the petals lay brown and crinkled on the moss. The bluebells had not faded yet, they made a solid carpet in the woods above the valley, and the young bracken was shooting up, curling and green. The moss smelt rich and deep, and the bluebells were earthy, bitter. I lay down in the long grass beside the bluebells with my hands behind my head, and

Jasper at my side. He looked down at me panting, his face foolish, saliva dripping from his tongue and his heavy jowl. There were pigeons somewhere in the trees above. It was very peaceful and quiet. I wondered why it was that places are so much lovelier when one is alone. How commonplace and stupid it would be if I had a friend now, sitting beside me, someone I had known at school, who would say 'By the way, I saw old Hilda the other day. You remember her, the one who was so good at tennis. She's married, with two children.' And the bluebells beside us unnoticed, and the pigeons overhead unheard. I did not want anyone with me. Not even Maxim. If Maxim had been there I should not be lying as I was now, chewing a piece of grass, my eyes shut. I should have been watching him, watching his eyes, his expression. Wondering if he liked it, if he was bored. Wondering what he was thinking. Now I could relax, none of these things mattered. Maxim was in London. How lovely it was to be alone again. No, I did not mean that. It was disloyal, wicked. It was not what I meant. Maxim was my life and my world. I got up from the bluebells and called sharply to Jasper. We set off together down the valley to the beach. The tide was out, the sea very calm and remote. It looked like a great placid lake out there in the bay. I could not imagine it rough now, any more than I could imagine winter in summer. There was no wind, and the sun shone on the lapping water where it ran into the little pools in the rocks. Jasper scrambled up the rocks immediately, glancing back at me, one ear blown back against his head, giving him an odd rakish appearance.

'Not that way, Jasper,' I said.

He cared nothing for me of course. He loped off, deliberately disobedient. 'What a nuisance he is,' I said aloud, and I scrambled up the rocks after him, pretending to myself I did not want to go to the other beach. 'Oh, well,' I thought, 'it can't be helped. After all, Maxim is not with me. It's nothing to do with me.'

I splashed through the pools on the rocks, humming a tune. The cove looked different when the tide was out. Less formidable. There was only about three foot of water in the tiny harbour. A boat would just float there comfortably I supposed, at dead low water. The buoy was still there. It was painted white and green, I had not noticed that before. Perhaps because it had been raining the colouring was indistinct. There was no one on the beach. I walked across the shingle to the other side of the cove, and climbed the low stone wall of the jetty-arm. Jasper ran on ahead as though it was his custom. There was a ring in the wall and an iron ladder descending to the water. That's where the dinghy would be tied, I suppose, and one would climb to it from the ladder. The buoy was just opposite, about thirty feet away. There was something written on it. I craned my neck sideways to read the lettering. 'Je Reviens'. What a funny name. Not like a boat. Perhaps it had been a French boat though, a fishing boat. Fishing boats sometimes had names like that; 'Happy Return', 'I'm Here', those sort of names. 'Je Reviens' – 'I come back.' Yes, I suppose it was quite a good name for a boat. Only it had not been right for that particular boat which would never come back again.

It must be cold sailing out there in the bay, beyond the beacon away on the headland. The sea was calm in the bay, but even today, when it was so still, out there round the headland there was a ripple of white foam on the surface of the water where the tide was racing. A small boat would heel to the wind when she rounded the headland and came out of the landlocked bay. The sea would splash inboard perhaps, run down the deck. The person at the tiller would wipe spray out of her eyes and hair, glance up at the straining mast. I wondered what colour the boat had been. Green and white perhaps, like the buoy. Not very big, Frank had said, with a little cabin.

Jasper was sniffing at the iron ladder. 'Come away,' I said. 'I don't want to go in after you.' I went back along the harbour wall to the beach. The cottage did not seem so remote and sinister at the edge of the wood as it had done before. The sun made such a difference. No rain today, pattering on the roof. I walked slowly up the beach towards it. After all, it was only a cottage, with nobody living in it. There was nothing to be frightened of. Nothing at all. Any place seemed damp and sinister when it had been uninhabited for a certain time. Even new bungalows and places. Besides, they had moonlight picnics and things here. Week-end visitors probably used to come and bathe, and then go for a sail in the boat. I stood looking into the neglected garden choked with nettles. Someone ought to come and tidy it up. One of the gardeners. There was no need to leave it like this. I pushed the little gate and went to the door of the cottage. It was not entirely closed. I was certain I had closed it the last time. Jasper began growling, sniffing under the door.

'Don't, Jasper,' I said. He went on sniffing deeply, his nose thrust to the crack. I pushed the door open and looked inside. It was very dark. Like it had been before. Nothing was changed. The cobwebs still clung to the rigging of the model boats. The door into the boat-store at the end of the room was open though. Jasper growled again, and there was a sound of something falling. Jasper barked furiously, and darting between my legs into the room he tore to the open door of the store. I followed him, heart beating, and then stood uncertainly in the middle of the room. 'Jasper, come back, don't be a fool,' I said. He stood in the doorway, still barking furiously, an hysterical note in his voice. Something was there then, inside the store. Not a rat. He would have gone for a rat. 'Jasper, Jasper. Come here,' I said. He would not come. I went slowly to the door of the store.

'Is there anybody there?' I said.

No one answered. I bent down to Jasper, putting my hand on his collar, and looked round the edge of the door. Someone was sitting in the corner against the wall. Someone who, from his crouching position, was even more frightened than me. It was Ben. He was trying to hide behind one of the sails. 'What is the matter? Do you want something?' I said. He blinked at me stupidly, his mouth slightly open.

'I'm not doing nothing,' he said.

'Quiet, Jasper,' I scolded, putting my hand over his muzzle,

172

and I took my belt off and ran it through his collar as a leash.

'What do you want, Ben?' I said, a little bolder this time.

He did not answer. He watched me with his sly idiot's eyes.

'I think you had better come out,' I said. 'Mr de Winter doesn't like people walking in and out of here.'

He shambled to his feet grinning furtively, wiping his nose with the back of his hand. The other hand he kept behind his back. 'What have you got, Ben?' I said. He obeyed me like a child, showing me the other hand. There was a fishing line in it. 'I'm not doing anything,' he repeated.

'Does that line belong here?' I asked.

'Eh?' he said.

'Listen, Ben,' I said. 'You can take that line if you want to, but you mustn't do it again. It's not honest, taking people's things.'

He said nothing. He blinked at me and wriggled.

'Come along,' I said firmly.

I went into the main room and he followed me. Jasper had stopped barking, and was now sniffing at Ben's heels. I did not want to stop any longer in the cottage. I walked quickly out into the sunshine, Ben shuffling behind me. Then I shut the door.

'You had better go home,' I said to Ben.

He held the fishing line clutched to his heart like a treasure. 'You won't put me to the asylum, will you?' he said.

I saw then that he was trembling with fright. His hands were shaking, and his eyes were fixed on mine in supplication, like a dumb thing.

'Of course not,' I said gently.

'I done nothing,' he repeated, 'I never told no one. I don't want to be put to the asylum.' A tear rolled down his dirty face.

'That's all right, Ben,' I said; 'no one will put you away. But you must not go to the cottage again.'

I turned away, and he came after me, pawing at my hand.

'Here,' he said. 'Here, I got something for you.'

He smiled foolishly, he beckoned with his finger, and turned towards the beach. I went with him, and he bent down and

173

picked up a flat stone by a rock. There was a little heap of shells under the stone. He chose one, and presented it to me. 'That's yourn,' he said.

'Thank you; it's very pretty,' I said.

He grinned again, rubbing his ear, his fright forgotten. 'You've got angel's eyes,' he said.

I glanced down at the shell again, rather taken aback. I did not know what to say.

'You're not like the other one,' he said.

'Who do you mean?' I said. 'What other one?'

He shook his head. His eyes were sly again. He laid his finger against his nose. 'Tall and dark she was,' he said. 'She gave you the feeling of a snake. I seen her here with me own eyes. Be night she'd come. I seen her.' He paused, watching me intently. I did not say anything. 'I looked in on her once,' he said, 'and she turned on me, she did. "You don't know me, do you?" she said. "You've never seen me here, and you won't again. If I catch you looking at me through the windows here I'll have you put to the asylum," she said. "You wouldn't like that would you? They're cruel to people in the asylum," she said. "I won't say nothing, M'am," I said. And I touched me cap, like this here.' He pulled at his sou'wester. 'She's gone now, ain't she?' he said anxiously.

'I don't know who you mean,' I said slowly; 'no one is going to put you in the asylum. Good afternoon, Ben.'

I turned away and walked up the beach to the path dragging Jasper by his belt. Poor wretch, he was potty, of course. He did not know what he was talking about. It was hardly likely that anyone would threaten him with the asylum. Maxim had said he was quite harmless, and so had Frank. Perhaps he had heard himself discussed once, amongst his own people, and the memory of it lingered, like an ugly picture in the mind of a child. He would have a child's mentality too, regarding likes and dislikes. He would take a fancy to a person for no reason, and be friendly one day perhaps and sullen the next. He had been friendly with me because I had said he could keep the fishing line. Tomorrow

174

if I met him he might not know me. It was absurd to notice anything said by an idiot. I glanced back over my shoulder at the cove. The tide had begun to run and was swirling slowly round the arm of the harbour wall. Ben had disappeared over the rocks. The beach was deserted again. I could just see the stone chimney of the cottage through a gap in the dark trees. I had a sudden unaccountable desire to run. I pulled at Jasper's leash and panted up the steep narrow path through the woods, not looking back any more. Had I been offered all the treasures in the world I could not have turned and gone down to the cottage or the beach again. It was as though someone waited down there, in the little garden where the nettles grew. Someone who watched and listened.

Jasper barked as we ran together. He thought it was some new kind of game. He kept trying to bite the belt and worry it. I had not realized how closely the trees grew together here, their roots stretching across the path like tendrils ready to trip one. They ought to clear all this, I thought as I ran, catching my breath, Maxim should get the men on to it. There is no sense or beauty in this undergrowth. That tangle of shrubs there should be cut down to bring light to the path. It was dark, much too dark. That naked eucalyptus tree stifled by brambles looked like the white bleached limb of a skeleton, and there was a black earthy stream running beneath it, choked with the muddied rains of years, trickling silently to the beach below. The birds did not sing here as they did in the valley. It was quiet in a different way. And even as I ran and panted up the path I could hear the wash of the sea as the tide crept into the cove. I understood why Maxim disliked the path and the cove. I disliked it too. I had been a fool to come this way. I should have stayed on the other beach, on the white shingle, and come home by the Happy Valley.

I was glad to come out on to the lawn and see the house there in the hollow, solid and secure. The woods were behind me. I would ask Robert to bring me my tea under the chestnut tree. I glanced at my watch. It was earlier than I thought, not yet four. I would have to wait a bit. It was not the routine at Manderley to have tea before half past. I was glad Frith was out. Robert would not make such a performance of bringing the tea out into the garden. As I wandered across the lawn to the terrace my eye was caught by a gleam of sunshine on something metal showing through the green of the rhododendron leaves at the turn in the drive. I shaded my eyes with my hand to see what it was. It looked like the radiator of a car. I wondered if someone had called. If they had though, they would have driven up to the house, not left their car concealed like that from the house, at the turn of the drive, by the shrubs. I went a little closer. Yes, it was a car all right. I could see the wings now and the hood. What a funny thing. Visitors never did that as a rule. And the tradesmen went round the back way by the old stables and the garage. It was not Frank's Morris. I knew that well. This was a long, low car, a sports car. I wondered what I had better do. If it was a caller Robert would have shown them into the library or the drawing-room. In the drawing-room they would be able to see me as I came across the lawn. I did not want to face a caller dressed like this. I should have to ask them to stay to tea. I hesitated, at the edge of the lawn. For no reason, perhaps because the sunlight flickered a moment on the glass, I looked up at the house, and as I did so I noticed with surprise that the shutters of one of the windows in the west wing had been opened up. Somebody stood by the window. A man. And then he must have caught sight of me because he drew back abruptly, and a figure behind him put up an arm and closed the shutters.

The arm belonged to Mrs Danvers. I recognized the black sleeve. I wondered for a minute if it was a public day and she was showing the rooms. It could not be so though because Frith always did that, and Frith was out. Besides, the rooms in the west wing were not shown to the public. I had not even been into them myself yet. No, I knew it was not a public day. The public never came on a Tuesday. Perhaps it was something to do with a repair in one of the rooms. It was odd though the way the man had been looking out and directly he saw me he whipped back into the room and the shutters were closed. And the car too, drawn up behind the rhododendrons, so that it could not be seen from the house. Still, that was up to Mrs Danvers. It was nothing to do with me. If she had friends she took to the west wing it was not exactly my affair. I had never known it happen before though. Odd that it should occur on the only day Maxim was from home.

I strolled rather self-consciously across the lawn to the house, aware that they might be watching me still from a chink in the shutters.

I went up the steps and through the big front door to the hall. There was no sign of a strange cap or stick, and no card on the salver. Evidently this was not an official visitor. Well, it was not my affair. I went into the flower room and washed my hands in the basin to save going upstairs. It would be awkward if I met them face to face on the stairs or somewhere. I remembered I had left my knitting in the morning-room before lunch, and I went along through the drawing-room to fetch it, the faithful Jasper at my heels. The morning-room door was open. And I noticed that my bag of knitting had been moved. I had left it on the divan, and it had been picked up and pushed behind a cushion. There was the imprint of a person on the fabric of the divan where my knitting had been before. Someone had sat down there recently, and picked up my knitting because it had been in the way. The chair by the desk had also been moved. It looked as though Mrs Danvers entertained her visitors in the morning-room when Maxim and I were out of the way. I felt rather uncomfortable. I would rather not know. Jasper was sniffing under the divan and wagging his tail. He was not suspicious of the visitor anyway. I took my bag of knitting and went out. As I did so the door in the large drawing-room that led to the stone passage and the back premises opened, and I heard voices. I darted back into the morning-room again, just in time. I had not been seen. I waited behind the door frowning at Jasper who stood in the doorway looking at me, his tongue hanging out, wagging his tail. The little wretch would give me away. I stood very still, holding my breath.

Then I heard Mrs Danvers speak. 'I expect she has gone to the library,' she said. 'She's come home early for some reason. If she has gone to the library you will be able to go through the hall without her seeing you. Wait here while I go and see.'

I knew they were talking about me. I began to feel more uncomfortable than ever. It was so furtive, the whole business. And I did not want to catch Mrs Danvers in the wrong. Then Jasper turned his head sharply towards the drawing-room. He trotted out, wagging his tail.

'Hullo, you little tyke,' I heard the man say. Jasper began to bark excitedly. I looked round desperately for somewhere to hide. Hopeless of course. And then I heard a footstep quite close to my ear, and the man came into the room. He did not see me at first because I was behind the door, but Jasper made a dive at me, still barking with delight.

The man wheeled round suddenly and saw me. I have never seen anyone look more astonished. I might have been the burglar and he the master of the house.

'I beg your pardon,' he said, looking me up and down.

He was a big, hefty fellow, good-looking in a rather flashy, sunburnt way. He had the hot, blue eyes usually associated with heavy drinking and loose living. His hair was reddish like his skin. In a few years he would run to fat, his neck bulging over the back of his collar. His mouth gave him away, it was too soft, too pink. I could smell the whisky in his breath from where I stood. He began to smile. The sort of smile he would give to every woman.

'I hope I haven't startled you,' he said.

I came out from behind the door looking no doubt as big a fool as I felt. 'No, of course not,' I said, 'I heard voices, I was not quite sure who it was. I did not expect any callers this afternoon.'

'What a shame,' he said heartily, 'it's too bad of me to butt in on you like this. I hope you'll forgive me. The fact is I just popped in to see old Danny, she's a very old friend of mine.'

'Oh, of course, it's quite all right,' I said.

'Dear old Danny,' he said, 'she's so anxious, bless her, not to disturb anyone. She didn't want to worry you.'

'Oh, it does not matter at all,' I said. I was watching Jasper who was jumping up and pawing at the man in delight.

'This little beggar hasn't forgotten me, has he?' he said. 'Grown into a jolly little beast. He was quite a youngster when I saw him last. He's too fat though. He needs more exercise.'

'I've just taken him for a long walk,' I said.

'Have you really? How sporting of you,' he said. He went on patting Jasper and smiling at me in a familiar way. Then he pulled out his cigarette case. 'Have one?' he said.

'I don't smoke,' I told him.

'Don't you really?' He took one himself and lighted it.

I never minded those things, but it seemed odd to me, in somebody else's room. It was surely rather bad manners? Not polite to me.

'How's old Max?' he said.

I was surprised at his tone. It sounded as though he knew him well. It was queer, to hear Maxim talked of as Max. No one called him that.

'He's very well, thank you,' I said. 'He's gone up to London.'

'And left the bride all alone? Why, that's too bad. Isn't he afraid someone will come and carry you off?'

He laughed, opening his mouth. I did not like his laugh. There was something offensive about it. I did not like him, either. Just then Mrs Danvers came into the room. She turned her eyes upon me and I felt quite cold. Oh, God, I thought, how she must hate me.

'Hullo, Danny, there you are,' said the man; 'all your precautions were in vain. The mistress of the house was hiding behind the door.' And he laughed again. Mrs Danvers did not say anything. She just went on looking at me. 'Well, aren't you going to introduce me?' he said; 'after all it's the usual thing to do, isn't it, to pay one's respect to a bride?'

'This is Mr Favell, Madam,' said Mrs Danvers. She spoke quietly, rather unwillingly. I don't think she wanted to introduce him to me.

'How do you do,' I said, and then, with an effort to be polite, 'Won't you stay to tea?'

He looked very amused. He turned to Mrs Danvers.

'Now isn't that a charming invitation?' he said. 'I've been asked to stay to tea? By heaven, Danny, I've a good mind to.'

I saw her flash a look of warning at him. I felt very uneasy. It was all wrong, this situation. It ought not to be happening at all.

'Well, perhaps you're right,' he said; 'it would have been a lot of fun, all the same. I suppose I had better be going, hadn't I? Come and have a look at my car.' He still spoke in a familiar rather offensive way. I did not want to go and look at his car. I felt very awkward and embarrassed. 'Come on,' he said, 'it's a jolly good little car. Much faster than anything poor old Max ever has.'

I could not think of an excuse. The whole business was so forced and stupid. I did not like it. And why did Mrs Danvers have to stand there looking at me with that smouldering look in her eyes?

'Where is the car?' I said feebly.

'Round the bend in the drive. I didn't drive to the door, I was afraid of disturbing you. I had some idea you probably rested in the afternoon.'

I said nothing. The lie was too obvious. We all walked out through the drawing-room and into the hall. I saw him glance over his shoulder and wink at Mrs Danvers. She did not wink in return. I hardly expected she would. She looked very hard and grim. Jasper frolicked out on to the drive. He seemed delighted with the sudden appearance of this visitor whom he appeared to know so well.

'I left my cap in the car, I believe,' said the man, pretending to glance round the hall. 'As a matter of fact, I didn't come in this way. I slipped round and bearded Danny in her den. Coming out to see the car too?'

He looked inquiringly at Mrs Danvers. She hesitated, watching me out of the tail of her eye.

'No,' she said. 'No, I don't think I'll come out now. Good-bye, Mr Jack.'

He seized her hand and shook it heartily. 'Good-bye, Danny: take care of yourself. You know where to get in touch with me always. It's done me a power of good to see you again.' He walked out on to the drive, Jasper dancing at his heels, and I followed him slowly, feeling very uncomfortable still.

'Dear old Manderley,' he said, looking up at the windows. 'The place hasn't changed much. I suppose Danny sees to that. What a wonderful woman she is, eh?'

'Yes, she's very efficient,' I said.

'And what do you think of it all? Like being buried down here?'

'I'm very fond of Manderley,' I said stiffly.

'Weren't you living somewhere down in the south of France when Max met you? Monte, wasn't it? I used to know Monte well.'

'Yes, I was in Monte Carlo,' I said.

We had come to his car now. A green sports thing, typical of its owner.

'What do you think of it?' he said.

'Very nice,' I said, politely.

'Come for a run to the lodge gates?' he said.

'No, I don't think I will,' I said. 'I'm rather tired.'

'You don't think it would look too good for the mistress of Manderley to be seen driving with someone like me, is that it?' he said, and he laughed, shaking his head at me.

'Oh, no,' I said, turning rather red. 'No, really.'

He went on looking me up and down in his amused way with those familiar, unpleasant blue eyes. I felt like a barmaid.

'Oh, well,' he said, 'we mustn't lead the bride astray, must we, Jasper? It wouldn't do at all.' He reached for his cap, and an enormous pair of motoring gloves. He threw his cigarette away on the drive.

181

'Good-bye,' he said, holding out his hand; 'it's been a lot of fun meeting you.'

'Good-bye,' I said.

'By the way,' he said carelessly, 'it would be very sporting and grand of you if you did not mention this little visit of mine to Max? He doesn't exactly approve of me, I'm afraid; I don't know why, and it might get poor old Danny into trouble.'

'No,' I said awkwardly. 'No, all right.'

'That's very sporting of you. Sure you won't change your mind and come for a run?'

'No, I don't think I will, if you don't mind.'

'Bye-bye, then. Perhaps I'll come and look you up one day. Get down, Jasper, you devil, you'll scratch my paint. I say, I call it a damn shame Max going up to London and leaving you alone like this!'

'I don't mind. I like being alone,' I said.

'Do you, by Jove? What an extraordinary thing. It's all wrong, you know. Against nature. How long have you been married? Three months, isn't it?'

'About that,' I said.

'I say, I wish I'd got a bride of three months waiting for me at home! I'm a poor lonesome bachelor.' He laughed again, and pulled his cap down over his eyes. 'Fare you well,' he said, starting up the engine, and the car shot down the drive snorting explosive fury from the exhaust, while Jasper stood looking after it, his ears drooping, his tail between his legs.

'Oh, come on, Jasper,' I said, 'don't be so idiotic.' I walked slowly back to the house. Mrs Danvers had disappeared. I stood in the hall and rang the bell. Nothing happened for about five minutes. I rang again. Presently Alice appeared, her face rather aggrieved. 'Yes, Madam?' she said.

'Oh, Alice,' I said, 'isn't Robert there? I rather fancied my tea out under the chestnut tree.'

'Robert went to the post this afternoon, and isn't back yet, Madam,' said Alice. 'Mrs Danvers gave him to understand you would be late for tea. Frith is out too of course. If you want your tea now I can get it for you. I don't think it's quite half past four yet.'

'Oh, it doesn't matter, Alice. I'll wait till Robert comes back,' I said. I supposed when Maxim was away things automatically became slack. I had never known Frith and Robert to be out at the same time. It was Frith's day of course. And Mrs Danvers had sent Robert to the post. And I myself was understood to have gone for a long walk. That man Favell had chosen his time well to pay his call on Mrs Danvers. It was almost too well chosen. There was something not right about it, I was certain of that. And then he had asked me not to say anything to Maxim. It was all very awkward. I did not want to get Mrs Danvers into trouble or make any sort of scene. More important still I did not want to worry Maxim.

I wondered who he was, this man Favell. He had called Maxim 'Max'. No one ever called him Max. I had seen it written once, on the fly-leaf of a book, the letters thin and slanting, curiously pointed, the tail of the M very definite, very long. I thought there was only one person who had ever called him Max . . .

As I stood there in the hall, undecided about my tea, wondering what to do, the thought suddenly came to me that perhaps Mrs Danvers was dishonest, that all this time she was engaged in some business behind Maxim's back, and coming back early as I had today I had discovered her and this man, an accomplice, who had then bluffed his way out by pretending to be familiar with the house and with Maxim. I wondered what they had been doing in the west wing. Why had they closed the shutters when they saw me on the lawn? I was filled with vague disquiet. Frith and Robert had been away. The maids were generally in their bedrooms changing during the afternoon. Mrs Danvers would have the run of the place. Supposing this man was a thief, and Mrs Danvers was in his pay? There were valuable things in the west wing. I had a sudden rather terrifying impulse to creep upstairs now to the west wing and go into those rooms and see for myself.

Robert was not yet back. I would just have time before tea.

I hesitated, glancing at the gallery. The house seemed very still and quiet. The servants were all in their own quarters beyond the kitchen. Jasper lapped noisily at his drinking bowl below the stairs, the sound echoing in the great stone hall. I began to walk upstairs. My heart was beating in a queer excited way.

# 14

I found myself in the corridor where I had stood that first morning. I had not been there since, nor had I wished to go. The sun streamed in from the window in the alcove and made gold patterns on the dark panelling.

There was no sound at all. I was aware of the same musty, unused smell that had been before. I was uncertain which way to go. The plan of the rooms was not familiar to me. I remembered then that last time Mrs Danvers had come out of a door here, just behind me, and it seemed to me that the position of the room would make it the one I wanted, whose windows looked out upon the lawns to the sea. I turned the handle of the door and went inside. It was dark of course, because of the shutters. I felt for the electric light switch on the wall and turned it on. I was standing in a little ante-room, a dressing-room I judged, with big wardrobes round the wall, and at the end of this room was another door, open, leading to a larger room. I went through to this room, and turned on the light. My first impression was one of shock because the room was fully furnished, as though in use.

I had expected to see chairs and tables swathed in dust-sheets, and dust-sheets too over the great double bed against the wall. Nothing was covered up. There were brushes and combs on the dressing-table, scent, and powder. The bed was made up, I saw the gleam of white linen on the pillow-case, and the tip of a blanket beneath the quilted coverlet. There were flowers on the dressing-table and on the table beside the bed. Flowers too on the carved mantelpiece. A satin dressing-gown lay on a chair, and a pair of bedroom slippers beneath. For one desperate moment I thought that something had happened to my brain, that I was seeing back into Time, and looking upon the room as it used to be, before she died . . . In a minute Rebecca herself would come back into the room, sit down before the looking-glass at her dressing-table, humming a tune, reach for her comb and run it through her hair. If she sat there I should see her reflection in the glass and she would see me too, standing like this by the door. Nothing happened. I went on standing there, waiting for something to happen. It was the clock ticking on the wall that brought me to reality again. The hands stood at twenty-five past four. My watch said the same. There was something sane and comforting about the ticking of the clock. It reminded me of the present, and that tea would soon be ready for me on the lawn. I walked slowly into the middle of the room. No, it was not used. It was not lived in any more. Even the flowers could not destroy the musty smell. The curtains were drawn and the shutters were closed. Rebecca would never come back to the room again. Even if Mrs Danvers did put the flowers on the mantelpiece and the sheets upon the bed, they would not bring her back. She was dead. She had been dead now for a year. She lay buried in the crypt of the church with all the other dead de Winters.

I could hear the sound of the sea very plainly. I went to the window and swung back the shutter. Yes, I was standing at the same window where Favell and Mrs Danvers had stood, half an hour ago. The long shaft of daylight made the electric light look false and yellow. I opened the shutter a little more. The daylight cast a white beam upon the bed. It shone upon the nighdress-case, lying on the pillow. It shone on the glass top of the dressing-table, on the brushes, and on the scent bottles.

The daylight gave an even greater air of reality to the room. When the shutter was closed and it had been lit by electricity the room had more the appearance of a setting on the stage. The scene set between performances. The curtain having fallen for the night, the evening over, and the first act set for tomorrow's matinée. But the daylight made the room vivid and alive. I forgot the musty smell and the drawn curtains of the other windows.

I was a guest again. An uninvited guest. I had strolled into my hostess's bedroom by mistake. Those were her brushes on the dressing-table, that was her dressing-gown and slippers laid out upon the chair.

I realized for the first time since I had come into the room that my legs were trembling, weak as straw. I sat down on the stool by the dressing-table. My heart no longer beat in a strange excited way. It felt as heavy as lead. I looked about me in the room with a sort of dumb stupidity. Yes, it was a beautiful room. Mrs Danvers had not exaggerated that first evening. It was the most beautiful room in the house. That exquisite mantelpiece, the ceiling, the carved bedstead, and the curtain hangings, even the clock on the wall and the candlesticks up on the dressing-table beside me, all were things I would have loved and almost worshipped had they been mine. They were not mine though. They belonged to somebody else. I put out my hand and touched the brushes. One was more worn than its fellow. I understood it well. There was always one brush that had the greater use. Often you forgot to use the other, and when they were taken to be washed there was one that was still quite clean and untouched. How white and thin my face looked in the glass, my hair hanging lank and straight. Did I always look like this? Surely I had more colour as a rule? The reflection stared back at me, sallow and plain.

I got up from the stool and went and touched the dressing-gown on the chair. I picked up the slippers and held them in my hand. I was aware of a growing sense of horror, of horror turning to despair. I touched the quilt on the bed, traced with my fingers the monogram on the nightdress case, R de W, interwoven and interlaced. The letters were corded and strong against the golden satin material. The nightdress was inside the case, thin as gossamer, apricot in colour. I touched it, drew it out from the case, put it against my face. It was cold, quite cold. But there was a dim mustiness about it still where the scent had been. The scent of the white azaleas. I folded it, and put it back into the case, and as I did so I noticed with a sick dull aching in my

187

heart that there were creases in the night-dress, the texture was ruffled, it had not been touched or laundered since it was last worn.

On a sudden impulse I moved away from the bed and went back to the little ante-room where I had seen the wardrobes. I opened one of them. It was as I thought. The wardrobe was full of clothes. There were evening dresses here, I caught the shimmer of silver over the top of the white bags that enfolded them. There was a piece of gold brocade. There, next to it, was velvet, wine-coloured and soft. There was a train of white satin, dripping on the floor of the wardrobe. Peeping out from a piece of tissue paper on a shelf above was an ostrich feather fan.

The wardrobe smelt stuffy, queer. The azalea scent, so fragrant and delicate in the air, had turned stale inside the wardrobe, tarnishing the silver dresses and the brocade, and the breath of it wafted towards me now from the open doors, faded and old. I shut the doors. I went back into the bedroom once again. The gleam of light from the shutter still shone white and clear on the golden coverlet of the bed, picking out clearly and distinctly the tall sloping R of the monogram.

Then I heard a step behind me and turning round I saw Mrs Danvers. I shall never forget the expression on her face. Triumphant, gloating, excited in a strange unhealthy way. I felt very frightened.

'Is anything the matter, Madam?' she said.

I tried to smile at her, and could not. I tried to speak.

'Are you feeling unwell?' she said, coming nearer to me, speaking very softly. I backed away from her. I believe if she had come any closer to me I should have fainted. I felt her breath on my face.

'I'm all right, Mrs Danvers,' I said, after a moment, 'I did not expect to see you. The fact is, I was looking up at the windows from the lawn. I noticed one of the shutters was not quite closed. I came up to see if I could fasten it.'

'I will fasten it,' she said, and she went silently across the room and clamped back the shutter. The daylight had gone. The room looked unreal again in the false yellow light. Unreal and ghastly.

Mrs Danvers came back and stood beside me. She smiled, and her manner, instead of being still and unbending as it usually was, became startlingly familiar, fawning even.

'Why did you tell me the shutter was open?' she asked. 'I closed it before I left the room. You opened it yourself, didn't you, now? You wanted to see the room. Why have you never asked me to show it to you before? I was ready to show it to you every day. You had only to ask me.'

I wanted to run away, but I could not move. I went on watching her eyes.

'Now you are here, let me show you everything,' she said, her voice ingratiating and sweet as honey, horrible, false. 'I know you want to see it all, you've wanted to for a long time, and you were too shy to ask. It's a lovely room, isn't it? The loveliest room you have ever seen.'

She took hold of my arm, and walked me towards the bed. I could not resist her, I was like a dumb thing. The touch of her hand made me shudder. And her voice was low and intimate, a voice I hated and feared.

'That was her bed. It's a beautiful bed, isn't it? I keep the golden coverlet on it always, it was her favourite. Here is her nightdress inside the case. You've been touching it, haven't you? This was the nightdress she was wearing for the last time, before she died. Would you like to touch it again?' She took the nightdress from the case and held it before me. 'Feel it, hold it,' she said, 'how soft and light it is, isn't it? I haven't washed it since she wore it for the last time. I put it out like this, and the dressing-gown and slippers, just as I put them out for her the night she never came back, the night she was drowned.' She folded up the nightgown and put it back in the case. 'I did everything for her, you know,' she said, taking my arm again, leading me to the dressing-gown and slippers. 'We tried maid after maid but not one of them suited. "You maid me better than anyone, Danny," she used to say, "I won't have anyone but you." Look, this is her dressing-gown. She was much taller than you, you

189

can see by the length. Put it up against you. It comes down to your ankles. She had a beautiful figure. These are her slippers. "Throw me my slips, Danny," she used to say. She had little feet for her height. Put your hands inside the slippers. They are quite small and narrow, aren't they?'

She forced the slippers over my hands, smiling all the while, watching my eyes. 'You never would have thought she was so tall, would you?' she said, 'these slippers would fit a tiny foot. She was so slim too. You would forget her height, until she stood beside you. She was every bit as tall as me. But lying there in bed she looked quite a slip of a thing, with her mass of dark hair, standing out from her face like a halo.'

She put the slippers back on the floor, and laid the dressing-gown on the chair. 'You've seen her brushes, haven't you?' she said, taking me to the dressing-table; 'there they are, just as she used them, unwashed and untouched. I used to brush her hair for her every evening. "Come on, Danny, hair-drill," she would say, and I'd stand behind her by the stool here, and brush away for twenty minutes at a time. She only wore it short the last few years, you know. It came down below the waist, when she was first married. Mr de Winter used to brush it for her then. I've come into this room time and time again and seen him, in his shirt sleeves, with the two brushes in his hand. "Harder, Max, harder," she would say, laughing up at him, and he would do as she told him. They would be dressing for dinner, you see, and the house filled with guests. "Here, I shall be late," he would say, throwing the brushes to me, and laughing back at her. He was always laughing and gay then.' She paused, her hand still resting on my arm.

'Everyone was angry with her when she cut her hair,' she said, 'but she did not care. "It's nothing to do with anyone but myself," she would say. And of course short hair was much easier for riding and sailing. She was painted on horseback, you know. A famous artist did it. The picture hung in the Academy. Did you ever see it?'

I shook my head. 'No,' I said. 'No.'

'I understood it was the picture of the year,' she went on, 'but Mr de Winter did not care for it, and would not have it at Manderley. I don't think he considered it did her justice. You would like to see her clothes, wouldn't you?' She did not wait for my answer. She led me to the little ante-room and opened the wardrobes, one by one.

'I keep her furs in here,' she said, 'the moths have not got to them yet, and I doubt if they ever will. I'm too careful. Feel that sable wrap. That was a Christmas present from Mr de Winter. She told me the cost once, but I've forgotten it now. This chin-chilla she wore in the evenings mostly. Round her shoulders, very often, when the evenings were cold. This wardrobe here is full of her evening clothes. You opened it, didn't you? The latch is not quite closed. I believe Mr de Winter liked her to wear silver mostly. But of course she could wear anything, stand any colour. She looked beautiful in this velvet. Put it against your face. It's soft, isn't it? You can feel it, can't you? The scent is still fresh, isn't it? You could almost imagine she had only just taken it off. I would always know when she had been before me in a room. There would be a little whiff of her scent in the room. These are her underclothes, in this drawer. This pink set here she had never worn. She was wearing slacks of course and a shirt when she died. They were torn from her body in the water though. There was nothing on the body when it was found, all those weeks afterwards.'

Her fingers tightened on my arm. She bent down to me, her skull's face close, her dark eyes searching mine. 'The rocks had battered her to bits, you know,' she whispered, 'her beautiful face unrecognizable, and both arms gone. Mr de Winter identified her. He went up to Edgecoombe to do it. He went quite alone. He was very ill at the time but he would go. No one could stop him. Not even Mr Crawley.'

She paused, her eyes never leaving my face. 'I shall always blame myself for the accident,' she said, 'it was my fault for being out that evening. I had gone into Kerrith for the afternoon and stayed there late, as Mrs de Winter was up in London and not expected back until much later. That's why I did not hurry back. When I came in, about half past nine, I heard she had returned just before seven, had her dinner, and then went out again. Down to the beach of course. I felt worried then. It was blowing from the south-west. She would never have gone if I'd been in. She always listened to me. 'I wouldn't go out this evening, it's not fit,' I should have said, and she would have answered me 'All right, Danny, you old fuss-pot.' And we would have sat up here talking no doubt, she telling me all she had done in London, like she always did.'

My arm was bruised and numb from the pressure of her fingers. I could see how tightly the skin was stretched across her face, showing the cheekbones. There were little patches of yellow beneath her ears.

'Mr de Winter had been dining with Mr Crawley down at his house,' she went on. 'I don't know what time he got back, I dare say it was after eleven. But it began to blow quite hard just before midnight, and she had not come back. I went down-stairs, but there were no lights under the library door. I came upstairs again and knocked on the dressing-room door. Mr de Winter answered at once, "Who is it, what do you want?" he said. I told him I was worried about Mrs de Winter not being back. He waited a moment, and then he came and opened the door in his dressing-gown. "She's spending the night down at the cottage I expect," he said. "I should go to bed if I were you. She won't come back here to sleep if it goes on like this." He looked tired, and I did not like to disturb him. After all, she spent many nights at the cottage, and had sailed in every sort of weather. She might not even have gone for a sail, but just wanted the night at the cottage as a change after London. I said good night to Mr de Winter and went back to my room. I did not sleep though. I kept wondering what she was doing.'

She paused again. I did not want to hear any more. I wanted to get away from her, away from the room.

'I sat on my bed until half past five,' she said, 'then I couldn't wait there any longer. I got up and put on my coat and went down through the woods to the beach. It was getting light, but there was still a misty sort of rain falling, although the wind had dropped. When I got to the beach I saw the buoy there in the water and the dinghy, but the boat had gone . . .' It seemed to me that I could see the cove in the grey morning light, feel the thin drizzle on my face, and peering through the mist could make out, shadowy and indistinct, the low dark outline of the buoy.

Mrs Danvers loosened the pressure on my arm. Her hand fell back again to her side. Her voice lost all expression, became the hard mechanical voice of every day.

'One of the life-buoys was washed up at Kerrith in the afternoon,' she said, 'and another was found the next day by some crabbers on the rocks below the headland. Bits and pieces of rigging too would come in with the tide.' She turned away from me, and closed the chest of drawers. She straightened one of the pictures on the wall. She picked up a piece of fluff from the carpet. I stood watching her, not knowing what to do.

'You know now', she said, 'why Mr de Winter does not use these rooms any more. Listen to the sea.'

Even with the windows closed and the shutters fastened I could hear it; a low sullen murmur as the waves broke on the white shingle in the cove. The tide would be coming in fast now and running up the beach nearly to the stone cottage.

'He has not used these rooms since the night she was drowned,' she said. 'He had his things moved out from the dressing-room. We made up one of the rooms at the end of the corridor. I don't think he slept much even there. He used to sit in the armchair. There would be cigarette ash all round it in the morning. And in the daytime Frith would hear him in the library pacing up and down. Up and down, up and down.'

I too could see the ash on the floor beside the chair. I too could hear his footsteps; one, two, one, two, backwards and forwards across the library . . . Mrs Danvers closed the door softly between the bedroom and the ante-room where we were standing, and put out the light. I could not see the bed any more, nor the nightdress case upon the pillow, nor the dressing-table, nor the slippers by the chair. She crossed the ante-room and put her hand on the knob of the door and stood waiting for me to follow her.

'I come to the rooms and dust them myself every day,' she said. 'If you want to come again you have only to tell me. Ring me on the house-telephone. I shall understand. I don't allow the maids up here. No one ever comes but me.'

Her manner was fawning again, intimate and unpleasant. The smile on her face was a false, unnatural thing. 'Sometimes when Mr de Winter is away, and you feel lonely, you might like to come up to these rooms and sit here. You have only to tell me. They are such beautiful rooms. You would not think she had gone now for so long, would you, not by the way the rooms are kept? You would think she had just gone out for a little while and would be back in the evening.'

I forced a smile. I could not speak. My throat felt dry and tight.

'It's not only this room,' she said. 'It's in many rooms in the house. In the morning-room, in the hall, even in the little flower-room. I feel her everywhere. You do too, don't you?'

She stared at me curiously. Her voice dropped to a whisper. 'Sometimes, when I walk along the corridor here, I fancy I hear her just behind me. That quick, light footstep. I could not mistake it anywhere. And in the minstrels' gallery above the hall. I've seen her leaning there, in the evenings in the old days, looking down at the hall below and calling to the dogs. I can fancy her there now from time to time. It's almost as though I catch the sound of her dress sweeping the stairs as she comes down to dinner.' She paused. She went on looking at me, watching my eyes. 'Do you think she can see us, talking to one another now?' she said slowly. 'Do you think the dead come back and watch the living?'

I swallowed. I dug my nails into my hands.

'I don't know,' I said. 'I don't know.' My voice sounded high-pitched and unnatural. Not my voice at all.

'Sometimes I wonder,' she whispered. 'Sometimes I wonder if she comes back here to Manderley and watches you and Mr de Winter together.'

We stood there by the door, staring at one another. I could not take my eyes away from hers. How dark and sombre they were in the white skull's face of hers, how malevolent, how full of hatred. Then she opened the door into the corridor. 'Robert is back now,' she said. 'He came back a quarter of an hour ago. He has orders to take your tea out under the chestnut tree.'

She stepped aside for me to pass. I stumbled out on to the corridor, not looking where I was going. I did not speak to her, I went down the stairs blindly, and turned the corner and pushed through the door that led to my own rooms in the east wing. I shut the door of my room and turned the key, and put the key in my pocket.

Then I lay down on my bed and closed my eyes. I felt deadly sick.

# 15

Maxim rang up the next morning to say he would be back about seven. Frith took the message. Maxim did not ask to speak to me himself. I heard the telephone ring while I was at breakfast and I thought perhaps Frith would come into the dining-room and say 'Mr de Winter on the telephone, Madam.' I had put down my napkin and had risen to my feet. And then Frith came back into the dining-room and gave me the message.

He saw me push back my chair and go to the door. 'Mr de Winter has rung off, Madam,' he said, 'there was no message. Just that he would be back about seven.'

I sat down in my chair again and picked up my napkin. Frith must have thought me eager and stupid rushing across the dining-room.

'All right, Frith. Thank you,' I said.

I went on eating my eggs and bacon, Jasper at my feet, the old dog in her basket in the corner. I wondered what I should do with my day. I had slept badly; perhaps because I was alone in the room. I had been restless, waking up often, and when I glanced at my clock I saw the hands had scarcely moved. When I did fall asleep I had varied, wandering dreams. We were walking through woods, Maxim and I, and he was always just a little ahead of me. I could not keep up with him. Nor could I see his face. Just his figure, striding away in front of me all the time. I must have cried while I slept, for when I woke in the morning the pillow was damp. My eyes were heavy too, when I looked in the glass. I looked plain, unattractive. I rubbed a little rouge on my cheeks in a wretched attempt to give myself colour. But it made me worse. It gave me a false clown look. Perhaps I did not know the best way to put it on. I noticed Robert staring at me as I crossed the hall and went into breakfast.

About ten o'clock as I was crumbling some pieces for the birds on the terrace the telephone rang again. This time it was for me. Frith came and said Mrs Lacy wanted to speak to me.

'Good morning, Beatrice,' I said.

'Well, my dear, how are you?' she said, her telephone voice typical of herself, brisk, rather masculine, standing no nonsense, and then not waiting for my answer. 'I thought of motoring over this afternoon and looking up Gran. I'm lunching with people about twenty miles from you. Shall I come and pick you up and we'll go together? It's time you met the old lady, you know.'

'I'd like to very much, Beatrice,' I said.

'Splendid. Very well, then. I'll come along for you about half past three. Giles saw Maxim at the dinner. Poor food, he said, but excellent wine. All right, my dear, see you later.'

The click of the receiver, and she was gone. I wandered back into the garden. I was glad she had rung up and suggested the plan of going over to see the grandmother. It made something to look forward to, and broke the monotony of the day. The hours had seemed so long until seven o'clock. I did not feel in my holiday mood today, and I had no wish to go off with Jasper to the Happy Valley and come to the cove and throw stones in the water. The sense of freedom had departed, and the childish desire to run across the lawns in sandshoes. I went and sat down with a book and *The Times* and my knitting in the rose-garden, domestic as a matron, yawning in the warm sun while the bees hummed amongst the flowers.

I tried to concentrate on the bald newspaper columns, and later to lose myself in the racy plot of the novel in my hands. I did not want to think of yesterday afternoon and Mrs Danvers. I tried to forget that she was in the house at this moment, perhaps looking down on me from one of the windows. And now and again, when I looked up from my book or glanced across the garden, I had the feeling I was not alone.

There were so many windows in Manderley, so many rooms

that were never used by Maxim and myself that were empty now; dust-sheeted, silent, rooms that had been occupied in the old days when his father and his grandfather had been alive, when there had been much entertaining, many servants. It would be easy for Mrs Danvers to open those doors softly and close them again, and then steal quietly across the shrouded room and look down upon me from behind the drawn curtains.

I should not know. Even if I turned in my chair and looked up at the windows I would not see her. I remembered a game I had played as a child that my friends next-door had called 'Grandmother's Steps' and myself 'Old Witch'. You had to stand at the end of the garden with your back turned to the rest, and one by one they crept nearer to you, advancing in short furtive fashion. Every few minutes you turned to look at them, and if you saw one of them moving the offender had to retire to the back line and begin again. But there was always one a little bolder than the rest, who came up very close, whose movement was impossible to detect, and as you waited there, your back turned, counting the regulation Ten, you knew, with a fatal terrifying certainty, that before long, before even the Ten was counted, this bold player would pounce upon you from behind, unheralded, unseen, with a scream of triumph. I felt as tense and expectant as I did then. I was playing 'Old Witch' with Mrs Danvers.

Lunch was a welcome break to the long morning. The calm efficiency of Frith, and Robert's rather foolish face, helped me more than my book and my newspaper had done. And at half past three, punctual to the moment, I heard the sound of Beatrice's car round the sweep of the drive and pull up at the steps before the house. I ran out to meet her, ready dressed, my gloves in my hand. 'Well, my dear, here I am, what a splendid day, isn't it?' She slammed the door of the car and came up the steps to meet me. She gave me a hard swift kiss, brushing me somewhere near the ear.

'You don't look well,' she said immediately, looking me up and down, 'much too thin in the face and no colour. What's wrong with you?'

'Nothing,' I said humbly, knowing the fault of my face too well. 'I'm not a person who ever has much colour.'

'Oh, bosh,' she replied, 'you looked quite different when I saw you before.'

'I expect the brown of Italy has worn off,' I said, getting into the car.

'H'mph,' she said shortly, 'you're as bad as Maxim. Can't stand any criticism about your health. Slam the door hard or it doesn't shut.' We started off down the drive, swerving at the corner, going rather too fast. 'You're not by any chance starting an infant, are you?' she said, turning her hawk-brown eyes upon me.

'No,' I said awkwardly. 'No, I don't think so.'

'No morning sickness or anything like that?'

'No.'

'Oh, well – of course it doesn't always follow. I never turned a hair when Roger was born. Felt as fit as a fiddle the whole nine months. I played golf the day before he arrived. There's nothing to be embarrassed about in the facts of nature, you know. If you have any suspicions you had better tell me.'

'No, really, Beatrice,' I said, 'there's nothing to tell.'

'I must say I do hope you will produce a son and heir before long. It would be so terribly good for Maxim. I hope you are doing nothing to prevent it.'

'Of course not,' I said. What an extraordinary conversation.

'Oh, don't be shocked,' she said, 'you must never mind what I say. After all, brides of today are up to everything. It's a damn nuisance if you want to hunt and you land yourself with an infant your first season. Quite enough to break a marriage up if you are both keen. Wouldn't matter in your case. Babies needn't interfere with sketching. How is the sketching, by the way?'

'I'm afraid I don't seem to do much,' I said.

'Oh, really? Nice weather, too, for sitting out of doors. You only need a camp-stool and a box of pencils, don't you? Tell me, were you interested in those books I sent you?'

'Yes, of course,' I said. 'It was a lovely present, Beatrice.'

She looked pleased. 'Glad you liked them,' she said.

199

The car sped along. She kept her foot permanently on the accelerator, and took every corner at an acute angle. Two motorists we passed looked out of their windows outraged as she swept by, and one pedestrian in a lane waved his stick at her. I felt rather hot for her. She did not seem to notice though. I crouched lower in my seat.

'Roger goes up to Oxford next term,' she said, 'heaven knows what he'll do with himself. Awful waste of time I think, and so does Giles, but we couldn't think what else to do with him. Of course he's just like Giles and myself. Thinks of nothing but horses. What on earth does this car in front think it's doing? Why don't you put out your hand, my good man? Really, some of these people on the road today ought to be shot.'

We swerved into a main road, narrowly avoiding the car ahead of us. 'Had any people down to stay?' she asked.

'No, we've been very quiet,' I said.

'Much better, too,' she said, 'awful bore, I always think, those big parties. You won't find it alarming if you come to stay with us. Very nice lot of people all round, and we all know one another frightfully well. We dine in one another's houses, and have our bridge, and don't bother with outsiders. You do play bridge, don't you?'

'I'm not very good, Beatrice.'

'Oh, we shan't mind that. As long as you can play. I've no patience with people who won't learn. What on earth can one do with them between tea and dinner in the winter, and after dinner? One can't just sit and talk.'

I wondered why. However, it was simpler not to say anything.

'It's quite amusing now Roger is a reasonable age,' she went on, 'because he brings his friends to stay, and we have really good fun. You ought to have been with us last Christmas. We had charades. My dear, it was the greatest fun. Giles was in his element. He adores dressing-up, you know, and after a glass or two of champagne he's the funniest thing you've ever seen. We often say he's missed his vocation and ought to have been on the stage.'

I thought of Giles, and his large moon face, his horn spectacles.

I felt the sight of him being funny after champagne would embarrass me. 'He and another man, a great friend of ours, Dickie Marsh, dressed up as women and sang a duet. What exactly it had to do with the word in the charade nobody knew, but it did not matter. We all roared.'

I smiled politely. 'Fancy, how funny,' I said.

I saw them all rocking from side to side in Beatrice's drawing-room. All these friends who knew one another so well. Roger would look like Giles. Beatrice was laughing again at the memory. 'Poor Giles,' she said. 'I shall never forget his face when Dick squirted the soda syphon down his back. We were all in fits.'

I had an uneasy feeling we might be asked to spend the approaching Christmas with Beatrice. Perhaps I could have influenza.

'Of course our acting was never very ambitious,' she said. 'It was just a lot of fun amongst ourselves. At Manderley now, there is scope for a really fine show. I remember a pageant they had there, some years ago. People from London came down to do it. Of course that type of thing needs terrific organization.'

'Yes,' I said.

She was silent for a while, and drove without speaking.

'How is Maxim?' she said, after a moment.

'Very well, thanks,' I said.

'Quite cheerful and happy?'

'Oh, yes. Yes, rather.'

A narrow village street engaged her attention. I wondered whether I should tell her about Mrs Danvers. About the man Favell. I did not want her to make a blunder though, and perhaps tell Maxim.

'Beatrice,' I said, deciding upon it, 'have you ever heard of someone called Favell? Jack Favell?'

'Jack Favell,' she repeated. 'Yes, I do know the name. Wait a minute. Jack Favell. Of course. An awful bounder. I met him once, ages ago.'

'He came to Manderley yesterday to see Mrs Danvers,' I said.

'Really? Oh, well, perhaps he would . . .'

'Why?' I said.

'I rather think he was Rebecca's cousin,' she said.

I was very surprised. That man her relation? It was not my idea of the sort of cousin Rebecca would have. Jack Favell her cousin. 'Oh,' I said. 'Oh, I hadn't realized that.'

'He probably used to go to Manderley a lot,' said Beatrice. 'I don't know. I couldn't tell you. I was very seldom there.' Her manner was abrupt. It gave me the impression she did not want to pursue the subject.

'I did not take to him much,' I said.

'No,' said Beatrice. 'I don't blame you.'

I waited, but she did not say any more. I thought it wiser not to tell her how Favell had asked me to keep the visit a secret. It might lead to some complication. Besides, we were just coming to our destination. A pair of white gates and a smooth gravel drive.

'Don't forget the old lady is nearly blind,' said Beatrice, 'and she's not very bright these days. I telephoned to the nurse that we were coming, so everything will be all right.'

The house was large, red-bricked, and gabled. Late Victorian I supposed. Not an attractive house. I could tell in a glance it was the sort of house that was aggressively well-kept by a big staff. And all for one old lady who was nearly blind.

A trim parlour-maid opened the door.

'Good afternoon, Norah, how are you?' said Beatrice.

'Very well, thank you, Madam. I hope you are keeping well?'

'Oh, yes, we are all flourishing. How has the old lady been, Norah?'

'Rather mixed, Madam. She has one good day, and then a bad. She's not too bad in herself, you know. She will be pleased to see you I'm sure.' She glanced curiously at me.

'This is Mrs Maxim,' said Beatrice.

'Yes, Madam. How do you do,' said Norah.

We went through a narrow hall and a drawing-room crowded with furniture to a veranda facing a square clipped lawn. There were many bright geraniums in stone vases on the steps of the veranda. In the corner was a bath chair. Beatrice's grandmother was sitting there, propped up with pillows and surrounded by shawls. When we came close to her I saw that she had a strong, rather uncanny, resemblance to Maxim. That was what Maxim would look like, if he was very old, if he was blind. The nurse by her side got up from her chair and put a mark in the book she was reading aloud. She smiled at Beatrice.

'How are you, Mrs Lacy?' she said.

Beatrice shook hands with her and introduced me. 'The old lady looks all right,' she said. 'I don't know how she does it, at eighty-six. Here we are, Gran,' she said, raising her voice, 'arrived safe and sound.'

The grandmother looked in our direction. 'Dear Bee,' she said, 'how sweet of you to come and visit me. We're so dull here, nothing for you to do.'

Beatrice leant over her and kissed her. 'I've brought Maxim's wife over to see you,' she said, 'she wanted to come and see you before, but she and Maxim have been so busy.'

Beatrice prodded me in the back. 'Kiss her,' she murmured. I too bent down and kissed her on the cheek.

The grandmother touched my face with her fingers. 'You nice thing,' she said, 'so good of you to come. I'm very pleased to see you, dear. You ought to have brought Maxim with you.'

'Maxim is in London,' I said, 'he's coming back tonight.'

'You might bring him next time,' she said. 'Sit down, dear, in this chair, where I can see you. And Bee, come the other side. How is dear Roger? He's a naughty boy, he doesn't come and see me.'

'He shall come during August,' shouted Beatrice; 'he's leaving Eton, you know, he's going up to Oxford.'

'Oh, dear, he'll be quite a young man, I shan't know him.'

'He's taller than Giles now,' said Beatrice.

She went on, telling her about Giles, and Roger, and the horses, and the dogs. The nurse brought out some knitting, and clicked her needles sharply. She turned to me, very bright, very cheerful.

'How are you liking Manderley, Mrs de Winter?'

'Very much, thank you,' I said.

'It's a beautiful spot, isn't it?' she said, the needles jabbing one another. 'Of course we don't get over there now, she's not up to it. I am sorry, I used to love our days at Manderley.'

'You must come over yourself some time,' I said.

'Thank you, I should love to. Mr de Winter is well, I suppose?'

'Yes, very well.'

'You spent your honeymoon in Italy, didn't you? We were so pleased with the picture-postcard Mr de Winter sent.'

I wondered whether she used 'we' in the royal sense, or if she meant that Maxim's grandmother and herself were one.

'Did he send one? I can't remember.'

'Oh, yes, it was quite an excitement. We love anything like that. We keep a scrap-book you know, and paste anything to do with the family inside it. Anything pleasant, that is.'

'How nice,' I said.

I caught snatches of Beatrice's conversation on the other side. 'We had to put old Marksman down,' she was saying. 'You remember old Marksman? The best hunter I ever had.'

'Oh, dear, not old Marksman?' said her grandmother.

'Yes, poor old man. Got blind in both eyes, you know.'

'Poor Marksman,' echoed the old lady.

I thought perhaps it was not very tactful to talk about blindness, and I glanced at the nurse. She was still busy clicking her needles.

'Do you hunt, Mrs de Winter?' she said.

'No, I'm afraid I don't,' I said.

'Perhaps you will come to it. We are all very fond of hunting in this part of the world.'

'Yes.'

'Mrs de Winter is very keen on art,' said Beatrice to the nurse. 'I tell her there are heaps of spots in Manderley that would make very jolly pictures.'

'Oh rather,' agreed the nurse, pausing a moment from the fury of knitting. 'What a nice hobby. I had a friend who was a wonder with her pencil. We went to Provence together one Easter and she did such pretty sketches.'

'How nice,' I said.

'We're talking about sketching,' shouted Beatrice to her grandmother, 'you did not know we had an artist in the family, did you?'

'Who's an artist?' said the old lady. 'I don't know any.'

'Your new granddaughter,' said Beatrice: 'you ask her what I gave her for a wedding-present.'

I smiled, waiting to be asked. The old lady turned her head in my direction. 'What's Bee talking about?' she said. 'I did not know you were an artist. We've never had any artists in the family.'

'Beatrice was joking,' I said: 'of course I'm not an artist really. I like drawing as a hobby. I've never had any lessons. Beatrice gave me some lovely books as a present.'

'Oh,' she said, rather bewildered. 'Beatrice gave you some books, did she? Rather like taking coals to Newcastle, wasn't it? There are so many books in the library at Manderley.' She laughed heartily. We all joined in her joke. I hoped the subject would be left at that, but Beatrice had to harp on it. 'You don't understand, Gran,' she said. 'They weren't ordinary books. They were volumes on art. Four of 'em.'

The nurse leant forward to add her tribute. 'Mrs Lacy is trying to explain that Mrs de Winter is very fond of sketching as a hobby. So she gave her four fine volumes all about painting as a wedding-present.'

'What a funny thing to do,' said the grandmother. 'I don't think much of books for a wedding-present. Nobody ever gave me any books when I was married. I should never have read them if they had.'

She laughed again. Beatrice looked rather offended. I smiled at her to show my sympathy. I don't think she saw. The nurse resumed her knitting.

'I want my tea,' said the old lady querulously, 'isn't it half past four yet? Why doesn't Norah bring the tea?'

'What? Hungry again after our big lunch?' said the nurse, rising to her feet and smiling brightly at her charge.

I felt rather exhausted, and wondered, rather shocked at my callous thought, why old people were sometimes such a strain. Worse than young children or puppies because one had to be polite. I sat with my hands in my lap ready to agree with what anybody said. The nurse was thumping the pillows and arranging the shawls.

Maxim's grandmother suffered her in patience. She closed her eyes as though she too were tired. She looked more like Maxim than ever. I knew how she must have looked when she was young, tall, and handsome, going round to the stables at Manderley with sugar in her pockets, holding her trailing skirt out of the mud. I pictured the nipped-in waist, the high collar, I heard her ordering the carriage for two o'clock. That was all finished now for her, all gone. Her husband had been dead for forty years, her son for fifteen. She had to live in this bright, red gabled house with the nurse until it was time for her to die. I thought how little we know about the feelings of old people. Children we understand, their fears and hopes and make-believe. I was a child yesterday. I had not forgotten. But Maxim's grandmother, sitting there in her shawl with her poor blind eyes, what did she feel, what was she thinking? Did she know that Beatrice was yawning and glancing at her watch? Did she guess that we had come to visit her because we felt it right, it was a duty, so that when she got home afterwards Beatrice would be able to say, 'Well, that clears my conscience for three months'?

Did she ever think about Manderley? Did she remember sitting at the dining-room table, where I sat? Did she too have tea under the chestnut-tree? Or was it all forgotten and laid aside, and was there nothing left behind that calm, pale face of hers but little aches and little strange discomforts, a blurred thankfulness when the sun shone, a tremor when the wind blew cold?

I wished that I could lay my hands upon her face and take the years away. I wished I could see her young, as she was once, with colour in her cheeks and chestnut hair, alert and active as

Beatrice by her side, talking as she did about hunting, hounds, and horses. Not sitting there with her eyes closed while the nurse thumped the pillows behind her head.

'We've got a treat today, you know,' said the nurse, 'water-cress sandwiches for tea. We love water-cress, don't we?'

'Is it water-cress day?' said Maxim's grandmother, raising her head from the pillows, and looking towards the door. 'You did not tell me that. Why does not Norah bring in the tea?'

'I wouldn't have your job, Sister, for a thousand a day,' said Beatrice *sotto voce* to the nurse.

'Oh, I'm used to it, Mrs Lacy,' smiled the nurse; 'it's very comfortable here, you know. Of course we have our bad days but they might be a great deal worse. She's very easy, not like some patients. The staff are obliging too, that's really the main thing. Here comes Norah.'

The parlour-maid brought out a little gate-legged table and a snowy cloth.

'What a time you've been, Norah,' grumbled the old lady.

'It's only just turned the half-hour, Madam,' said Norah in a special voice, bright and cheerful like the nurse. I wondered if Maxim's grandmother realized that people spoke to her in this way. I wondered when they had done so for the first time, and if she had noticed then. Perhaps she had said to herself, 'They think I'm getting old, how very ridiculous', and then little by little she had become accustomed to it, and now it was as though they had always done so, it was part of her background. But the young woman with the chestnut hair and the narrow waist who gave sugar to the horses, where was she?

We drew our chairs to the gate-legged table and began to eat the water-cress sandwiches. The nurse prepared special ones for the old lady.

'There, now, isn't that a treat?' she said.

I saw a slow smile pass over the calm, placid face. 'I like water-cress day,' she said.

The tea was scalding, much too hot to drink. The nurse drank hers in tiny sips.

'Boiling water today,' she said, nodding at Beatrice. 'I have such trouble about it. They will let the tea stew. I've told them time and time again about it. They will not listen.'

'Oh, they're all the same,' said Beatrice. 'I've given it up as a bad job.' The old lady stirred hers with a spoon, her eyes very far and distant. I wished I knew what she was thinking about.

'Did you have fine weather in Italy?' said the nurse.

'Yes, it was very warm,' I said.

Beatrice turned to her grandmother. 'They had lovely weather in Italy for their honeymoon, she says. Maxim got quite sunburnt.'

'Why isn't Maxim here today?' said the old lady.

'We told you, darling, Maxim had to go to London,' said Beatrice impatiently. 'Some dinner, you know. Giles went too.'

'Oh, I see. Why did you say Maxim was in Italy?'

'He was in Italy, Gran. In April. They're back at Manderley now.' She glanced at the nurse, shrugging her shoulders.

'Mr and Mrs de Winter are in Manderley now,' repeated the nurse.

'It's been lovely there this month,' I said, drawing nearer to Maxim's grandmother. 'The roses are in bloom now. I wish I had brought you some.'

'Yes, I like roses,' she said vaguely, and then peering closer at me with her dim blue eyes. 'Are you staying at Manderley too?'

I swallowed. There was a slight pause. Then Beatrice broke in with her loud, impatient voice, 'Gran, darling, you know perfectly well she lives there now. She and Maxim are married.'

I noticed the nurse put down her cup of tea and glance swiftly at the old lady. She had relaxed against the pillows, plucking at her shawl, and her mouth began to tremble. 'You talk too much, all of you. I don't understand.' Then she looked across at me, a frown on her face, and began shaking her head. 'Who are you, my dear, I haven't seen you before? I don't know your face. I don't remember you at Manderley. Bee, who is this child? Why did not Maxim bring Rebecca? I'm so fond of Rebecca. Where is dear Rebecca?'

There was a long pause, a moment of agony. I felt my cheeks

grow scarlet. The nurse got to her feet very quickly and went to the bath-chair.

'I want Rebecca,' repeated the old lady, 'what have you done with Rebecca?' Beatrice rose clumsily from the table, shaking the cups and saucers. She too had turned very red, and her mouth twitched.

'I think you'd better go, Mrs Lacy,' said the nurse, rather pink and flustered. 'She's looking a little tired, and when she wanders like this it sometimes lasts a few hours. She does get excited like this from time to time. It's very unfortunate it should happen today. I'm sure you will understand, Mrs de Winter?' She turned apologetically to me.

'Of course,' I said quickly, 'it's much better we should go.'

Beatrice and I groped for our bags and gloves. The nurse had turned to her patient again. 'Now, what's all this about? Do you want your nice water-cress sandwich that I've cut for you?'

'Where is Rebecca? Why did not Maxim come and bring Rebecca?' replied the thin, querulous voice.

We went through the drawing-room to the hall and let ourselves out of the front door. Beatrice started up the car without a word. We drove down the smooth gravel drive and out of the white gates.

I stared straight in front of me down the road. I did not mind for myself. I should not have cared if I had been alone. I minded for Beatrice.

The whole thing had been so wretched and awkward for Beatrice.

She spoke to me when we turned out of the village. 'My dear,' she began, 'I'm so dreadfully sorry. I don't know what to say.'

'Don't be absurd, Beatrice,' I said hurriedly, 'it doesn't matter a bit. It's absolutely all right.'

'I had no idea she would do that,' said Beatrice. 'I would never have dreamt of taking you to see her. I'm so frightfully sorry.'

'There's nothing to be sorry about. Please don't say any more.'

'I can't make it out. She knew all about you. I wrote and told her, and so did Maxim. She was so interested in the wedding abroad.'

'You forget how old she is,' I said. 'Why should she remember that? She doesn't connect me with Maxim. She only connects him with Rebecca.' We went on driving in silence. It was a relief to be in the car again. I did not mind the jerky motion and the swaying corners.

'I'd forgotten she was so fond of Rebecca,' said Beatrice slowly, 'I was a fool not to expect something like this. I don't believe she ever took it in properly about the accident. Oh, Lord, what a ghastly afternoon. What on earth will you think of me?'

'Please, Beatrice, don't. I tell you I don't mind.'

'Rebecca made a great fuss of her always. And she used to have the old lady over to Manderley. Poor darling Gran was much more alert then. She used to rock with laughter at whatever Rebecca said. Of course she was always very amusing, and the old lady loved that. She had an amazing gift, Rebecca I mean, of being attractive to people; men, women, children, dogs. I suppose the old lady has never forgotten her. My dear, you won't thank me for this afternoon.'

'I don't mind, I don't mind,' I repeated mechanically. If only Beatrice could leave the subject alone. It did not interest me. What did it matter after all? What did anything matter?

'Giles will be very upset,' said Beatrice. 'He will blame me for taking you over. "What an idiotic thing to do, Bee." I can hear him saying it. I shall get into a fine row.'

'Don't say anything about it,' I said. 'I would much rather it was forgotten. The story will only get repeated and exaggerated.'

'Giles will know something is wrong from my face. I never have been able to hide anything from him.'

I was silent. I knew how the story would be tossed about in their immediate circle of friends. I could imagine the little crowd at Sunday lunch. The round eyes, the eager ears, and the gasps and exclamations—

'My Lord, how awful, what on earth did you do?' and then, 'How did she take it? How terribly embarrassing for everyone!'

210

The only thing that mattered to me was that Maxim should never come to hear of it. One day I might tell Frank Crawley, but not yet, not for quite a while.

It was not long before we came to the high road at the top of the hill. In the distance I could see the first grey roofs of Kerrith, while to the right, in a hollow, lay the deep woods of Manderley and the sea beyond.

'Are you in a frightful hurry to get home?' said Beatrice.

'No,' I said. 'I don't think so. Why?'

'Would you think me a perfect pig if I dropped you at the lodge gates? If I drive like hell now I shall just be in time to meet Giles by the London train, and it will save him taking the station taxi.'

'Of course,' I said. 'I can walk down the drive.'

'Thanks awfully,' she said gratefully.

I felt the afternoon had been too much for her. She wanted to be alone again, and did not want to face another belated tea at Manderley.

I got out of the car at the lodge gates and we kissed goodbye.

'Put on some weight next time I see you,' she said; 'it doesn't suit you to be so thin. Give Maxim my love, and forgive me for today.' She vanished in a cloud of dust and I turned in down the drive.

I wondered if it had altered much since Maxim's grandmother had driven down it in her carriage. She had ridden here as a young woman, she had smiled at the woman at the lodge as I did now. And in her day the lodge-keeper's wife had curtseyed, sweeping the path with her full wide skirt. This woman nodded to me briefly, and then called to her little boy, who was grubbing with some kittens at the back. Maxim's grandmother had bowed her head to avoid the sweeping branches of the trees, and the horse had trotted down the twisting drive where I now walked. The drive had been wider then, and smoother too, better kept. The woods did not encroach upon it.

I did not think of her as she was now, lying against those pillows, with that shawl around her. I saw her when she was young, and when Manderley was her home. I saw her wandering in the gardens with a small boy, Maxim's father, clattering behind her on his hobby horse. He would wear a stiff Norfolk jacket and a round white collar. Picnics to the cove would be an expedition, a treat that was not indulged in very often. There would be a photograph somewhere, in an old album – all the family sitting very straight and rigid round a tablecloth set upon the beach, the servants in the background beside a huge lunchbasket. And I saw Maxim's grandmother when she was older too, a few years ago. Walking on the terrace at Manderley, leaning on a stick. And someone walked beside her, laughing, holding her arm. Someone tall and slim and very beautiful, who had a gift, Beatrice said, of being attractive to people. Easy to like, I supposed, easy to love.

When I came to the end of the long drive at last I saw that Maxim's car was standing in front of the house. My heart lifted, I ran quickly into the hall. His hat and gloves were lying on the table. I went towards the library, and as I came near I heard the sound of voices, one raised louder than the other, Maxim's voice. The door was shut. I hesitated a moment before going in.

'You can write and tell him from me to keep away from Manderley in future, do you hear? Never mind who told me, that's of no importance. I happen to know his car was seen here yesterday afternoon. If you want to meet him you can meet him outside Manderley. I won't have him inside the gates, do you understand? Remember, I'm warning you for the last time.'

I slipped away from the door to the stairs. I heard the door of the library open. I ran swiftly up the stairs and hid in the gallery. Mrs Danvers came out of the library, shutting the door behind her. I crouched against the wall of the gallery so that I should not be seen. I had caught one glimpse of her face. It was grey with anger, distorted, horrible.

She passed up the stairs swiftly and silently and disappeared through the door leading to the west wing.

I waited a moment. Then I went slowly downstairs to the library. I opened the door and went in. Maxim was standing by the window, some letters in his hand. His back was turned to me. For a moment I thought of creeping out again, and going upstairs to my room and sitting there. He must have heard me though, for he swung round impatiently.

'Who is it now?' he said.

I smiled, holding out my hands. 'Hullo!' I said.

'Oh, it's you . . .'

I could tell in a glance that something had made him very angry. His mouth was hard, his nostrils white and pinched. 'What have you been doing with yourself?' he said. He kissed the top of my head and put his arm round my shoulder. I felt as if a very long time had passed since he had left me yesterday.

'I've been to see your grandmother,' I said. 'Beatrice drove me over this afternoon.'

'How was the old lady?'

'All right.'

'What's happened to Bee?'

'She had to get back to meet Giles.'

We sat down together on the window-seat. I took his hand in mine. 'I hated you being away, I've missed you terribly,' I said.

'Have you?' he said.

We did not say anything for a bit. I just held his hand.

'Was it hot up in London?' I said.

'Yes, pretty awful. I always hate the place.'

I wondered if he would tell me what had happened just now in the library with Mrs Danvers. I wondered who had told him about Favell.

'Are you worried about something?' I said.

'I've had a long day,' he said, 'that drive twice in twenty-four hours is too much for anyone.'

He got up and wandered away, lighting a cigarette. I knew then that he was not going to tell me about Mrs Danvers.

'I'm tired too,' I said slowly, 'it's been a funny sort of day.'

# 16

It was one Sunday, I remember, when we had an invasion of visitors during the afternoon, that the subject of the fancy dress ball was first brought up. Frank Crawley had come over to lunch, and we were all three of us looking forward to a peaceful afternoon under the chestnut tree when we heard the fatal sound of a car rounding the sweep in the drive. It was too late to warn Frith, the car itself came upon us standing on the terrace with cushions and papers under our arms.

We had to come forward and welcome the unexpected guests. As often happens in such cases, these were not to be the only visitors. Another car arrived about half an hour afterwards, followed by three local people who had walked from Kerrith, and we found ourselves, with the peace stripped from our day, entertaining group after group of dreary acquaintances, doing the regulation walk in the grounds, the tour of the rose-garden, the stroll across the lawns, and the formal inspection of the Happy Valley.

They stayed for tea of course, and instead of a lazy nibbling of cucumber sandwiches under the chestnut tree, we had the paraphernalia of a stiff tea in the drawing-room, which I always loathed. Frith in his element of course, directing Robert with a lift of his eyebrows, and myself rather hot and flustered with a monstrous silver tea-pot and kettle that I never knew how to manage. I found it very difficult to gauge the exact moment when it became imperative to dilute the tea with the boiling water, and more difficult still to concentrate on the small talk that was going on at my side.

Frank Crawley was invaluable at a moment like this. He took the cups from me and handed them to people, and when my answers seemed more than usually vague owing to my concentration on the silver tea-pot he quietly and unobtrusively put in his small wedge to the conversation, relieving me of responsibility. Maxim was always at the other end of the room, showing a book to a bore, or pointing out a picture, playing the perfect host in his own inimitable way, and the business of tea was a side-issue that did not matter to him. His own cup of tea grew cold, left on a side table behind some flowers, and I, steaming behind my kettle, and Frank gallantly juggling with scones and angel cake, were left to minister to the common wants of the herd. It was Lady Crowan, a tiresome gushing woman who lived in Kerrith, who introduced the matter. There was one of those pauses in conversation that happen in every tea-party, and I saw Frank's lips about to form the inevitable and idiotic remark about an angel passing overhead, when Lady Crowan, balancing a piece of cake on the edge of her saucer, looked up at Maxim who happened to be beside her.

'Oh, Mr de Winter,' she said, 'there is something I've been wanting to ask you for ages. Now tell me, is there any chance of you reviving the Manderley fancy dress ball?' She put her head on one side as she spoke, flashing her too prominent teeth in what she supposed was a smile. I lowered my head instantly, and became very busy with the emptying of my own tea-cup, screening myself behind the cosy.

It was a moment or two before Maxim replied, and when he did his voice was quite calm and matter-of-fact. 'I haven't thought about it,' he said, 'and I don't think anyone else has.'

'Oh, but I assure you we have all thought of it so much,' continued Lady Crowan. 'It used to make the summer for all of us in this part of the world. You have no idea of the pleasure it used to give. Can't I persuade you to think about it again?'

'Well, I don't know,' said Maxim drily. 'It was all rather a business to organize. You had better ask Frank Crawley, he'd have to do it.'

'Oh, Mr Crawley, do be on my side,' she persisted, and one or two of the others joined in. 'It would be a most popular

215

move, you know, we all miss the Manderley gaiety.'

I heard Frank's quiet voice beside me. 'I don't mind organizing the ball if Maxim has no objection to giving it. It's up to him and Mrs de Winter. It's nothing to do with me.'

Of course I was bombarded at once. Lady Crowan moved her chair so that the cosy no longer hid me from view. 'Now, Mrs de Winter, you get round your husband. You are the person he will listen to. He should give the ball in your honour as the bride.'

'Yes, of course,' said somebody else, a man. 'We missed the fun of the wedding, you know; it's a shame to deprive us of all excitement. Hands up for the Manderley fancy-dress ball. There you see, de Winter? Carried unanimously.' There was much laughter and clapping of hands.

Maxim lit a cigarette and his eyes met mine over the tea-pot. 'What do you think about it?' he said.

'I don't know,' I said uncertainly. 'I don't mind.'

'Of course she longs to have a ball in her honour,' gushed Lady Crowan. 'What girl wouldn't? You'd look sweet, Mrs de Winter, dressed as a little Dresden shepherdess, your hair tucked under a big three-cornered hat.'

I thought of my clumsy hands and feet and the slope of my shoulders. A fine Dresden shepherdess I should make! What an idiot the woman was. I was not surprised when nobody agreed with her, and once more I was grateful to Frank for turning the conversation away from me.

'As a matter of fact, Maxim, someone was talking about it the other day. "I suppose we shall be having some sort of celebration for the bride, shan't we, Mr Crawley?" he said. "I wish Mr de Winter would give a ball again. It was rare fun for all of us." It was Tucker at the Home farm,' he added, to Lady Crowan. 'Of course they do adore a show of any kind. I don't know, I told him. Mr de Winter hasn't said anything to me.'

'There you are,' said Lady Crowan triumphantly to the drawing-room in general. 'What did I say? Your own people are asking for a ball. If you don't care for us, surely you care about them.'

Maxim still watched me doubtfully over the tea-pot. It occurred to me that perhaps he thought I could not face it, that being shy, as he knew only too well, I should find myself unable to cope. I did not want him to think that. I did not want him to feel I should let him down.

'I think it would be rather fun,' I said.

Maxim turned away, shrugging his shoulders. 'That settles it of course,' he said. 'All right, Frank, you will have to go ahead with the arrangements. Better get Mrs Danvers to help you. She will remember the form.'

'That amazing Mrs Danvers is still with you then?' said Lady Crowan.

'Yes,' said Maxim shortly, 'have some more cake, will you? Or have you finished? Then let's all go into the garden.'

We wandered out on to the terrace, everyone discussing the prospect of the ball and suitable dates, and then, greatly to my relief, the car parties decided it was time to take their departure, and the walkers went too, on being offered a lift. I went back into the drawing-room and had another cup of tea which I thoroughly enjoyed now that the burden of entertaining had been taken from me, and Frank came too, and we crumbled up the remains of the scones and ate them, feeling like conspirators.

Maxim was throwing sticks for Jasper on the lawn. I wondered if it was the same in every home, this feeling of exuberance when visitors had gone. We did not say anything about the ball for a little while, and then, when I had finished my cup of tea and wiped my sticky fingers on a handkerchief, I said to Frank: 'What do you truthfully think about this fancy dress business?'

Frank hesitated, half glancing out of the window at Maxim on the lawn. 'I don't know,' he said. 'Maxim did not seem to object, did he? I thought he took the suggestion very well.'

'It was difficult for him to do anything else,' I said. 'What a tiresome person Lady Crowan is. Do you really believe all the people round here are talking and dreaming of nothing but a fancy dress ball at Manderley?'

'I think they would all enjoy a show of some sort,' said Frank.

217

'We're very conventional down here, you know, about these things. I don't honestly think Lady Crowan was exaggerating when she said something should be done in your honour. After all, Mrs de Winter, you are a bride.'

How pompous and stupid it sounded. I wished Frank would not always be so terribly correct.

'I'm not a bride,' I said. 'I did not even have a proper wedding. No white dress or orange blossom or trailing bridesmaids. I don't want any silly dance given in my honour.'

'It's a very fine sight, Manderley *en fête*,' said Frank. 'You'll enjoy it, you see. You won't have to do anything alarming. You just receive the guests and there's nothing in that. Perhaps you'll give me a dance?'

Dear Frank. I loved his little solemn air of gallantry.

'You shall have as many dances as you like,' I said. 'I shan't dance with anyone except you and Maxim.'

'Oh, but that would not look right at all,' said Frank seriously. 'People would be very offended. You must dance with the people who ask you.'

I turned away to hide my smile. It was a joy to me the way he never knew when his leg had been pulled.

'Do you think Lady Crowan's suggestion about the Dresden shepherdess was a good one?' I said slyly.

He considered me solemnly without the trace of a smile. 'Yes, I do,' he said. 'I think you'd look very well indeed.'

I burst into laughter. 'Oh, Frank, dear, I do love you,' I said, and he turned rather pink, a little shocked I think at my impulsive words, and a little hurt too that I was laughing at him.

'I don't see that I've said anything funny,' he said stiffly.

Maxim came in at the window, Jasper dancing at his heels. 'What's all the excitement about?' he said.

'Frank is being so gallant,' I said. 'He thinks Lady Crowan's idea of my dressing up as a Dresden shepherdess is nothing to laugh at.'

'Lady Crowan is a damned nuisance,' said Maxim. 'If she had to write out all the invitations and organize the affair she would

218

not be so enthusiastic. It's always been the same though. The locals look upon Manderley as if it was a pavilion on the end of a pier, and expect us to put up a turn for their benefit. I suppose we shall have to ask the whole county.'

'I've got the records in the office,' said Frank. 'It won't really entail much work. Licking the stamps is the longest job.'

'We'll give that to you to do,' said Maxim, smiling at me.

'Oh, we'll do that in the office,' said Frank. 'Mrs de Winter need not bother her head about anything at all.' I wondered what they would say if I suddenly announced my intention of running the whole affair. Laugh, I supposed, and then begin talking of something else. I was glad, of course, to be relieved of responsibility, but it rather added to my sense of humility to feel that I was not even capable of licking stamps. I thought of the writing-desk in the morning-room, the docketed pigeon-holes all marked in ink by that slanting pointed hand.

'What will you wear?' I said to Maxim.

'I never dress up,' said Maxim. 'It's the one perquisite allowed to the host, isn't it, Frank?'

'I can't really go as a Dresden shepherdess,' I said, 'what on earth shall I do? I'm not much good at dressing-up.'

'Put a ribbon round your hair and be Alice-in-Wonderland,' said Maxim lightly; 'you look like it now, with your finger in your mouth.'

'Don't be so rude,' I said. 'I know my hair is straight, but it isn't as straight as that. I tell you what, I'll give you and Frank the surprise of your lives, and you won't know me.'

'As long as you don't black your face and pretend to be a monkey I don't mind what you do,' said Maxim.

'All right, that's a bargain,' I said. 'I'll keep my costume a secret to the last minute, and you won't know anything about it. Come on, Jasper, we don't care what they say, do we?' I heard Maxim laughing as I went out into the garden, and he said something to Frank which I did not catch.

I wished he would not always treat me as a child, rather spoilt, rather irresponsible, someone to be petted from time to time when the mood came upon him but more often forgotten, more often patted on the shoulder and told to run away and play. I wished something would happen to make me look wiser, more mature. Was it always going to be like this? He away ahead of me, with his own moods that I did not share, his secret troubles that I did not know? Would we never be together, he a man and I a woman, standing shoulder to shoulder, hand in hand, with no gulf between us? I did not want to be a child. I wanted to be his wife, his mother. I wanted to be old.

I stood on the terrace, biting my nails, looking down towards the sea, and as I stood there I wondered for the twentieth time that day whether it was by Maxim's orders that those rooms in the west wing were kept furnished and untouched. I wondered if he went, as Mrs Danvers did, and touched the brushes on the dressing-table, opened the wardrobe doors, and put his hands amongst the clothes.

'Come on, Jasper,' I shouted, 'run, run with me, come on, can't you?' and I tore across the grass, savagely, angrily, the bitter tears behind my eyes, with Jasper leaping at my heels and barking hysterically.

The news soon spread about the fancy dress ball. My little maid Clarice, her eyes shining with excitement, talked of nothing else. I gathered from her that the servants in general were delighted. 'Mr Frith says it will be like old times,' said Clarice eagerly. 'I heard him saying so to Alice in the passage this morning. What will you wear, Madam?'

'I don't know, Clarice, I can't think,' I said.

'Mother said I was to be sure and tell her,' said Clarice. 'She remembers the last ball they gave at Manderley, and she has never forgotten it. Will you be hiring a costume from London, do you think?'

'I haven't made up my mind, Clarice,' I said. 'But I tell you what. When I do decide, I shall tell you and nobody else. It will be a dead secret between us both.'

'Oh, Madam, how exciting,' breathed Clarice. 'I don't know how I am going to wait for the day.'

I was curious to know Mrs Danvers' reaction to the news. Since that afternoon I dreaded even the sound of her voice down the house telephone, and by using Robert as mediator between us I was spared this last ordeal. I could not forget the expression of her face when she left the library after that interview with Maxim. I thanked God she had not seen me crouching in the gallery. And I wondered too, if she thought that it was I who had told Maxim about Favell's visit to the house. If so, she would hate me more than ever. I shuddered now when I remembered the touch of her hand on my arm, and that dreadful soft, intimate pitch of her voice close to my ear. I did not want to remember anything about that afternoon. That was why I did not speak to her, not even on the house telephone.

The preparations went on for the ball. Everything seemed to be done down at the estate office. Maxim and Frank were down there every morning. As Frank had said, I did not have to bother my head about anything. I don't think I licked one stamp. I began to get in a panic about my costume. It seemed so feeble not to be able to think of anything, and I kept remembering all the people who would come, from Kerrith and round about, the bishop's wife who had enjoyed herself so much, the last time, Beatrice and Giles, that tiresome Lady Crowan, and many more people I did not know and who had never seen me, they would every one of them have some criticism to offer, some curiosity to know what sort of effort I should make. At last, in desperation, I remembered the books that Beatrice had given me for a wedding-present, and I sat down in the library one morning turning over the pages as a last hope, passing from illustration to illustration in a sort of frenzy. Nothing seemed suitable, they were all so elaborate and pretentious, those gorgeous costumes of velvet and silk in the reproductions given of Rubens, Rembrandt and others. I got hold of a piece of paper and a pencil and copied one or two of them, but they did not please me, and I threw the sketches into the waste paper basket in disgust, thinking no more about them.

In the evening, when I was changing for dinner, there was a

knock at my bedroom door. I called 'Come in,' thinking it was Clarice. The door opened and it was not Clarice. It was Mrs Danvers. She held a piece of paper in her hand. 'I hope you will forgive me disturbing you,' she said, 'but I was not sure whether you meant to throw these drawings away. All the waste paper baskets are always brought to me to check, at the end of the day, in case of mislaying anything of value. Robert told me this was thrown into the library basket.'

I had turned quite cold all over at the sight of her, and at first I could not find my voice. She held out the paper for me to see. It was the rough drawing I had done during the morning.

'No, Mrs Danvers,' I said, after a moment, 'it doesn't matter throwing that away. It was only a rough sketch. I don't want it.'

'Very good,' she said, 'I thought it better to inquire from you personally to save any misunderstanding.'

'Yes,' I said. 'Yes, of course.' I thought she would turn and go, but she went on standing there by the door.

'So you have not decided yet what you will wear?' she said. There was a hint of derision in her voice, a trace of odd satisfaction. I supposed she had heard of my efforts through Clarice in some way.

'No,' I said. 'No, I haven't decided.'

She continued watching me, her hand on the handle of the door.

'I wonder you don't copy one of the pictures in the gallery,' she said.

I pretended to file my nails. They were too short and too brittle, but the action gave me something to do and I did not have to look at her.

'Yes, I might think about that,' I said. I wondered privately why such an idea had never come to me before. It was an obvious and very good solution to my difficulty. I did not want her to know this though. I went on filing my nails.

'All the pictures in the gallery would make good costumes,' said Mrs Danvers, 'especially that one of the young lady in white, with her hat in her hand. I wonder Mr de Winter does not make

222

it a period ball, everyone dressed more or less the same, to be in keeping. I never think it looks right to see a clown dancing with a lady in powder and patches.'

'Some people enjoy the variety,' I said. 'They think it makes it all the more amusing.'

'I don't like it myself,' said Mrs Danvers. Her voice was surprisingly normal and friendly, and I wondered why it was she had taken the trouble to come up with my discarded sketch herself. Did she want to be friends with me at last? Or did she realize that it had not been me at all who had told Maxim about Favell, and this was her way of thanking me for my silence?

'Has not Mr de Winter suggested a costume for you?' she said.

'No,' I said, after a moment's hesitation. 'No, I want to surprise him and Mr Crawley. I don't want them to know anything about it.'

'It's not for me to make a suggestion, I know,' she said, 'but when you do decide, I should advise you to have your dress made in London. There is no one down here can do that sort of thing well. Voce, in Bond Street, is a good place I know.'

'I must remember that,' I said.

'Yes,' she said, and then, as she opened the door, 'I should study the pictures in the gallery, Madam, if I were you, especially the one I mentioned. And you need not think I will give you away. I won't say a word to anyone.'

'Thank you, Mrs Danvers,' I said. She shut the door very gently behind her. I went on with my dressing, puzzled at her attitude, so different from our last encounter, and wondering whether I had the unpleasant Favell to thank for it.

Rebecca's cousin. Why should Maxim dislike Rebecca's cousin? Why had he forbidden him to come to Manderley? Beatrice had called him a bounder. She had not said much about him. And the more I considered him the more I agreed with her. Those hot blue eyes, that loose mouth, and the careless familiar laugh. Some people would consider him attractive. Girls in sweet shops giggling behind the counter, and girls who gave

223

one programmes in a cinema. I knew how he would look at them, smiling, and half whistling a tune under his breath. The sort of look and the type of whistle that would make one feel uncomfortable. I wondered how well he knew Manderley. He seemed quite at home, and Jasper certainly recognized him, but these two facts did not fit in with Maxim's words to Mrs Danvers. And I could not connect him with my idea of Rebecca. Rebecca, with her beauty, her charm, her breeding, why did she have a cousin like Jack Favell? It was wrong, out of all proportion. I decided he must be the skeleton in the family cupboard, and Rebecca with her generosity had taken pity on him from time to time and invited him to Manderley, perhaps when Maxim was from home, knowing his dislike. There had been some argument about it probably, Rebecca defending him, and ever after this perhaps a slight awkwardness whenever his name was mentioned.

As I sat down to dinner in the dining-room in my accustomed place, with Maxim at the head of the table, I pictured Rebecca sitting in where I sat now, picking up her fork for the fish, and then the telephone ringing and Frith coming into the room and saying 'Mr Favell on the phone, Madam, wishing to speak to you,' and Rebecca would get up from her chair with a quick glance at Maxim, who would not say anything, who would go on eating his fish. And when she came back, having finished her conversation, and sat down in her place again, Rebecca would begin talking about something different, in a gay, careless way, to cover up the little cloud between them. At first Maxim would be glum, answering in monosyllables, but little by little she would win his humour back again, telling him some story of her day, about someone she had seen in Kerrith, and when they had finished the next course he would be laughing again, looking at her and smiling, putting out his hand to her across the table.

'What the devil are you thinking about?' said Maxim.

I started, the colour flooding my face, for in that brief moment, sixty seconds in time perhaps, I had so identified myself with

Rebecca that my own dull self did not exist, had never come to Manderley. I had gone back in thought and in person to the days that were gone.

'Do you know you were going through the most extraordinary antics instead of eating your fish?' said Maxim. 'First you listened, as though you heard the telephone, and then your lips moved, and you threw half a glance at me. And you shook your head, and smiled, and shrugged your shoulders. All in about a second. Are you practising your appearance for the fancy dress ball?' He looked across at me, laughing, and I wondered what he would say if he really knew my thoughts, my heart, and my mind, and that for one second he had been the Maxim of another year, and I had been Rebecca. 'You look like a little criminal,' he said, 'what is it?'

'Nothing,' I said quickly, 'I wasn't doing anything.'

'Tell me what you were thinking?'

'Why should I? You never tell me what you are thinking about.'

'I don't think you've ever asked me, have you?'

'Yes, I did once.'

'I don't remember.'

'We were in the library.'

'Very probably. What did I say?'

'You told me you were wondering who had been chosen to play for Surrey against Middlesex.'

Maxim laughed again. 'What a disappointment to you. What did you hope I was thinking?'

'Something very different.'

'What sort of thing?'

'Oh, I don't know.'

'No, I don't suppose you do. If I told you I was thinking about Surrey and Middlesex I was thinking about Surrey and Middlesex. Men are simpler than you imagine, my sweet child. But what goes on in the twisted tortuous minds of women would baffle anyone. Do you know, you did not look a bit like yourself just now? You had quite a different expression on your face.'

'I did? What sort of expression?'

'I don't know that I can explain. You looked older suddenly, deceitful. It was rather unpleasant.'

'I did not mean to.'

'No, I don't suppose you did.'

I drank some water, watching him over the rim of my glass.

'Don't you want me to look older?' I said.

'No.'

'Why not?'

'Because it would not suit you.'

'One day I shall. It can't be helped. I shall have grey hair, and lines and things.'

'I don't mind that.'

'What do you mind then?'

'I don't want you to look like you did just now. You had a twist to your mouth and a flash of knowledge in your eyes. Not the right sort of knowledge.'

I felt very curious, rather excited. 'What do you mean, Maxim? What isn't the right sort of knowledge?'

He did not answer for a moment. Frith had come back into the room and was changing the plates. Maxim waited until Frith had gone behind the screen and through the service door before speaking again.

'When I met you first you had a certain expression on your face,' he said slowly, 'and you have it still. I'm not going to define it, I don't know how to. But it was one of the reasons why I married you. A moment ago, when you were going through that curious little performance, the expression had gone. Something else had taken its place.'

'What sort of thing? Explain to me, Maxim,' I said eagerly.

He considered me a moment, his eyebrows raised, whistling softly. 'Listen, my sweet. When you were a little girl, were you ever forbidden to read certain books, and did your father put those books under lock and key?'

'Yes,' I said.

'Well, then. A husband is not so very different from a father

226

after all. There is a certain type of knowledge I prefer you not to have. It's better kept under lock and key. So that's that. And now eat up your peaches, and don't ask me any more questions, or I shall put you in the corner.'

'I wish you would not treat me as if I was six,' I said.

'How do you want to be treated?'

'Like other men treat their wives.'

'Knock you about, you mean?'

'Don't be absurd. Why must you make a joke of everything?'

'I'm not joking. I'm very serious.'

'No, you're not. I can tell by your eyes. You're playing with me all the time, just as if I was a silly little girl.'

'Alice-in-Wonderland. That was a good idea of mine. Have you bought your sash and your hair-ribbon yet?'

'I warn you. You'll get the surprise of your life when you do see me in my fancy dress.'

'I'm sure I shall. Get on with your peach and don't talk with your mouth full. I've got a lot of letters to write after dinner.'

He did not wait for me to finish. He got up and strolled about the room, and asked Frith to bring the coffee in the library. I sat still, sullenly, being as slow as I could, hoping to keep things back and irritate him, but Frith took no notice of me and my peach, he brought the coffee at once and Maxim went off to the library by himself.

When I had finished I went upstairs to the minstrel's gallery to have a look at the pictures. I knew them well of course by now, but had never studied them with a view to reproducing one of them as a fancy-dress. Mrs Danvers was right of course. What an idiot I had been not to think of it before. I always loved the girl in white, with a hat in her hand. It was a Raeburn, and the portrait was of Caroline de Winter, a sister of Maxim's great-great grandfather. She married a great Whig politician, and was a famous London beauty for many years, but this portrait was painted before that, when she was still unmarried. The white dress should be easy to copy. Those puffed sleeves, the flounce, and the little bodice. The hat might be rather difficult, and I should have to wear a wig. My straight hair would never curl in that way. Perhaps that Voce place in London that Mrs Danvers had told me about would do the whole thing. I would send them a sketch of the portrait and tell them to copy it faithfully, sending my measurements.

What a relief it was to have decided at last! Quite a weight off my mind. I began almost to look forward to the ball. Perhaps I should enjoy it after all, almost as much as little Clarice.

I wrote to the shop in the morning, enclosing a sketch of the portrait, and I had a very favourable reply, full of honour at my esteemed order, and saying the work would be put in hand right away, and they would manage the wig as well.

Clarice could hardly contain herself for excitement, and I, too, began to get party fever as the great day approached. Giles and Beatrice were coming for the night, but nobody else, thank heaven, although a lot of people were expected to dinner first. I had imagined we should have to hold a large house-party for the occasion, but Maxim decided against it. 'Having the dance alone is quite enough effort,' he said; and I wondered whether he did it for my sake alone, or whether a large crowd of people really bored him as he said. I had heard so much of the Manderley parties in the old days, with people sleeping in bathrooms and on sofas because of the squash. And here we were alone in the vast house, with only Beatrice and Giles to count as guests.

The house began to wear a new, expectant air. Men came to lay the floor for dancing in the great hall, and in the drawing-room some of the furniture was moved so that the long buffet tables could be placed against the wall. Lights were put up on the terrace, and in the rose-garden too, wherever one walked there would be some sign of preparation for the ball. Workmen from the estate were everywhere, and Frank came to lunch nearly every day. The servants talked of nothing else, and Frith stalked about as though the whole of the evening would depend on him alone. Robert rather lost his head, and kept forgetting things, napkins at lunch, and handing vegetables. He wore a harassed expression, like someone who has got to catch a train. The dogs were miserable. Jasper trailed about the hall with his tail between his legs, and nipped every workman on sight. He used to stand on the terrace, barking idiotically, and then dash madly to one corner of the lawn and eat grass in a sort of frenzy. Mrs Danvers never obtruded herself, but I was aware of her continually. It was her voice I heard in the drawing-room when they came to put the tables, it was she who gave directions for the laying of the floor in the hall. Whenever I came upon the scene she had always just disappeared; I would catch a glimpse of her skirt brushing the door, or hear the sound of her footsteps on the stairs. I was a lay-figure, no use to man or beast. I used to stand about doing nothing except get in the way. 'Excuse me, Madam,' I would hear a man say, just behind me, and he would pass, with a smile of apology, carrying two chairs on his back, his face dripping with perspiration.

'I'm awfully sorry,' I would say, getting quickly to one side, and then as a cover to my idleness, 'Can I help you? What about putting those chairs in the library?' The man would look bewildered. 'Mrs Danvers' orders, Madam, was that we were to take the chairs round to the back, to be out of the way.'

'Oh,' I said, 'yes, of course. How silly of me. Take them round to the back, as she said.' And I would walk quickly away murmuring something about finding a piece of paper and a pencil, in a vain attempt to delude the man into thinking I was busy, while he went on across the hall, looking rather astonished, and I would feel I had not deceived him for a moment.

The great day dawned misty and overcast, but the glass was high and we, had no fears. The mist was a good sign. It cleared about eleven, as Maxim had foretold, and we had a glorious still summer's day without a cloud in the blue sky. All the morning the gardeners were bringing flowers into the house, the last of the white lilac, and great lupins and delphiniums, five foot high, roses in hundreds, and every sort of lily.

Mrs Danvers showed herself at last; quietly, calmly, she told the gardeners where to put the flowers, and she herself arranged them, stacking the vases with quick, deft fingers. I watched her in fascination, the way she did vase after vase, carrying them herself through the flower-room to the drawing-room and the various corners of the house, massing them in just the right numbers and profusion, putting colour where colour was needed, leaving the walls bare where severity paid.

Maxim and I had lunch with Frank at his bachelor establishment next-door to the office to be out of the way. We were all three in the rather hearty, cheerful humour of people after a funeral. We made pointless jokes about nothing at all, our minds eternally on the thought of the next few hours. I felt very much the same as I did the morning I was married. The same stifled feeling that I had gone too far now to turn back.

The evening had got to be endured. Thank heaven Messrs Voce had sent my dress in time. It looked perfect, in its folds of tissue paper. And the wig was a triumph. I had tried it on after breakfast, and was amazed at the transformation. I looked quite attractive, quite different altogether. Not me at all. Someone much more interesting, more vivid and alive. Maxim and Frank kept asking me about my costume.

'You won't know me,' I told them, 'you will both get the shock of your lives.'

'You are not going to dress up as a clown, are you?' said Maxim gloomily. 'No frightful attempt to be funny?'

'No, nothing like that,' I said, full of importance.

'I wish you had kept to Alice-in-Wonderland,' he said.

'Or Joan of Arc with your hair,' said Frank shyly.

'I never thought of that,' I said blankly, and Frank went rather pink. 'I'm sure we shall like whatever you wear,' he said in his most pompous Frank-ish voice.

'Don't encourage her, Frank,' said Maxim. 'She's so full of her precious disguise already there's no holding her. Bee will put you in your place, that's one comfort. She'll soon tell you if she doesn't like your dress. Dear old Bee always looks just wrong on these occasions, bless her. I remember her once as Madame Pompadour and she tripped up going in to supper and her wig came adrift. "I can't stand this damned thing," she said, in that blunt voice of hers, and chucked it on a chair and went through the rest of the evening with her own cropped hair. You can imagine what it looked like, against a pale blue satin crinoline, or whatever the dress was. Poor Giles did not cope that year. He came as a cook, and sat about in the bar all night looking perfectly miserable. I think he felt Bee had let him down.'

'No, it wasn't that,' said Frank, 'he'd lost his front teeth trying out a new mare, don't you remember, and he was so shy about it he wouldn't open his mouth.'

'Oh, was that it? Poor Giles. He generally enjoys dressing-up.'

'Beatrice says he loves playing charades,' I said. 'She told me they always have charades at Christmas.'

'I know,' said Maxim, 'that's why I've never spent Christmas with her.'

'Have some more asparagus, Mrs de Winter, and another potato?'

'No, really, Frank, I'm not hungry, thank you.'

'Nerves,' said Maxim, shaking his head. 'Never mind, this time tomorrow it will all be over.'

'I sincerely hope so,' said Frank seriously. 'I was going to give orders that all cars should stand by for 5 a.m.'

I began to laugh weakly, the tears coming into my eyes. 'Oh dear,' I said, 'let's send wires to everybody not to come.'

'Come on, be brave and face it,' said Maxim. 'We need not give another one for years. Frank, I have an uneasy feeling we ought to be going up to the house. What do you think?'

Frank agreed, and I followed them unwillingly, reluctant to leave the cramped, rather uncomfortable little dining-room that was so typical of Frank's bachelor establishment, and which seemed to me today the embodiment of peace and quietude. When we came to the house we found that the band had arrived, and were standing about in the hall rather pink in the face and self-conscious, while Frith, more important than ever, offered refreshments. The band were to be our guests for the night, and after we had welcomed them and exchanged a few slightly obvious jokes proper to the occasion, the band were borne off

231

to their quarters to be followed by a tour of the grounds.

The afternoon dragged, like the last hour before a journey when one is packed up and keyed to departure, and I wandered from room to room almost as lost as Jasper, who trailed reproachfully at my heels.

There was nothing I could do to help, and it would have been wiser on my part to have kept clear of the house altogether and taken the dog and myself for a long walk. By the time I decided upon this it was too late, Maxim and Frank were demanding tea, and when tea was over Beatrice and Giles arrived. The evening had come upon us all too soon.

'This is like old times,' said Beatrice, kissing Maxim, and looking about her. 'Congratulations to you for remembering every detail. The flowers are exquisite,' she added, turning to me. 'Did you do them?'

'No,' I said, rather ashamed, 'Mrs Danvers is responsible for everything.'

'Oh. Well, after all . . .' Beatrice did not finish her sentence, she accepted a light for her cigarette from Frank, and once it was lit she appeared to have forgotten what she was going to say.

'Have you got Mitchell's to do the catering as usual?' asked Giles.

'Yes,' said Maxim. 'I don't think anything has been altered, has it, Frank? We had all the records down at the office. Nothing has been forgotten, and I don't think we have left anyone out.'

'What a relief to find only ourselves,' said Beatrice. 'I remember once arriving about this time, and there were about twenty-five people in the place already. All going to stop the night.'

'What's everyone going to wear? I suppose Maxim, as always, refuses to play?'

'As always,' said Maxim.

'Such a mistake I think. The whole thing would go with much more swing if you did.'

'Have you ever known a ball at Manderley not to go with a swing?'

'No, my dear boy, the organization is too good. But I do think the host ought to give the lead himself.'

'I think it's quite enough if the hostess makes the effort,' said Maxim. 'Why should I make myself hot and uncomfortable and a damn fool into the bargain?'

'Oh, but that's absurd. There's no need to look a fool. With your appearance, my dear Maxim, you could get away with any costume. You don't have to worry about your figure like poor Giles.'

'What is Giles going to wear tonight?' I asked, 'or is it a dead secret?'

'No, rather not,' beamed Giles; 'as a matter-of-fact it's a pretty good effort. I got our local tailor to rig it up. I'm coming as an Arabian sheik.'

'Good God,' said Maxim.

'It's not at all bad,' said Beatrice warmly. 'He stains his face of course, and leaves off his glasses. The head-dress is authentic. We borrowed it off a friend who used to live in the East, and the rest the tailor copied from some paper. Giles looks very well in it.'

'What are you going to be, Mrs Lacy?' said Frank.

'Oh, I'm afraid I haven't coped much,' said Beatrice, 'I've got some sort of Eastern get-up to go with Giles, but I don't pretend it's genuine. Strings of beads, you know, and a veil over my face.'

'It sounds very nice,' I said politely.

'Oh, it's not bad. Comfortable to wear, that's one blessing. I shall take off the veil if I get too hot. What are you wearing?'

'Don't ask her,' said Maxim. 'She won't tell any of us. There has never been such a secret. I believe she even wrote to London for it.'

'My dear,' said Beatrice, rather impressed, 'don't say you have gone a bust and will put us all to shame? Mine is only home-made, you know.'

'Don't worry,' I said, laughing, 'it's quite simple really. But Maxim would tease me, and I've promised to give him the surprise of his life.'

'Quite right too,' said Giles. 'Maxim is too superior altogether. The fact is he's jealous. Wishes he was dressing up like the rest of us, and doesn't like to say so.'

'Heaven forbid,' said Maxim.

'What are you doing, Crawley?' asked Giles.

Frank looked rather apologetic. 'I've been so busy I'm afraid I've left things to the last moment. I hunted up an old pair of trousers last night, and a striped football jersey, and thought of putting a patch over one eye and coming as a pirate.'

'Why on earth didn't you write to us and borrow a costume?' said Beatrice. 'There's one of a Dutchman that Roger had last winter in Switzerland. It would have suited you excellently.'

'I refuse to allow my agent to walk about as a Dutchman,' said Maxim. 'He'd never get rents out of anybody again. Let him stick to his pirate. It might frighten some of them.'

'Anything less like a pirate,' murmured Beatrice in my ear.

I pretended not to hear. Poor Frank, she was always rather down on him.

'How long will it take me to paint my face?' asked Giles.

'Two hours at least,' said Beatrice. 'I should begin thinking about it if I were you. How many shall we be at dinner?'

'Sixteen,' said Maxim, 'counting ourselves. No strangers. You know them all.'

'I'm beginning to get dress fever already,' said Beatrice. 'What fun it all is. I'm so glad you decided to do this again, Maxim.'

'You've got her to thank for it,' said Maxim, nodding at me.

'Oh, it's not true,' I said. 'It was all the fault of Lady Crowan.'

'Nonsense,' said Maxim, smiling at me, 'you know you're as excited as a child at its first party.'

'I'm not.'

'I'm longing to see your dress,' said Beatrice.

'It's nothing out of the way. Really it's not,' I insisted.

'Mrs de Winter says we shan't know her,' said Frank.

Everybody looked at me and smiled. I felt pleased and flushed and rather happy. People were being nice. They were all so

234

friendly. It was suddenly fun, the thought of the dance, and that I was to be the hostess.

The dance was being given for me, in my honour, because I was the bride. I sat on the table in the library, swinging my legs, while the rest of them stood round, and I had a longing to go upstairs and put on my dress, try the wig in front of the looking-glass, turn this way and that before the long mirror on the wall. It was new this sudden unexpected sensation of being important, of having Giles, and Beatrice, and Frank and Maxim all looking at me and talking about my dress. All wondering what I was going to wear. I thought of the soft white dress in its folds of tissue paper, and how it would hide my flat dull figure, my rather sloping shoulders. I thought of my own lank hair covered by the sleek and gleaming curls.

'What's the time?' I said carelessly, yawning a little, pretending I did not care. 'I wonder if we ought to think about going upstairs . . . ?'

As we crossed the great hall on the way to our rooms I realized for the first time how the house lent itself to the occasion, and how beautiful the rooms were looking. Even the drawing-room, formal and cold to my consideration when we were alone, was a blaze of colour now, flowers in every corner, red roses in silver bowls on the white cloth of the supper table, the long windows open to the terrace, where, as soon as it was dusk, the fairy lights would shine. The band had stacked their instruments ready in the minstrel's gallery above the hall, and the hall itself wore a strange, waiting air; there was a warmth about it I had never known before, due to the night itself, so still and clear, to the flowers beneath the pictures, to our own laughter as we hovered on the wide stone stairs.

The old austerity had gone. Manderley had come alive in a fashion I would not have believed possible. It was not the still quiet Manderley I knew. There was a certain significance about it now that had not been before. A reckless air, rather triumphant, rather pleasing. It was as if the house remembered other days, long, long ago, when the hall was a banqueting hall indeed, with weapons and tapestry hanging upon the walls, and men sat at a long narrow table in the centre laughing louder than we laughed now, calling for wine, for song, throwing great pieces of meat upon the flags to the slumbering dogs. Later, in other years, it would still be gay, but with a certain grace and dignity, and Caroline de Winter, whom I should present tonight, would walk down the wide stone stairs in her white dress to dance the minuet. I wished we could sweep away the years and see her. I wished we did not have to degrade the house with our modern jig-tunes, so out-of-place and unromantic. They would not suit Manderley. I found myself in sudden agreement with Mrs Danvers. We should have made it a period ball, not the hotchpotch of humanity it was bound to be, with Giles, poor fellow, well-meaning and hearty in his guise of Arabian sheik. I found Clarice waiting for me in my bedroom, her round face scarlet with excitement. We giggled at one another like school-girls, and I bade her lock my door. There was much sound of tissue paper, rustling and mysterious. We spoke to one another softly like conspirators, we walked on tiptoe. I felt like a child again on the eve of Christmas. This padding to and fro in my room with bare feet, the little furtive bursts of laughter, the stifled exclamations, reminded me of hanging up my stocking long ago. Maxim was safe in his dressing-room, and the way through was barred against him. Clarice alone was my ally and favoured friend. The dress fitted perfectly. I stood still, hardly able to restrain my impatience while Clarice hooked me up with fumbling fingers.

'It's handsome, Madam,' she kept saying, leaning back on her heels to look at me. 'It's a dress fit for the Queen of England.'

'What about under the left shoulder there,' I said, anxiously. 'That strap of mine, is it going to show?'

'No, Madam, nothing shows.'

'How is it? How do I look?' I did not wait for her answer, I twisted and turned in front of the mirror, I frowned, I smiled. I felt different already, no longer hampered by my appearance. My own dull personality was submerged at last. 'Give me the

wig,' I said excitedly, 'careful, don't crush it, the curls mustn't be
flat. They are supposed to stand out from the face.' Clarice stood
behind my shoulder, I saw her round face beyond mine in the
reflection of the looking-glass, her eyes shining, her mouth a
little open. I brushed my own hair sleek behind my ears. I took
hold of the soft gleaming curls with trembling fingers, laughing
under my breath, looking up at Clarice.

'Oh, Clarice,' I said, 'what will Mr de Winter say?'

I covered my own mousy hair with the curled wig, trying to
hide my triumph, trying to hide my smile. Somebody came and
hammered on the door.

'Who's there?' I called in panic. 'You can't come in.'

'It's me, my dear, don't alarm yourself,' said Beatrice, 'how far
have you got? I want to look at you.'

'No, no,' I said, 'you can't come in, I'm not ready.'

The flustered Clarice stood beside me, her hand full of hair-
pins, while I took them from her one by one, controlling the
curls that had become fluffed in the box.

'I'll come down when I am ready,' I called. 'Go on down, all
of you. Don't wait for me. Tell Maxim he can't come in.'

'Maxim's down,' she said. 'He came along to us. He said he
hammered on your bathroom door and you never answered.
Don't be too long, my dear, we are all so intrigued. Are you sure
you don't want any help?'

'No,' I shouted impatiently, losing my head, 'go away, go on
down.'

Why did she have to come and bother just at this moment?
It fussed me, I did not know what I was doing. I jabbed with
a hair-pin, flattening it against a curl. I heard no more from
Beatrice, she must have gone along the passage. I wondered if
she was happy in her Eastern robes and if Giles had succeeded
in painting his face. How absurd it was, the whole thing. Why
did we do it, I wonder, why were we such children?

I did not recognize the face that stared at me in the glass.
The eyes were larger surely, the mouth narrower, the skin white
and clear? The curls stood away from the head in a little cloud.

I watched this self that was not me at all and then smiled; a new, slow smile.

'Oh, Clarice!' I said. 'Oh, Clarice!' I took the skirt of my dress in my hands and curtseyed to her, the flounces sweeping the ground. She giggled excitedly, rather embarrassed, flushed though, very pleased. I paraded up and down in front of my glass watching my reflection.

'Unlock the door,' I said. 'I'm going down. Run ahead and see if they are there.' She obeyed me, still giggling, and I lifted my skirts off the ground and followed her along the corridor.

She looked back at me and beckoned. 'They've gone down,' she whispered, 'Mr de Winter, and Major and Mrs Lacy. Mr Crawley has just come. They are all standing in the hall.' I peered through the archway at the head of the big staircase, and looked down on the hall below.

Yes, there they were. Giles, in his white Arab dress, laughing loudly, showing the knife at his side; Beatrice swathed in an extraordinary green garment and hung about the neck with trailing beads; poor Frank self-conscious and slightly foolish in his striped jersey and sea-boots; Maxim, the only normal one of the party, in his evening clothes.

'I don't know what she's doing,' he said, 'she's been up in her bedroom for hours. What's the time, Frank? The dinner crowd will be upon us before we know where we are.'

The band were changed, and in the gallery already. One of the men was tuning his fiddle. He played a scale softly, and then plucked at a string. The light shone on the picture of Caroline de Winter.

Yes, the dress had been copied exactly from my sketch of the portrait. The puffed sleeve, the sash and the ribbon, the wide floppy hat I held in my hand. And my curls were her curls, they stood out from my face as hers did in the picture. I don't think I have ever felt so excited before, so happy and so proud. I waved my hand at the man with the fiddle, and then put my finger to my lips for silence. He smiled and bowed. He came across the gallery to the archway where I stood.

'Make the drummer announce me,' I whispered, 'make him beat the drum, you know how they do, and then call out Miss Caroline de Winter. I want to surprise them below.' He nodded his head, he understood. My heart fluttered absurdly, and my cheeks were burning. What fun it was, what mad ridiculous childish fun! I smiled at Clarice still crouching on the corridor. I picked up my skirt in my hands. Then the sound of the drum echoed in the great hall, startling me for a moment, who had waited for it, who knew that it would come. I saw them look up surprised and bewildered from the hall below.

'Miss Caroline de Winter,' shouted the drummer.

I came forward to the head of the stairs and stood there, smiling, my hat in my hand, like the girl in the picture. I waited for the clapping and laughter that would follow as I walked slowly down the stairs. Nobody clapped, nobody moved.

They all stared at me like dumb things. Beatrice uttered a little cry and put her hand to her mouth. I went on smiling, I put one hand on the banister.

'How do you do, Mr de Winter,' I said.

Maxim had not moved. He stared up at me, his glass in his hand. There was no colour in his face. It was ashen white. I saw Frank go to him as though he would speak, but Maxim shook him off. I hesitated, one foot already on the stairs. Something was wrong, they had not understood. Why was Maxim looking like that? Why did they all stand like dummies, like people in a trance?

Then Maxim moved forward to the stairs, his eyes never leaving my face.

'What the hell do you think you are doing?' he asked. His eyes blazed in anger. His face was still ashen white.

I could not move, I went on standing there, my hand on the banister.

'It's the picture,' I said, terrified at his eyes, at his voice. 'It's the picture, the one in the gallery.'

There was a long silence. We went on staring at each other. Nobody moved in the hall. I swallowed, my hand moved to my throat. 'What is it?' I said. 'What have I done?'

239

If only they would not stare at me like that with dull blank faces. If only somebody would say something. When Maxim spoke again I did not recognize his voice. It was still and quiet, icy cold, not a voice I knew.

'Go and change,' he said, 'it does not matter what you put on. Find an ordinary evening frock, anything will do. Go now, before anybody comes.'

I could not speak, I went on staring at him. His eyes were the only living things in the white mask of his face.

'What are you standing there for?' he said, his voice harsh and queer. 'Didn't you hear what I said?'

I turned and ran blindly through the archway to the corridors beyond. I caught a glimpse of the astonished face of the drummer who had announced me. I brushed past him, stumbling, not looking where I went. Tears blinded my eyes. I did not know what was happening. Clarice had gone. The corridor was deserted. I looked about me stunned and stupid like a haunted thing. Then I saw that the door leading to the west wing was open wide, and that someone was standing there.

It was Mrs Danvers. I shall never forget the expression on her face, loathsome, triumphant. The face of an exulting devil. She stood there, smiling at me.

And then I ran from her, down the long narrow passage to my own room, tripping, stumbling over the flounces of my dress.

# 17

Clarice was waiting for me in my bedroom. She looked pale and scared. As soon as she saw me she burst into tears. I did not say anything. I began tearing at the hooks of my dress, ripping the stuff. I could not manage them properly, and Clarice came to help me, still crying noisily.

'It's all right, Clarice, it's not your fault,' I said, and she shook her head, the tears still running down her cheeks.

'Your lovely dress, Madam,' she said, 'your lovely white dress.'

'It doesn't matter,' I said. 'Can't you find the hook? There it is, at the back. And another one somewhere, just below.'

She fumbled with the hooks, her hands trembling, making worse trouble with it than I did myself, and all the time catching at her breath.

'What will you wear instead, Madam?' she said.

'I don't know,' I said, 'I don't know.' She had managed to unfasten the hooks, and I struggled out of the dress. 'I think I'd rather like to be alone, Clarice,' I said, 'would you be a dear and leave me? Don't worry, I shall manage all right. Forget what's happened. I want you to enjoy the party.'

'Can't I press out a dress for you, Madam?' she said, looking up at me with swollen streaming eyes. 'It won't take me a moment.'

'No,' I said, 'don't bother, I'd rather you went, and Clarice . . .'

'Yes, Madam?'

'Don't – don't say anything about what's just happened.'

'No, Madam.' She burst into another torrent of weeping.

'Don't let the others see you like that,' I said. 'Go to your bedroom and do something to your face. There's nothing to cry about, nothing at all.' Somebody knocked on the door. Clarice threw me a quick frightened glance.

'Who is it?' I said. The door opened and Beatrice came into the room. She came to me at once, a strange, rather ludicrous figure in her Eastern drapery, the bangles jangling on her wrists.

'My dear,' she said, 'my dear,' and held out her hands to me.

Clarice slipped out of the room. I felt tired suddenly, and unable to cope. I went and sat down on the bed. I put my hand up to my head and took off the curled wig. Beatrice stood watching me.

'Are you all right?' she said. 'You look very white.'

'It's the light,' I said. 'It never gives one any colour.'

'Sit down for a few minutes and you'll be all right,' she said; 'wait, I'll get a glass of water.'

She went into the bathroom, her bangles jangling with her every movement, and then she came back, the glass of water in her hands.

I drank some to please her, not wanting it a bit. It tasted warm from the tap; she had not let it run.

'Of course I knew at once it was just a terrible mistake,' she said. 'You could not possibly have known, why should you?'

'Known what?' I said.

'Why, the dress, you poor dear, the picture you copied of the girl in the gallery. It was what Rebecca did at the last fancy dress ball at Manderley. Identical. The same picture, the same dress. You stood there on the stairs, and for one ghastly moment I thought . . .'

She did not go on with her sentence, she patted me on the shoulder.

'You poor child, how wretchedly unfortunate, how were you to know?'

'I ought to have known,' I said stupidly, staring at her, too stunned to understand. 'I ought to have known.'

'Nonsense, how could you know? It was not the sort of thing that could possibly enter any of our heads. Only it was such a shock, you see. We none of us expected it, and Maxim . . .'

'Yes, Maxim?' I said.

'He thinks, you see, it was deliberate on your part. You had

242

some bet that you would startle him, didn't you? Some foolish joke. And of course, he doesn't understand. It was such a frightful shock for him. I told him at once you could not have done such a thing, and that it was sheer appalling luck that you had chosen that particular picture.'

'I ought to have known,' I repeated again. 'It's all my fault, I ought to have seen. I ought to have known.'

'No, no. Don't worry, you'll be able to explain the whole thing to him quietly. Everything will be quite all right. The first lot of people were arriving just as I came upstairs to you. They are having drinks. Everything's all right. I've told Frank and Giles to make up a story about your dress not fitting, and you are very disappointed.'

I did not say anything. I went on sitting on the bed with my hands in my lap.

'What can you wear instead?' said Beatrice, going to my wardrobe and flinging open the doors. 'Here. What's this blue? It looks charming. Put this on. Nobody will mind. Quick. I'll help you.'

'No,' I said. 'No, I'm not coming down.'

Beatrice stared at me in great distress, my blue frock over her arm.

'But, my dear, you must,' she said in dismay. 'You can't possibly not appear.'

'No, Beatrice, I'm not coming down. I can't face them, not after what's happened.'

'But nobody will know about the dress,' she said. 'Frank and Giles will never breathe a word. We've got the story all arranged. The shop sent the wrong dress, and it did not fit, so you are wearing an ordinary evening dress instead. Everyone will think it perfectly natural. It won't make any difference to the evening.'

'You don't understand,' I said. 'I don't care about the dress. It's not that at all. It's what has happened, what I did. I can't come down now, Beatrice, I can't.'

'But, my dear, Giles and Frank understand perfectly. They are full of sympathy. And Maxim too. It was just the first shock . . .

243

I'll try and get him alone a minute, I'll explain the whole thing.'

'No!' I said. 'No!'

She put my blue frock down beside me on the bed. 'Everyone will be arriving,' she said, very worried, very upset. 'It will look so extraordinary if you don't come down. I can't say you've suddenly got a headache.'

'Why not?' I said wearily. 'What does it matter? Make anything up. Nobody will mind, they don't any of them know me.'

'Come now, my dear,' she said, patting my hand, 'try and make the effort. Put on this charming blue. Think of Maxim. You must come down for his sake.'

'I'm thinking about Maxim all the time,' I said.

'Well, then, surely . . . ?'

'No,' I said, tearing at my nails, rocking backwards and forwards on the bed. 'I can't, I can't.'

Somebody else knocked on the door. 'Oh, dear, who on earth is that?' said Beatrice, walking to the door. 'What is it?'

She opened the door. Giles was standing just outside. 'Everyone has turned up. Maxim sent me up to find out what's happening,' he said.

'She says she won't come down,' said Beatrice. 'What on earth are we going to say?'

I caught sight of Giles peering at me through the open door. 'Oh, Lord, what a frightful mix-up,' he whispered. He turned away embarrassed when he noticed that I had seen him.

'What shall I say to Maxim?' he asked Beatrice. 'It's five past eight now.'

'Say she's feeling rather faint, but will try and come down later. Tell them not to wait dinner. I'll be down directly, I'll make it all right.'

'Yes, right you are.' He half glanced in my direction again, sympathetic but rather curious, wondering why I sat there on the bed, and his voice was low, as it might be after an accident, when people are waiting for the doctor.

'Is there anything else I can do?' he said.

244

'No,' said Beatrice, 'go down now, I'll follow in a minute.'

He obeyed her, shuffling away in his Arabian robes. This is the sort of moment, I thought, that I shall laugh at years afterwards, that I shall say 'Do you remember how Giles was dressed as an Arab, and Beatrice had a veil over her face, and jangling bangles on her wrist?' And time will mellow it, make it a moment for laughter. But now it was not funny, now I did not laugh. It was not the future, it was the present. It was too vivid and too real. I sat on the bed, plucking at the eiderdown, pulling a little feather out of a slit in one corner.

'Would you like some brandy?' said Beatrice, making a last effort. 'I know it's only Dutch courage, but it sometimes works wonders.'

'No,' I said. 'No, I don't want anything.'

'I shall have to go down. Giles says they are waiting dinner. Are you sure it's all right for me to leave you?'

'Yes. And thank you, Beatrice.'

'Oh, my dear, don't thank me. I wish I could do something.' She stooped swiftly to my looking-glass and dabbed her face with powder. 'God, what a sight I look,' she said, 'this damn veil is crooked I know. However it can't be helped.' She rustled out of the room, closing the door behind her. I felt I had forfeited her sympathy by my refusal to go down. I had shown the white feather. She had not understood. She belonged to another breed of men and women, another race than I. They had guts, the women of her race. They were not like me. If it had been Beatrice who had done this thing instead of me she would have put on her other dress and gone down again to welcome her guests. She would have stood by Giles's side, and shaken hands with people, a smile on her face. I could not do that. I had not the pride, I had not the guts. I was badly bred.

I kept seeing Maxim's eyes blazing in his white face, and behind him Giles, and Beatrice and Frank standing like dummies, staring at me.

I got up from my bed and went and looked out of the window. The gardeners were going round to the lights in the rose garden, testing them to see if they all worked. The sky was pale, with a few salmon clouds of evening streaking to the west. When it was dusk the lamps would all be lit. There were tables and chairs in the rose-garden, for the couples who wanted to sit out. I could smell the roses from my window. The men were talking to one another and laughing. 'There's one here gone,' I heard a voice call out; 'can you get me another small bulb? One of the blue ones, Bill.' He fixed the light into position. He whistled a popular tune of the moment with easy confidence, and I thought how tonight perhaps the band would play the same tune in the minstrel's gallery above the hall. 'That's got it,' said the man, switching the light on and off, 'they're all right here. No others gone. We'd better have a look at those on the terrace.' They went off round the corner of the house, still whistling the song. I wished I could be the man. Later in the evening he would stand with his friend in the drive and watch the cars drive up to the house, his hands in his pockets, his cap on the back of his head. He would stand in a crowd with other people from the estate, and then drink cider at the long table arranged for them in one corner of the terrace. 'Like the old days, isn't it?' he would say. But his friend would shake his head, puffing at his pipe. 'This new one's not like our Mrs de Winter, she's different altogether.' And a woman next them in the crowd would agree, other people too, all saying 'That's right,' and nodding their heads.

'Where is she tonight? She's not been on the terrace once.'

'I can't say, I'm sure. I've not seen her.'

'Mrs de Winter used to be here, there, and everywhere.'

'Aye, that's right.'

And the woman would turn to her neighbours nodding mysteriously.

'They say she's not appearing tonight at all.'

'Go on.'

'That's right. One of the servants from the house told me Mrs de Winter hasn't come down from her room all evening.'

'What's wrong with the maid, is she bad?'

'No, sulky I reckon. They say her dress didn't please her.'

A squeal of laughter and a murmur from the little crowd.

'Did you ever hear of such a thing? It's a shame for Mr de Winter.'

'I wouldn't stand for it, not from a chit like her.'

'Maybe it's not true at all.'

'It's true all right. They're full of it up at the house.' One to the other. This one to the next. A smile, a wink, a shrug of the shoulder. One group, and then another group. And then spreading to the guests who walked on the terrace and strolled across the lawns. The couple who in three hours' time would sit in those chairs beneath me in the rose-garden.

'Do you suppose it's true what I heard?'

'What did you hear?'

'Why, that there's nothing wrong with her at all, they've had a colossal row, and she won't appear!'

'I say!' A lift of the eyebrows, a long whistle.

'I know. Well, it does look rather odd, don't you think? What I mean is, people don't suddenly for no reason have violent headaches. I call the whole thing jolly fishy.'

'I thought he looked a bit grim.'

'So did I.'

'Of course I have heard before the marriage is not a wild success.'

'Oh, really?'

'H'm. Several people have said so. They say he's beginning to realize he's made a big mistake. She's nothing to look at, you know.'

'No, I've heard there's nothing much to her. Who was she?'

'Oh, no one at all. Some pick-up in the south of France, a nursery gov., or something.'

'Good Lord!'

'I know. And when you think of Rebecca . . .'

I went on staring at the empty chairs. The salmon sky had turned to grey. Above my head was the evening star. In the woods beyond the rose-garden the birds were making their last little rustling noises before nightfall. A lone gull flew across the sky.

I went away from the window, back to the bed again. I picked up the white dress I had left on the floor and put it back in the box with the tissue paper. I put the wig back in its box too. Then I looked in one of my cupboards for the little portable iron I used to have in Monte Carlo for Mrs Van Hopper's dresses. It was lying at the back of a shelf with some woollen jumpers I had not worn for a long time. The iron was one of those universal kinds that go on any voltage and I fitted it to the plug in the wall. I began to iron the blue dress that Beatrice had taken from the wardrobe, slowly, methodically, as I used to iron Mrs Van Hopper's dresses in Monte Carlo.

When I had finished I laid the dress ready on the bed. Then I cleaned the make-up off my face that I had put on for the fancy dress. I combed my hair, and washed my hands. I put on the blue dress and the shoes that went with it. I might have been my old self again, going down to the lounge of the hotel with Mrs Van Hopper. I opened the door of my room and went along the corridor. Everything was still and silent. There might not have been a party at all. I tiptoed to the end of the passage and turned the corner. The door to the west wing was closed. There was no sound of anything at all. When I came to the archway by the gallery and the staircase I heard the murmur and hum of conversation coming from the dining-room. They were still having dinner. The great hall was deserted. There was nobody in the gallery either. The band must be having their dinner too. I did not know what arrangements had been made for them. Frank had done it – Frank or Mrs Danvers.

From where I stood I could see the picture of Caroline de Winter facing me in the gallery. I could see the curls framing her face, and I could see the smile on her lips. I remembered the bishop's wife who had said to me that day I called, 'I shall never forget her, dressed all in white, with that cloud of dark hair.' I ought to have remembered that, I ought to have known. How queer the instruments looked in the gallery, the little stands for the music, the big drum. One of the men had left his handkerchief on a chair. I leant over the rail and looked down at the hall below. Soon it would be filled with people, like the bishop's wife had said, and Maxim would stand at the bottom of the stairs shaking hands with them as they came into the hall. The sound of their voices would echo to the ceiling, and then the band would play from the gallery where I was leaning now, the man with the violin smiling, swaying to the music.

It would not be quiet like this any more. A board creaked in the gallery. I swung round, looking at the gallery behind me. There was nobody there. The gallery was empty, just as it had been before. A current of air blew in my face though, somebody must have left a window open in one of the passages. The hum of voices continued in the dining-room. I wondered why the board creaked when I had not moved at all. The warmth of the night perhaps, a swelling somewhere in the old wood. The draught still blew in my face though. A piece of music on one of the stands fluttered to the floor. I looked towards the archway above the stairs. The draught was coming from there. I went beneath the arch again, and when I came out on to the long corridor I saw that the door to the west wing had blown open and swung back against the wall. It was dark in the west passage, none of the lights had been turned on. I could feel the wind blowing on my face from an open window. I fumbled for a switch on the wall and could not find one. I could see the window in an angle of the passage, the curtain blowing softly, backwards and forwards. The grey evening light cast queer shadows on the floor. The sound of the sea came to me through the open window, the soft hissing sound of the ebb-tide leaving the shingle.

I did not go and shut the window. I stood there shivering a moment in my thin dress, listening to the sea as it sighed and left the shore. Then I turned quickly and shut the door of the west wing behind me, and came out again through the archway by the stairs.

The murmur of voices had swollen now and was louder than before. The door of the dining-room was open. They were coming out of dinner. I could see Robert standing by the open door, and there was a scraping of chairs, a babble of conversation, and laughter.

I walked slowly down the stairs to meet them.


When I look back at my first party at Manderley, my first and my last, I can remember little isolated things standing alone out of the vast blank canvas of the evening. The background was hazy, a sea of dim faces none of whom I knew, and there was the slow drone of the band harping out a waltz that never finished, that went on and on. The same couples swung by in rotation, with the same fixed smiles, and to me, standing with Maxim at the bottom of the stairs to welcome the late-comers, these dancing couples seemed like marionettes twisting and turning on a piece of string, held by some invisible hand.

There was a woman, I never knew her name, never saw her again, but she wore a salmon-coloured gown hooped in crinoline form, a vague gesture to some past century but whether seventeenth, eighteenth, or nineteenth I could not tell, and every time she passed me it coincided with a sweeping bar of the waltz to which she dipped and swayed, smiling as she did so in my direction. It happened again and again until it became automatic, a matter of routine, like those promenades on board ship when we meet the same people bent on exercise like ourselves, and know with deadly certainty that we will pass them by the bridge.

I can see her now, the prominent teeth, the gay spot of rouge placed high upon her cheek-bones, and her smile, vacant, happy, enjoying her evening. Later I saw her by the supper table, her keen eyes searching the food, and she heaped a plate high with salmon and lobster mayonnaise and went off into a corner. There was Lady Crowan too, monstrous in purple, disguised as I know not what romantic figure of the past, it might have been Marie Antoinette or Nell Gwynne for all I knew, or a strange erotic combination of the two, and she kept exclaiming in excited high-pitch tones, a little higher than usual because of the champagne she had consumed, 'You all have me to thank for this, not the de Winters at all.'

I remember Robert dropping a tray of ices, and the expression of Frith's face when he saw Robert was the culprit and not one of the minions hired for the occasion. I wanted to go to Robert and stand beside him and say 'I know how you feel. I understand. I've done worse than you tonight.' I can feel now the stiff, set smile on my face that did not match the misery in my eyes. I can see Beatrice, dear friendly tactless Beatrice, watching me from her partner's arms, nodding encouragement, the bangles jangling on her wrists, the veil slipping continually from her overheated forehead. I can picture myself once more whirled round the room in a desperate dance with Giles, who with dog-like sympathy and kind heart would take no refusal, but must steer me through the stamping crowd as he would one of his own horses at a meet. 'That's a jolly pretty dress you're wearing,' I can hear him say, 'it makes all these people look damn silly,' and I blessed him for his pathetic simple gesture of understanding and sincerity, thinking, dear Giles, that I was disappointed in my dress, that I was worrying about my appearance, that I cared.

It was Frank who brought me a plate of chicken and ham that I could not eat, and Frank who stood by my elbow with a glass of champagne I would not drink.

'I wish you would,' he said quietly, 'I think you need it,' and I took three sips of it to please him. The black patch over his eye gave him a pale odd appearance, it made him look older, different. There seemed to be lines on his face I had not seen before.

He moved amongst the guests like another host, seeing to their comfort, that they were supplied with drink, and food, and cigarettes, and he danced too in solemn painstaking fashion, walking his partners round the room with a set face. He did not wear his pirate costume with abandon, and there was something rather tragic about the side-whiskers he had fluffed under the scarlet handkerchief on his head. I thought of him standing before the looking-glass in his bare bachelor bedroom curling them round his fingers. Poor Frank. Dear Frank. I never asked, I never knew, how much he hated the last fancy dress ball given at Manderley.

The band played on, and the swaying couples twisted like bobbing marionettes, to and fro, to and fro, across the great hall and back again, and it was not I who watched them at all, not someone with feelings, made of flesh and blood, but a dummy-stick of a person in my stead, a prop who wore a smile screwed to its face. The figure who stood beside it was wooden too. His face was a mask, his smile was not his own. The eyes were not the eyes of the man I loved, the man I knew. They looked through me and beyond me, cold, expressionless, to some place of pain and torture I could not enter, to some private, inward hell I could not share.

He never spoke to me. He never touched me. We stood beside one another, the host and the hostess, and we were not together. I watched his courtesy to his guests. He flung a word to one, a jest to another, a smile to a third, a call over his shoulder to a fourth, and no one but myself could know that every utterance he made, every movement, was automatic and the work of a machine. We were like two performers in a play, but we were divided, we were not acting with one another. We had to endure it alone, we had to put up this show, this miserable, sham perform-ance, for the sake of all these people I did not know and did not want to see again.

'I hear your wife's frock never turned up in time,' said someone with a mottled face and a sailor's pigtail, and he laughed, and dug Maxim in the ribs. 'Damn shame, what? I should sue the shop for fraud. Same thing happened to my wife's cousin once.'

'Yes, it was unfortunate,' said Maxim.

'I tell you what,' said the sailor, turning to me, 'you ought to say you are a forget-me-not. They're blue aren't they? Jolly little flowers, forget-me-nots. That's right, isn't it, de Winter? Tell your wife she must call herself a "forget-me-not".' He swept away, roaring with laughter, his partner in his arms. 'Pretty good idea, what? A forget-me-not.' Then Frank again hovering just behind me, another glass in his hand, lemonade this time. 'No, Frank, I'm not thirsty.'

'Why don't you dance? Or come and sit down a moment; there's a corner in the terrace.'

'No, I'm better standing. I don't want to sit down.'

'Can't I get you something, a sandwich, a peach?'

'No, I don't want anything.'

There was the salmon lady again; she forgot to smile at me this time. She was flushed after her supper. She kept looking up into her partner's face. He was very tall, very thin, he had a chin like a fiddle.

The Destiny waltz, the Blue Danube, the Merry Widow, one-two-three, one-two-three, round-and-round, one-two-three, one-two-three, round-and-round. The salmon lady, a green lady, Beatrice again, her veil pushed back off her forehead; Giles, his face streaming with perspiration, and that sailor once more, with another partner; they stopped beside me, I did not know her; she was dressed as a Tudor woman, any Tudor woman; she wore a ruffle round her throat and a black velvet dress.

'When are you coming to see us?' she said, as though we were old friends, and I answered, 'Soon of course; we were talking about it the other day,' wondering why I found it so easy to lie suddenly, no effort at all. 'Such a delightful party; I do congratulate you,' she said, and 'Thank you very much,' I said. 'It's fun, isn't it?'

'I hear they sent you the wrong dress?'

'Yes; absurd, wasn't it?'

'These shops are all the same. No depending on them. But you look delightfully fresh in that pale blue. Much more comfortable than this hot velvet. Don't forget, you must both come and dine at the Palace soon.'

'We should love to.'

What did she mean, where, what palace? Were we entertaining royalty? She swept on to the Blue Danube in the arms of the sailor, her velvet frock brushing the ground like a carpet-sweeper, and it was not until long afterwards, in the middle of some night, when I could not sleep, that I remembered the Tudor woman was the bishop's wife who liked walking in the Pennines.

What was the time? I did not know. The evening dragged on, hour after hour, the same faces and the same tunes. Now and again the bridge people crept out of the library like hermits to watch the dancers, and then returned again. Beatrice, her draperies trailing behind her, whispered in my ear.

'Why don't you sit down? You look like death.'

'I'm all right.'

Giles, the make-up running on his face, poor fellow, and stifling in his Arab blanket, came up to me and said, 'Come and watch the fireworks on the terrace.'

I remember standing on the terrace and staring up at the sky as the foolish rockets burst and fell. There was little Clarice in a corner with some boy off the estate; she was smiling happily, squealing with delight as a squib spluttered at her feet. She had forgotten her tears.

'Hullo, this will be a big 'un.' Giles, his large face upturned, his mouth open. 'Here she comes. Bravo, jolly fine show.'

The slow hiss of the rocket as it sped into the air, the burst of the explosion, the stream of little emerald stars. A murmur of approval from the crowd, cries of delight, and a clapping of hands.

The salmon lady well to the front, her face eager with expectation, a remark for every star that fell. 'Oh, what a beauty . . . look at that one now; I say, how pretty . . . Oh, that one didn't burst . . . take care, it's coming our way . . . what are those men doing over there?' . . . Even the hermits left their lair and came to join the dancers on the terrace. The lawns were black with people. The bursting stars shone on their upturned faces.

Again and again the rockets sped into the air like arrows, and the sky became crimson and gold. Manderley stood out like an enchanted house, every window aflame, the grey walls coloured by the falling stars. A house bewitched, carved out of the dark woods. And when the last rocket burst and the cheering died away, the night that had been fine before seemed dull and heavy in contrast, the sky became a pall. The little groups on the lawns and in the drive broke up and scattered. The guests crowded the long windows in the terrace back to the drawing-room again. It was anti-climax, the aftermath had come. We stood about with blank faces. Someone gave me a glass of champagne. I heard the sound of cars starting up in the drive.

'They're beginning to go,' I thought. 'Thank God, they're beginning to go.' The salmon lady was having some more supper. It would take time yet to clear the hall. I saw Frank make a signal to the band. I stood in the doorway between the drawing-room and the hall beside a man I did not know.

'What a wonderful party it's been,' he said.

'Yes,' I said.

'I've enjoyed every minute of it,' he said.

'I'm so glad,' I said.

'Molly was wild with fury at missing it,' he said.

'Was she?' I said.

The band began to play Auld Lang Syne. The man seized my hand and started swinging it up and down. 'Here,' he said, 'come on, some of you.' Somebody else swung my other hand, and more people joined us. We stood in a great circle singing at the top of our voices. The man who had enjoyed his evening and said Molly would be wild at missing it was dressed as a Chinese mandarin, and his false nails got caught up in his sleeve as we swung our hands up and down. He roared with laughter. We all laughed. 'Should auld acquaintance be forgot,' we sang.

The hilarious gaiety changed swiftly at the closing bars, and the drummer rattled his sticks in the inevitable prelude to God Save the King. The smiles left our faces as though wiped clean by a sponge. The Mandarin sprang to attention, his hands stiff to his sides. I remember wondering vaguely if he was in the Army. How queer he looked with his long poker face, and his drooping Mandarin moustache. I caught the salmon lady's eye. God Save the King had taken her unawares, she was still holding a plate heaped with chicken in aspic. She held it stiffly out in front of her like a church collection. All animation had gone from her face. As the last note of God Save the King died away she relaxed again, and attacked her chicken in a sort of frenzy, chattering over her shoulder to her partner. Somebody came and wrung me by the hand.

'Don't forget, you're dining with us on the fourteenth of next month.'

'Oh, are we?' I stared at him blankly.

'Yes, we've got your sister-in-law to promise too.'

'Oh. Oh, what fun.'

'Eight-thirty, and black tie. So looking forward to seeing you.'

'Yes. Yes, rather.'

People began to form up in queues to say good-bye. Maxim was at the other side of the room. I put on my smile again, which had worn thin after Auld Lang Syne.

'The best evening I've spent for a long time.'

'I'm so glad.'

'Many thanks for a grand party.'

'I'm so glad.'

'Here we are, you see, staying to the bitter end.'

'Yes, I'm so glad.'

Was there no other sentence in the English language? I bowed and smiled like a dummy, my eyes searching for Maxim above their heads. He was caught up in a knot of people by the library. Beatrice too was surrounded, and Giles had led a team of stragglers to the buffet table in the drawing-room. Frank was out in the drive seeing that people got their cars. I was hemmed in by strangers.

'Good-bye, and thanks tremendously.'

'I'm so glad.'

The great hall began to empty. Already it wore that drab deserted air of a vanished evening and the dawn of a tired day. There was a grey light on the terrace, I could see the shapes of the blown firework stands taking form on the lawns.

'Good-bye; a wonderful party.'

'I'm so glad.'

Maxim had gone out to join Frank in the drive. Beatrice came up to me, pulling off her jangling bracelets. 'I can't stand

256

these things a moment longer. Heavens, I'm dead beat. I don't believe I've missed a dance. Anyway, it was a tremendous success.'

'Was it?' I said.

'My dear, hadn't you better go to bed? You look worn out. You've been standing nearly all the evening. Where are the men?'

'Out on the drive.'

'I shall have some coffee, and eggs and bacon. What about you?'

'No, Beatrice, I don't think I will.'

'You looked very charming in your blue. Everyone said so. And nobody had an inkling about − about the other things, so you mustn't worry.'

'No.'

'If I were you I should have a good long lie tomorrow morning. Don't attempt to get up. Have your breakfast in bed.'

'Yes, perhaps.'

'I'll tell Maxim you've gone up, shall I?'

'Please, Beatrice.'

'All right, my dear. Sleep well.' She kissed me swiftly, patting my shoulder at the same time, and then went off to find Giles in the supper room. I walked slowly up the stairs, one step at a time. The band had turned the lights off in the gallery, and had gone down to have eggs and bacon too. Pieces of music lay about the floor. One chair had been upturned. There was an ashtray full of the stubs of their cigarettes. The aftermath of the party. I went along the corridor to my room. It was getting lighter every moment, and the birds had started singing. I did not have to turn on the light to undress. A little chill wind blew in from the open window. It was rather cold. Many people must have used the rose-garden during the evening, for all the chairs were moved, and dragged from their places. There was a tray of empty glasses on one of the tables. Someone had left a bag behind on a chair. I pulled the curtain to darken the room, but the grey morning light found its way through the gaps at the side.

I got into bed, my legs very weary, a niggling pain in the

small of my back. I lay back and closed my eyes, thankful for the cool white comfort of clean sheets. I wished my mind would rest like my body, relax, and pass to sleep. Not hum round in the way it did, jigging to music, whirling in a sea of faces. I pressed my hands over my eyes but they would not go.

I wondered how long Maxim would be. The bed beside me looked stark and cold. Soon there would be no shadows in the room at all, the walls and the ceiling and the floor would be white with the morning. The birds would sing their songs, louder, gayer, less subdued. The sun would make a yellow pattern on the curtain. My little bed-side clock ticked out the minutes one by one. The hand moved round the dial. I lay on my side watching it. It came to the hour and passed it again. It started afresh on its journey. But Maxim did not come.

# 18

I think I fell asleep a little after seven. It was broad daylight, I remember, there was no longer any pretence that the drawn curtains hid the sun. The light streamed in at the open window and made patterns on the wall. I heard the men below in the rose-garden clearing away the tables and the chairs, and taking down the chain of fairy lights. Maxim's bed was still bare and empty. I lay across my bed, my arms over my eyes, a strange, mad position and the least likely to bring sleep, but I drifted to the border-line of the unconscious and slipped over it at last. When I awoke it was past eleven, and Clarice must have come in and brought me my tea without my hearing her, for there was a tray by my side, and a stone-cold teapot, and my clothes had been tidied, my blue frock put away in the wardrobe.

I drank my cold tea, still blurred and stupid from my short heavy sleep, and stared at the blank wall in front of me. Maxim's empty bed brought me to realization with a queer shock to my heart, and the full anguish of the night before was upon me once again. He had not come to bed at all. His pyjamas lay folded on the turned-down sheet untouched. I wondered what Clarice had thought when she came into the room with my tea. Had she noticed? Would she have gone out and told the other servants, and would they all discuss it over their breakfast? I wondered why I minded that, and why the thought of the servants talking about it in the kitchen should cause me such distress. It must be that I had a small mean mind, a conventional, petty hatred of gossip.

That was why I had come down last night in my blue dress and had not stayed hidden in my room. There was nothing brave or fine about it, it was a wretched tribute to convention. I had not come down for Maxim's sake, for Beatrice's, for the sake of Manderley. I had come down because I did not want the people at the ball to think I had quarrelled with Maxim. I didn't want them to go home and say, 'Of course you know they don't get on. I hear he's not at all happy.' I had come for my own sake, my own poor personal pride. As I sipped my cold tea I thought with a tired bitter feeling of despair that I would be content to live in one corner of Manderley and Maxim in the other so long as the outside world should never know. If he had no more tenderness for me, never kissed me again, did not speak to me except on matters of necessity, I believed I could bear it if I were certain that nobody knew of this but our two selves. If we could bribe servants not to tell, play our part before relations, before Beatrice, and then when we were alone sit apart in our separate rooms, leading our separate lives.

It seemed to me, as I sat there in bed, staring at the wall, at the sunlight coming in at the window, at Maxim's empty bed, that there was nothing quite so shaming, so degrading as a marriage that had failed. Failed after three months, as mine had done. For I had no illusions left now, I no longer made any effort to pretend. Last night had shown me too well. My marriage was a failure. All the things that people would say about it if they knew, were true. We did not get on. We were not companions. We were not suited to one another. I was too young for Maxim, too inexperienced, and, more important still, I was not of his world. The fact that I loved him in a sick, hurt, desperate way, like a child or a dog, did not matter. It was not the sort of love he needed. He wanted something else that I could not give him, something he had had before. I thought of the youthful almost hysterical excitement and conceit with which I had gone into this marriage, imagining I would bring happiness to Maxim, who had known much greater happiness before. Even Mrs Van Hopper, with her cheap views and common outlook, had known I was making a mistake. 'I'm afraid you will regret it,' she said. 'I believe you are making a big mistake.'

I would not listen to her, I thought her hard and cruel. But she was right. She was right in everything. That last mean thrust thrown at me before she said good-bye, 'You don't flatter yourself he's in love with you, do you? He's lonely, he can't bear that great empty house,' was the sanest, most truthful statement she had ever made in her life. Maxim was not in love with me, he had never loved me. Our honeymoon in Italy had meant nothing at all to him, nor our living here together. What I had thought was love for me, for myself as a person, was not love. It was just that he was a man, and I was his wife and was young, and he was lonely. He did not belong to me at all, he belonged to Rebecca. He still thought about Rebecca. He would never love me because of Rebecca. She was in the house still, as Mrs Danvers had said; she was in that room in the west wing, she was in the library, in the morning-room, in the gallery above the hall. Even in the little flower-room, where her mackintosh still hung. And in the garden, and in the woods, and down in the stone cottage on the beach. Her footsteps sounded in the corridors, her scent lingered on the stairs. The servants obeyed her orders still, the food we ate was the food she liked. Her favourite flowers filled the rooms. Her clothes were in the wardrobes in her room, her brushes were on the table, her shoes beneath the chair, her night-dress on her bed. Rebecca was still mistress of Manderley. Rebecca was still Mrs de Winter. I had no business here at all. I had come blundering like a poor fool on ground that was preserved. 'Where is Rebecca?' Maxim's grandmother had cried. 'I want Rebecca. What have you done with Rebecca?' She did not know me, she did not care about me. Why should she? I was a stranger to her. I did not belong to Maxim or to Manderley. And Beatrice at our first meeting, looking me up and down, frank, direct, 'You're so very different from Rebecca.' Frank, reserved, embarrassed when I spoke of her, hating those questions I had poured upon him, even as I had hated them myself, and then answering that final one as we came towards the house, his voice grave and quiet. 'Yes, she was the most beautiful creature I have ever seen.'

Rebecca, always Rebecca. Wherever I walked in Manderley, wherever I sat, even in my thoughts and in my dreams, I met

Rebecca. I knew her figure now, the long slim legs, the small and narrow feet. Her shoulders, broader than mine, the capable clever hands. Hands that could steer a boat, could hold a horse. Hands that arranged flowers, made the models of ships, and wrote 'Max from Rebecca' on the fly-leaf of a book. I knew her face too, small and oval, the clear white skin, the cloud of dark hair. I knew the scent she wore, I could guess her laughter and her smile. If I heard it, even among a thousand others, I should recognize her voice. Rebecca, always Rebecca. I should never be rid of Rebecca.

Perhaps I haunted her as she haunted me; she looked down on me from the gallery as Mrs Danvers had said, she sat beside me when I wrote my letters at her desk. That mackintosh I wore, that handkerchief I used. They were hers. Perhaps she knew and had seen me take them. Jasper had been her dog, and he ran at my heels now. The roses were hers and I cut them. Did she resent me and fear me as I resented her? Did she want Maxim alone in the house again? I could fight the living but I could not fight the dead. If there was some woman in London that Maxim loved, someone he wrote to, visited, dined with, slept with, I could fight with her. We would stand on common ground. I should not be afraid. Anger and jealousy were things that could be conquered. One day the woman would grow old or tired or different, and Maxim would not love her any more. But Rebecca would never grow old. Rebecca would always be the same. And her I could not fight. She was too strong for me.

I got out of bed and pulled the curtains. The sun streamed into the room. The men had cleared the mess away from the rose-garden. I wondered if people were talking about the ball in the way they do the day after a party.

'Did you think it quite up to their usual standard?'

'Oh, I think so.'

'The band dragged a bit, I thought.'

'The supper was damn good.'

'Fireworks weren't bad.'

'Bee Lacy is beginning to look old.'

'Who wouldn't in that get-up?'

'I thought he looked rather ill.'

'He always does.'

'What did you think of the bride?'

'Not much. Rather dull.'

'I wonder if it's a success.'

'Yes, I wonder . . .'

Then I noticed for the first time there was a note under my door. I went and picked it up. I recognized the square hand of Beatrice. She had scribbled it in pencil after breakfast.

I knocked at your door but had no answer so gather you've taken my advice and are sleeping off last night. Giles is anxious to get back early as they have rung up from home to say he's wanted to take somebody's place in a cricket match, and it starts at two. How he is going to see the ball after all the champagne he put away last night heaven only knows! I'm feeling a bit weak in the legs, but slept like a top. Frith says Maxim was down to an early breakfast, and there's now no sign of him! So please give him our love, and many thanks to you both for our evening, which we thoroughly enjoyed. Don't think any more about the dress. [*This last was heavily underlined*] Yours affectionately, Bee. [*And a postscript*] You must both come over and see us soon.

She had scribbled nine-thirty a.m. at the top of the paper, and it was now nearly half past eleven. They had been gone about two hours. They would be home by now, Beatrice with her suitcase unpacked, going out into her garden and taking up her ordinary routine, and Giles preparing for his match, renewing the whipping on his bat.

In the afternoon Beatrice would change into a cool frock and a shady hat and watch Giles play cricket. They would have tea afterwards in a tent, Giles very hot and red in the face, Beatrice laughing and talking to her friends. 'Yes, we went over for the

263

dance at Manderley; it was great fun. I wonder Giles was able to run a yard.' Smiling at Giles, patting him on the back. They were both middle-aged and unromantic. They had been married for twenty years and had a grown-up son who was going to Oxford. They were very happy. Their marriage was a success. It had not failed after three months as mine had done.

I could not go on sitting in my bedroom any longer. The maids would want to come and do the room. Perhaps Clarice would not have noticed about Maxim's bed after all. I rumpled it, to make it look as though he had slept there. I did not want the housemaids to know, if Clarice had not told them.

I had a bath and dressed, and went downstairs. The men had taken up the floor already in the hall and the flowers had been carried away. The music stands were gone from the gallery. The band must have caught an early train. The gardeners were sweeping the lawns and the drive clear of the spent fireworks. Soon there would be no trace left of the fancy dress ball at Manderley. How long the preparations had seemed, and how short and swift the clearance now.

I remembered the salmon lady standing by the drawing-room door with her plate of chicken, and it seemed to me a thing I must have fancied, or something that had happened very long ago. Robert was polishing the table in the dining-room. He was normal again, stolid, dull, not the fey excited creature of the past few weeks.

'Good morning, Robert,' I said.

'Good morning, Madam.'

'Have you seen Mr de Winter anywhere?'

'He went out soon after breakfast, Madam, before Major and Mrs Lacy were down. He has not been in since.'

'You don't know where he went?'

'No, Madam, I could not say.'

I wandered back again into the hall. I went through the drawing-room to the morning-room. Jasper rushed at me and licked my hands in a frenzy of delight as if I had been away for a long time. He had spent the evening on Clarice's bed and I had not seen him since tea-time yesterday. Perhaps the hours had been as long for him as they had for me.

I picked up the telephone and asked for the number of the estate office. Perhaps Maxim was with Frank. I felt I must speak to him, even if it was only for two minutes. I must explain to him that I had not meant to do what I had done last night. Even if I never spoke to him again, I must tell him that. The clerk answered the telephone, and told me that Maxim was not there.

'Mr Crawley is here, Mrs de Winter,' said the clerk; 'would you speak to him?' I would have refused, but he gave me no chance, and before I could put down the receiver I heard Frank's voice.

'Is anything the matter?' It was a funny way to begin a conversation. The thought flashed through my mind. He did not say good-morning, or did you sleep well? Why did he ask if something was the matter?

'Frank, it's me,' I said; 'where's Maxim?'

'I don't know, I haven't seen him. He's not been in this morning.'

'Not been to the office?'

'No.'

'Oh! Oh, well, it doesn't matter.'

'Did you see him at breakfast?' Frank said.

'No, I did not get up.'

'How did he sleep?'

I hesitated, Frank was the only person I did not mind knowing. 'He did not come to bed last night.'

There was silence at the other end of the line, as though Frank was thinking hard for an answer.

'Oh,' he said at last, very slowly. 'Oh, I see,' and then, after a minute, 'I was afraid something like that would happen.'

'Frank,' I said desperately, 'what did he say last night when everyone had gone? What did you all do?'

'I had a sandwich with Giles and Mrs Lacy,' said Frank. 'Maxim did not come. He made some excuse and went into the library.

I came back home almost at once. Perhaps Mrs Lacy can tell you.'

'She's gone,' I said, 'they went after breakfast. She sent up a note. She had not seen Maxim, she said.'

'Oh,' said Frank. I did not like it. I did not like the way he said it. It was sharp, ominous.

'Where do you think he's gone?' I said.

'I don't know,' said Frank; 'perhaps he's gone for a walk.' It was the sort of voice doctors used to relatives at a nursing-home when they came to inquire.

'Frank, I must see him,' I said. 'I've got to explain about last night.'

Frank did not answer. I could picture his anxious face, the lines on his forehead.

'Maxim thinks I did it on purpose,' I said, my voice breaking in spite of myself, and the tears that had blinded me last night and I had not shed came coursing down my cheeks sixteen hours too late. 'Maxim thinks I did it as a joke, a beastly damnable joke!'

'No,' said Frank. 'No.'

'He does, I tell you. You didn't see his eyes, as I did. You didn't stand beside him all the evening, watching him, as I did. He didn't speak to me, Frank. He never looked at me again. We stood there together the whole evening and we never spoke to one another.'

'There was no chance,' said Frank. 'All those people. Of course I saw, don't you think I know Maxim well enough for that? Look here . . .'

'I don't blame him,' I interrupted. 'If he believes I played that vile hideous joke he has a right to think what he likes of me, and never talk to me again, never see me again.'

'You mustn't talk like that,' said Frank. 'You don't know what you're saying. Let me come up and see you. I think I can explain.'

What was the use of Frank coming to see me, and us sitting in the morning-room together, Frank smoothing me down, Frank being tactful, Frank being kind? I did not want kindness from anybody now. It was too late.

266

'No,' I said. 'No, I don't want to go over it and over it again. It's happened, it can't be altered now. Perhaps it's a good thing; it's made me realize something I ought to have known before, that I ought to have suspected when I married Maxim.'

'What do you mean?' said Frank.

His voice was sharp, queer. I wondered why it should matter to him about Maxim not loving me. Why did he not want me to know?

'About him and Rebecca,' I said, and as I said her name it sounded strange and sour like a forbidden word, a relief to me no longer, not a pleasure, but hot and shaming as a sin confessed.

Frank did not answer for a moment. I heard him draw in his breath at the other end of the wire.

'What do you mean?' he said again, shorter and sharper than before. 'What do you mean?'

'He doesn't love me, he loves Rebecca,' I said. 'He's never forgotten her, he thinks about her still, night and day. He's never loved me, Frank. It's always Rebecca, Rebecca, Rebecca.'

I heard Frank give a startled cry but I did not care how much I shocked him now. 'Now you know how I feel,' I said, 'now you understand.'

'Look here,' he said; 'I've got to come and see you, I've got to, do you hear? It's vitally important; I can't talk to you down the telephone. Mrs de Winter? Mrs de Winter?'

I slammed down the receiver, and got up from the writing-desk. I did not want to see Frank. He could not help me over this. No one could help me but myself. My face was red and blotchy from crying. I walked about the room biting the corner of my handkerchief, tearing at the edge.

The feeling was strong within me that I should never see Maxim again. It was certainty, born of some strange instinct. He had gone away and would not come back. I knew in my heart that Frank believed this too and would not admit it to me on the telephone. He did not want to frighten me. If I rang him up again at the office now I should find that he had gone. The clerk would say, 'Mr Crawley has just gone out, Mrs de Winter', and I could see Frank, hatless, climbing into his small, shabby Morris, driving off in search of Maxim.

I went and stared out of the window at the little clearing where the satyr played his pipes. The rhododendrons were all over now. They would not bloom again for another year. The tall shrubs looked dark and drab now that the colour had gone. A fog was rolling up from the sea, and I could not see the woods beyond the bank. It was very hot, very oppressive. I could imagine our guests of last night saying to one another, 'What a good thing this fog kept off for yesterday, we should never have seen the fireworks.' I went out of the morning-room and through the drawing-room to the terrace. The sun had gone in now behind a wall of mist. It was as though a blight had fallen upon Manderley taking the sky away and the light of the day. One of the gardeners passed me with a barrow full of bits of paper, and litter, and the skins of fruit left on the lawns by the people last night.

'Good morning,' I said.

'Good morning, Madam.'

'I'm afraid the ball last night has made a lot of work for you,' I said.

'That's all right, Madam,' he said. 'I think everyone enjoyed themselves good and hearty, and that's the main thing, isn't it?'

'Yes, I suppose so,' I said.

He looked across the lawns to the clearing in the woods where the valley sloped to the sea. The dark trees loomed thin and indistinct.

'It's coming up very thick,' he said.

'Yes,' I said.

'A good thing it wasn't like this last night,' he said.

'Yes,' I said.

He waited a moment, and then he touched his cap and went off trundling his barrow. I went across the lawns to the edge of the woods. The mist in the trees had turned to moisture and dripped upon my bare head like a thin rain. Jasper stood by my feet dejected, his tail downcast, his pink tongue hanging from his mouth. The clammy oppression of the day made him listless and heavy. I could hear the sea from where I stood, sullen and slow, as it broke in the coves below the woods. The white fog rolled on past me towards the house smelling of damp salt and seaweed. I put my hand on Jasper's coat. It was wringing wet. When I looked back at the house I could not see the chimneys or the contour of the walls, I could only see the vague substance of the house, the windows in the west wing, and the flower tubs on the terrace. The shutter had been pulled aside from the window of the large bedroom in the west wing, and someone was standing there, looking down upon the lawns. The figure was shadowy and indistinct and for one moment of shock and fear I believed it to be Maxim. Then the figure moved, I saw the arm reach up to fold the shutter, and I knew it was Mrs Danvers. She had been watching me as I stood at the edge of the woods bathed in that white wall of fog. She had seen me walk slowly from the terrace to the lawns. She may have listened to my conversation with Frank on the telephone from the connecting line in her own room. She would know that Maxim had not been with me last night. She would have heard my voice, known about my tears. She knew the part I had played through the long hours, standing by Maxim's side in my blue dress at the bottom of the stairs, and that he had not looked at me nor spoken to me. She knew because she had meant it to happen. This was her triumph, hers and Rebecca's.

I thought of her as I had seen her last night, watching me through the open door to the west wing, and that diabolical smile on her white skull's face, and I remembered that she was a living breathing woman like myself, she was made of flesh and blood. She was not dead, like Rebecca. I could speak to her, but I could not speak to Rebecca.

I walked back across the lawns on sudden impulse to the house. I went through the hall and up the great stairs, I turned in under the archway by the gallery, I passed through the door to the west wing, and so along the dark silent corridor to Rebecca's room. I turned the handle of the door and went inside.

Mrs Danvers was still standing by the window, and the shutter was folded back.

'Mrs Danvers,' I said. 'Mrs Danvers.' She turned to look at me, and I saw her eyes were red and swollen with crying, even as mine were, and there were dark shadows in her white face.

'What is it?' she said, and her voice was thick and muffled from the tears she had shed, even as mine had been.

I had not expected to find her so. I had pictured her smiling as she had smiled last night, cruel and evil. Now she was none of these things, she was an old woman who was ill and tired.

I hesitated, my hand still on the knob of the open door, and I did not know what to say to her now or what to do.

She went on staring at me with those red, swollen eyes and I could not answer her. 'I left the menu on the desk as usual,' she said. 'Do you want something changed?' Her words gave me courage, and I left the door and came to the middle of the room.

'Mrs Danvers,' I said. 'I have not come to talk about the menu. You know that, don't you?'

She did not answer me. Her left hand opened and shut.

'You've done what you wanted, haven't you?' I said, 'you meant this to happen, didn't you? Are you pleased now? Are you happy?'

She turned her head away, and looked out of the window as she had done when I first came into the room. 'Why did you ever come here?' she said. 'Nobody wanted you at Manderley. We were all right until you came. Why did you not stay where you were out in France?'

'You seem to forget I love Mr de Winter,' I said.

'If you loved him you would never have married him,' she said.

I did not know what to say. The situation was mad, unreal. She kept talking in that choked muffled way with her head turned from me.

'I thought I hated you but I don't now,' she said; 'it seems to have spent itself, all the feeling I had.'

'Why should you hate me?' I asked; 'what have I ever done to you that you should hate me?'

'You tried to take Mrs de Winter's place,' she said.

Still she would not look at me. She stood there sullen, her head turned from me. 'I had nothing changed,' I said. 'Manderley went on as it had always been. I gave no orders, I left everything to you. I would have been friends with you, if you had let me, but you set yourself against me from the first. I saw it in your face, the moment I shook hands with you.'

She did not answer, and her hand kept opening and shutting against her dress. 'Many people marry twice, men and women,' I said. 'There are thousands of second marriages taking place every day. You talk as though my marrying Mr de Winter was a crime, a sacrilege against the dead. Haven't we as much right to be happy as anyone else?'

'Mr de Winter is not happy,' she said, turning to look at me at last; 'any fool can see that. You have only to look at his eyes. He's still in hell, and he's looked like that ever since she died.'

'It's not true,' I said. 'It's not true. He was happy when we were in France together; he was younger, much younger, and laughing and gay.'

'Well, he's a man, isn't he?' she said. 'No man denies himself on a honeymoon, does he? Mr de Winter's not forty-six yet.'

She laughed contemptuously, and shrugged her shoulders.

'How dare you speak to me like that? How dare you?' I said.

I was not afraid of her any more. I went up to her, shook her by the arm. 'You made me wear that dress last night,' I said, 'I should never have thought of it but for you. You did it because you wanted to hurt Mr de Winter, you wanted to make him suffer. Hasn't he suffered enough without your playing that vile hideous joke upon him? Do you think his agony and pain will bring Mrs de Winter back again?'

She shook herself clear of me, the angry colour flooded her dead white face. 'What do I care for his suffering?' she said, 'he's never cared about mine. How do you think I've liked it, watching you sit in her place, walk in her footsteps, touch the things that were hers? What do you think it's meant to me all these months knowing that you wrote at her desk in the morning-room, using the very pen that she used, speaking down the house telephone, where she used to speak every morning of her life to me, ever since she first came to Manderley? What do you think it meant to me to hear Frith and Robert and the rest of the servants talking about you as "Mrs de Winter"? "Mrs de Winter has gone out for a walk." "Mrs de Winter wants the car this afternoon at three o'clock." "Mrs de Winter won't be in to tea till five o'clock." And all the while my Mrs de Winter, my lady with her smile and her lovely face and brave ways, the real Mrs de Winter, lying dead and cold and forgotten in the church crypt. If he suffers then he deserves to suffer, marrying a young girl like you not ten months afterwards. Well, he's paying for it now, isn't he? I've seen his face, I've seen his eyes. He's made his own hell and there's no one but himself to thank for it. He knows she sees him, he knows she comes by night and watches him. And she doesn't come kindly, not she, not my lady. She was never one to stand mute and still and be wronged. "I'll see them in hell, Danny," she'd say, "I'll see them in hell first." "That's right, my dear," I'd tell her, "no one will put upon you. You were born into this world to take what you could out of it," and she did, she didn't care, she wasn't afraid. She had all the courage and spirit of a boy, had my Mrs de Winter. She ought to have been a boy, I often told her that. I had the care of her as a child. You knew that, didn't you?'

'No!' I said, 'no. Mrs Danvers, what's the use of all this? I don't want to hear any more, I don't want to know. Haven't I got feelings as well as you? Can't you understand what it means to me, to hear her mentioned, to stand here and listen while you tell me about her?'

She did not hear me, she went on raving like a mad woman, a fanatic, her long fingers twisting and tearing the black stuff of her dress.

'She was lovely then,' she said. 'Lovely as a picture; men turning to stare at her when she passed, and she not twelve years old. She knew then, she used to wink at me like the little devil she was. "I'm going to be a beauty, aren't I, Danny?" she said, and

"We'll see about that, my love, we'll see about that," I told her. She had all the knowledge then of a grown person; she'd enter into conversation with men and women as clever and full of tricks as someone of eighteen. She twisted her father round her little finger, and she'd have done the same with her mother, had she lived. Spirit, you couldn't beat my lady for spirit. She drove a four-in-hand on her fourteenth birthday, and her cousin, Mr Jack, got up on the box beside her and tried to take the reins from her hands. They fought it out there together, for three minutes, like a couple of wild cats, and the horses galloping to glory. She won though, my lady won. She cracked her whip over his head and down he came, head-over-heels, cursing and laughing. They were a pair, I tell you, she and Mr Jack. They sent him in the Navy, but he wouldn't stand the discipline, and I don't blame him. He had too much spirit to obey orders, like my lady.'

I watched her, fascinated, horrified; a queer ecstatic smile was on her lips, making her older than ever, making her skull's face vivid and real. 'No one got the better of her, never, never,' she said. 'She did what she liked, she lived as she liked. She had the strength of a little lion too. I remember her at sixteen getting up on one of her father's horses, a big brute of an animal too, that the groom said was too hot for her to ride. She stuck to him, all right. I can see her now, with her hair flying out behind her, slashing at him, drawing blood, digging the spurs into his side, and when she got off his back he was trembling all over, full of froth and blood. "That will teach him, won't it, Danny?" she said, and walked off to wash her hands as cool as you please. And that's how she went at life, when she grew up. I saw her, I was with her. She cared for nothing and for no one. And then she was beaten in the end. But it wasn't a man, it wasn't a woman. The sea got her. The sea was too strong for her. The sea got her in the end.'

She broke off, her mouth working strangely, and dragging at the corners. She began to cry noisily, harshly, her mouth open and her eyes dry.

273

'Mrs Danvers,' I said. 'Mrs Danvers.' I stood before her help-lessly, not knowing what to do. I mistrusted her no longer, I was afraid of her no more, but the sight of her sobbing there, dry-eyed, made me shudder, made me ill. 'Mrs Danvers,' I said, 'you're not well, you ought to be in bed. Why don't you go to your room and rest? Why don't you go to bed?'

She turned on me fiercely. 'Leave me alone, can't you?' she said. 'What's it to do with you if I show my grief? I'm not ashamed of it, I don't shut myself up in my room to cry. I don't walk up and down, up and down, in my room like Mr de Winter, with the door locked on me.'

'What do you mean?' I said. 'Mr de Winter does not do that.'

'He did,' she said, 'after she died. Up and down, up and down in the library. I heard him. I watched him too, through the key-hole, more than once. Backwards and forwards, like an animal in a cage.'

'I don't want to hear,' I said. 'I don't want to know.'

'And then you say you made him happy on his honeymoon,' she said; 'made him happy – you, a young ignorant girl, young enough to be his daughter. What do you know about life? What do you know about men? You come here and think you can take Mrs de Winter's place. You. You take my lady's place. Why, even the servants laughed at you when you came to Manderley. Even the little scullery-maid you met in the back passage there on your first morning. I wonder what Mr de Winter thought when he got you back here at Manderley, after his precious honeymoon was over. I wonder what he thought when he saw you sitting at the dining-room table for the first time.'

'You'd better stop this, Mrs Danvers,' I said; 'you'd better go to your room.'

'Go to my room,' she mimicked, 'go to my room. The mistress of the house thinks I had better go to my room. And after that, what then? You'll go running to Mr de Winter and saying, "Mrs Danvers has been unkind to me, Mrs Danvers has been rude." You'll go running to him like you did before when Mr Jack came to see me.'

'I never told him,' I said.

'That's a lie,' she said. 'Who else told him, if you didn't? No one else was here. Frith and Robert were out, and none of the other servants knew. I made up my mind then I'd teach you a lesson, and him too. Let him suffer, I say. What do I care? What's his suffering to me? Why shouldn't I see Mr Jack here at Manderley? He's the only link I have left now with Mrs de Winter. "I'll not have him here," he said. "I'm warning you, it's the last time." He's not forgotten to be jealous, has he?'

I remembered crouching in the gallery when the library door was open. I remembered Maxim's voice raised in anger, using the words that Mrs Danvers had just repeated. Jealous, Maxim jealous . . .

'He was jealous while she lived, and now he's jealous when she's dead,' said Mrs Danvers. 'He forbids Mr Jack the house now like he did then. That shows you he's not forgotten her, doesn't it? Of course he was jealous. So was I. So was everyone who knew her. She didn't care. She only laughed. "I shall live as I please, Danny," she told me, "and the whole world won't stop me." A man had only to look at her once and be mad about her. I've seen them here, staying in the house, men she'd meet up in London and bring for week-ends. She would take them bathing from the boat, she would have a picnic supper at her cottage in the cove. They made love to her of course; who would not? She laughed, she would come back and tell me what they had said, and what they'd done. She did not mind, it was like a game to her. Like a game. Who wouldn't be jealous? They were all jealous, all mad for her. Mr de Winter, Mr Jack, Mr Crawley, everyone who knew her, everyone who came to Manderley.'

'I don't want to know,' I said. 'I don't want to know.'

Mrs Danvers came close to me, she put her face near to mine. 'It's no use, is it?' she said. 'You'll never get the better of her. She's still mistress here, even if she is dead. She's the real Mrs de Winter, not you. It's you that's the shadow and the ghost. It's you that's forgotten and not wanted and pushed aside. Well, why don't you leave Manderley to her? Why don't you go?'

I backed away from her towards the window, my old fear and horror rising up in me again. She took my arm and held it like a vice.

'Why don't you go?' she said. 'We none of us want you. He doesn't want you, he never did. He can't forget her. He wants to be alone in the house again, with her. It's you that ought to be lying there in the church crypt, not her. It's you who ought to be dead, not Mrs de Winter.'

She pushed me towards the open window. I could see the terrace below me grey and indistinct in the white wall of fog. 'Look down there,' she said. 'It's easy, isn't it? Why don't you jump? It wouldn't hurt, not to break your neck. It's a quick, kind way. It's not like drowning. Why don't you try it? Why don't you go?'

The fog filled the open window, damp and clammy, it stung my eyes, it clung to my nostrils. I held on to the window-sill with my hands.

'Don't be afraid,' said Mrs Danvers. 'I won't push you. I won't stand by you. You can jump of your own accord. What's the use of your staying here at Manderley? You're not happy. Mr de Winter doesn't love you. There's not much for you to live for, is there? Why don't you jump now and have done with it? Then you won't be unhappy any more.'

I could see the flower tubs on the terrace and the blue of the hydrangeas clumped and solid. The paved stones were smooth and grey. They were not jagged and uneven. It was the fog that made them look so far away. They were not far really, the window was not so very high.

'Why don't you jump?' whispered Mrs Danvers. 'Why don't you try?'

The fog came thicker than before and the terrace was hidden from me. I could not see the flower tubs any more, nor the smooth paved stones. There was nothing but the white mist about me, smelling of sea-weed dank and chill. The only reality was the window-sill beneath my hands and the grip of Mrs Danvers on my left arm. If I jumped I should not see the stones rise up to meet me, the fog would hide them from me. The pain would be sharp and sudden as she said. The fall would break my neck. It would not be slow, like drowning. It would soon be over. And Maxim did not love me. Maxim wanted to be alone again, with Rebecca.

'Go on,' whispered Mrs Danvers. 'Go on, don't be afraid.'

I shut my eyes. I was giddy from staring down at the terrace, and my fingers ached from holding to the ledge. The mist entered my nostrils and lay upon my lips rank and sour. It was stifling, like a blanket, like an anaesthetic. I was beginning to forget about being unhappy, and about loving Maxim. I was beginning to forget Rebecca. Soon I would not have to think about Rebecca any more . . .

As I relaxed my hands and sighed, the white mist and the silence that was part of it was shattered suddenly, was rent in two by an explosion that shook the window where we stood. The glass shivered in its frame. I opened my eyes. I stared at Mrs Danvers. The burst was followed by another, and yet a third and fourth. The sound of the explosions stung the air and the birds rose unseen from the woods around the house and made an echo with their clamour.

'What is it?' I said stupidly. 'What has happened?'

Mrs Danvers relaxed her grip upon my arm. She stared out of the window into the fog. 'It's the rockets,' she said; 'there must be a ship gone ashore there in the bay.'

We listened, staring into the white fog together. And then we heard the sound of footsteps running on the terrace beneath us.

# 19

It was Maxim. I could not see him but I could hear his voice. He was shouting for Frith as he ran. I heard Frith answer from the hall and come out on the terrace. Their figures loomed out of the mist beneath us.

'She's ashore all right,' said Maxim. 'I was watching her from the headland and I saw her come right into the bay, and head for the reef. They'll never shift her, not with these tides. She must have mistaken the bay for Kerrith harbour. It's like a wall out there, in the bay. Tell them in the house to stand by with food and drink in case these fellows want anything, and ring through to the office to Mr Crawley and tell him what's happened. I'm going back to the cove to see if I can do anything. Get me some cigarettes, will you?'

Mrs Danvers drew back from the window. Her face was expressionless once more, the cold white mask that I knew.

'We had better go down,' she said, 'Frith will be looking for me to make arrangements. Mr de Winter may bring the men back to the house as he said. Be careful of your hands, I'm going to shut the window.' I stepped back into the room still dazed and stupid, not sure of myself or of her. I watched her close the window and fasten the shutters, and draw the curtains in their place.

'It's a good thing there is no sea running,' she said, 'there wouldn't have been much chance for them then. But on a day like this there's no danger. The owners will lose their ship, though, if she's run on the reef as Mr de Winter said.'

She glanced round the room to make certain that nothing was disarranged or out of place. She straightened the cover on the double bed. Then she went to the door and held it open for me. 'I will tell them in the kitchen to serve cold lunch in the dining-room after all,' she said, 'and then it won't matter what time you come for it. Mr de Winter may not want to rush back at one o'clock if he's busy down there in the cove.'

I stared at her blankly and then passed out of the open door, stiff and wooden like a dummy.

'When you see Mr de Winter, Madam, will you tell him it will be quite all right if he wants to bring the men back from the ship? There will be a hot meal ready for them any time.'

'Yes,' I said. 'Yes, Mrs Danvers.'

She turned her back on me and went along the corridor to the service staircase, a weird gaunt figure in her black dress, the skirt just sweeping the ground like the full, wide skirts of thirty years ago. Then she turned the corner of the corridor and disappeared.

I walked slowly along the passage to the door by the archway, my mind still blunt and slow as though I had just woken from a long sleep. I pushed through the door and went down the stairs with no set purpose before me. Frith was crossing the hall towards the dining-room. When he saw me he stopped, and waited until I came down into the hall.

'Mr de Winter was in a few moments ago, Madam,' he said. 'He took some cigarettes, and then went back again to the beach. It appears there is a ship gone ashore.'

'Yes,' I said.

'Did you hear the rockets, Madam?' said Frith.

'Yes, I heard the rockets,' I said.

'I was in the pantry with Robert, and we both thought at first that one of the gardeners had let off a firework left over from last night,' said Frith, 'and I said to Robert, "What do they want to do that for in this weather? Why don't they keep them for the kiddies on Saturday night?" And then the next one came, and then the third. "That's not fireworks," says Robert, "that's a ship in distress." "I believe you're right," I said, and I went out to the hall and there was Mr de Winter calling me from the terrace.'

'Yes,' I said.

'Well, it's hardly to be wondered at in this fog, Madam. That's what I said to Robert just now. It's difficult to find your way on the road, let alone on the water.'

'Yes,' I said.

'If you want to catch Mr de Winter he went straight across the lawn only two minutes ago,' said Frith.

'Thank you, Frith,' I said.

I went out on the terrace. I could see the trees taking shape beyond the lawns. The fog was lifting, it was rising in little clouds to the sky above. It whirled above my head in wreaths of smoke. I looked up at the windows above my head. They were tightly closed, and the shutters were fastened. They looked as though they would never open, never be thrown wide.

It was by the large window in the centre that I had stood five minutes before. How high it seemed above my head, how lofty and remote. The stones were hard and solid under my feet. I looked down at my feet and then up again to the shuttered window, and as I did so I became aware suddenly that my head was swimming and I felt hot. A little trickle of perspiration ran down the back of my neck. Black dots jumped about in the air in front of me. I went into the hall again and sat down on a chair. My hands were quite wet. I sat very still, holding my knees.

'Frith,' I called, 'Frith, are you in the dining-room?'

'Yes, Madam?' He came out at once, and crossed the hall towards me.

'Don't think me very odd, Frith, but I rather think I'd like a small glass of brandy.'

'Certainly, Madam.'

I went on holding my knees and sitting very still. He came back with a liqueur glass on a silver salver.

'Do you feel a trifle unwell, Madam?' said Frith. 'Would you like me to call Clarice?'

'No, I'll be all right, Frith,' I said. 'I felt a bit hot, that's all.'

'It's a very warm morning, Madam. Very warm indeed. Oppressive, one might almost say.'

'Yes, Frith. Very oppressive.'

I drank the brandy and put the glass back on the silver salver.

'Perhaps the sound of those rockets alarmed you,' said Frith; 'they went off so very sudden.'

'Yes, they did,' I said.

'And what with the hot morning and standing about all last night, you are not perhaps feeling quite like yourself, Madam,' said Frith.

'No, perhaps not,' I said.

'Will you lie down for half an hour? It's quite cool in the library.'

'No. No, I think I'll go out in a moment or two. Don't bother, Frith.'

'No. Very good, Madam.'

He went away and left me alone in the hall. It was quiet sitting there, quiet and cool. All trace of the party had been cleared away. It might never have happened. The hall was as it had always been, grey and silent and austere, with the portraits and the weapons on the wall. I could scarcely believe that last night I had stood there in my blue dress at the bottom of the stairs, shaking hands with five hundred people. I could not believe that there had been music-stands in the minstrel's gallery, and a band playing there, a man with a fiddle, a man with a drum. I got up and went out on to the terrace again.

The fog was rising, lifting to the tops of the trees. I could see the woods at the end of the lawns. Above my head a pale sun tried to penetrate the heavy sky. It was hotter than ever. Oppressive, as Frith had said. A bee hummed by me in search of scent, bumbling, noisy, and then creeping inside a flower was suddenly silent. On the grass banks above the lawns the gardener started his mowing machine. A startled linnet fled from the whirring blades towards the rose-garden. The gardener bent to the handles of the machine and walked slowly along the bank scattering the short-tipped grass and the pin-point daisy-heads. The smell of the sweet warm grass came towards me on the air, and the sun shone down upon me full and strong from out of the white mist. I whistled for Jasper but he did not come. Perhaps he had followed Maxim when he went down to the beach. I glanced at my watch. It was after half past twelve, nearly twenty to one. This time yesterday Maxim and I were standing with Frank in the little garden in front of his house, waiting for his house-keeper to serve lunch.

Twenty-four hours ago. They were teasing me, baiting me about my dress. 'You'll both get the surprise of your lives,' I had said.

I felt sick with shame at the memory of my words. And then I realized for the first time that Maxim had not gone away as I had feared. The voice I had heard on the terrace was calm and practical. The voice I knew. Not the voice of last night when I stood at the head of the stairs. Maxim had not gone away. He was down there in the cove somewhere. He was himself, normal and sane. He had just been for a walk, as Frank had said. He had been on the headland, he had seen the ship closing in towards the shore. All my fears were without foundation. Maxim was safe. Maxim was all right. I had just experienced something that was degrading and horrible and mad, something that I did not fully understand even now, that I had no wish to remember, that I wanted to bury for evermore, deep in the shadows of my mind with old forgotten terrors of childhood; but even this did not matter as long as Maxim was all right.

Then I, too, went down the steep twisting path through the dark woods to the beach below.

The fog had almost gone, and when I came to the cove I could see the ship at once, lying about two miles off-shore with her bows pointed towards the cliffs. I went along the breakwater and stood at the end of it, leaning against the rounded wall. There was a crowd of people on the cliffs already who must have walked along the coast-guard path from Kerrith. The cliffs and the headland were part of Manderley, but the public had always used the right-of-way along the cliffs. Some of them were scrambling down the cliff face to get a closer view of the stranded ship. She lay at an awkward angle, her stern tilted, and there were a number of rowing-boats already pulling round her. The life-boat was standing off. I saw someone stand up in her and shout through a megaphone. I could not hear what he was saying. It was still misty out in the bay, and I could not see the horizon. Another motor-boat chugged into the light with some men aboard. The motor-boat was dark grey. I could see someone in uniform. That would be the harbour-master from Kerrith, and the Lloyd's agent with him. Another motor-boat followed, a party of holiday-makers from Kerrith aboard. They circled round and round the stranded steamer chatting excitedly. I could hear their voices echoing across the still water.

I left the breakwater and the cove and climbed up the path over the cliffs towards the rest of the people. I did not see Maxim anywhere. Frank was there, talking to one of the coast-guards. I hung back when I saw him, momentarily embarrassed. Barely an hour ago I had been crying to him, down the telephone. I was not sure what I ought to do. He saw me at once and waved his hand. I went over to him and the coast-guard. The coast-guard knew me.

'Come to see the fun, Mrs de Winter?' he said smiling. 'I'm afraid it will be a hard job. The tugs may shift her, but I doubt it. She's hard and fast where she is on that ledge.'

'What will they do?' I said.

'They'll send a diver down directly to see if she's broken her back,' he replied. 'There's the fellow there in the red stocking cap. Like to see through these glasses?'

I took his glasses and looked at the ship. I could see a group of men staring over her stern. One of them was pointing at something. The man in the life-boat was still shouting through the megaphone.

The harbour-master from Kerrith had joined the group of men in the stern of the stranded ship. The diver in his stocking cap was sitting in the grey motor-boat belonging to the harbour-master.

The pleasure-boat was still circling round the ship. A woman was standing up taking a snapshot. A group of gulls had settled on the water and were crying foolishly, hoping for scraps.

I gave the glasses back to the coast-guard.

'Nothing seems to be happening,' I said.

'They'll send him down directly,' said the coast-guard. 'They'll argue a bit first, like all foreigners. Here come the tugs.'

'They'll never do it,' said Frank. 'Look at the angle she's lying at. It's much shallower there than I thought.'

'That reef runs out quite a way,' said the coast-guard; 'you don't notice it in the ordinary way, going over that piece of water in a small boat. But a ship with her depth would touch all right.'

'I was down in the first cove by the valley when they fired the rockets,' said Frank. 'I could scarcely see three yards in front of me where I was. And then the things went off out of the blue.'

I thought how alike people were in a moment of common interest. Frank was Frith all over again, giving his version of the story, as though it mattered, as though we cared. I knew that he had gone down to the beach to look for Maxim. I knew that he had been frightened, as I had been. And now all this was forgotten and put aside: our conversation down the telephone, our mutual anxiety, his insistence that he must see me. All because a ship had gone ashore in the fog.

A small boy came running up to us. 'Will the sailors be drowned?' he asked.

'Not them. They're all right, sonny,' said the coast-guard. 'The sea's as flat as the back of my hand. No one's going to be hurt this time.'

'If it had happened last night we should never have heard them,' said Frank. 'We must have let off more than fifty rockets at our show, beside all the smaller things.'

'We'd have heard all right,' said the coast-guard. 'We'd have seen the flash and known the direction. There's the diver, Mrs de Winter. See him putting on his helmet?'

'I want to see the diver,' said the small boy.

'There he is,' said Frank, bending and pointing – 'that chap there putting on the helmet. They're going to lower him into the water.'

'Won't he be drowned?' said the child.

'Divers don't drown,' said the coast-guard. 'They have air pumped into them all the time. Watch him disappear. There he goes.'

The surface of the water was disturbed a minute and then was clear again. 'He's gone,' said the small boy.

'Where's Maxim?' I said.

'He's taken one of the crew into Kerrith,' said Frank; 'the fellow lost his head and jumped for it apparently when the ship struck. We found him clinging on to one of the rocks here under the cliff. He was soaked to the skin of course and shaking like a jelly. Couldn't speak a word of English, of course. Maxim went down to him, and found him bleeding like a pig from a scratch on the rocks. He spoke to him in German. Then he hailed one of the motor-boats from Kerrith that was hanging around like a hungry shark, and he's gone off with him to get him bandaged by a doctor. If he's lucky he'll just catch old Phillips sitting down to lunch.'

'When did he go?' I said.

'He went just before you turned up,' said Frank, 'about five minutes ago. I wonder you didn't see the boat. He was sitting in the stern with this German fellow.'

'He must have gone while I was climbing up the cliff,' I said.

'Maxim is splendid at anything like this,' said Frank. 'He always gives a hand if he can. You'll find he will invite the whole crew back to Manderley, and feed them, and give them beds into the bargain.'

'That's right,' said the coast-guard. 'He'd give the coat off his back for any of his own people, I know that. I wish there was more like him in the county.'

'Yes, we could do with them,' said Frank.

We went on staring at the ship. The tugs were standing off still, but the life-boat had turned and gone back towards Kerrith.

'It's not their turn today,' said the coast-guard.

'No,' said Frank, 'and I don't think it's a job for the tugs either. It's the ship-breaker who's going to make money this time.'

The gulls wheeled overhead, mewing like hungry cats; some of them settled on the ledges of the cliff, while others, bolder, rode the surface of the water beside the ship.

The coast-guard took off his cap and mopped his forehead.

'Seems kind of airless, doesn't it?' he said.

'Yes,' I said.

The pleasure-boat with the camera people went chugging off towards Kerrith. 'They've got fed up,' said the coast-guard.

'I don't blame them,' said Frank. 'I don't suppose anything will happen for hours. The diver will have to make his report before they try to shift her.'

'That's right,' said the coast-guard.

'I don't think there's much sense in hanging about here,' said Frank; 'we can't do anything. I want my lunch.'

I did not say anything. He hesitated. I felt his eyes upon me.

'What are you going to do?' he said.

'I think I shall stay here a bit,' I said. 'I can have lunch any time. It's cold. It doesn't matter. I want to see what the diver's going to do.' Somehow I could not face Frank just at the moment. I wanted to be alone, or with someone I did not know, like the coast-guard.

'You won't see anything,' said Frank; 'there won't be anything to see. Why not come back and have some lunch with me?'

'No,' I said. 'No, really . . .'

'Oh, well,' said Frank, 'you know where to find me if you do want me. I shall be at the office all the afternoon.'

'All right,' I said.

He nodded to the coast-guard and went off down the cliff towards the cove. I wondered if I had offended him. I could not help it. All these things would be settled some day, one day. So much seemed to have happened since I spoke to him on the telephone, and I did not want to think about anything any more. I just wanted to sit there on the cliff and stare at the ship.

'He's a good sort, Mr Crawley,' said the coast-guard.

'Yes,' I said.

'He'd give his right hand for Mr de Winter too,' he said.

286

'Yes, I think he would,' I said.

The small boy was still hopping around on the grass in front of us.

'When's the diver coming up again?' he said.

'Not yet, sonny,' said the coast-guard.

A woman in a pink striped frock and a hair-net came across the grass towards us. 'Charlie? Charlie? Where are you?' she called.

'Here's your mother coming to give you what-for,' said the coast-guard.

'I've seen the diver, Mum,' shouted the boy.

The woman nodded to us and smiled. She did not know me. She was a holiday-maker from Kerrith. 'The excitement all seems to be over doesn't it?' she said; 'they are saying down on the cliff there the ship will be there for days.'

'They're waiting for the diver's report,' said the coast-guard.

'I don't know how they get them to go down under the water like that,' said the woman; 'they ought to pay them well.'

'They do that,' said the coast-guard.

'I want to be a diver, Mum,' said the small boy.

'You must ask your Daddy, dear,' said the woman, laughing at us. 'It's a lovely spot up here, isn't it?' she said to me. 'We brought a picnic lunch, never thinking it would turn foggy and we'd have a wreck into the bargain. We were just thinking of going back to Kerrith when the rockets went off under our noses, it seemed. I nearly jumped out of my skin. "Why, whatever's that?" I said to my husband. "That's a distress signal," he said; "let's stop and see the fun." There's no dragging him away; he's as bad as my little boy. I don't see anything in it myself.'

'No, there's not much to see now,' said the coast-guard.

'Those are nice-looking woods over there; I suppose they're private,' said the woman.

The coast-guard coughed awkwardly, and glanced at me. I began eating a piece of grass and looked away.

'Yes, that's all private in there,' he said.

'My husband says all these big estates will be chopped up in time and bungalows built,' said the woman. 'I wouldn't mind a nice little bungalow up here facing the sea. I don't know that I'd care for this part of the world in the winter though.'

'No, it's very quiet here winter times,' said the coast-guard.

I went on chewing my piece of grass. The little boy kept running round in circles. The coast-guard looked at his watch. 'Well, I must be getting on,' he said; 'good afternoon!' He saluted me, and turned back along the path towards Kerrith. 'Come on, Charlie, come and find Daddy,' said the woman.

She nodded to me in friendly fashion, and sauntered off to the edge of the cliff, the little boy running at her heels. A thin man in khaki shorts and a striped blazer waved to her. They sat down by a clump of gorse bushes and the woman began to undo paper packages.

I wished I could lose my own identity and join them. Eat hard-boiled eggs and potted meat sandwiches, laugh rather loudly, enter their conversation, and then wander back with them during the afternoon to Kerrith and paddle on the beach, run races across the stretch of sand, and so to their lodgings and have shrimps for tea. Instead of which I must go back alone through the woods to Manderley and wait for Maxim. And I did not know what we should say to one another, how he would look at me, what would be his voice. I went on sitting there on the cliff. I was not hungry. I did not think about lunch.

More people came and wandered over the cliffs to look at the ship. It made an excitement for the afternoon. There was nobody I knew. They were all holiday-makers from Kerrith. The sea was glassy calm. The gulls no longer wheeled overhead, they had settled on the water a little distance from the ship. More pleasure boats appeared during the afternoon. It must be a field day for Kerrith boat-men. The diver came up and then went down again. One of the tugs steamed away while the other still stood by. The harbour-master went back in his grey motor-boat, taking some men with him, and the diver who had come to the surface for the second time. The crew of the ship leant against the side throwing scraps to the gulls, while visitors in pleasure-boats rowed slowly round the ship. Nothing happened at all. It was dead low water now, and the ship was heeled at an angle, the propeller showing clean. Little ridges of white cloud formed in the western sky and the sun became pallid. It was still very hot. The woman in the pink striped frock with the little boy got up and wandered off along the path towards Kerrith, the man in the shorts following with the picnic basket.

I glanced at my watch. It was after three o'clock. I got up and went down the hill to the cove. It was quiet and deserted as always. The shingle was dark and grey. The water in the little harbour was glassy like a mirror. My feet made a queer crunching noise as I crossed the shingle. The ridges of white cloud now covered all the sky above my head, and the sun was hidden. When I came to the further side of the cove I saw Ben crouching by a little pool between two rocks scraping winkles into his hand. My shadow fell upon the water as I passed, and he looked up and saw me.

'G' day,' he said, his mouth opening in a grin.

'Good afternoon,' I said.

He scrambled to his feet and opened a dirty handkerchief he had filled with winkles.

'You eat winkles?' he said.

I did not want to hurt his feelings. 'Thank you,' I said.

He emptied about a dozen winkles into my hand, and I put them in the two pockets of my skirt. 'They'm all right with bread-an'-butter,' he said, 'you must boil 'em first.'

'Yes, all right,' I said.

He stood there grinning at me. 'Seen the steamer?' he said.

'Yes,' I said, 'she's gone ashore, hasn't she?'

'Eh?' he said.

'She's run aground,' I repeated. 'I expect she's got a hole in her bottom.'

His face went blank and foolish. 'Aye,' he said, 'she's down there all right. She'll not come back again.'

'Perhaps the tugs will get her off when the tide makes,' I said.

He did not answer. He was staring out towards the stranded ship. I could see her broadside on from here, the red underwater

289

section showing against the black of the top-sides, and the single funnel leaning rakishly towards the cliffs beyond. The crew were still leaning over her side feeding the gulls and staring into the water. The rowing boats were pulling back to Kerrith.

'She's a Dutchman, ain't she?' said Ben.

'I don't know,' I said. 'German or Dutch.'

'She'll break up there where she's to,' he said.

'I'm afraid so,' I said.

He grinned again, and wiped his nose with the back of his hand.

'She'll break up bit by bit,' he said, 'she'll not sink like a stone like the little 'un.' He chuckled to himself, picking his nose. I did not say anything. 'The fishes have eaten her up by now, haven't they?' he said.

'Who?' I said.

He jerked his thumb towards the sea. 'Her,' he said, 'the other one.'

'Fishes don't eat steamers, Ben,' I said.

'Eh?' he said. He stared at me, foolish and blank once more.

'I must go home now,' I said; 'good-afternoon.'

I left him and walked towards the path through the woods. I did not look at the cottage. I was aware of it on my right hand; grey and quiet. I went straight to the path and up through the trees. I paused to rest half-way and looking through the trees I could still see the stranded ship leaning towards the shore. The pleasure boats had all gone. Even the crew had disappeared below. The ridges of cloud covered the whole sky. A little wind sprang from nowhere and blew into my face. A leaf fell onto my hand from the tree above. I shivered for no reason. Then the wind went again, it was hot and sultry as before. The ship looked desolate there upon her side, with no one on her decks, and her thin black funnel pointing to the shore. The sea was so calm that when it broke upon the shingle in the cove it was like a whisper, hushed and still. I turned once more to the steep path through the woods, my legs reluctant, my head heavy, a strange sense of foreboding in my heart.

The house looked very peaceful as I came upon it from the woods and crossed the lawns. It seemed sheltered and protected, more beautiful than I had ever seen it. Standing there, looking down upon it from the banks, I realized, perhaps for the first time, with a funny feeling of bewilderment and pride that it was my home, I belonged there, and Manderley belonged to me. The trees and the grass and the flower tubs on the terrace were reflected in the mullioned windows. A thin column of smoke rose in the air from one of the chimneys. The new-cut grass on the lawn smelt sweet as hay. A blackbird was singing on the chestnut tree. A yellow butterfly winged his foolish way before me to the terrace.

I went into the hall and through to the dining-room. My place was still laid, but Maxim's had been cleared away. The cold meat and salad awaited me on the sideboard. I hesitated, and then rang the dining-room bell. Robert came in from behind the screen.

'Has Mr de Winter been in?' I said.

'Yes, Madam,' said Robert; 'he came in just after two, and had a quick lunch, and then went out again. He asked for you and Frith said he thought you must have gone down to see the ship.'

'Did he say when he would be back again?' I asked.

'No, Madam.'

'Perhaps he went to the beach another way,' I said; 'I may have missed him.'

'Yes, Madam,' said Robert.

I looked at the cold meat and the salad. I felt empty but not hungry. I did not want cold meat now. 'Will you be taking lunch?' said Robert.

'No,' I said, 'No, you might bring me some tea, Robert, in the library. Nothing like cakes or scones. Just tea and bread-and-butter.'

'Yes, Madam.'

I went and sat on the window-seat in the library. It seemed funny without Jasper. He must have gone with Maxim. The old dog lay asleep in her basket. I picked up *The Times* and turned the pages without reading it. It was queer this feeling of marking time, like sitting in a waiting-room at a dentist's. I knew I should never settle to my knitting or to a book. I was waiting for something to happen, something unforeseen. The horror of my morning and the stranded ship and not having any lunch had all combined to give birth to a latent sense of excitement at the back of my mind that I did not understand. It was as though I had entered into a new phase of my life and nothing would be quite the same again. The girl who had dressed for the fancy dress ball the night before had been left behind. It had all happened a very long time ago. This self who sat on the window-seat was new, was different . . . Robert brought in my tea, and I ate my bread-and-butter hungrily. He had brought scones as well, and some sandwiches, and an angel cake. He must have thought it derogatory to bring bread-and-butter alone, nor was it Manderley routine. I was glad of the scones and the angel cake. I remembered I had only had cold tea at half past eleven, and no breakfast. Just after I had drunk my third cup Robert came in again.

'Mr de Winter is not back yet is he, Madam?' he said.

'No,' I said. 'Why? Does someone want him?'

'Yes, Madam,' said Robert, 'it's Captain Searle, the harbour-master of Kerrith, on the telephone. He wants to know if he can come up and see Mr de Winter personally.'

'I don't know what to say,' I said. 'He may not be back for ages.'

'No, Madam.'

'You'd better tell him to ring again at five o'clock,' I said. Robert went out of the room and came back again in a few minutes.

'Captain Searle would like to see you, if it would be conven-ient, Madam,' said Robert. 'He says the matter is rather urgent. He tried to get Mr Crawley, but there was no reply.'

'Yes, of course I must see him if it's urgent,' I said. 'Tell him to come along at once if he likes. Has he got a car?'

'Yes, I believe so, Madam.'

Robert went out of the room. I wondered what I should say to Captain Searle. His business must be something to do with the stranded ship. I could not understand what concern it was of Maxim's. It would have been different if the ship had gone ashore in the cove. That was Manderley property. They might have to ask Maxim's permission to blast away rocks or whatever it was that was done to move a ship. But the open bay and the ledge of rock under the water did not belong to Maxim. Captain Searle would waste his time talking to me about it all.

He must have got into his car right away after talking to Robert because in less than quarter of an hour he was shown into the room.

He was still in his uniform as I had seen him through the glasses in the early afternoon. I got up from the window-seat and shook hands with him. 'I'm sorry my husband isn't back yet, Captain Searle,' I said; 'he must have gone down to the cliffs again, and he went into Kerrith before that. I haven't seen him all day.'

'Yes, I heard he'd been to Kerrith but I missed him there,' said the harbour-master. 'He must have walked back across the cliffs when I was in my boat. And I can't get hold of Mr Crawley either.'

'I'm afraid the ship has disorganized everybody,' I said. 'I was out on the cliffs and went without my lunch, and I know Mr Crawley was there earlier on. What will happen to her? Will tugs get her off, do you think?'

Captain Searle made a great circle with his hands. 'There's a hole that deep in her bottom,' he said, 'she'll not see Hamburg again. Never mind the ship. Her owner and Lloyd's agent will settle that between them. No, Mrs de Winter, it's not the ship that's brought me here. Indirectly of course she's the cause of my coming. The fact is, I've got some news for Mr de Winter, and I hardly know how to break it to him.' He looked at me very straight with his bright blue eyes.

'What sort of news, Captain Searle?'

He brought a large white handkerchief out of his pocket and

293

blew his nose. 'Well, Mrs de Winter, it's not very pleasant for me to tell you either. The last thing I want to do is to cause distress or pain to you and your husband. We're all very fond of Mr de Winter in Kerrith, you know, and the family has always done a lot of good. It's hard on him and hard on you that we can't let the past lie quiet. But I don't see how we can under the circumstances.' He paused, and put his handkerchief back in his pocket. He lowered his voice, although we were alone in the room.

'We sent the diver down to inspect the ship's bottom,' he said, 'and while he was down there he made a discovery. It appears he found the hole in the ship's bottom and was working round to the other side to see what further damage there was when he came across the hull of a little sailing boat, lying on her side, quite intact and not broken up at all. He's a local man, of course, and he recognized the boat at once. It was the little boat belonging to the late Mrs de Winter.'

My first feeling was one of thankfulness that Maxim was not there to hear. This fresh blow coming swiftly upon my masquerade of the night before was ironic, and rather horrible.

'I'm so sorry,' I said slowly, 'it's not the sort of thing one expected would happen. Is it necessary to tell Mr de Winter? Couldn't the boat be left there, as it is? It's not doing any harm, is it?'

'It would be left, Mrs de Winter, in the ordinary way. I'm the last man in the world to want to disturb it. And I'd give anything, as I said before, to spare Mr de Winter's feelings. But that wasn't all, Mrs de Winter. My man poked round the little boat and he made another, more important discovery. The cabin door was tightly closed, it was not stove in, and the portlights were closed too. He broke one of the ports with a stone from the sea bed, and looked into the cabin. It was full of water, the sea must have come through some hole in the bottom, there seemed no damage elsewhere. And then he got the fright of his life, Mrs de Winter.'

Captain Searle paused, he looked over his shoulder as though one of the servants might hear him. 'There was a body in there, lying on the cabin floor,' he said quietly. 'It was dissolved of course, there was no flesh on it. But it was a body all right. He saw the head and the limbs. He came up to the surface then and reported it direct to me. And now you understand, Mrs de Winter, why I've got to see your husband.'

I stared at him, bewildered at first, then shocked, then rather sick.

'She was supposed to be sailing alone?' I whispered, 'there must have been someone with her then, all the time, and no one ever knew?'

'It looks like it,' said the harbour-master.

'Who could it have been?' I said. 'Surely relatives would know if anyone had been missing? There was so much about it at the time, it was all in the papers. Why should one of them be in the cabin and Mrs de Winter herself be picked up many miles away, months afterwards?'

Captain Searle shook his head. 'I can't tell any more than you,' he said. 'All we know is that the body is there, and it has got to be reported. There'll be publicity, I'm afraid, Mrs de Winter. I don't know how we're going to avoid it. It's very hard on you and Mr de Winter. Here you are, settled down quietly, wanting to be happy, and this has to happen.'

I knew now the reason for my sense of foreboding. It was not the stranded ship that was sinister, nor the crying gulls, nor the thin black funnel pointing to the shore. It was the stillness of the black water, and the unknown things that lay beneath. It was the diver going down into those cool quiet depths and stumbling upon Rebecca's boat, and Rebecca's dead companion. He had touched the boat, had looked into the cabin, and all the while I sat on the cliffs and had not known.

'If only we did not have to tell him,' I said. 'If only we could keep the whole thing from him.'

'You know I would if it were possible, Mrs de Winter,' said the harbour-master, 'but my personal feelings have to go, in a matter like this. I've got to do my duty. I've got to report that body.' He broke off short as the door opened, and Maxim came into the room.

'Hullo,' he said, 'what's happening? I didn't know you were here, Captain Searle? Is anything the matter?'

I could not stand it any longer. I went out of the room like the coward I was and shut the door behind me. I had not even glanced at Maxim's face. I had the vague impression that he looked tired, untidy, hatless.

I went and stood in the hall by the front door. Jasper was drinking noisily from his bowl. He wagged his tail when he saw me and went on drinking. Then he loped towards me, and stood up, pawing at my dress. I kissed the top of his head and went and sat on the terrace. The moment of crisis had come, and I must face it. My old fears, my diffidence, my shyness, my hopeless sense of inferiority, must be conquered now and thrust aside. If I failed now I should fail for ever. There would never be another chance. I prayed for courage in a blind despairing way, and dug my nails into my hands. I sat there for five minutes staring at the green lawns and the flower tubs on the terrace. I heard the sound of a car starting up in the drive. It must be Captain Searle. He had broken his news to Maxim and had gone. I got up from the terrace and went slowly through the hall to the library. I kept turning over in my pockets the winkles that Ben had given me. I clutched them tight in my hands.

Maxim was standing by the window. His back was turned to me. I waited by the door. Still he did not turn round. I took my hands out of my pockets and went and stood beside him. I reached out for his hand and laid it against my cheek. He did not say anything. He went on standing there.

'I'm so sorry,' I whispered, 'so terribly, terribly sorry.' He did not answer. His hand was icy cold. I kissed the back of it, and then the fingers, one by one. 'I don't want you to bear this alone,' I said. 'I want to share it with you. I've grown up, Maxim, in twenty-four hours. I'll never be a child again.'

He put his arm round me and pulled me to him very close. My reserve was broken, and my shyness too. I stood there with my face against his shoulder. 'You've forgiven me, haven't you?' I said.

He spoke to me at last. 'Forgiven you?' he said. 'What have I got to forgive you for?'

'Last night,' I said; 'you thought I did it on purpose.'

'Ah, that,' he said. 'I'd forgotten. I was angry with you, wasn't I?'

'Yes,' I said.

He did not say any more. He went on holding me close to his shoulder. 'Maxim,' I said, 'can't we start all over again? Can't we begin from today, and face things together? I don't want you to love me, I won't ask impossible things. I'll be your friend and your companion, a sort of boy. I don't ever want more than that.'

He took my face between his hands and looked at me. For the first time I saw how thin his face was, how lined and drawn. And there were great shadows beneath his eyes.

'How much do you love me?' he said.

I could not answer. I could only stare back at him, at his dark tortured eyes, and his pale drawn face.

'It's too late, my darling, too late,' he said. 'We've lost our little chance of happiness.'

'No, Maxim. No,' I said.

'Yes,' he said. 'It's all over now. The thing has happened.'

'What thing?' I said.

'The thing I've always foreseen. The thing I've dreamt about, day after day, night after night. We're not meant for happiness, you and I.' He sat down on the window-seat, and I knelt in front of him, my hands on his shoulders.

'What are you trying to tell me?' I said.

He put his hands over mine and looked into my face. 'Rebecca has won,' he said.

I stared at him, my heart beating strangely, my hands suddenly cold beneath his hands.

'Her shadow between us all the time,' he said. 'Her damned shadow keeping us from one another. How could I hold you like this, my darling, my little love, with the fear always in my heart that this would happen? I remembered her eyes as she looked at me before she died. I remembered that slow treacherous smile.

She knew this would happen even then. She knew she would win in the end.'

'Maxim,' I whispered, 'what are you saying, what are you trying to tell me?'

'Her boat,' he said, 'they've found it. The diver found it this afternoon.'

'Yes,' I said. 'I know. Captain Searle came to tell me. You are thinking about the body, aren't you, the body the diver found in the cabin?'

'Yes,' he said.

'It means she was not alone,' I said. 'It means there was somebody sailing with Rebecca at the time. And you have to find out who it was. That's it, isn't it, Maxim?'

'No,' he said. 'No, you don't understand.'

'I want to share this with you, darling,' I said. 'I want to help you.'

'There was no one with Rebecca, she was alone,' he said.

I knelt there watching his face, watching his eyes.

'It's Rebecca's body lying there on the cabin floor,' he said.

'No,' I said. 'No.'

'The woman buried in the crypt is not Rebecca,' he said. 'It's the body of some unknown woman, unclaimed, belonging nowhere. There never was an accident. Rebecca was not drowned at all. I killed her. I shot Rebecca in the cottage in the cove. I carried her body to the cabin, and took the boat out that night and sunk it there, where they found it today. It's Rebecca who's lying dead there on the cabin floor. Will you look into my eyes and tell me that you love me now?'

# 20

It was very quiet in the library. The only sound was that of Jasper licking his foot. He must have caught a thorn in his pads, for he kept biting and sucking at the skin. Then I heard the watch on Maxim's wrist ticking close to my ear. The little normal sounds of every day. And for no reason the stupid proverb of my schooldays ran through my mind, 'Time and Tide wait for no man.' The words repeated themselves over and over again. 'Time and Tide wait for no man.' These were the only sounds then, the ticking of Maxim's watch and Jasper licking his foot on the floor beside me.

When people suffer a great shock, like death, or the loss of a limb, I believe they don't feel it just at first. If your hand is taken from you you don't know, for a few minutes, that your hand is gone. You go on feeling the fingers. You stretch and beat them on the air, one by one, and all the time there is nothing there, no hand, no fingers. I knelt there by Maxim's side, my body against his body, my hands upon his shoulders, and I was aware of no feeling at all, no pain and no fear, there was no horror in my heart. I thought how I must take the thorn out of Jasper's foot and I wondered if Robert would come in and clear the tea-things. It seemed strange to me that I should think of these things, Jasper's foot, Maxim's watch, Robert and the tea things. I was shocked at my lack of emotion and this queer cold absence of distress. Little by little the feeling will come back to me, I said to myself, little by little I shall understand. What he has told me and all that has happened will tumble into place like pieces of a jig-saw puzzle. They will fit themselves into a pattern. At the moment I am nothing, I have no heart, and no mind, and no senses, I am just a wooden thing in Maxim's arms.

Then he began to kiss me. He had not kissed me like this before. I put my hands behind his head and shut my eyes.

'I love you so much,' he whispered. 'So much.'

This is what I have wanted him to say every day and every night, I thought, and now he is saying it at last. This is what I imagined in Monte Carlo, in Italy, here in Manderley. He is saying it now. I opened my eyes and looked at a little patch of curtain above his head. He went on kissing me, hungry, desperate, murmuring my name. I kept on looking at the patch of curtain, and saw where the sun had faded it, making it lighter than the piece above. 'How calm I am,' I thought. 'How cool. Here I am looking at the piece of curtain, and Maxim is kissing me. For the first time he is telling me he loves me.'

Then he stopped suddenly, he pushed me away from him, and got up from the window-seat. 'You see, I was right,' he said. 'It's too late. You don't love me now. Why should you?' He went and stood over by the mantelpiece. 'We'll forget that,' he said, 'it won't happen again.'

Realization flooded me at once, and my heart jumped in quick and sudden panic. 'It's not too late,' I said swiftly, getting up from the floor and going to him, putting my arms about him; 'you're not to say that, you don't understand. I love you more than anything in the world. But when you kissed me just now I felt stunned and shaken. I could not feel anything. I could not grasp anything. It was just as though I had no more feeling left in me at all.'

'You don't love me,' he said, 'that's why you did not feel anything. I know. I understand. It's come too late for you, hasn't it?'

'No,' I said.

'This ought to have happened four months ago,' he said. 'I should have known. Women are not like men.'

'I want you to kiss me again,' I said; 'please, Maxim.'

'No,' he said, 'it's no use now.'

'We can't lose each other now,' I said. 'We've got to be together always, with no secrets, no shadows. Please, darling, please.'

'There's no time,' he said. 'We may only have a few hours, a few days. How can we be together now that this has happened? I've told you they've found the boat. They've found Rebecca.'

I stared at him stupidly, not understanding. 'What will they do?' I said.

'They'll identify her body,' he said, 'there's everything to tell them, there in the cabin. The clothes she had, the shoes, the rings on her fingers. They'll identify her body; and then they will remember the other one, the woman buried up there, in the crypt.'

'What are you going to do?' I whispered.

'I don't know,' he said. 'I don't know.'

The feeling was coming back to me, little by little, as I knew it would. My hands were cold no longer. They were clammy, warm. I felt a wave of colour come into my face, my throat. My cheeks were burning hot. I thought of Captain Searle, the diver, the Lloyd's agent, all those men on the stranded ship leaning against the side, staring down into the water. I thought of the shopkeepers in Kerrith, of errand boys whistling in the street, of the vicar walking out of church, of Lady Crowan cutting roses in her garden, of the woman in the pink dress and her little boy on the cliffs. Soon they would know. In a few hours. By breakfast time tomorrow. 'They've found Mrs de Winter's boat, and they say there is a body in the cabin.' A body in the cabin. Rebecca was lying there on the cabin floor. She was not in the crypt at all. Some other woman was lying in the crypt. Maxim had killed Rebecca. Rebecca had not been drowned at all. Maxim had killed her. He had shot her in the cottage in the woods. He had carried her body to the boat, and sunk the boat there in the bay. That grey, silent cottage, with the rain pattering on the roof. The jig-saw pieces came tumbling thick and fast upon me. Disjointed pictures flashed one by one through my bewildered mind. Maxim sitting in the car beside me in the south of France. 'Something happened nearly a year ago that altered my whole life. I had to begin living all over again . . .' Maxim's silence, Maxim's moods. The way he never

301

talked about Rebecca. The way he never mentioned her name. Maxim's dislike of the cove, the stone cottage. 'If you had my memories you would not go there either.' The way he climbed the path through the woods not looking behind him. Maxim pacing up and down the library after Rebecca died. Up and down. Up and down. 'I came away in rather a hurry,' he said to Mrs Van Hopper, a line, thin as gossamer, between his brows. 'They say he can't get over his wife's death.' The fancy dress dance last night, and I coming down to the head of the stairs, in Rebecca's dress. 'I killed Rebecca,' Maxim had said. 'I shot Rebecca in the cottage in the woods.' and the diver had found her lying there, on the cabin floor . . .

'What are we going to do?' I said. 'What are we going to say?'

Maxim did not answer. He stood there by the mantelpiece, his eyes wide and staring, looking in front of him, not seeing anything.

'Does anyone know?' I said, 'anyone at all?'

He shook his head. 'No,' he said.

'No one but you and me?' I asked.

'No one but you and me,' he said.

'Frank,' I said suddenly, 'are you sure Frank does not know?'

'How could he?' said Maxim. 'There was nobody there but myself. It was dark . . .' He stopped. He sat down on a chair, he put his hand up to his forehead. I went and knelt beside him. He sat very still a moment. I took his hands away from his face and looked into his eyes. 'I love you,' I whispered, 'I love you. Will you believe me now?' He kissed my face and my hands. He held my hands very tightly like a child who would gain confidence.

'I thought I should go mad,' he said, 'sitting here, day after day, waiting for something to happen. Sitting down at the desk there, answering those terrible letters of sympathy. The notices in the papers, the interviews, all the little aftermath of death. Eating and drinking, trying to be normal, trying to be sane. Frith, the servants, Mrs Danvers. Mrs Danvers, who I had not the courage to turn away, because with her knowledge of

Rebecca she might have suspected, she might have guessed . . . Frank, always by my side, discreet, sympathetic. "Why don't you get away?" he used to say, "I can manage here. You ought to get away." And Giles, and Bee, poor dear tactless Bee. "You're looking frightfully ill, can't you go and see a doctor?" I had to face them all, these people, knowing every word I uttered was a lie.'

I went on holding his hands very tight. I leant close to him, quite close. 'I nearly told you, once,' he said, 'that day Jasper ran to the cove, and you went to the cottage for some string. We were sitting here, like this, and then Frith and Robert came in with the tea.'

'Yes,' I said. 'I remember. Why didn't you tell me? The time we've wasted when we might have been together. All these weeks and days.'

'You were so aloof,' he said, 'always wandering into the garden with Jasper, going off on your own. You never came to me like this.'

'Why didn't you tell me?' I whispered. 'Why didn't you tell me?'

'I thought you were unhappy, bored,' he said. 'I'm so much older than you. You seemed to have more to say to Frank than you ever had to me. You were funny with me, awkward, shy.'

'How could I come to you when I knew you were thinking about Rebecca?' I said. 'How could I ask you to love me when I knew you loved Rebecca still?'

He pulled me close to him and searched my eyes.

'What are you talking about? What do you mean?' he said.

I knelt up straight beside him. 'Whenever you touched me I thought you were comparing me to Rebecca,' I said. 'Whenever you spoke to me or looked at me, walked with me in the garden, sat down to dinner, I felt you were saying to yourself, "This I did with Rebecca, and this, and this."' He stared at me bewildered as though he did not understand.

'It was true, wasn't it?' I said.

'Oh, my God,' he said. He pushed me away, he got up and began walking up and down the room, clasping his hands.

303

'What is it? What's the matter?' I said.

He whipped round and looked at me as I sat there huddled on the floor. 'You thought I loved Rebecca?' he said. 'You thought I killed her, loving her? I hated her, I tell you. Our marriage was a farce from the very first. She was vicious, damnable, rotten through and through. We never loved each other, never had one moment of happiness together. Rebecca was incapable of love, of tenderness, of decency. She was not even normal.'

I sat on the floor, clasping my knees, staring at him.

'She was clever of course,' he said. 'Damnably clever. No one would guess meeting her that she was not the kindest, most generous, most gifted person in the world. She knew exactly what to say to different people, how to match her mood to theirs. Had she met you, she would have walked off into the garden with you, arm-in-arm, calling to Jasper, chatting about flowers, music, painting, whatever she knew to be your particular hobby; and you would have been taken in, like the rest. You would have sat at her feet and worshipped her.'

Up and down he walked, up and down across the library floor.

'When I married her I was told I was the luckiest man in the world,' he said. 'She was so lovely, so accomplished, so amusing. Even Gran, the most difficult person to please in those days, adored her from the first. "She's got the three things that matter in a wife," she told me: "breeding, brains, and beauty." And I believed her, or forced myself to believe her. But all the time I had a seed of doubt at the back of my mind. There was something about her eyes . . .'

The jig-saw pieces came together piece by piece, the real Rebecca took shape and form before me, stepping from her shadow world like a living figure from a picture frame. Rebecca slashing at her horse; Rebecca seizing life with her two hands; Rebecca, triumphant, leaning down from the minstrel's gallery with a smile on her lips.

Once more I saw myself standing on the beach beside poor startled Ben. 'You're kind,' he said, 'not like the other one. You won't put me to the asylum, will you?' There was someone who walked through the woods by night, someone tall and slim. She gave you the feeling of a snake . . .

Maxim was talking though. Maxim was walking up and down the library floor. 'I found her out at once,' he was saying, 'five days after we were married. You remember that time I drove you in the car, to the hills above Monte Carlo? I wanted to stand there again, to remember. She sat there, laughing, her black hair blowing in the wind; she told me about herself, told me things I shall never repeat to a living soul. I knew then what I had done, what I had married. Beauty, brains, and breeding. Oh, my God!'

He broke off abruptly. He went and stood by the window, looking out upon the lawns. He began to laugh. He stood there laughing. I could not bear it, it made me frightened, ill. I could not stand it.

'Maxim!' I cried. 'Maxim!'

He lit a cigarette, and stood there smoking, not saying anything. Then he turned away again, and paced up and down the room once more. 'I nearly killed her then,' he said. 'It would have been so easy. One false step, one slip. You remember the precipice. I frightened you, didn't I? You thought I was mad. Perhaps I was. Perhaps I am. It doesn't make for sanity, does it, living with the devil.'

I sat there watching him, up and down, up and down.

'She made a bargain with me up there, on the side of the precipice,' he said. '"I'll run your house for you," she told me, "I'll look after your precious Manderley for you, make it the most famous show-place in all the country, if you like. And people will visit us, and envy us, and talk about us; they'll say we are the luckiest, happiest, handsomest couple in all England. What a leg-pull, Max!" she said, "what a God-damn triumph!" She sat there on the hillside, laughing, tearing a flower to bits in her hands.'

Maxim threw his cigarette away, a quarter smoked, into the empty grate.

'I did not kill her,' he said. 'I watched her, I said nothing, I let her laugh. We got into the car together and drove away. And she knew I would do as she suggested: come here to Manderley, throw the place open, entertain, have our marriage spoken of as the success of the century. She knew I would sacrifice pride, honour, personal feelings, every damned quality on earth, rather than stand before our little world after a week of marriage and have them know the things about her that she had told me then. She knew I would never stand in a divorce court and give her away, have fingers pointing at us, mud flung at us in the newspapers, all the people who belong down here whispering when my name was mentioned, all the trippers from Kerrith trooping to the lodge gates, peering into the grounds and saying, "That's where he lives, in there. That's Manderley. That's the place that belongs to the chap who had that divorce case we read about. Do you remember what the judge said about his wife . . . ?"'

He came and stood before me. He held out his hands. 'You despise me, don't you?' he said. 'You can't understand my shame, and loathing and disgust?'

I did not say anything. I held his hands against my heart. I did not care about his shame. None of the things that he had told me mattered to me at all. I clung to one thing only, and repeated it to myself, over and over again. Maxim did not love Rebecca. He had never loved her, never, never. They had never known one moment's happiness together. Maxim was talking and I listened to him, but his words meant nothing to me. I did not really care. 'I thought about Manderley too much,' he said. 'I put Manderley first, before anything else. And it does not prosper, that sort of love. They don't preach about it in the churches. Christ said nothing about stones, and bricks, and walls, the love that a man can bear for his plot of earth, his soil, his little kingdom. It does not come into the Christian creed.'

'My darling,' I said, 'my Maxim, my love.' I laid his hands against my face, I put my lips against them.

'Do you understand?' he said, 'do you, do you?'

306

'Yes,' I said, 'my sweet, my love.' But I looked away from him so he should not see my face. What did it matter whether I understood him or not? My heart was light like a feather floating in the air. He had never loved Rebecca.

'I don't want to look back on those years,' he said slowly. 'I don't want even to tell you about them. The shame and the degradation. The lie we lived, she and I. The shabby, sordid farce we played together. Before friends, before relations, even before the servants, before faithful, trusting creatures like old Frith. They all believed in her down here, they all admired her, they never knew how she laughed at them behind their backs, jeered at them, mimicked them. I can remember days when the place was full for some show or other, a garden-party, a pageant, and she walked about with a smile like an angel on her face, her arm through mine, giving prizes afterwards to a little troop of children; and then the day afterwards she would be up at dawn driving to London, streaking to that flat of hers by the river like an animal to its hole in the ditch, coming back here at the end of the week, after five unspeakable days. Oh, I kept to my side of the bargain all right. I never gave her away. Her blasted taste made Manderley the thing it is today. The gardens, the shrubs, even the azaleas in the Happy Valley; do you think they existed when my father was alive? God, the place was a wilderness; lovely, yes, wild and lonely with a beauty of its own, yes, but crying out for skill and care and the money that he would never give to it, that I would not have thought of giving to it – but for Rebecca. Half the stuff you see here in the rooms was never here originally. The drawing room as it is today, the morning-room – that's all Rebecca. Those chairs that Frith points out so proudly to the visitors on the public day, and that panel of tapestry – Rebecca again. Oh, some of the things were here admittedly, stored away in back rooms – my father knew nothing about furniture or pictures – but the majority was bought by Rebecca. The beauty of Manderley that you see today, the Manderley that people talk about and photograph and paint, it's all due to her, to Rebecca.'

I did not say anything. I held him close. I wanted him to go on talking like this, that his bitterness might loosen and come away, carrying with it all the pent-up hatred and disgust and muck of the lost years.

'And so we lived,' he said, 'month after month, year after year. I accepted everything – because of Manderley. What she did in London did not touch me – because it did not hurt Manderley. And she was careful those first years; there was never a murmur about her, never a whisper. Then little by little she began to grow careless. You know how a man starts drinking? He goes easy at first, just a little at a time, a bad bout perhaps every five months or so. And then the period between grows less and less. Soon it's every month, every fortnight, every few days. There's no margin of safety left and all his secret cunning goes. It was like that with Rebecca. She began to ask her friends down here. She would have one or two of them and mix them up at a week-end party so that at first I was not quite sure, not quite certain. She would have picnics down at her cottage in the cove. I came back once, having been away shooting in Scotland, and found her there, with half a dozen of them; people I had never seen before. I warned her, and she shrugged her shoulders. "What the hell's it got to do with you?" she said. I told her she could see her friends in London, but Manderley was mine. She must stick to that part of the bargain. She smiled, she did not say anything. Then she started on Frank, poor shy faithful Frank. He came to me one day and said he wanted to leave Manderley and take another job. We argued for two hours, here in the library, and then I understood. He broke down and told me. She never left him alone, he said, she was always going down to his house, trying to get him to the cottage. Dear, wretched Frank, who had not understood, who had always thought we were the normal happy married couple we pretended to be.

'I accused Rebecca of this, and she flared up at once, cursing me, using every filthy word in her particular vocabulary. We had a sickening, loathsome scene. She went up to London after that and stayed there for a month. When she came back again she

308

was quiet at first; I thought she had learnt her lesson. Bee and Giles came for a week-end, and I realized then what I had sometimes suspected before, that Bee did not like Rebecca. I believe, in her funny abrupt, downright way she saw through her, guessed something was wrong. It was a tricky, nervy sort of week-end. Giles went out sailing with Rebecca, Bee and I lazed on the lawn. And when they came back I could tell by Giles's rather hearty jovial manner and by a look in Rebecca's eye that she had started on him, as she had done on Frank. I saw Bee watching Giles at dinner, who laughed louder than usual, talked a little too much. And all the while Rebecca sitting there at the head of the table, looking like an angel.'

They were all fitting into place, the jig-saw pieces. The odd strained shapes that I had tried to piece together with my fumbling fingers and they had never fitted. Frank's odd manner when I spoke about Rebecca. Beatrice, and her rather diffident negative attitude. The silence that I had always taken for sympathy and regret was a silence born of shame and embarrassment. It seemed incredible to me now that I had never understood. I wondered how many people there were in the world who suffered, and continued to suffer, because they could not break out from their own web of shyness and reserve, and in their blindness and folly built up a great distorted wall in front of them that hid the truth. This was what I had done. I had built up false pictures in my mind and sat before them. I had never had the courage to demand the truth. Had I made one step forward out of my own shyness, Maxim would have told me these things four months, five months ago.

'That was the last week-end Bee and Giles ever spent at Manderley,' said Maxim. 'I never asked them alone again. They came officially, to garden-parties, and dances. Bee never said a word to me or I to her. But I think she guessed my life, I think she knew. Even as Frank did. Rebecca grew cunning again. Her behaviour was faultless, outwardly. But if I happened to be away when she was here at Manderley I could never be certain what might happen. There had been Frank, and Giles. She might get hold of one of the workmen on the estate, someone from Kerrith, anyone . . . And then the bomb would have to fall. The gossip, the publicity I dreaded.'

It seemed to me I stood again by the cottage in the woods, and I heard the drip-drip of the rain upon the roof. I saw the dust on the model ships, the rat holes on the divan. I saw Ben with his poor staring idiot's eyes. 'You'll not put me to the asylum, will you?' And I thought of the dark steep path through the woods, and how, if a woman stood there behind the trees, her evening dress would rustle in the thin night breeze.

'She had a cousin,' said Maxim slowly, 'a fellow who had been abroad, and was living in England again. He took to coming here, if ever I was away. Frank used to see him. A fellow called Jack Favell.'

'I know him,' I said; 'he came here the day you went to London.'

'You saw him too?' said Maxim. 'Why didn't you tell me? I heard it from Frank, who saw his car turn in at the lodge gates.'

'I did not like to,' I said, 'I thought it would remind you of Rebecca.'

'Remind me?' whispered Maxim. 'Oh, God, as if I needed reminding.'

He stared in front of him, breaking off from his story, and I wondered if he was thinking, as I was, of that flooded cabin beneath the waters in the bay.

'She used to have this fellow Favell down to the cottage,' said Maxim, 'she would tell the servants she was going to sail, and would not be back before the morning. Then she would spend the night down there with him. Once again I warned her. I said if I found him here, anywhere on the estate, I'd shoot him. He had a black, filthy record . . . The very thought of him walking about the woods in Manderley, in places like the Happy Valley, made me mad. I told her I would not stand for it. She shrugged her shoulders. She forgot to blaspheme. And I noticed she was looking paler than usual, nervy, rather haggard. I wondered then what the hell would happen to her when she began to look old, feel old. Things drifted on. Nothing very much happened. Then one day she went up to London, and came back again the same day, which she did not do as a rule. I did not expect her. I dined that night with Frank at his house, we had a lot of work on at the time.' He was speaking now in short, jerky sentences. I had his hands very tightly between my two hands.

'I came back after dinner, about half past ten, and I saw her scarf and gloves lying on a chair in the hall. I wondered what the devil she had come back for. I went into the morning-room, but she was not there. I guessed she had gone off there then, down to the cove. And I knew then I could not stand this life of lies and filth and deceit any longer. The thing had got to be settled, one way or the other. I thought I'd take a gun and frighten the fellow, frighten them both. I went down right away to the cottage. The servants never knew I had come back to the house at all. I slipped out into the garden and through the woods. I saw the light in the cottage window, and I went straight in. To my surprise Rebecca was alone. She was lying on the divan with an ash-tray full of cigarette stubs beside her. She looked ill, queer.

'I began at once about Favell and she listened to me without a word. "We've lived this life of degradation long enough, you and I," I said. "This is the end, do you understand? What you do in London does not concern me. You can live with Favell there, or with anyone you like. But not here. Not at Manderley."

'She said nothing for a moment. She stared at me, and then she smiled. "Suppose it suits me better to live here, what then?" she said.

'"You know the conditions," I said. "I've kept my part of our dirty, damnable bargain, haven't I? But you've cheated. You think you can treat my house and my home like your own sink in London. I've stood enough, but my God, Rebecca, this is your last chance."

'I remember she squashed out her cigarette in the tub by the divan, and then she got up, and stretched herself, her arms above her head.

311

'"You're right, Max," she said. "It's time I turned over a new leaf."

'She looked very pale, very thin. She began walking up and down the room, her hands in the pockets of her trousers. She looked like a boy in her sailing kit, a boy with a face like a Botticelli angel.

'"Have you ever thought", she said, "how damned hard it would be for you to make a case against me? In a court of law, I mean. If you wanted to divorce me. Do you realize that you've never had one shred of proof against me, from the very first? All your friends, even the servants, believe our marriage to be a success."

'"What about Frank?" I said. "What about Beatrice?"

'She threw back her head and laughed. "What sort of a story could Frank tell against mine?" she said. "Don't you know me well enough for that? As for Beatrice, wouldn't it be the easiest thing in the world for her to stand in a witness-box as the ordinary jealous woman whose husband once lost his head and made a fool of himself? Oh, no, Max, you'd have a hell of a time trying to prove anything against me."

'She stood watching me, rocking on her heels, her hands in her pockets and a smile on her face. "Do you realize that I could get Danny, as my personal maid, to swear anything I asked her to swear, in a court of law? And that the rest of the servants, in blind ignorance, would follow her example and swear too? They think we live together at Manderley as husband and wife, don't they? And so does everyone, your friends, all our little world. Well, how are you going to prove that we don't?"

'She sat down on the edge of the table, swinging her legs, watching me.

'"Haven't we acted the parts of a loving husband and wife rather too well?" she said. I remember watching that foot of hers in its striped sandal swinging backwards and forwards, and my eyes and brain began to burn in a strange quick way.

'"We could make you look very foolish, Danny and I," she said softly. "We could make you look so foolish that no one

312

would believe you, Max, nobody at all." Still that foot of hers, swinging to and fro, that damned foot in its blue and white striped sandal.

'Suddenly she slipped off the table and stood in front of me, smiling still, her hands in her pockets.

'"If I had a child, Max," she said, "neither you, nor anyone in the world, would ever prove that it was not yours. It would grow up here in Manderley, bearing your name. There would be nothing you could do. And when you died Manderley would be his. You could not prevent it. The property's entailed. You would like an heir, wouldn't you, for your beloved Manderley? You would enjoy it, wouldn't you, seeing my son lying in his pram under the chestnut tree, playing leap-frog on the lawn, catching butterflies in the Happy Valley? It would give you the biggest thrill of your life, wouldn't it, Max, to watch my son grow bigger day by day, and to know that when you died, all this would be his?"

'She waited a minute, rocking on her heels, and then she lit a cigarette and went and stood by the window. She began to laugh. She went on laughing. I thought she would never stop. "God, how funny," she said, "how supremely, wonderfully funny! Well, you heard me say I was going to turn over a new leaf, didn't you? Now you know the reason. They'll be happy, won't they, all these smug locals, all your blasted tenants? 'It's what we've always hoped for, Mrs de Winter,' they will say. I'll be the perfect mother, Max, like I've been the perfect wife. And none of them will ever guess, none of them will ever know."

'She turned round and faced me, smiling, one hand in her pocket, the other holding her cigarette. When I killed her she was smiling still. I fired at her heart. The bullet passed right through. She did not fall at once. She stood there, looking at me, that slow smile on her face, her eyes wide open . . .'

Maxim's voice had sunk low, so low that it was like a whisper. The hand that I held between my own was cold. I did not look at him. I watched Jasper's sleeping body on the carpet beside me, the little thump of his tail, now and then, upon the floor.

'I'd forgotten,' said Maxim, and his voice was slow now, tired,

313

without expression, 'that when you shot a person there was so much blood.'

There was a hole there on the carpet beneath Jasper's tail. The burnt hole from a cigarette. I wondered how long it had been there. Some people said ash was good for the carpets.

'I had to get water from the cove,' said Maxim. 'I had to keep going backwards and forwards to the cove for water. Even by the fireplace, where she had not been, there was a stain. It was all round where she lay on the floor. It began to blow too. There was no catch on the window. The window kept banging backwards and forwards, while I knelt there on the floor with that dishcloth, and the bucket beside me.'

And the rain on the roof, I thought, he does not remember the rain on the roof. It pattered thin and light and very fast.

'I carried her out to the boat,' he said; 'it must have been half past eleven by then, nearly twelve. It was quite dark. There was no moon. The wind was squally, from the west. I carried her down to the cabin and left her there. Then I had to get under way, with the dinghy astern, and beat out of the little harbour against the tide. The wind was with me, but it came in puffs, and I was in the lee there, under cover of the headland. I remember I got the mainsail jammed half-way up the mast. I had not done it, you see, for a long time. I never went out with Rebecca.

'And I thought of the tide, how swift it ran and strong into the little cove. The wind blew down from the headland like a funnel. I got the boat out into the bay. I got her out there, beyond the beacon, and I tried to go about, to clear the ridge of rocks. The little jib fluttered. I could not sheet it in. A puff of wind came and the sheet tore out of my hands, went twisting round the mast. The sail thundered and shook. It cracked like a whip above my head. I could not remember what one had to do. I could not remember. I tried to reach that sheet and it blew above me in the air. Another blast of wind came straight ahead. We began to drift sideways, closer to the ridge. It was dark, so damned dark I couldn't see anything on the black, slippery deck.

Somehow I blundered down into the cabin. I had a spike with me. If I didn't do it now it would be too late. We were getting so near to the ridge, and in six or seven minutes, drifting like this, we should be out of deep water. I opened the sea-cocks. The water began to come in. I drove the spike into the bottom boards. One of the planks split right across. I took the spike out and began to drive in another plank. The water came up over my feet. I left Rebecca lying on the floor. I fastened both the scuttles. I bolted the door. When I came up on deck I saw we were within twenty yards of the ridge. I threw some of the loose stuff on the deck into the water. There was a lifebuoy, a pair of sweeps, a coil of rope. I climbed into the dinghy. I pulled away, and lay back on the paddles, and watched. The boat was drifting still. She was sinking too. Sinking by the head. The jib was still shaking and cracking like a whip. I thought someone must hear it, someone walking the cliffs late at night, some fisherman from Kerrith away beyond me in the bay, whose boat I could not see. The boat was smaller, like a black shadow on the water. The mast began to shiver, began to crack. Suddenly she heeled right over and as she went the mast broke in two, split right down the centre. The lifebuoy and the sweeps floated away from me on the water. The boat was not there any more. I remember staring at the place where she had been. Then I pulled back to the cove. It started raining.'

Maxim waited. He stared in front of him still. Then he looked at me, sitting beside him on the floor.

'That's all,' he said, 'there's no more to tell. I left the dinghy on the buoy, as she would have done. I went back and looked at the cottage. The floor was wet with the salt water. She might have done it herself. I walked up the path through the woods. I went into the house. Up the stairs to the dressing-room. I remember undressing. It began to blow and rain very hard. I was sitting there, on the bed, when Mrs Danvers knocked on the door. I went and opened it, in my dressing-gown, and spoke to her. She was worried about Rebecca. I told her to go back to bed. I shut the door again. I went back and sat by the window in my dressing-gown, watching the rain, listening to the sea as it broke there, in the cove.'

We sat there together without saying anything. I went on holding his cold hands. I wondered why Robert did not come to clear the tea.

'She sank too close in,' said Maxim. 'I meant to take her right out in the bay. They would never have found her there. She was too close in.'

'It was the ship,' I said; 'it would not have happened but for the ship. No one would have known.'

'She was too close in,' said Maxim.

We were silent again. I began to feel very tired.

'I knew it would happen one day,' said Maxim, 'even when I went up to Edgecoombe and identified that body as hers. I knew it meant nothing, nothing at all. It was only a question of waiting, of marking time. Rebecca would win in the end. Finding you has not made any difference has it? Loving you does not alter things at all. Rebecca knew she would win in the end. I saw her smile, when she died.'

'Rebecca is dead,' I said. 'That's what we've got to remember. Rebecca is dead. She can't speak, she can't bear witness. She can't harm you any more.'

'There's her body,' he said, 'the diver has seen it. It's lying there, on the cabin floor.'

'We've got to explain it,' I said. 'We've got to think out a way to explain it. It's got to be the body of someone you don't know. Someone you've never seen before.'

'Her things will be there still,' he said. 'The rings on her fingers. Even if her clothes have rotted in the water there will be something there to tell them. It's not like a body lost at sea, battered against rocks. The cabin is untouched. She must be lying there on the floor as I left her. The boat has been there, all these months. No one has moved anything. There is the boat, lying on the sea-bed where she sank.'

'A body rots in water, doesn't it?' I whispered; 'even if it's lying there, undisturbed, the water rots it, doesn't it?'

'I don't know,' he said. 'I don't know.'

'How will you find out? how will you know?' I said.

'The diver is going down again at five-thirty tomorrow morning,' said Maxim. 'Searle has made all the arrangements. They are going to try to raise the boat. No one will be about. I'm going with them. He's sending his boat to pick me up in the cove. Five-thirty tomorrow morning.'

'And then?' I said, 'if they get it up, what then?'

'Searle's going to have his big lighter anchored there, just out in the deep water. If the boat's wood has not rotted, if it still holds together, his crane will be able to lift it on to the lighter. They'll go back to Kerrith then. Searle says he will moor the lighter at the head of that disused creek half-way up Kerrith harbour. It drives out very easily. It's mud there at low water and the trippers can't row up there. We shall have the place to ourselves. He says we'll have to let the water drain out of the boat, leaving the cabin bare. He's going to get hold of a doctor.'

'What will he do?' I said. 'What will the doctor do?'

'I don't know,' he said.

'If they find out it's Rebecca you must say the other body was a mistake,' I said. 'You must say that the body in the crypt was a mistake, a ghastly mistake. You must say that when you went to Edgecoombe you were ill, you did not know what you were doing. You were not sure, even then. You could not tell. It was a mistake, just a mistake. You will say that, won't you?'

'Yes,' he said. 'Yes.'

'They can't prove anything against you,' I said. 'Nobody saw you that night. You had gone to bed. They can't prove anything. No one knows but you and I. No one at all. Not even Frank. We are the only two people in the world to know, Maxim. You and I.'

'Yes,' he said. 'Yes.'

'They will think the boat capsized and sank when she was in the cabin,' I said; 'they will think she went below for a rope, for something, and while she was there the wind came from the

317

headland, and the boat heeled over, and Rebecca was trapped. They'll think that, won't they?'

'I don't know,' he said. 'I don't know.'

Suddenly the telephone began ringing in the little room behind the library.

# 21

Maxim went into the little room and shut the door. Robert came in a few minutes afterwards to clear away the tea. I stood up, my back turned to him so that he should not see my face. I wondered when they would begin to know, on the estate, in the servants' hall, in Kerrith itself. I wondered how long it took for news to trickle through.

I could hear the murmur of Maxim's voice in the little room beyond. I had a sick expectant feeling at the pit of my stomach. The sound of the telephone ringing seemed to have woken every nerve in my body. I had sat there on the floor beside Maxim in a sort of dream, his hand in mine, my face against his shoulder. I had listened to his story, and part of me went with him like a shadow in his tracks. I too had killed Rebecca, I too had sunk the boat there in the bay. I had listened beside him to the wind and water. I had waited for Mrs Danvers' knocking on the door. All this I had suffered with him, all this and more beside. But the rest of me sat there on the carpet, unmoved and detached, thinking and caring for one thing only, repeating a phrase over and over again, 'He did not love Rebecca, he did not love Rebecca.' Now, at the ringing of the telephone, these two selves merged and became one again. I was the self that I had always been, I was not changed. But something new had come upon me that had not been before. My heart, for all its anxiety and doubt, was light and free. I knew then that I was no longer afraid of Rebecca. I did not hate her any more. Now that I knew her to have been evil and vicious and rotten I did not hate her any more. She could not hurt me. I could go to the morning-room and sit down at her desk and touch her pen and look at her writing on the pigeon-holes, and I should not mind. I could go to her room in the west wing, stand by the window even as I had done this morning, and I should not be afraid. Rebecca's power had dissolved into the air, like the mist had done. She would never haunt me again. She would never stand behind me on the stairs, sit beside me in the dining-room, lean down from the gallery and watch me standing in the hall. Maxim had never loved her. I did not hate her any more. Her body had come back, her boat had been found with its queer prophetic name, *Je Reviens*, but I was free of her forever.

I was free now to be with Maxim, to touch him, and hold him, and love him. I would never be a child again. It would not be I, I, I any longer; it would be we, it would be us. We would be together. We would face this trouble together, he and I. Captain Searle, and the diver, and Frank, and Mrs Danvers, and Beatrice, and the men and women of Kerrith reading their newspapers, could not break us now. Our happiness had not come too late. I was not young any more. I was not shy. I was not afraid. I would fight for Maxim. I would lie and perjure and swear, I would blaspheme and pray. Rebecca had not won. Rebecca had lost.

Robert had taken away the tea and Maxim came back into the room.

'It was Colonel Julyan,' he said; 'he's just been talking to Searle. He's coming out with us to the boat tomorrow. Searle has told him.'

'Why Colonel Julyan, why?' I said.

'He's the magistrate for Kerrith. He has to be present.'

'What did he say?'

'He asked me if I had any idea whose body it could be.'

'What did you say?'

'I said I did not know. I said we believed Rebecca to be alone. I said I did not know of any friend.'

'Did he say anything after that?'

'Yes.'

'What did he say?'

'He asked me if I thought it possible that I made a mistake when I went up to Edgecoombe?'

'He said that? He said that already?'

'Yes.'

'And you?'

'I said it might be possible. I did not know.'

'He'll be with you then tomorrow when you look at the boat? He, and Captain Searle, and a doctor.'

'Inspector Welch too.'

'Inspector Welch?'

'Yes.'

'Why? Why Inspector Welch?'

'It's the custom, when a body has been found.'

I did not say anything. We stared at one another. I felt the little pain come again at the pit of my stomach.

'They may not be able to raise the boat,' I said.

'No.' he said.

'They couldn't do anything then about the body, could they?' I said.

'I don't know,' he said.

He glanced out of the window. The sky was white and over-cast as it had been when I came away from the cliffs. There was no wind though. It was still and quiet.

'I thought it might blow from the south-west about an hour ago but the wind has died away again,' he said.

'Yes,' I said.

'It will be a flat calm tomorrow for the diver,' he said.

The telephone began ringing again from the little room. There was something sickening about the shrill urgent summons of the bell. Maxim and I looked at one another. Then he went into the room to answer it, shutting the door behind him as he had done before. The queer nagging pain had not left me yet. It returned again in greater force with the ringing of the bell. The feel of it took me back across the years to my childhood. This was the pain I had known when I was very small and the maroons had sounded in the streets of London, and I had sat, shivering, not understanding, under a little cupboard beneath the stairs. It was the same feeling, the same pain.

Maxim came back into the library. 'It's begun,' he said slowly.

'What do you mean? What's happened?' I said, grown suddenly cold.

'It was a reporter,' he said, 'the fellow from the *County Chronicle*. Was it true, he said, that the boat belonging to the late Mrs de Winter had been found.'

'What did you say?'

'I said yes, a boat had been found, but that was all we know. It might not be her boat at all.'

'Was that all he said?'

'No. He asked if I could confirm the rumour that a body had been found in the cabin.'

'No!'

'Yes. Someone must have been talking. Not Searle, I know that. The diver, one of his friends. You can't stop these people. The whole story will be all over Kerrith by breakfast time tomorrow.'

'What did you say, about the body?'

'I said I did not know. I had no statement to make. And I should be obliged if he did not ring me up again.'

'You will irritate them. You will have them against you.'

'I can't help that. I don't make statements to newspapers. I won't have those fellows ringing up and asking questions.'

'We might want them on our side,' I said.

'If it comes to fighting, I'll fight alone,' he said. 'I don't want a newspaper behind me.'

'The reporter will ring up someone else,' I said. 'He will get on to Colonel Julyan or Captain Searle.'

'He won't get much change out of them,' said Maxim.

'If only we could do something,' I said, 'all these hours ahead of us, and we sit here, idle, waiting for tomorrow morning.'

'There's nothing we can do,' said Maxim.

We went on sitting in the library. Maxim picked up a book but I know he did not read. Now and again I saw him lift his

322

head and listen, as though he heard the telephone again. But it did not ring again. No one disturbed us. We dressed for dinner as usual. It seemed incredible to me that this time last night I had been putting on my white dress, sitting before the mirror at my dressing-table, arranging the curled wig. It was like an old forgotten nightmare, something remembered months afterwards with doubt and disbelief. We had dinner. Frith served us, returned from his afternoon. His face was solemn, expressionless. I wondered if he had been in Kerrith, if he had heard anything.

After dinner we went back again to the library. We did not talk much. I sat on the floor at Maxim's feet, my head against his knees. He ran his fingers through my hair. Different from his old abstracted way. It was not like stroking Jasper any more. I felt his finger tips on the scalp of my head. Sometimes he kissed me. Sometimes he said things to me. There were no shadows between us any more, and when we were silent it was because the silence came to us of our own asking. I wondered how it was I could be so happy when our little world about us was so black. It was a strange sort of happiness. Not what I had dreamt about or expected. It was not the sort of happiness I had imagined in the lonely hours. There was nothing feverish or urgent about this. It was a quiet, still happiness. The library windows were open wide, and when we did not talk or touch one another we looked out at the dark dull sky.

It must have rained in the night, for when I woke the next morning, just after seven, and got up, and looked out of the window, I saw the roses in the garden below were folded and drooping, and the grass banks leading to the woods were wet and silver. There was a little smell in the air of mist and damp, the smell that comes with the first fall of the leaf. I wondered if autumn would come upon us two months before her time. Maxim had not woken me when he got up at five. He must have crept from his bed and gone through the bathroom to his dressing-room without a sound. He would be down there now, in the bay, with Colonel Julyan, and Captain Searle, and the men from the lighter. The lighter would be there, the crane and the chain, and Rebecca's boat coming to the surface. I thought about it calmly, coolly, without feeling. I pictured them all down there in the bay, and the little dark hull of the boat rising slowly to the surface, sodden, dripping, the grass-green seaweed and shells clinging to her sides. When they lifted her on to the lighter the water would stream from her sides, back into the sea again. The wood of the little boat would look soft and grey, pulpy in places. She would smell of mud and rust, and that dark weed that grows deep beneath the sea beside rocks that are never uncovered. Perhaps the name-board still hung upon her stern. *Je Reviens.* The lettering green and faded. The nails rusted through. And Rebecca herself was there, lying on the cabin floor.

I got up and had my bath and dressed, and went down to breakfast at nine o'clock as usual. There were a lot of letters on my plate. Letters from people thanking us for the dance. I skimmed through them, I did not read them all. Frith wanted to know whether to keep the breakfast hot for Maxim. I told him I did not know when he would be back. He had to go out very early, I said. Frith did not say anything. He looked very solemn, very grave. I wondered again if he knew.

After breakfast I took my letters along to the morning-room. The room smelt fusty, the windows had not been opened. I flung them wide, letting in the cool fresh air. The flowers on the mantelpiece were drooping, many of them dead. The petals lay on the floor. I rang the bell, and Maud, the under-housemaid, came into the room.

'This room has not been touched this morning,' I said, 'even the windows were shut. And the flowers are dead. Will you please take them away?'

She looked nervous and apologetic. 'I'm very sorry, Madam,' she said. She went to the mantelpiece and took the vases.

'Don't let it happen again,' I said.

'No, Madam,' she said. She went out of the room, taking the flowers with her. I had not thought it would be so easy to be severe. I wondered why it had seemed hard for me before. The menu for the day lay on the writing-desk. Cold salmon and mayonnaise, cutlets in aspic, galantine of chicken, soufflé. I recognized them all from the buffet-supper of the night of the ball. We were evidently still living on the remains. This must be the cold lunch that was put out in the dining-room yesterday and I had not eaten. The staff were taking things easily, it seemed. I put a pencil through the list and rang for Robert. 'Tell Mrs Danvers to order something hot,' I said. 'If there's still a lot of cold stuff to finish we don't want it in the dining-room.'

'Very good, Madam,' he said.

I followed him out of the room and went to the little flower-room for my scissors. Then I went into the rose-garden and cut some young buds. The chill had worn away from the air. It was going to be as hot and airless as yesterday had been. I wondered if they were still down in the bay or whether they had gone back to the creek in Kerrith harbour. Presently I should hear. Presently Maxim would come back and tell me. Whatever happened I must be calm and quiet. Whatever happened I must not be afraid. I cut my roses and took them back into the morning-room. The carpet had been dusted, and the fallen petals removed. I began to arrange the flowers in the vases that Robert had filled with water. When I had nearly finished there was a knock on the door.

'Come in,' I said.

It was Mrs Danvers. She had the menu list in her hand. She looked pale and tired. There were great rings round her eyes.

'Good morning, Mrs Danvers,' I said.

'I don't understand', she began, 'why you sent the menu out and the message by Robert. Why did you do it?'

I looked across at her, a rose in my hand.

'Those cutlets and that salmon were sent in yesterday,' I said. 'I saw them on the side-board. I should prefer something hot today. If they won't eat the cold in the kitchen you had better throw the stuff away. So much waste goes on in this house anyway that a little more won't make any difference.'

She stared at me. She did not say anything. I put the rose in the vase with the others.

'Don't tell me you can't think of anything to give us, Mrs Danvers,' I said. 'You must have menus for all occasions in your room.'

'I'm not used to having messages sent to me by Robert,' she said. 'If Mrs de Winter wanted anything changed she would ring me personally on the house telephone.'

'I'm afraid it does not concern me very much what Mrs de Winter used to do,' I said. 'I am Mrs de Winter now, you know. And if I choose to send a message by Robert I shall do so.'

Just then Robert came into the room. 'The *County Chronicle* on the telephone, Madam,' he said.

'Tell the *County Chronicle* I'm not at home,' I said.

'Yes, Madam,' he said. He went out of the room.

'Well, Mrs Danvers, is there anything else?' I said.

She went on staring at me. Still she did not say anything. 'If you have nothing else to say you had better go and tell the cook about the hot lunch,' I said. 'I'm rather busy.'

'Why did the *County Chronicle* want to speak to you?' she said.

'I haven't the slightest idea, Mrs Danvers,' I said.

'Is it true,' she said slowly, 'the story Frith brought back with him from Kerrith last night, that Mrs de Winter's boat has been found?'

'Is there such a story?' I said. 'I'm afraid I don't know anything about it.'

'Captain Searle, the Kerrith harbour-master, called here yesterday, didn't he?' she said. 'Robert told me, Robert showed him in. Frith says the story in Kerrith is that the diver who went down about the ship there in the bay found Mrs de Winter's boat.'

'Perhaps so,' I said. 'You had better wait until Mr de Winter himself comes in and ask him about it.'

'Why was Mr de Winter up so early?' she asked.

'That was Mr de Winter's business,' I said.

She went on staring at me. 'Frith said the story goes that there was a body in the cabin of the little boat,' she said. 'Why should there be a body there? Mrs de Winter always sailed alone.'

'It's no use asking me, Mrs Danvers,' I said. 'I don't know any more than you do.'

'Don't you?' she said slowly. She kept on looking at me. I turned away, I put the vase back on the table by the window.

'I will give the orders about the lunch,' she said. She waited a moment. I did not say anything. Then she went out of the room. She can't frighten me any more, I thought. She has lost her power with Rebecca. Whatever she said or did now it could not matter to me or hurt me. I knew she was my enemy and I did not mind. But if she should learn the truth about the body in the boat and become Maxim's enemy too – what then? I sat down in the chair. I put the scissors on the table. I did not feel like doing any more roses. I kept wondering what Maxim was doing. I wondered why the reporter from the *County Chronicle* had rung us up again. The old sick feeling came back inside me. I went and leant out of the window. It was very hot. There was thunder in the air. The gardeners began to mow the grass again. I could see one of the men with his machine walk backwards and forwards on the top of the bank. I could not go on sitting in the morning-room. I left my scissors and my roses and went out on to the terrace. I began to walk up and down. Jasper padded after me, wondering why I did not take him for a walk. I went on walking up and down the terrace. About half past eleven Frith came out to me from the hall.

'Mr de Winter on the telephone, Madam,' he said.

I went through the library to the little room beyond. My hands were shaking as I lifted the receiver.

'Is that you?' he said. 'It's Maxim. I'm speaking from the office. I'm with Frank.'

'Yes?' I said.

There was a pause. 'I shall be bringing Frank and Colonel Julyan back to lunch at one o'clock,' he said.

327

'Yes,' I said.

I waited. I waited for him to go on. 'They were able to raise the boat,' he said. 'I've just got back from the creek.'

'Yes,' I said.

'Searle was there, and Colonel Julyan, and Frank, and the others,' he said. I wondered if Frank was standing beside him at the telephone, and if that was the reason he was so cool, so distant.

'All right then,' he said; 'expect us about one o'clock.'

I put back the receiver. He had not told me anything. I still did not know what had happened. I went back again to the terrace, telling Frith first that we should be four to lunch instead of two.

An hour dragged past, slow, interminable. I went upstairs and changed into a thinner frock. I came down again. I went and sat in the drawing-room and waited. At five minutes to one I heard the sound of a car in the drive, and then voices in the hall. I patted my hair in front of the looking-glass. My face was very white. I pinched some colour into my cheeks and stood up waiting for them to come into the room. Maxim came in, and Frank, and Colonel Julyan. I remembered seeing Colonel Julyan at the ball dressed as Cromwell. He looked shrunken now, different. A smaller man altogether.

'How do you do?' he said. He spoke quietly, gravely, like a doctor.

'Ask Frith to bring the sherry,' said Maxim. 'I'm going to wash.'

'I'll have a wash too,' said Frank. Before I rang the bell Frith appeared with the sherry. Colonel Julyan did not have any. I took some to give me something to hold. Colonel Julyan came and stood beside me by the window.

'This is a most distressing thing, Mrs de Winter,' he said gently. 'I do feel for you and your husband most acutely.'

'Thank you,' I said. I began to sip my sherry. Then I put the glass back again on the table. I was afraid he would notice that my hand was shaking.

'What makes it so difficult was the fact of your husband identifying that first body, over a year ago,' he said.

'I don't quite understand,' I said.

'You did not hear, then, what we found this morning?' he said.

'I knew there was a body. The diver found a body,' I said.

'Yes,' he said. And then, half glancing over his shoulder towards the hall, 'I'm afraid it was her, without a doubt,' he said, lowering his voice. 'I can't go into details with you, but the evidence was sufficient for your husband and Doctor Phillips to identify.'

He stopped suddenly, and moved away from me. Maxim and Frank had come back into the room.

'Lunch is ready; shall we go in?' said Maxim.

I led the way into the hall, my heart like a stone, heavy, numb. Colonel Julyan sat on my right, Frank on my left. I did not look at Maxim. Frith and Robert began to hand the first course. We all talked about the weather. 'I see in *The Times* they had it well over eighty in London yesterday,' said Colonel Julyan.

'Really?' I said.

'Yes. Must be frightful for the poor devils who can't get away.'

'Yes, frightful,' I said.

'Paris can be hotter than London,' said Frank. 'I remember staying a week-end in Paris in the middle of August, and it was quite impossible to sleep. There was not a breath of air in the whole city. The temperature was over ninety.'

'Of course the French always sleep with their windows shut, don't they?' said Colonel Julyan.

'I don't know,' said Frank. 'I was staying in a hotel. The people were mostly Americans.'

'You know France of course, Mrs de Winter?' said Colonel Julyan.

'Not so very well,' I said.

'Oh, I had the idea you had lived many years out there.'

'No,' I said.

'She was staying in Monte Carlo when I met her,' said Maxim. 'You don't call that France, do you?'

'No, I suppose not,' said Colonel Julyan; 'it must be very cosmopolitan. The coast is pretty though, isn't it?'

'Very pretty,' I said.

'Not so rugged as this, eh? Still, I know which I'd rather have. Give me England every time, when it comes to settling down. You know where you are over here.'

'I dare say the French feel that about France,' said Maxim.

'Oh, no doubt,' said Colonel Julyan.

We went on eating awhile in silence. Frith stood behind my chair. We were all thinking of one thing, but because of Frith we had to keep up our little performance. I suppose Frith was thinking about it too, and I thought how much easier it would be if we cast aside convention and let him join in with us, if he had anything to say. Robert came with the drinks. Our plates were changed. The second course was handed. Mrs Danvers had not forgotten my wish for hot food. I took something out of a casserole covered in mushroom sauce.

'I think everyone enjoyed your wonderful party the other night,' said Colonel Julyan.

'I'm so glad,' I said.

'Does an immense amount of good locally, that sort of thing,' he said.

'Yes, I suppose it does,' I said.

'It's a universal instinct of the human species, isn't it, that desire to dress up in some sort of disguise?' said Frank.

'I must be very inhuman, then,' said Maxim.

'It's natural, I suppose,' said Colonel Julyan, 'for all of us to wish to look different. We are all children in some ways.'

I wondered how much pleasure it had given him to disguise himself as Cromwell. I had not seen much of him at the ball. He had spent most of the evening in the morning-room, playing bridge.

'You don't play golf, do you, Mrs de Winter?' said Colonel Julyan.

'No, I'm afraid I don't,' I said.

'You ought to take it up,' he said. 'My eldest girl is very keen, and she can't find young people to play with her. I gave her a small car for her birthday, and she drives herself over to the north coast nearly every day. It gives her something to do.'

'How nice,' I said.

'She ought to have been the boy,' he said. 'My lad is different altogether. No earthly use at games. Always writing poetry. I suppose he'll grow out of it.'

'Oh, rather,' said Frank. 'I used to write poetry myself when I was his age. Awful nonsense too. I never write any now.'

'Good heavens, I should hope not,' said Maxim.

'I don't know where my boy gets it from,' said Colonel Julyan; 'certainly not from his mother or from me.'

There was another long silence. Colonel Julyan had a second dip into the casserole. 'Mrs Lacy looked very well the other night,' he said.

'Yes,' I said.

'Her dress came adrift as usual,' said Maxim.

'Those Eastern garments must be the devil to manage,' said Colonel Julyan, 'and yet they say, you know, they are far more comfortable and far cooler than anything you ladies wear in England.'

'Really?' I said.

'Yes, so they say. It seems all that loose drapery throws off the hot rays of the sun.'

'How curious,' said Frank; 'you'd think it would have just the opposite effect.'

'No, apparently not,' said Colonel Julyan.

'Do you know the East, sir?' said Frank.

'I know the Far East,' said Colonel Julyan. 'I was in China for five years. Then Singapore.'

'Isn't that where they make the curry?' I said.

'Yes, they gave us very good curry in Singapore,' he said.

'I'm fond of curry,' said Frank.

'Ah, it's not curry at all in England, it's hash,' said Colonel Julyan.

The plates were cleared away. A soufflé was handed, and a

331

bowl of fruit salad. 'I suppose you are coming to the end of your raspberries,' said Colonel Julyan. 'It's been a wonderful summer for them, hasn't it? We've put down pots and pots of jam.'

'I never think raspberry jam is a great success,' said Frank; 'there are always so many pips.'

'You must come and try some of ours,' said Colonel Julyan. 'I don't think we have a great lot of pips.'

'We're going to have a mass of apples this year at Manderley,' said Frank. 'I was saying to Maxim a few days ago we ought to have a record season. We shall be able to send a lot up to London.'

'Do you really find it pays?' said Colonel Julyan; 'by the time you've paid your men for the extra labour, and then the packing, and carting, do you make any sort of profit worth while?'

'Oh, Lord, yes,' said Frank.

'How interesting. I must tell my wife,' said Colonel Julyan.

The soufflé and the fruit salad did not take long to finish. Robert appeared with cheese and biscuits, and a few minutes later Frith came with the coffee and cigarettes. Then they both went out of the room and shut the door. We drank our coffee in silence. I gazed steadily at my plate.

'I was saying to your wife before luncheon, de Winter,' began Colonel Julyan, resuming his first quiet confidential tone, 'that the awkward part of this whole distressing business is the fact that you identified that original body.'

'Yes, quite,' said Maxim.

'I think the mistake was very natural under the circumstances,' said Frank quickly. 'The authorities wrote to Maxim, asking him to go up to Edgecoombe, presupposing before he arrived there that the body was hers. And Maxim was not well at the time. I wanted to go with him, but he insisted on going alone. He was not in a fit state to undertake anything of the sort.'

'That's nonsense,' said Maxim. 'I was perfectly well.'

'Well, it's no use going into all that now,' said Colonel Julyan. 'You made that first identification, and now the only thing to do is to admit the error. There seems to be no doubt about it this time.'

332

'No,' said Maxim.

'I wish you could be spared the formality and the publicity of an inquest,' said Colonel Julyan, 'but I'm afraid that's quite impossible.'

'Naturally,' said Maxim.

'I don't think it need take very long,' said Colonel Julyan. 'It's just a case of you re-affirming identification, and then getting Tabb, who you say converted the boat when your wife brought her from France, just to give his piece of evidence that the boat was seaworthy and in good order when he last had her in his yard. It's just red-tape, you know. But it has to be done. No, what bothers me is the wretched publicity of the affair. So sad and unpleasant for you and your wife.'

'That's quite all right,' said Maxim. 'We understand.'

'So unfortunate that wretched ship going ashore there,' said Colonel Julyan, 'but for that the whole matter would have rested in peace.'

'Yes,' said Maxim.

'The only consolation is that now we know poor Mrs de Winter's death must have been swift and sudden, not the dreadful slow lingering affair we all believed it to be. There can have been no question of trying to swim.'

'None,' said Maxim.

'She must have gone down for something, and then the door jammed, and a squall caught the boat without anyone at the helm,' said Colonel Julyan. 'A dreadful thing.'

'Yes,' said Maxim.

'That seems to be the solution, don't you think, Crawley?' said Colonel Julyan, turning to Frank.

'Oh, yes, undoubtedly,' said Frank.

I glanced up, and I saw Frank looking at Maxim. He looked away again immediately but not before I had seen and understood the expression in his eyes. Frank knew. And Maxim did not know that he knew. I went on stirring my coffee. My hand was hot, damp.

'I suppose sooner or later we all make a mistake in judgement,' said Colonel Julyan, 'and then we are for it. Mrs de Winter must have known how the wind comes down like a funnel in that bay, and that it was not safe to leave the helm of a small boat like that. She must have sailed alone over that spot scores of times. And then the moment came, she took a chance – and the chance killed her. It's a lesson to all of us.'

'Accidents happen so easily,' said Frank, 'even to the most experienced people. Think of the number killed out hunting every season.'

'Oh, I know. But then it's the horse falling generally that lets you down. If Mrs de Winter had not left the helm of her boat the accident would never have happened. An extraordinary thing to do. I must have watched her many times in the handicap race on Saturdays from Kerrith, and I never saw her make an elementary mistake. It's the sort of thing a novice would do. In that particular place too, just by the ridge.'

'It was very squally that night,' said Frank; 'something may have happened to the gear. Something may have jammed. And then she slipped down for a knife.'

'Of course. Of course. Well, we shall never know. And I don't suppose we should be any the better for it if we did. As I said before, I wish I could stop this inquest but I can't. I'm trying to arrange it for Tuesday morning, and it will be as short as possible. Just a formal matter. But I'm afraid we shan't be able to keep the reporters out of it.'

There was another silence. I judged the time had come to push back my chair.

'Shall we go into the garden?' I said.

We all stood up, and then I led the way to the terrace. Colonel Julyan patted Jasper.

'He's grown into a nice-looking dog,' he said.

'Yes,' I said.

'They make nice pets,' he said.

'Yes,' I said.

We stood about for a minute. Then he glanced at his watch.

'Thank you for your most excellent lunch,' he said. 'I have

334

rather a busy afternoon in front of me, and I hope you will excuse me dashing away.'

'Of course,' I said.

'I'm so very sorry this should have happened. You have all my sympathy. I consider it's almost harder for you than for your husband. However, once the inquest is over you must both forget all about it.'

'Yes,' I said, 'yes, we must try to.'

'My car is here in the drive. I wonder whether Crawley would like a lift. Crawley? I can drop you at your office if it's any use.'

'Thank you, sir,' said Frank.

He came and took my hand. 'I shall be seeing you again,' he said.

'Yes,' I said.

I did not look at him. I was afraid he would understand my eyes. I did not want him to know that I knew. Maxim walked with them to the car. When they had gone he came back to me on the terrace. He took my arm. We stood looking down at the green lawns towards the sea and the beacon on the headland.

'It's going to be all right,' he said. 'I'm quite calm, quite confident. You saw how Julyan was at lunch, and Frank. There won't be any difficulty at the inquest. It's going to be all right.'

I did not say anything. I held his arm tightly.

'There was never any question of the body being someone unknown,' he said. 'What we saw was enough for Doctor Phillips even to make the identification alone without me. It was straightforward, simple. There was no trace of what I'd done. The bullet had not touched the bone.'

A butterfly sped past us on the terrace, silly and inconsequent.

'You heard what they said,' he went on; 'they think she was trapped there, in the cabin. The jury will believe that at the inquest too. Phillips will tell them so.' He paused. Still I did not speak.

'I only mind for you,' he said. 'I don't regret anything else. If it had to come all over again I should not do anything different. I'm glad I killed Rebecca. I shall never have any remorse for that, never, never. But you. I can't forget what it has done to you. I was looking at you, thinking of nothing else all through lunch. It's gone forever, that funny, young, lost look that I loved. It won't come back again. I killed that too, when I told you about Rebecca . . . It's gone, in twenty-four hours. You are so much older . . .'

# 22

That evening, when Frith brought in the local paper, there were great headlines right across the top of the page. He brought the paper and laid it down on the table. Maxim was not there; he had gone up early to change for dinner. Frith stood a moment, waiting for me to say something, and it seemed to me stupid and insulting to ignore a matter that must mean so much to everyone in the house.

'This is a very dreadful thing, Frith,' I said.

'Yes, Madam; we are all most distressed outside,' he said.

'It's so sad for Mr de Winter,' I said, 'having to go through it all again.'

'Yes, Madam. Very sad. Such a shocking experience, Madam, having to identify the second body having seen the first. I suppose there is no doubt then, that the remains in the boat are genuinely those of the late Mrs de Winter?'

'I'm afraid not, Frith. No doubt at all.'

'It seems so odd to us, Madam, that she should have let herself be trapped like that in the cabin. She was so experienced in a boat.'

'Yes, Frith. That's what we all feel. But accidents will happen. And how it happened I don't suppose any of us will ever know.'

'I suppose not, Madam. But it's a great shock, all the same. We are most distressed about it outside. And coming suddenly just after the party. It doesn't seem right somehow, does it?'

'No, Frith.'

'It seems there is to be an inquest, Madam?'

'Yes. A formality, you know.'

'Of course, Madam. I wonder if any of us will be required to give evidence?'

'I don't think so.'

'I shall be only too pleased to do anything that might help the family; Mr de Winter knows that.'

'Yes, Frith. I'm sure he does.'

'I've told them outside not to discuss the matter, but it's very difficult to keep an eye on them, especially the girls. I can deal with Robert, of course. I'm afraid the news has been a great shock to Mrs Danvers.'

'Yes, Frith. I rather expected it would.'

'She went up to her room straight after lunch, and has not come down again. Alice took her a cup of tea and the paper a few minutes ago. She said Mrs Danvers looked very ill indeed.'

'It would be better really if she stayed where she is,' I said. 'It's no use her getting up and seeing to things if she is ill. Perhaps Alice would tell her that. I can very well manage the ordering. The cook and I between us.'

'Yes, Madam. I don't think she is physically ill, Madam; it's just the shock of Mrs de Winter being found. She was very devoted to Mrs de Winter.'

'Yes,' I said. 'Yes, I know.'

Frith went out of the room after that, and I glanced quickly at the paper before Maxim came down. There was a great column, all down the front page, and an awful blurred photograph of Maxim that must have been taken at least fifteen years ago. It was dreadful, seeing it there on the front page staring at me. And the little line about myself at the bottom, saying whom Maxim had married as his second wife, and how we had just given the fancy dress ball at Manderley. It sounded so crude and callous, in the dark print of the newspaper. Rebecca, whom they described as beautiful, talented, and loved by all who knew her, having been drowned a year ago, and then Maxim marrying again the following spring, bringing his bride straight to Manderley (so it said) and giving the big fancy dress ball in her honour. And then the following morning the body of his first wife being found, trapped in the cabin of her sailing boat, at the bottom of the bay.

It was true of course, though sprinkled with the little inaccuracies that added to the story, making it strong meat for the hundreds of readers who wanted value for their pennies. Maxim sounded vile in it, a sort of satyr. Bringing back his 'young bride', as it described me, to Manderley, and giving the dance, as though we wanted to display ourselves before the world.

I hid the paper under the cushion of the chair so that Maxim should not see it. But I could not keep the morning editions from him. The story was in our London papers too. There was a picture of Manderley, and the story underneath. Manderley was news, and so was Maxim. They talked about him as Max de Winter. It sounded racy, horrible. Each paper made great play of the fact that Rebecca's body had been found the day after the fancy dress ball, as though there was something deliberate about it. Both papers used the same word, 'ironic'. Yes, I suppose it was ironic. It made a good story. I watched Maxim at the breakfast table getting whiter and whiter as he read the papers, one after the other, and then the local one as well. He did not say anything. He just looked across at me, and I stretched out my hand to him. 'Damn them,' he whispered, 'damn them, damn them.'

I thought of all the things they could say, if they knew the truth. Not one column, but five or six. Placards in London. Newsboys shouting in the streets, outside the underground stations. That frightful word of six letters, in the middle of the placard, large and black.

Frank came up after breakfast. He looked pale and tired, as though he had not slept. 'I've told the exchange to put all calls for Manderley through to the office,' he said to Maxim. 'It doesn't matter who it is. If reporters ring up I can deal with them. And anyone else too. I don't want either of you to be worried at all. We've had several calls already from locals. I gave the same answer to each. Mr and Mrs de Winter were grateful for all sympathetic inquiries, and they hoped their friends would understand that they were not receiving calls during the next few days. Mrs Lacy rang up about eight-thirty. Wanted to come over at once.'

'Oh, my God . . .' began Maxim.

'It's all right, I prevented her. I told her quite truthfully that I did not think she would do any good coming over. That you did not want to see anyone but Mrs de Winter. She wanted to know when they were holding the inquest, but I told her it had not been settled. I don't know that we can stop her from coming to that, if she finds it in the papers.'

'Those blasted reporters,' said Maxim.

'I know,' said Frank; 'we all want to wring their necks, but you've got to see their point of view. It's their bread-and-butter; they've got to do the job for their paper. If they don't get a story the editor probably sacks them. If the editor does not produce a saleable edition the proprietor sacks him. And if the paper doesn't sell, the proprietor loses all his money. You won't have to see them or speak to them, Maxim. I'm going to do all that for you. All you have to concentrate on is your statement at the inquest.'

'I know what to say,' said Maxim.

'Of course you do, but don't forget old Horridge is the Coroner. He's a sticky sort of chap, goes into details that are quite irrelevant, just to show the jury how thorough he is at his job. You must not let him rattle you.'

'Why the devil should I be rattled? I have nothing to be rattled about.'

'Of course not. But I've attended these coroner's inquests before, and it's so easy to get nervy and irritable. You don't want to put the fellow's back up.'

'Frank's right,' I said. 'I know just what he means. The swifter and smoother the whole thing goes the easier it will be for everyone. Then once the wretched thing is over we shall forget all about it, and so will everyone else, won't they, Frank?'

'Yes, of course,' said Frank.

I still avoided his eye, but I was more convinced than ever that he knew the truth. He had always known it. From the very first. I remembered the first time I met him, that first day of mine at Manderley, when he, and Beatrice, and Giles had all

340

been at lunch, and Beatrice had been tactless about Maxim's health. I remembered Frank, his quiet turning of the subject, the way he had come to Maxim's aid in his quiet unobtrusive manner if there was ever any question of difficulty. That strange reluctance of his to talk about Rebecca, his stiff, funny, pompous way of making conversation whenever we had approached anything like intimacy. I understood it all. Frank knew, but Maxim did not know that he knew. And Frank did not want Maxim to know that he knew. And we all stood there, looking at one another, keeping up these little barriers between us.

We were not bothered with the telephone again. All the calls were put through to the office. It was just a question of waiting now. Waiting until the Tuesday.

I saw nothing of Mrs Danvers. The menu was sent through as usual, and I did not change it. I asked little Clarice about her. She said she was going about her work as usual but she was not speaking to anybody. She had all her meals alone in her sitting-room.

Clarice was wide-eyed, evidently curious, but she did not ask me any questions, and I was not going to discuss it with her. No doubt they talked of nothing else, out in the kitchen, and on the estate too, in the lodge, on the farms. I supposed all Kerrith was full of it. We stayed in Manderley, in the gardens close to the house. We did not even walk in the woods. The weather had not broken yet. It was still hot, oppressive. The air was full of thunder, and there was rain behind the white dull sky, but it did not fall. I could feel it, and smell it, pent up there, behind the clouds. The inquest was to be on the Tuesday afternoon at two o'clock.

We had lunch at a quarter to one. Frank came. Thank heaven Beatrice had telephoned that she could not get over. The boy Roger had arrived home with measles; they were all in quarantine. I could not help blessing the measles. I don't think Maxim could have borne it, with Beatrice sitting here, staying in the house, sincere, anxious, and affectionate, but asking questions all the time. Forever asking questions.

341

Lunch was a hurried, nervous meal. We none of us talked very much. I had that nagging pain again. I did not want anything to eat. I could not swallow. It was a relief when the farce of the meal was over, and I heard Maxim go out on to the drive and start up the car. The sound of the engine steadied me. It meant we had to go, we had to be doing something. Not just sitting at Manderley. Frank followed us in his own car. I had my hand on Maxim's knee all the way as he drove. He seemed quite calm. Not nervous in any way. It was like going with someone to a nursing-home, someone who was to have an operation. And not knowing what would happen. Whether the operation would be successful. My hands were very cold. My heart was beating in a funny, jerky way. And all the time that little nagging pain beneath my heart. The inquest was to be held at Lanyon, the market town six miles the other side of Kerrith. We had to park the cars in the big cobbled square by the market-place. Doctor Phillips' car was there already, and also Colonel Julyan's. Other cars too. I saw a passer-by stare curiously at Maxim, and then nudge her companion's arm.

'I think I shall stay here,' I said. 'I don't think I'll come in with you after all.'

'I did not want you to come,' said Maxim. 'I was against it from the first. You'd much better have stayed at Manderley.'

'No,' I said. 'No, I'll be all right here, sitting in the car.'

Frank came and looked in at the window. 'Isn't Mrs de Winter coming?' he said.

'No,' said Maxim. 'She wants to stay in the car.'

'I think she's right,' said Frank; 'there's no earthly reason why she should be present at all. We shan't be long.'

'It's all right,' I said.

'I'll keep a seat for you,' said Frank, 'in case you should change your mind.'

They went off together and left me sitting there. It was early-closing day. The shops looked drab and dull. There were not many people about. Lanyon was not much of a holiday centre anyway; it was too far inland. I sat looking at the silent shops.

The minutes went by. I wondered what they were doing, the Coroner, Frank, Maxim, Colonel Julyan. I got out of the car and began walking up and down the market square. I went and looked in a shop window. Then I walked up and down again. I saw a policeman watching me curiously. I turned up a side-street to avoid him.

Somehow, in spite of myself, I found I was coming to the building where the inquest was being held. There had been little publicity about the actual time, and because of this there was no crowd waiting, as I had feared and expected. The place seemed deserted. I went up the steps and stood just inside the door.

A policeman appeared from nowhere. 'Do you want anything?' he said.

'No,' I said. 'No.'

'You can't wait here,' he said.

'I'm sorry,' I said. I went back towards the steps into the street.

'Excuse me, Madam,' he said, 'aren't you Mrs de Winter?'

'Yes,' I said.

'Of course that's different,' he said; 'you can wait here if you like. Would you like to take a seat just inside this room?'

'Thank you,' I said.

He showed me into a little bare room with a desk in it. It was like a waiting-room at a station. I sat there, with my hands on my lap. Five minutes passed. Nothing happened. It was worse than being outside, than sitting in the car. I got up and went into the passage. The policeman was still standing there.

'How long will they be?' I said.

'I'll go and inquire if you like,' he said.

He disappeared along the passage. In a moment he came back again. 'I don't think they will be very much longer,' he said. 'Mr de Winter has just given his evidence. Captain Searle, and the diver, and Doctor Phillips have already given theirs. There's only one more to speak. Mr Tabb, the boat-builder from Kerrith.'

'Then it's nearly over,' I said.

'I expect so, Madam,' he said. Then he said, on a sudden thought, 'Would you like to hear the remaining evidence? There

343

is a seat there, just inside the door. If you slip in now nobody will notice you.'

'Yes,' I said. 'Yes, I think I will.'

It was nearly over. Maxim had finished giving his evidence. I did not mind hearing the rest. It was Maxim I had not wanted to hear. I had been nervous of listening to his evidence. That was why I had not gone with him and Frank in the first place. Now it did not matter. His part of it was over.

I followed the policeman, and he opened a door at the end of the passage. I slipped in, I sat down just by the door. I kept my head low so that I did not have to look at anybody. The room was smaller than I had imagined. Rather hot and stuffy. I had pictured a great bare room with benches, like a church. Maxim and Frank were sitting down at the other end. The Coroner was a thin, elderly man in pince-nez. There were people there I did not know. I glanced at them out of the tail of my eye. My heart gave a jump suddenly as I recognized Mrs Danvers. She was sitting right at the back. And Favell was beside her. Jack Favell, Rebecca's cousin. He was leaning forward, his chin in his hands, his eyes fixed on the Coroner, Mr Horridge. I had not expected him to be there. I wondered if Maxim had seen him. James Tabb, the boat-builder, was standing up now and the Coroner was asking him a question.

'Yes, sir,' answered Tabb, 'I converted Mrs de Winter's little boat. She was a French fishing boat originally, and Mrs de Winter bought her for next to nothing over in Brittany, and had her shipped over. She gave me the job of converting her and doing her up like a little yacht.'

'Was the boat in a fit state to put to sea?' said the Coroner.

'She was when I fitted her out in April of last year,' said Tabb. 'Mrs de Winter laid her up as usual at my yard in the October, and then in March I had word from her to fit her up as usual, which I did. That would be Mrs de Winter's fourth season with the boat since I did the conversion job for her.'

'Had the boat ever been known to capsize before?' asked the Coroner.

'No, sir. I should soon have heard of it from Mrs de Winter had there been any question of it. She was delighted with the boat in every way, according to what she said to me.'

'I suppose great care was needed to handle the boat?' said the Coroner.

'Well, sir, everyone has to have their wits about them, when they go sailing boats, I won't deny it. But Mrs de Winter's boat wasn't one of those cranky little craft that you can't leave for a moment, like some of the boats you see in Kerrith. She was a stout seaworthy boat, and could stand a lot of wind. Mrs de Winter had sailed her in worse weather than she ever found that night. Why, it was only blowing in fits and starts at the time. That's what I've said all along. I couldn't understand Mrs de Winter's boat being lost on a night like that.'

'But surely, if Mrs de Winter went below for a coat, as is supposed, and a sudden puff of wind was to come down from that headland, it would be enough to capsize the boat?' asked the Coroner.

James Tabb shook his head. 'No,' he said stubbornly, 'I don't see that it would.'

'Well, I'm afraid that is what must have happened,' said the Coroner. 'I don't think Mr de Winter or any of us suggest that your workmanship was to blame for the accident at all. You fitted the boat out at the beginning of the season, you reported her sound and seaworthy, and that's all I want to know. Unfortunately the late Mrs de Winter relaxed her watchfulness for a moment and she lost her life, the boat sinking with her aboard. Such accidents have happened before. I repeat again we are not blaming you.'

'Excuse me, sir,' said the boat-builder, 'but there is a little bit more to it than that. And if you would allow me I should like to make a further statement.'

'Very well, go on,' said the Coroner.

'It's like this, sir. After the accident last year a lot of people in Kerrith made unpleasantness about my work. Some said I had let Mrs de Winter start the season in a leaky, rotten boat. I lost two or three orders because of it. It was very unfair, but the boat had sunk, and there was nothing I could say to clear myself. Then that steamer went ashore, as we all know, and Mrs de Winter's little boat was found, and brought to the surface. Captain Searle himself gave me permission yesterday to go and look at her, and I did. I wanted to satisfy myself that the work I had put in to her was sound, in spite of the fact that she had been waterlogged for twelve months or more.'

'Well, that was very natural,' said the Coroner, 'and I hope you were satisfied.'

'Yes, sir, I was. There was nothing wrong with that boat as regards the work I did to her. I examined every corner of her there on the lighter up the pill where Captain Searle had put her. She had sunk on sandy bottom. I asked the diver about that, and he told me so. She had not touched the ridge at all. The ridge was a clear five feet away. She was lying on sand, and there wasn't the mark of a rock on her.'

He paused. The Coroner looked at him expectantly.

'Well?' he said, 'is that all you want to say?'

'No, sir,' said Tabb emphatically, 'it's not. What I want to know is this. Who drove the holes in her planking? Rocks didn't do it. The nearest rock was five feet away. Besides, they weren't the sort of marks made by a rock. They were holes. Done with a spike.'

I did not look at him. I was looking at the floor. There was oil-cloth laid on the boards. Green oil-cloth. I looked at it.

I wondered why the Coroner did not say something. Why did the pause last so long? When he spoke at last his voice sounded rather far away.

'What do you mean?' he said, 'what sort of holes?'

'There were three of them altogether,' said the boat-builder, 'one right for'ard, by her chain locker, on her starboard planking, below the water-line. The other two close together amidships, underneath her floor boards in the bottom. The ballast had been shifted too. It was lying loose. And that's not all. The sea-cocks had been turned on.'

'The sea-cocks? What are they?' asked the Coroner.

'The fitting that plugs the pipes leading from a washbasin or lavatory, sir. Mrs de Winter had a little place fitted up right aft. And there was a sink for'ard, where the washing-up was done. There was a sea-cock there, and another in the lavatory. These are always kept tight closed when you're under way, otherwise the water would flow in. When I examined the boat yesterday both sea-cocks were turned full on.'

It was hot, much too hot. Why didn't they open a window? We should be suffocated if we sat here with the air like this, and there were so many people, all breathing the same air, so many people.

'With those holes in her planking, sir, and the sea-cocks not closed, it wouldn't take long for a small boat like her to sink. Not much more than ten minutes, I should say. Those holes weren't there when the boat left my yard. I was proud of my work and so was Mrs de Winter. It's my opinion, sir, that the boat never capsized at all. She was deliberately scuttled.'

I must try and get out of the door. I must try and go back to the waiting-room again. There was no air left in this place, and the person next to me was pressing close, close . . . Someone in front of me was standing up, and they were talking, too, they were all talking. I did not know what was happening. I could not see anything. It was hot, so very hot. The Coroner was asking everybody to be silent. And he said something about 'Mr de Winter'. I could not see. That woman's hat was in front of me. Maxim was standing up now. I could not look at him. I must not look at him. I felt like this once before. When was it? I don't know. I don't remember. Oh, yes, with Mrs Danvers. The time Mrs Danvers stood with me by the window. Mrs Danvers was in this place now, listening to the Coroner. Maxim was standing up over there. The heat was coming up at me from the floor, rising in slow waves. It reached my hands, wet and slippery, it touched my neck, my chin, my face.

'Mr de Winter, you heard the statement from James Tabb, who

had the care of Mrs de Winter's boat? Do you know anything of these holes driven in the planking?'

'Nothing whatever.'

'Can you think of any reason why they should be there?'

'No, of course not.'

'It's the first time you have heard them mentioned?'

'Yes.'

'It's a shock to you, of course?'

'It was shock enough to learn that I made a mistake in identification over twelve months ago, and now I learn that my late wife was not only drowned in the cabin of her boat, but that holes were bored in the boat with the deliberate intent of letting in the water so that the boat should sink. Does it surprise you that I should be shocked?'

No, Maxim. No. You will put his back up. You heard what Frank said. You must not put his back up. Not that voice. Not that angry voice, Maxim. He won't understand. Please, darling, please. Oh, God, don't let Maxim lose his temper. Don't let him lose his temper.

'Mr de Winter, I want you to believe that we all feel very deeply for you in this matter. No doubt you have suffered a shock, a very severe shock, in learning that your late wife was drowned in her own cabin, and not at sea as you supposed. And I am inquiring into the matter for you. I want, for your sake, to find out exactly how and why she died. I don't conduct this inquiry for my own amusement.'

'That's rather obvious, isn't it?'

'I hope that it is. James Tabb has just told us that the boat which contained the remains of the late Mrs de Winter had three holes hammered through her bottom. And that the seacocks were open. Do you doubt his statement?'

'Of course not. He's a boat-builder, he knows what he is talking about.'

'Who looked after Mrs de Winter's boat?'

'She looked after it herself.'

'She employed no hand?'

'No, nobody at all.'

'The boat was moored in the private harbour belonging to Manderley?'

'Yes.'

'Any stranger who tried to tamper with the boat would be seen? There is no access to the harbour by public footpath?'

'No, none at all.'

'The harbour is quiet, is it not, and surrounded by trees?'

'Yes.'

'A trespasser might not be noticed?'

'Possibly not.'

'Yet James Tabb has told us, and we have no reason to disbelieve him, that a boat with those holes drilled in her bottom and the sea-cocks open could not float for more than ten or fifteen minutes.'

'Quite.'

'Therefore we can put aside the idea that the boat was tampered with maliciously before Mrs de Winter went for her evening sail. Had that been the case the boat would have sunk at her moorings.'

'No doubt.'

'Therefore we must assume that whoever took the boat out that night drove in the planking and opened the sea-cocks.'

'I suppose so.'

'You have told us already that the door of the cabin was shut, the port-holes closed, and your wife's remains were on the floor. This was in your statement, and in Doctor Phillips', and in Captain Searle's?'

'Yes.'

'And now added to this is the information that a spike was driven through the bottom, and the sea-cocks were open. Does not this strike you, Mr de Winter, as being very strange?'

'Certainly.'

'You have no suggestion to make?'

'No, none at all.'

'Mr de Winter, painful as it may be, it is my duty to ask you a very personal question.'

'Yes.'

'Were relations between you and the late Mrs de Winter perfectly happy?'

They had to come of course, those black spots in front of my eyes, dancing, flickering, stabbing the hazy air, and it was hot, so hot, with all these people, all these faces, and no open window; the door, from being near to me, was farther away than I had thought, and all the time the ground coming up to meet me.

And then, out of the queer mist around me, Maxim's voice, clear and strong. 'Will someone take my wife outside? She is going to faint.'

# 23

I was sitting in the little room again. The room like a waiting-room at the station. The policeman was there, bending over me, giving me a glass of water, and someone's hand was on my arm, Frank's hand. I sat quite still, the floor, the walls, the figures of Frank and the policeman taking solid shape before me.

'I'm so sorry,' I said, 'such a stupid thing to do. It was so hot in that room, so very hot.'

'It gets very airless in there,' said the policeman, 'there's been complaints about it often, but nothing's ever done. We've had ladies fainting in there before.'

'Are you feeling better, Mrs de Winter?' said Frank.

'Yes. Yes, much better. I shall be all right again. Don't wait with me.'

'I'm going to take you back to Manderley.'

'No.'

'Yes. Maxim has asked me to.'

'No. You ought to stay with him.'

'Maxim told me to take you back to Manderley.'

He put his arm through mine and helped me to get up. 'Can you walk as far as the car or shall I bring it round?'

'I can walk. But I'd much rather stay. I want to wait for Maxim.'

'Maxim may be a long time.'

Why did he say that? What did he mean? Why didn't he look at me? He took my arm and walked with me along the passage to the door, and so down the steps into the street. Maxim may be a long time . . .

We did not speak. We came to the little Morris car belonging to Frank. He opened the door, and helped me in. Then he got in himself and started up the engine. We drove away from the cobbled market-place, through the empty town, and out on to the road to Kerrith.

'Why will they be a long time? What are they going to do?'

'They may have to go over the evidence again.' Frank looked straight in front of him along the hard white road.

'They've had all the evidence,' I said. 'There's nothing more anyone can say.'

'You never know,' said Frank, 'the Coroner may put his questions in a different way. Tabb has altered the whole business. The Coroner will have to approach it now from another angle.'

'What angle? How do you mean?'

'You heard the evidence? You heard what Tabb said about the boat? They won't believe in an accident any more.'

'It's absurd, Frank, it's ridiculous. They should not listen to Tabb. How can he tell, after all these months, how holes came to be in a boat? What are they trying to prove?'

'I don't know.'

'That Coroner will go on and on harping at Maxim, making him lose his temper, making him say things he doesn't mean. He will ask question after question, Frank, and Maxim won't stand it, I know he won't stand it.'

Frank did not answer. He was driving very fast. For the first time since I had known him he was at a loss for the usual conventional phrase. That meant he was worried, very worried. And usually he was such a slow careful driver, stopping dead at every cross-roads, peering to right and left, blowing his horn at every bend in the road.

'That man was there,' I said, 'that man who came once to Manderley to see Mrs Danvers.'

'You mean Favell?' asked Frank. 'Yes, I saw him.'

'He was sitting there, with Mrs Danvers.'

'Yes, I know.'

'Why was he there? What right had he to go to the inquest?'

'He was her cousin.'

'It's not right that he and Mrs Danvers should sit there, listening to that evidence. I don't trust them, Frank.'

'No.'

'They might do something; they might make mischief.'

Again Frank did not answer. I realized that his loyalty to Maxim was such that he would not let himself be drawn into a discussion, even with me. He did not know how much I knew. Nor could I tell for certainty how much he knew. We were allies, we travelled the same road, but we could not look at one another. We neither of us dared risk a confession. We were turning in now at the lodge gates, and down the long twisting narrow drive to the house. I noticed for the first time how the hydrangeas were coming into bloom, their blue heads thrusting themselves from the green foliage behind. For all their beauty there was something sombre about them, funereal; they were like the wreaths, stiff and artificial, that you see beneath glass cases in a foreign churchyard. There they were, all the way along the drive, on either side of us, blue, monotonous, like spectators lined up in a street to watch us pass.

We came to the house at last and rounded the great sweep before the steps. 'Will you be all right now?' said Frank. 'You can lie down, can't you?'

'Yes,' I said, 'yes, perhaps.'

'I shall go back to Lanyon,' he said, 'Maxim may want me.'

He did not say anything more. He got quickly back into the car again and drove away. Maxim might want him. Why did he say Maxim might want him? Perhaps the Coroner was going to question Frank as well. Ask him about that evening, over twelve months ago, when Maxim had dined with Frank. He would want to know the exact time that Maxim left his house. He would want to know if anybody saw Maxim when he returned to the house. Whether the servants knew that he was there. Whether anybody could prove that Maxim went straight up to bed and undressed. Mrs Danvers might be questioned. They might ask Mrs Danvers to give evidence. And Maxim beginning to lose his temper, beginning to go white . . .

I went into the hall. I went upstairs to my room, and lay down upon my bed, even as Frank had suggested. I put my hands over my eyes. I kept seeing that room and all the faces. The lined, painstaking, aggravating face of the Coroner, the gold pince-nez on his nose.

'I don't conduct this inquiry for my own amusement.' His slow, careful mind, easily offended. What were they all saying now? What was happening? Suppose in a little while Frank came back to Manderley alone?

I did not know what happened. I did not know what people did. I remembered pictures of men in the papers, leaving places like that, and being taken away. Suppose Maxim was taken away? They would not let me go to him. They would not let me see him. I should have to stay here at Manderley day after day, night after night, waiting, as I was waiting now. People like Colonel Julyan being kind. People saying 'You must not be alone. You must come to us.' The telephone, the newspapers, the telephone again. 'No, Mrs de Winter can't see anyone. Mrs de Winter has no story to give the *County Chronicle*.' And another day. And another day. Weeks that would be blurred and non-existent. Frank at last taking me to see Maxim. He would look thin, queer, like people in hospital . . .

Other women had been through this. Women I had read about in papers. They sent letters to the Home Secretary and it was not any good. The Home Secretary always said that justice must take its course. Friends sent petitions too, everybody signed them, but the Home Secretary could never do anything. And the ordinary people who read about it in the papers said why should the fellow get off, he murdered his wife, didn't he? What about the poor, murdered wife? This sentimental business about abolishing the death penalty simply encourages crime. This fellow ought to have thought about that before he killed his wife. It's too late now. He will have to hang for it, like any other murderer. And serve him right too. Let it be a warning to others.

I remember seeing a picture on the back of a paper once, of a little crowd collected outside a prison gate, and just after nine o'clock a policeman came and pinned a notice on the gate for the people to read. The notice said something about the sentence being carried out. 'Sentence of death was carried out this morning at nine o'clock. The Governor, the Prison Doctor, and the Sheriff of the County were present.' Hanging was quick. Hanging did not hurt. It broke your neck at once. No, it did not. Someone said once it did not always work. Someone who had known the Governor of a prison. They put that bag over your head, and you stand on the little platform, and then the floor gives way beneath you. It takes exactly three minutes to go from the cell to the moment you are hanged. No, fifty seconds, someone said. No, that's absurd. It could not be fifty seconds. There's a little flight of steps down the side of the shed, down to the pit. The doctor goes down there to look. They die instantly. No, they don't. The body moves for some time, the neck is not always broken. Yes, but even so they don't feel anything. Someone said they did. Someone who had a brother who was a prison doctor said it was not generally known, because it would be such a scandal, but they did not always die at once. Their eyes were open, they stay open for quite a long time.

God, don't let me go on thinking about this. Let me think about something else. About other things. About Mrs Van Hopper in America. She must be staying with her daughter now. They had that house on Long Island in the summer. I expect they played a lot of bridge. They went to the races. Mrs Van Hopper was fond of the races. I wonder if she still wears that little yellow hat. It was too small for her. Much too small on that big face. Mrs Van Hopper sitting about in the garden of that house on Long Island, with novels, and magazines, and papers on her lap. Mrs Van Hopper putting up her lorgnette and calling to her daughter. 'Look at this, Helen. They say Max de Winter murdered his first wife. I always did think there was something peculiar about him. I warned that fool of a girl she was making a mistake, but she wouldn't listen to me. Well, she's cooked her goose now all right. I suppose they'll make her a big offer to go on the pictures.'

355

Something was touching my hand. It was Jasper. It was Jasper, thrusting his cold damp nose in my hands. He had followed me up from the hall. Why did dogs make one want to cry? There was something so quiet and hopeless about their sympathy. Jasper, knowing something was wrong, as dogs always do. Trunks being packed. Cars being brought to the door. Dogs standing with drooping tails, dejected eyes. Wandering back to their baskets in the hall when the sound of the car dies away . . .

I must have fallen asleep because I woke suddenly with a start, and heard that first crack of thunder in the air. I sat up. The clock said five. I got up and went to the window. There was not a breath of wind. The leaves hung listless on the trees, waiting. The sky was slatey grey. The jagged lightning split the sky. Another rumble in the distance. No rain fell. I went out into the corridor and listened. I could not hear anything. I went to the head of the stairs. There was no sign of anybody. The hall was dark because of the menace of thunder overhead. I went down and stood on the terrace. There was another burst of thunder. One spot of rain fell on my hand. One spot. No more. It was very dark. I could see the sea beyond the dip in the valley like a black lake. Another spot fell on my hands, and another crack of thunder came. One of the housemaids began shutting the windows in the rooms upstairs. Robert appeared and shut the windows of the drawing-room behind me.

'The gentlemen are not back yet, are they, Robert?' I asked.

'No, Madam, not yet. I thought you were with them, Madam.'

'No. No, I've been back some time.'

'Will you have tea, Madam?'

'No, no, I'll wait.'

'It looks as though the weather was going to break at last, Madam.'

'Yes.'

No rain fell. Nothing since those two drops on my hand. I went back and sat in the library. At half past five Robert came into the room.

'The car has just driven up to the door now, Madam,' he said.

'Which car?' I said.

'Mr de Winter's car, Madam,' he said.

'Is Mr de Winter driving it himself?'

'Yes, Madam.'

I tried to get up but my legs were things of straw, they would not bear me. I stood leaning against the sofa. My throat was very dry. After a minute Maxim came into the room. He stood just inside the door.

He looked very tired, old. There were lines at the corner of his mouth I had never noticed before.

'It's all over,' he said.

I waited. Still I could not speak or move towards him.

'Suicide,' he said, 'without sufficient evidence to show the state of mind of the deceased. They were all at sea of course, they did not know what they were doing.'

I sat down on the sofa. 'Suicide,' I said, 'but the motive? Where was the motive?'

'God knows,' he said. 'They did not seem to think a motive was necessary. Old Horridge, peering at me, wanting to know if Rebecca had any money troubles. Money troubles. God in heaven.'

He went and stood by the window, looking out at the green lawns. 'It's going to rain,' he said. 'Thank God it's going to rain at last.'

'What happened?' I said, 'what did the Coroner say? Why have you been there all this time?'

'He went over and over the same ground again,' said Maxim. 'Little details about the boat that no one cared about a damn. Were the sea-cocks hard to turn on? Where exactly was the first hole in relation to the second? What was ballast? What effect upon the stability of the boat would the shifting of the ballast have? Could a woman do this unaided? Did the cabin door shut firmly? What pressure of water was necessary to burst open the door? I thought I should go mad. I kept my temper though. Seeing you there, by the door, made me remember what I had to do. If you had not fainted like that, I should never have done it. It brought me up with a jerk. I knew exactly what I was going to say. I faced Horridge all the time. I never took my eyes off his thin, pernickety, little face and those gold-rimmed pince-nez. I shall remember that face of his to my dying day. I'm tired, darling; so tired I can't see, or hear or feel anything.'

He sat down on the window-seat. He leant forward, his head in his hands. I went and sat beside him. In a few minutes Frith came in, followed by Robert carrying the table for tea. The solemn ritual went forward as it always did, day after day, the leaves of the table pulled out, the legs adjusted, the laying of the snowy cloth, the putting down of the silver tea-pot and the kettle with the little flame beneath. Scones, sandwiches, three different sorts of cake. Jasper sat close to the table, his tail thumping now and again upon the floor, his eyes fixed expectantly on me. It's funny, I thought, how the routine of life goes on, whatever happens, we do the same things, go through the little performance of eating, sleeping, washing. No crisis can break through the crust of habit. I poured out Maxim's tea, I took it to him on the window-seat, gave him his scone, and buttered one for myself.

'Where's Frank?' I asked.

'He had to go and see the vicar. I would have gone too but I wanted to come straight back to you. I kept thinking of you, waiting here, all by yourself, not knowing what was going to happen.'

'Why the vicar?' I said.

'Something has to happen this evening,' he said. 'Something at the church.'

I stared at him blankly. Then I understood. They were going to bury Rebecca. They were going to bring Rebecca back from the mortuary.

'It's fixed for six-thirty,' he said. 'No one knows but Frank, and Colonel Julyan, and the vicar, and myself. There won't be anyone hanging about. This was arranged yesterday. The verdict doesn't make any difference.'

'What time must you go?'

'I'm meeting them there at the church at twenty-five past six.'

I did not say anything. I went on drinking my tea. Maxim put his sandwich down untasted. 'It's still very hot, isn't it,' he said.

'It's the storm,' I said. 'It won't break. Only little spots at a time. It's there in the air. It won't break.'

'It was thundering when I left Lanyon,' he said, 'the sky was like ink over my head. Why in the name of God doesn't it rain?'

The birds were hushed in the trees. It was still very dark.

'I wish you did not have to go out again,' I said.

He did not answer. He looked tired, so deathly tired.

'We'll talk over things this evening when I get back,' he said presently. 'We've got so much to do together, haven't we? We've got to begin all over again. I've been the worst sort of husband for you.'

'No!' I said. 'No!'

'We'll start again, once this thing is behind us. We can do it, you and I. It's not like being alone. The past can't hurt us if we are together. You'll have children too.' After a while he glanced at his watch. 'It's ten past six,' he said, 'I shall have to be going. It won't take long, not more than half an hour. We've got to go down to the crypt.'

I held his hand. 'I'll come with you. I shan't mind. Let me come with you.'

'No,' he said. 'No, I don't want you to come.'

Then he went out of the room. I heard the sound of the car starting up in the drive. Presently the sound died away, and I knew he had gone.

Robert came to clear away the tea. It was like any other day. The routine was unchanged. I wondered if it would have been so had Maxim not come back from Lanyon. I wondered if Robert would have stood there, that wooden expression on his young sheep's face, brushing the crumbs from the snow-white cloth, picking up the table, carrying it from the room.

It seemed very quiet in the library when he had gone. I began to think of them down at the church, going through that door and down the flight of stairs to the crypt. I had never been there. I had only seen the door. I wondered what a crypt was like, if there were coffins standing there. Maxim's father and mother. I wondered what would happen to the coffin of that other woman who had been put there by mistake. I wondered who she was, poor unclaimed soul, washed up by the wind and tide. Now another coffin would stand there. Rebecca would lie there in the crypt as well. Was the vicar reading the burial service there, with Maxim, and Frank, and Colonel Julyan standing by his side? Ashes to ashes. Dust to dust. It seemed to me that Rebecca had no reality any more. She had crumbled away when they had found her on the cabin floor. It was not Rebecca who was lying in the crypt, it was dust. Only dust.

Just after seven the rain began to fall. Gently at first, a light pattering in the trees, and so thin I could not see it. Then louder and faster, a driving torrent falling slantways from the slate sky, like water from a sluice. I left the windows open wide. I stood in front of them and breathed the cold clean air. The rain splashed into my face and on my hands. I could not see beyond the lawns, the falling rain came thick and fast. I heard it sputtering in the gutter-pipes above the window, and splashing on the stones of the terrace. There was no more thunder. The rain smelt of moss and earth and of the black bark of trees.

I did not hear Frith come in at the door. I was standing by the window, watching the rain. I did not see him until he was beside me.

'Excuse me, Madam,' he said, 'do you know if Mr de Winter will be long?'

'No,' I said, 'not very long.'

'There's a gentleman to see him, Madam,' said Frith after a moment's hesitation. 'I'm not quite sure what I ought to say. He's very insistent about seeing Mr de Winter.'

'Who is it?' I said. 'Is it anyone you know?'

Frith looked uncomfortable. 'Yes, Madam,' he said, 'it's a gentleman who used to come here frequently at one time, when Mrs de Winter was alive. A gentleman called Mr Favell.'

I knelt on the window-seat and shut the window. The rain was coming in on the cushions. Then I turned round and looked at Frith.

'I think perhaps I had better see Mr Favell,' I said.

'Very good, Madam.'

I went and stood over on the rug beside the empty fireplace. It was just possible that I should be able to get rid of Favell before Maxim came back. I did not know what I was going to say to him, but I was not frightened.

In a few moments Frith returned and showed Favell into the library. He looked much the same as before but a little rougher if possible, a little more untidy. He was the sort of man who invariably went hatless, his hair was bleached from the sun of the last days and his skin was deeply tanned. His eyes were rather bloodshot. I wondered if he had been drinking.

'I'm afraid Maxim is not here,' I said. 'I don't know when he will be back. Wouldn't it be better if you made an appointment to see him at the office in the morning?'

'Waiting doesn't worry me,' said Favell, 'and I don't think I shall have to wait very long, you know. I had a look in the dining-room as I came along, and I see Max's place is laid for dinner all right.'

'Our plans have been changed,' I said. 'It's quite possible Maxim won't be home at all this evening.'

'He's run off, has he?' said Favell, with a half smile I did not like. 'I wonder if you really mean it. Of course under the circumstances it's the wisest thing he can do. Gossip is an unpleasant thing to some people. It's more pleasant to avoid it, isn't it?'

'I don't know what you mean,' I said.

'Don't you?' he said. 'Oh, come, you don't expect me to believe that, do you? Tell me, are you feeling better? Too bad fainting like that at the inquest this afternoon. I would have come and helped you out but I saw you had one knight-errant already. I bet Frank Crawley enjoyed himself. Did you let him drive you home? You wouldn't let me drive you five yards when I offered to.'

361

'What do you want to see Maxim about?' I asked.

Favell leant forward to the table and helped himself to a cigarette. 'You don't mind my smoking, I suppose?' he said, 'it won't make you sick, will it? One never knows with brides.'

He watched me over his lighter. 'You've grown up a bit since I saw you last, haven't you?' he said. 'I wonder what you have been doing. Leading Frank Crawley up the garden-path?' He blew a cloud of smoke in the air. 'I say, do you mind asking old Frith to get me a whisky-and-soda?'

I did not say anything. I went and rang the bell. He sat down on the edge of the sofa, swinging his legs, that half-smile on his lips. Robert answered the bell. 'A whisky-and-soda for Mr Favell,' I said.

'Well, Robert?' said Favell, 'I haven't seen you for a very long time. Still breaking the hearts of the girls in Kerrith?'

Robert flushed. He glanced at me, horribly embarrassed.

'All right, old chap, I won't give you away. Run along and get me a double whisky, and jump on it.'

Robert disappeared. Favell laughed, dropping ash all over the floor.

'I took Robert out once on his half-day,' he said. 'Rebecca bet me a fiver I wouldn't ask him. I won my fiver all right. Spent one of the funniest evenings of my life. Did I laugh? Oh, boy! Robert on the razzle takes a lot of beating, I tell you. I must say he's got a good eye for a girl. He picked the prettiest of the bunch we saw that night.'

Robert came back again with the whisky-and-soda on a tray. He still looked very red, very uncomfortable. Favell watched him with a smile as he poured out his drink, and then he began to laugh, leaning back on the arm of the sofa. He whistled the bar of a song, watching Robert all the while.

'That was the one, wasn't it?' he said, 'that was the tune? Do you still like ginger hair, Robert?'

Robert gave him a flat weak smile. He looked miserable. Favell laughed louder still. Robert turned and went out of the room.

'Poor kid,' said Favell. 'I don't suppose he's been on the loose since. That old ass Frith keeps him on a leading string.'

He began drinking his whisky-and-soda, glancing round the room, looking at me every now and again, and smiling.

'I don't think I shall mind very much if Max doesn't get back to dinner,' he said. 'What say you?'

I did not answer. I stood by the fireplace my hands behind my back. 'You wouldn't waste that place at the dining-room table, would you?' he said. He looked at me, smiling still, his head on one side.

'Mr Favell,' I said, 'I don't want to be rude, but as a matter of fact I'm very tired. I've had a long and fairly exhausting day. If you can't tell me what you want to see Maxim about it's not much good your sitting here. You had far better do as I suggest, and go round to the estate office in the morning.'

He slid off the arm of the sofa and came towards me, his glass in his hand. 'No, no,' he said. 'No, no, don't be a brute. I've had an exhausting day too. Don't run away and leave me, I'm quite harmless, really I am. I suppose Max has been telling tales about me to you?'

I did not answer. 'You think I'm the big, bad wolf, don't you?' he said, 'but I'm not, you know. I'm a perfectly ordinary, harmless bloke. And I think you are behaving splendidly over all this, perfectly splendidly. I take off my hat to you, I really do.' This last speech of his was very slurred and thick. I wished I had never told Frith I would see him.

'You come down here to Manderley,' he said, waving his arm vaguely, 'you take on all this place, meet hundreds of people you've never seen before, you put up with old Max and his moods, you don't give a fig for anyone, you just go your own way. I call it a damn good effort, and I don't care who hears me say so. A damn good effort.' He swayed a little as he stood. He steadied himself, and put the empty glass down on the table. 'This business has been a shock to me, you know,' he said. 'A bloody awful shock. Rebecca was my cousin. I was damn fond of her.'

363

'Yes,' I said. 'I'm very sorry for you.'

'We were brought up together,' he went on. 'Always tremendous pals. Liked the same things, the same people. Laughed at the same jokes. I suppose I was fonder of Rebecca than anyone else in the world. And she was fond of me. All this has been a bloody shock.'

'Yes,' I said. 'Yes, of course.'

'And what is Max going to do about it, that's what I want to know? Does he think he can sit back quietly now that sham inquest is over? Tell me that?' He was not smiling any more. He bent towards me.

'I'm going to see justice is done to Rebecca,' he said, his voice growing louder. 'Suicide . . . God Almighty, that doddering old fool of a Coroner got the jury to say suicide. You and I know it wasn't suicide, don't we?' He leant closer to me still. 'Don't we?' he said slowly.

The door opened and Maxim came into the room, with Frank just behind him. Maxim stood quite still, with the door open, staring at Favell. 'What the hell are you doing here?' he said.

Favell turned round, his hands in his pockets. He waited a moment, and then he began to smile. 'As a matter of fact, Max, old chap, I came to congratulate you on the inquest this afternoon.'

'Do you mind leaving the house?' said Max, 'or do you want Crawley and me to chuck you out?'

'Steady a moment, steady a moment,' said Favell. He lit another cigarette, and sat down once more on the arm of the sofa.

'You don't want Frith to hear what I'm going to say, do you?' he said. 'Well, he will, if you don't shut that door.'

Maxim did not move. I saw Frank close the door very quietly.

'Now, listen here, Max,' said Favell, 'you've come very well out of this affair, haven't you? Better than you ever expected. Oh, yes, I was in the court this afternoon, and I dare say you saw me. I was there from start to finish. I saw your wife faint, at a rather critical moment, and I don't blame her. It was touch and go, then, wasn't it, Max, what way the inquiry would go?

364

And luckily for you it went the way it did. You hadn't squared those thick-headed fellows who were acting jury, had you? It looked damn like it to me.'

Maxim made a move towards Favell, but Favell held up his hand.

'Wait a bit, can't you?' he said. 'I haven't finished yet. You realize, don't you, Max, old man, that I can make things damned unpleasant for you if I choose. Not only unpleasant, but shall I say dangerous?'

I sat down on the chair beside the fireplace. I held the arms of the chair very tight. Frank came over and stood behind the chair. Still Maxim did not move. He never took his eyes off Favell.

'Oh, yes?' he said, 'in what way can you make things dangerous?'

'Look here, Max,' said Favell, 'I suppose there are no secrets between you and your wife and from the look of things Crawley there just makes the happy trio. I can speak plainly then, and I will. You all know about Rebecca and me. We were lovers, weren't we? I've never denied it, and I never will. Very well then. Up to the present I believed, like every other fool, that Rebecca was drowned sailing in the bay, and that her body was picked up at Edgecoombe weeks afterwards. It was a shock to me then, a bloody shock. But I said to myself, That's the sort of death Rebecca would choose, she'd go out like she lived, fighting.' He paused, he sat there on the edge of the sofa, looking at all of us in turn. 'Then I pick up the evening paper a few days ago and I read that Rebecca's boat had been stumbled on by the local diver and that there was a body in the cabin. I couldn't understand it. Who the hell would Rebecca have as a sailing companion? It didn't make sense. I came down here, and put up at a pub just outside Kerrith. I got in touch with Mrs Danvers. She told me then that the body in the cabin was Rebecca's. Even so I thought like everyone else that the first body was a mistake and Rebecca had somehow got shut in the cabin when she went to fetch a coat. Well, I attended that inquest today, as you know. And everything went smoothly, didn't it, until Tabb gave his evidence? But after that? Well, Max, old man, what have you got to say about those holes in the floor-boards, and those sea-cocks turned full on?'

'Do you think,' said Maxim slowly, 'that after those hours of talk this afternoon I am going into it again – with you? You heard the evidence, and you heard the verdict. It satisfied the Coroner, and it must satisfy you.'

'Suicide, eh?' said Favell. 'Rebecca committing suicide. The sort of thing she would do, wasn't it? Listen; you never knew I had this note, did you? I kept it, because it was the last thing she ever wrote to me. I'll read it to you. I think it will interest you.'

He took a piece of paper out of his pocket. I recognized that thin, pointed, slanting hand.

I tried to ring you from the flat, but could get no answer [*he read*]. I'm going down to Manders right away. I shall be at the cottage this evening, and if you get this in time will you get the car and follow me. I'll spend the night at the cottage, and leave the door open for you. I've got something to tell you and I want to see you as soon as possible. Rebecca.

He put the note back in his pocket. 'That's not the sort of note you write when you're going to commit suicide, is it?' he said. 'It was waiting for me at my flat when I got back about four in the morning. I had no idea Rebecca was to be in London that day or I should have got in touch with her. It happened, by a vile stroke of fortune, I was on a party that night. When I read the note at four in the morning I decided it was too late to go crashing down on a six-hour run to Manderley. I went to bed, determined to put a call through later in the day. I did. About twelve o'clock. And I heard Rebecca had been drowned!'

He sat there, staring at Maxim. None of us spoke.

'Supposing the Coroner this afternoon had read that note, it would have made it a little bit more tricky for you, wouldn't it, Max, old man?' said Favell.

'Well,' said Maxim, 'why didn't you get up and give it to him?'

'Steady, old boy, steady. No need to get rattled. I don't want to smash you, Max. God knows you've never been a friend to me, but I don't bear malice about it. All married men with lovely wives are jealous, aren't they? And some of 'em just can't help playing Othello. They're made that way. I don't blame them. I'm sorry for them. I'm a bit of a Socialist in my way, you know, and I can't think why fellows can't share their women instead of killing them. What difference does it make? You can get your fun just the same. A lovely woman isn't like a motor tyre, she doesn't wear out. The more you use her the better she goes. Now, Max, I've laid all my cards on the table. Why can't we come to some agreement? I'm not a rich man. I'm too fond of gambling for that. But what gets me down is never having any capital to fall back upon. Now if I had a settlement of two or three thousand a year for life I could jog along comfortably. And I'd never trouble you again. I swear before God I would not.'

'I've asked you before to leave the house,' said Maxim. 'I'm not going to ask you again. There's the door behind me. You can open it yourself.'

'Half a minute, Maxim,' said Frank; 'it's not quite so easy as all that.' He turned to Favell. 'I see what you're driving at. It happens, very unfortunately, that you could, as you say, twist things round and make it difficult for Maxim. I don't think he sees it as clearly as I do. What is the exact amount you propose Maxim should settle on you?'

I saw Maxim go very white, and a little pulse began to show on his forehead. 'Don't interfere with this, Frank,' he said, 'this is my affair entirely. I'm not going to give way to blackmail.'

'I don't suppose your wife wants to be pointed out as Mrs de Winter, the widow of a murderer, of a fellow who was hanged,' said Favell. He laughed, and glanced towards me.

'You think you can frighten me, don't you, Favell?' said Maxim. 'Well, you are wrong. I'm not afraid of anything you can do.

There is the telephone, in the next room. Shall I ring up Colonel Julyan and ask him to come over? He's the magistrate. He'll be interested in your story.'

Favell stared at him, and laughed.

'Good bluff,' he said, 'but it won't work. You wouldn't dare ring up old Julyan. I've got enough evidence to hang you, Max, old man.'

Maxim walked slowly across the room and passed through to the little room beyond. I heard the click of the telephone.

'Stop him!' I said to Frank. 'Stop him, for God's sake.'

Frank glanced at my face, he went swiftly towards the door.

I heard Maxim's voice, very cool, very calm. 'I want Kerrith 17,' he said.

Favell was watching the door, his face curiously intense.

'Leave me alone,' I heard Maxim say to Frank. And then, two minutes afterwards. 'Is that Colonel Julyan speaking? It's de Winter here. Yes. Yes, I know. I wonder if you could possibly come over here at once. Yes, to Manderley. It's rather urgent. I can't explain why on the telephone, but you shall hear everything directly you come. I'm very sorry to have to drag you out. Yes. Thank you very much. Good-bye.'

He came back again into the room. 'Julyan is coming right away,' he said. He crossed over and threw open the windows. It was still raining very hard. He stood there, with his back to us, breathing the cold air.

'Maxim,' said Frank quietly. 'Maxim.'

He did not answer. Favell laughed, and helped himself to another cigarette. 'If you want to hang yourself, old fellow, it's all the same to me,' he said. He picked up a paper from the table and flung himself down on the sofa, crossed his legs, and began to turn over the pages. Frank hesitated, glancing from me to Maxim. Then he came beside me.

'Can't you do something?' I whispered. 'Go out and meet Colonel Julyan, prevent him from coming, say it was all a mistake?'

Maxim spoke from the window without turning round.

'Frank is not to leave this room,' he said. 'I'm going to manage

368

this thing alone. Colonel Julyan will be here in exactly ten minutes.'

We none of us said anything. Favell went on reading his paper. There was no sound but the steady falling rain. It fell without a break, steady, straight, and monotonous. I felt helpless, without strength. There was nothing I could do. Nothing that Frank could do. In a book or in a play I would have found a revolver, and we should have shot Favell, hidden his body in a cupboard. There was no revolver. There was no cupboard. We were ordinary people. These things did not happen. I could not go to Maxim now and beg him on my knees to give Favell the money. I had to sit there, with my hands in my lap, watching the rain, watching Maxim with his back turned to me, standing by the window.

It was raining too hard to hear the car. The sound of the rain covered all other sounds. We did not know Colonel Julyan had arrived until the door opened, and Frith showed him into the room.

Maxim swung round from the window. 'Good evening,' he said. 'We meet again. You've made very good time.'

'Yes,' said Colonel Julyan, 'you said it was urgent, so I came at once. Luckily, my man had left the car handy. What an evening.'

He glanced at Favell uncertainly, and then came over and shook hands with me, nodding to Maxim. 'A good thing the rain has come,' he said. 'It's been hanging about too long. I hope you're feeling better.'

I murmured something, I don't know what, and he stood there looking from one to the other of us, rubbing his hands.

'I think you realize,' Maxim said, 'that I haven't brought you out on an evening like this for a social half-hour before dinner. This is Jack Favell, my late wife's first cousin. I don't know if you have ever met.'

Colonel Julyan nodded. 'Your face seems familiar. I've probably met you here in the old days.'

'Quite,' said Maxim. 'Go ahead, Favell.'

Favell got up from the sofa and chucked the paper back on the table. The ten minutes seemed to have sobered him. He walked quite steadily. He was not smiling any longer. I had the impression that he was not entirely pleased with the turn in the events, and he was ill-prepared for the encounter with Colonel Julyan. He began speaking in a loud, rather domineering voice. 'Look here, Colonel Julyan,' he said, 'there's no sense in beating about the bush. The reason why I'm here is that I'm not satisfied with the verdict given at the inquest this afternoon.'

'Oh?' said Colonel Julyan, 'isn't that for de Winter to say, not you?'

'No, I don't think it is,' said Favell. 'I have a right to speak, not only as Rebecca's cousin, but as her prospective husband, had she lived.'

Colonel Julyan looked rather taken aback. 'Oh,' he said. 'Oh, I see. That's rather different. Is this true, de Winter?'

Maxim shrugged his shoulders. 'It's the first I've heard of it,' he said.

Colonel Julyan looked from one to the other doubtfully. 'Look here, Favell,' he said, 'what exactly is your trouble?'

Favell stared at him a moment. I could see he was planning something in his mind, and he was still not sober enough to carry it through. He put his hand slowly in his waistcoat pocket and brought out Rebecca's note. 'This note was written a few hours before Rebecca was supposed to have set out on that suicidal sail. Here it is. I want you to read it, and say whether you think a woman who wrote that note had made up her mind to kill herself.'

Colonel Julyan took a pair of spectacles from a case in his pocket and read the note. Then he handed it back to Favell. 'No,' he said, 'on the face of it, no. But I don't know what the note refers to. Perhaps you do. Or perhaps de Winter does?'

Maxim did not say anything. Favell twisted the piece of paper in his fingers, considering Colonel Julyan all the while. 'My cousin made a definite appointment in that note, didn't she?' he said. 'She deliberately asked me to drive down to Manderley that night because she had something to tell me. What it actually was I don't suppose we shall ever know, but that's beside the point.

370

She made the appointment, and she was to spend the night in the cottage on purpose to see me alone. The mere fact of her going for a sail never surprised me. It was the sort of thing she did, for an hour or so, after a long day in London. But to plug holes in the cabin and deliberately drown herself, the hysterical impulsive freak of a neurotic girl – oh, no, Colonel Julyan, by Christ no!' The colour had flooded into his face, and the last words were shouted. His manner was not helpful to him, and I could see by the thin line of Colonel Julyan's mouth that he had not taken to Favell.

'My dear fellow,' he said, 'it's not the slightest use your losing your temper with me. I'm not the Coroner who conducted the inquiry this afternoon, nor am I a member of the jury who gave the verdict. I'm merely the magistrate of the district. Naturally I want to help you all I can, and de Winter, too. You say you refuse to believe your cousin committed suicide. On the other hand you heard, as we all did, the evidence of the boat-builder. The sea-cocks were open, the holes were there. Very well. Suppose we get to the point. What do you suggest really happened?'

Favell turned his head and looked slowly towards Maxim. He was still twisting the note between his fingers. 'Rebecca never opened those sea-cocks, nor split the holes in the planking. Rebecca never committed suicide. You've asked for my opinion, and by God you shall have it. Rebecca was murdered. And if you want to know who the murderer is, why there he stands, by the window there, with that God-damned superior smile on his face. He couldn't even wait could he, until the year was out, before marrying the first girl he set eyes on? There he is, there's your murderer for you, Mr Maximilian de Winter. Take a good long look at him. He'd look well hanging, wouldn't he?'

And Favell began to laugh, the laugh of a drunkard, high-pitched, forced, and foolish, and all the while twisting Rebecca's note between his fingers.

## 24

Thank God for Favell's laugh. Thank God for his pointing finger, his flushed face, his staring bloodshot eyes. Thank God for the way he stood there swaying on his two feet. Because it made Colonel Julyan antagonistic, it put him on our side. I saw the disgust on his face, the quick movement of his lips. Colonel Julyan did not believe him. Colonel Julyan was on our side.

'The man's drunk,' he said quickly. 'He doesn't know what he's saying.'

'Drunk, am I?' shouted Favell. 'Oh, no, my fine friend. You may be a magistrate and a colonel into the bargain, but it won't cut any ice with me. I've got the law on my side for a change, and I'm going to use it. There are other magistrates in this bloody county besides you. Fellows with brains in their heads, who understand the meaning of justice. Not soldiers who got the sack years ago for incompetence and walk about with a string of putty medals on their chest. Max de Winter murdered Rebecca and I'm going to prove it.'

'Wait a minute, Mr Favell,' said Colonel Julyan quietly, 'you were present at the inquiry this afternoon, weren't you? I remember you now. I saw you sitting there. If you felt so deeply about the injustice of the verdict why didn't you say so then, to the jury, to the Coroner himself? Why didn't you produce that letter in court?'

Favell stared at him, and laughed. 'Why?' he said, 'because I did not choose to, that's why. I preferred to come and tackle de Winter personally.'

'That's why I rang you up,' said Maxim, coming forward from the window; 'we've already heard Favell's accusations. I asked him the same question. Why didn't he tell his suspicions to the Coroner? He said he was not a rich man, and that if I cared to settle two or three thousand on him for life he would never worry me again. Frank was here, and my wife. They both heard him. Ask them.'

'It's perfectly true, sir,' said Frank. 'It's blackmail, pure and simple.'

'Yes, of course,' said Colonel Julyan, 'the trouble is that blackmail is not very pure, nor is it particularly simple. It can make a lot of unpleasantness for a great many people, even if the blackmailer finds himself in jail at the end of it. Sometimes innocent people find themselves in jail as well. We want to avoid that, in this case. I don't know whether you are sufficiently sober, Favell, to answer my questions, and if you keep off irrelevant personalities we may get through with the business quicker. You have just made a serious accusation against de Winter. Have you any proof to back that accusation?'

'Proof?' said Favell. 'What the hell do you want with proof? Aren't those holes in the boat proof enough?'

'Certainly not,' said Colonel Julyan, 'unless you can bring a witness who saw him do it. Where's your witness?'

'Witness be damned,' said Favell. 'Of course de Winter did it. Who else would kill Rebecca?'

'Kerrith has a large population,' said Colonel Julyan. 'Why not go from door to door making inquiries? I might have done it myself. You appear to have no more proof against de Winter there than you would have against me.'

'Oh, I see,' said Favell, 'you're going to hold his hand through this. You're going to back de Winter. You won't let him down because you've dined with him, and he's dined with you. He's a big name down here. He's the owner of Manderley. You poor bloody little snob.'

'Take care, Favell, take care.'

'You think you can get the better of me, don't you? You think I've got no case to bring to a court of law. I'll get my proof for you all right. I tell you de Winter killed Rebecca because of me.

He knew I was her lover; he was jealous, madly jealous. He knew she was waiting for me at the cottage on the beach, and he went down that night and killed her. Then he put her body in the boat and sank her.'

'Quite a clever story, Favell, in its way, but I repeat again you have no proof. Produce your witness who saw it happen and I might begin to take you seriously. I know that cottage on the beach. A sort of picnic place, isn't it? Mrs de Winter used to keep the gear there for the boat. It would help your story if you could turn it into a bungalow with fifty replicas alongside of it. There would be a chance then that one of the inhabitants might have seen the whole affair.'

'Hold on,' said Favell slowly, 'hold on . . . There is a chance de Winter might have been seen that night. Quite a good chance too. It's worth finding out. What would you say if I did produce a witness?'

Colonel Julyan shrugged his shoulders. I saw Frank glance inquiringly at Maxim. Maxim did not say anything. He was watching Favell. I suddenly knew what Favell meant. I knew who he was talking about. And in a flash of fear and horror I knew that he was right. There had been a witness that night. Little sentences came back to me. Words I had not understood, phrases I believed to be the fragments of a poor idiot's mind. 'She's down there isn't she? She won't come back again.' 'I didn't tell no one.' 'They'll find her there, won't they? The fishes have eaten her, haven't they?' 'She'll not come back no more.' Ben knew. Ben had seen. Ben, with his queer crazed brain, had been a witness all the time. He had been hiding in the woods that night. He had seen Maxim take the boat from the moorings, and pull back in the dinghy, alone. I knew all the colour was draining away from my face. I leant back against the cushion of the chair.

'There's a local half-wit who spends his time on the beach,' said Favell. 'He was always hanging about, when I used to come down and meet Rebecca. I've often seen him. He used to sleep in the woods, or on the beach when the nights were hot. The

374

fellow's cracked, he would never have come forward on his own. But I could make him talk if he did see anything that night. And there's a bloody big chance he did.'

'Who is this? What's he talking about?' said Colonel Julyan.

'He must mean Ben,' said Frank, with another glance at Maxim. 'He's the son of one of our tenants. But the man's not responsible for what he says or does. He's been an idiot since birth.'

'What the hell does that matter?' said Favell. 'He's got eyes, hasn't he? He knows what he sees. He's only got to answer yes or no. You're getting windy now, aren't you? Not so mighty confident?'

'Can we get hold of this fellow and question him?' asked Colonel Julyan.

'Of course,' said Maxim. 'Tell Robert to cut down to his mother's cottage, Frank, and bring him back.'

Frank hesitated. I saw him glance at me out of the tail of his eye.

'Go on, for God's sake,' said Maxim. 'We want to end this thing, don't we?' Frank went out of the room. I began to feel the old nagging pain beneath my heart.

In a few minutes Frank came back again into the room.

'Robert's taken my car,' he said. 'If Ben is at home he won't be more than ten minutes.'

'The rain will keep him at home all right,' said Favell; 'he'll be there. And I think you will find I shall be able to make him talk.' He laughed, and looked at Maxim. His face was still very flushed. Excitement had made him sweat; there were beads of perspiration on his forehead. I noticed how his neck bulged over the back of his collar, and how low his ears were set on his head. Those florid good looks would not last him very long. Already he was out of condition, puffy. He helped himself to another cigarette. 'You're like a little trade union here at Manderley, aren't you?' he said; 'no one going to give anyone else away. Even the local magistrate is on the same racket. We must exempt the bride of course. A wife doesn't give evidence

375

against her husband. Crawley of course has been squared. He knows he would lose his job if he told the truth. And if I guess rightly there's a spice of malice in his soul towards me too. You didn't have much success with Rebecca, did you, Crawley? That garden path wasn't quite long enough, eh? It's a bit easier this time, isn't it. The bride will be grateful for your fraternal arm every time she faints. When she hears the judge sentence her husband to death that arm of yours will come in very handy.'

It happened very quickly. Too quick for me to see how Maxim did it. But I saw Favell stagger and fall against the arm of the sofa, and down on to the floor. And Maxim was standing just beside him. I felt rather sick. There was something degrading in the fact that Maxim had hit Favell. I wished I had not known. I wished I had not been there to see. Colonel Julyan did not say anything. He looked very grim. He turned his back on them and came and stood beside me.

'I think you had better go upstairs,' he said quietly.

I shook my head. 'No,' I whispered. 'No.'

'That fellow is in a state capable of saying anything,' he said. 'What you have just seen was not very attractive, was it? Your husband was right of course, but it's a pity you saw it.'

I did not answer. I was watching Favell who was getting slowly to his feet. He sat down heavily on the sofa and put his hand-kerchief to his face.

'Get me a drink,' he said, 'get me a drink.'

Maxim looked at Frank. Frank went out of the room. None of us spoke. In a moment Frank came back with the whisky and soda on a tray. He mixed some in a glass and gave it to Favell. Favell drank it greedily, like an animal. There was something sensual and horrible the way he put his mouth to the glass. His lips folded upon the glass in a peculiar way. There was a dark red patch on his jaw where Maxim had hit him. Maxim had turned his back on him again and had returned to the window. I glanced at Colonel Julyan and saw that he was looking at Maxim. His gaze was curious, intent. My heart began beating very quickly. Why did Colonel Julyan look at Maxim in that way?

Did it mean that he was beginning to wonder, to suspect?

Maxim did not see. He was watching the rain. It fell straight and steady as before. The sound filled the room. Favell finished his whisky and soda and put the glass back on the table beside the sofa. He was breathing heavily. He did not look at any of us. He was staring straight in front of him at the floor.

The telephone began ringing in the little room. It struck a shrill, discordant note. Frank went to answer it.

He came back at once and looked at Colonel Julyan. 'It's your daughter,' he said; 'they want to know if they are to keep dinner back.'

Colonel Julyan waved his hand impatiently. 'Tell them to start,' he said, 'tell them I don't know when I shall be back.' He glanced at his watch. 'Fancy ringing up,' he muttered; 'what a moment to choose.'

Frank went back into the little room to give the message. I thought of the daughter at the other end of the telephone. It would be the one who played golf. I could imagine her calling to her sister, 'Dad says we're to start. What on earth can he be doing? The steak will be like leather.' Their little household disorganized because of us. Their evening routine upset. All these foolish inconsequent threads hanging upon one another, because Maxim had killed Rebecca. I looked at Frank. His face was pale and set.

'I heard Robert coming back with the car,' he said to Colonel Julyan. 'The window in there looks on to the drive.'

He went out of the library to the hall. Favell had lifted his head when he spoke. Then he got to his feet once more and stood looking towards the door. There was a queer ugly smile on his face.

The door opened, and Frank came in. He turned and spoke to someone in the hall outside.

'All right, Ben,' he said quietly, 'Mr de Winter wants to give you some cigarettes. There's nothing to be frightened of.'

Ben stepped awkwardly into the room. He had his sou'wester in his hands. He looked odd and naked without his hat. I realized for the first time that his head was shaved all over, and he had no hair. He looked different, dreadful.

The light seemed to daze him. He glanced foolishly round the room, blinking his small eyes. He caught sight of me, and I gave him a weak, rather tremulous smile. I don't know if he recognized me or not. He just blinked his eyes. Then Favell walked slowly towards him and stood in front of him.

'Hullo,' he said; 'how's life treated you since we last met?'

Ben stared at him. There was no recognition on his face. He did not answer.

'Well?' said Favell, 'you know who I am, don't you?'

Ben went on twisting his sou'wester. 'Eh?' he said.

'Have a cigarette,' said Favell, handing him the box. Ben glanced at Maxim and Frank.

'All right,' said Maxim, 'take as many as you like.'

Ben took four and stuck two behind each ear. Then he stood twisting his cap again.

'You know who I am don't you?' repeated Favell.

Still Ben did not answer. Colonel Julyan walked across to him. 'You shall go home in a few moments, Ben,' he said. 'No one is going to hurt you. We just want you to answer one or two questions. You know Mr Favell, don't you?'

This time Ben shook his head. 'I never seen 'un,' he said.

'Don't be a bloody fool,' said Favell roughly; 'you know you've seen me. You've seen me go to the cottage on the beach, Mrs de Winter's cottage. You've seen me there, haven't you?'

'No,' said Ben. 'I never seen no one.'

'You damned half-witted liar,' said Favell, 'are you going to stand there and say you never saw me, last year, walk through those woods with Mrs de Winter, and go into the cottage? Didn't we catch you once, peering at us from the window?'

'Eh?' said Ben.

'A convincing witness,' said Colonel Julyan sarcastically.

Favell swung round on him. 'It's a put-up job,' he said. 'Someone has got at this idiot and bribed him too. I tell you he's seen me scores of times. Here. Will this make you remember?' He fumbled in his hip-pocket and brought out a note-case. He flourished a pound note in front of Ben. 'Now do you remember me?' he said.

Ben shook his head. 'I never seen 'un,' he said, and then he took hold of Frank's arm. 'Has he come here to take me to the asylum?' he said.

'No,' said Frank. 'No, of course not, Ben.'

'I don't want to go to the asylum,' said Ben. 'They'm cruel to folk in there. I want to stay home. I done nothing.'

'That's all right, Ben,' said Colonel Julyan. 'No one's going to put you in the asylum. Are you quite sure you've never seen this man before?'

'No,' said Ben. 'I've never seen 'un.'

'You remember Mrs de Winter, don't you?' said Colonel Julyan.

Ben glanced doubtfully towards me.

'No,' said Colonel Julyan gently, 'not this lady. The other lady, who used to go to the cottage.'

'Eh?' said Ben.

'You remember the lady who had the boat?'

Ben blinked his eyes. 'She's gone,' he said.

'Yes, we know that,' said Colonel Julyan. 'She used to sail the boat, didn't she? Were you on the beach when she sailed the boat the last time? One evening, over twelve months ago. When she didn't come back again?'

Ben twisted his sou'wester. He glanced at Frank, and then at Maxim.

'Eh?' he said.

'You were there, weren't you?' said Favell, leaning forward. 'You saw Mrs de Winter come down to the cottage, and presently you saw Mr de Winter too. He went into the cottage after her. What happened then? Go on. What happened?'

Ben shrank back against the wall. 'I seen nothing,' he said. 'I want to stay home. I'm not going to the asylum. I never seen you. Never before. I never seen you and she in the woods.' He began to blubber like a child.

'You crazy little rat,' said Favell slowly, 'you bloody crazy little rat.'

Ben was wiping his eyes with the sleeve of his coat.

'Your witness does not seem to have helped you,' said Colonel Julyan. 'The performance has been rather a waste of time, hasn't it? Do you want to ask him anything else?'

'It's a plot,' shouted Favell. 'A plot against me. You're all in it, every one of you. Someone's paid this half-wit, I tell you. Paid him to tell his string of dirty lies.'

'I think Ben might be allowed to go home,' said Colonel Julyan.

'All right, Ben,' said Maxim. 'Robert shall take you back. And no one will put you in the asylum, don't be afraid. Tell Robert to find him something in the kitchen,' he added to Frank. 'Some cold meat, whatever he fancies.'

'Payment for services rendered, eh?' said Favell. 'He's done a good day's work for you, Max, hasn't he?'

Frank took Ben out of the room. Colonel Julyan glanced at Maxim. 'The fellow appeared to be scared stiff,' he said; 'he was shaking like a leaf. I was watching him. He's never been ill-treated, has he?'

'No,' said Maxim, 'he's perfectly harmless, and I've always let him have the run of the place.'

'He's been frightened at some time,' said Colonel Julyan. 'He was showing the whites of his eyes, just like a dog does when you're going to whip him.'

'Well, why didn't you?' said Favell. 'He'd have remembered me all right if you'd whipped him. Oh, no, he's going to be given a good supper for his work tonight. Ben's not going to be whipped.'

'He has not helped your case, has he?' said Colonel Julyan quietly; 'we're still where we were. You can't produce one shred of evidence against de Winter and you know it. The very motive you gave won't stand the test. In a court of law, Favell, you wouldn't have a leg to stand on. You say you were Mrs de Winter's prospective husband, and that you held clandestine meetings with her in that cottage on the beach. Even the poor idiot we have just had in this room swears he never saw you. You can't even prove your own story, can you?'

'Can't I?' said Favell. I saw him smile. He came across to the fireplace and rang the bell.

'What are you doing?' said Colonel Julyan.

'Wait a moment and you'll see,' said Favell.

I guessed already what was going to happen. Frith answered the bell.

'Ask Mrs Danvers to come here,' said Favell.

Frith glanced at Maxim. Maxim nodded shortly.

Frith went out of the room. 'Isn't Mrs Danvers the house-keeper?' said Colonel Julyan.

'She was also Rebecca's personal friend,' said Favell. 'She was with her for years before she married and practically brought her up. You are going to find Danny a very different sort of witness to Ben.'

Frank came back into the room. 'Packed Ben off to bed?' said Favell. 'Given him his supper and told him he was a good boy? This time it won't be quite so easy for the trade union.'

'Mrs Danvers is coming down,' said Colonel Julyan. 'Favell seems to think he will get something out of her.'

Frank glanced quickly at Maxim. Colonel Julyan saw the glance. I saw his lips tighten. I did not like it. No, I did not like it. I began biting my nails.

We all waited, watching the door. And Mrs Danvers came into the room. Perhaps it was because I had generally seen her alone, and beside me she had seemed tall and gaunt, but she looked shrunken now in size, more wizened, and I noticed she had to look up to Favell and to Frank and Maxim. She stood by the door, her hands folded in front of her, looking from one to the other of us.

'Good evening, Mrs Danvers,' said Colonel Julyan.

'Good evening, sir,' she said.

Her voice was that old, dead, mechanical one I had heard so often.

'First of all, Mrs Danvers, I want to ask you a question,' said Colonel Julyan, 'and the question is this. Were you aware of the relationship between the late Mrs de Winter and Mr Favell here?'

'They were first cousins,' said Mrs Danvers.

'I was not referring to blood-relationship, Mrs Danvers,' said Colonel Julyan. 'I mean something closer than that.'

'I'm afraid I don't understand, sir,' said Mrs Danvers.

'Oh, come off it, Danny,' said Favell; 'you know damn well what he's driving at. I've told Colonel Julyan already, but he doesn't seem to believe me. Rebecca and I had lived together off and on for years, hadn't we? She was in love with me, wasn't she?'

To my surprise Mrs Danvers considered him a moment without speaking, and there was something of scorn in the glance she gave him.

'She was not,' she said.

'Listen here, you old fool . . .' began Favell, but Mrs Danvers cut him short.

'She was not in love with you, or with Mr de Winter. She was not in love with anyone. She despised all men. She was above all that.'

Favell flushed angrily. 'Listen here. Didn't she come down the path through the woods to meet me, night after night? Didn't you wait up for her? Didn't she spend the week-ends with me in London?'

'Well?' said Mrs Danvers, with sudden passion, 'and what if she did? She had a right to amuse herself, hadn't she. Love-making was a game with her, only a game. She told me so. She did it because it made her laugh. It made her laugh, I tell you. She laughed at you like she did at the rest. I've known her come back and sit upstairs in her bed and rock with laughter at the lot of you.'

There was something horrible in the sudden torrent of words, something horrible and unexpected. It revolted me, even though I knew. Maxim had gone very white. Favell stared at her blankly, as though he had not understood. Colonel Julyan tugged at his small moustache. No one said anything for a few minutes. And there was no sound but that inevitable falling rain. Then Mrs Danvers began to cry. She cried like she had done that morning in the bedroom. I could not look at her. I had to turn away. No one said anything. There were just the two sounds in the room, the falling rain and Mrs Danvers crying. It made me want to scream. I wanted to run out of the room and scream and scream.

No one moved towards her, to say anything, or to help her. She went on crying. Then at last, it seemed eternity, she began to control herself. Little by little the crying ceased. She stood quite still, her face working, her hands clutching the black stuff of her frock. At last she was silent again. Then Colonel Julyan spoke, quietly, slowly.

'Mrs Danvers,' he said, 'can you think of any reason, however remote, why Mrs de Winter should have taken her own life?'

Mrs Danvers swallowed. She went on clutching at her frock. She shook her head. 'No,' she said. 'No.'

'There, you see?' Favell said swiftly. 'It's impossible. She knows that as well as I do. I've told you already.'

'Be quiet, will you?' said Colonel Julyan. 'Give Mrs Danvers time to think. We all of us agree that on the face of it the thing's absurd, out of the question. I'm not disputing the truth or veracity of that note of yours. It's plain for us to see. She wrote you that note some time during those hours she spent in London. There was something she wanted to tell you. It's just possible that if we knew what that something was we might have the answer to the whole appalling problem. Let Mrs Danvers read the note. She may be able to throw light on it.' Favell shrugged his shoulders. He felt in his pocket for the note and threw it on the floor at Mrs Danvers' feet. She stooped and picked it up. We watched her lips move as she read the words. She read it twice. Then she shook her head. 'It's no use,' she said. 'I don't know what she meant. If there was something important she had to tell Mr Jack she would have told me first.'

'You never saw her that night?'

'No, I was out. I was spending the afternoon and evening in Kerrith. I shall never forgive myself for that. Never till my dying day.'

'Then you know of nothing on her mind, you can't suggest a solution, Mrs Danvers? Those words "*I have something to tell you*" do not convey anything to you at all?'

'No,' she answered. 'No, sir, nothing at all.'

'Does anybody know how she spent that day in London?'

Nobody answered. Maxim shook his head. Favell swore under his breath. 'Look here, she left that note at my flat at three in the afternoon,' he said. 'The porter saw her. She must have driven down here straight after that, and gone like the wind too.'

'Mrs de Winter had a hair appointment from twelve until one thirty,' said Mrs Danvers. 'I remember that, because I had to telephone through to London from here earlier in the week and book it for her. I remember doing it. Twelve to one thirty. She always lunched at her club after a hair appointment so that she could leave the pins in her hair. It's almost certain she lunched there that day.'

'Say it took her half-an-hour to have lunch; what was she doing from two until three? We ought to verify that,' said Colonel Julyan.

'Oh, Christ Jesus, who the hell cares what she was doing?' shouted Favell. 'She didn't kill herself, that's the only thing that matters, isn't it?'

'I've got her engagement diary locked in my room,' said Mrs Danvers slowly. 'I kept all those things. Mr de Winter never asked me for them. It's just possible she may have noted down her appointments for that day. She was methodical in that way. She used to put everything down and then tick the items off with a cross. If you think it would be helpful I'll go and fetch the diary.'

'Well, de Winter?' said Colonel Julyan, 'what do you say? Do you mind us seeing this diary?'

'Of course not,' said Maxim. 'Why on earth should I?'

Once again I saw Colonel Julyan give him that swift, curious glance. And this time Frank noticed it. I saw Frank look at Maxim too. And then back again to me. This time it was I who got up and went towards the window. It seemed to me that it was no longer raining quite so hard. The fury was spent. The rain that was falling now had a quieter, softer note. The grey light of evening had come into the sky. The lawns were dark and drenched with the heavy rain, and the trees had a shrouded humped appearance. I could hear the housemaid overhead drawing the curtains for the night, shutting down the windows that had not been closed already. The little routine of the day going on inevitably as it had always done. The curtains drawn, shoes taken down to be cleaned, the towel laid out on the chair in the bathroom, and the water run for my bath. Beds turned down, slippers put beneath a chair. And here were we in the library, none of us speaking, knowing in our hearts that Maxim was standing trial here for his life.

I turned round when I heard the soft closing of the door. It was Mrs Danvers. She had come back again with the diary in her hand.

'I was right,' she said quietly. 'She had marked down the engagements as I said she would. Here they are on the date she died.'

She opened the diary, a small, red leather book. She gave it to Colonel Julyan. Once more he brought his spectacles from his case. There was a long pause while he glanced down the page. It seemed to me then that there was something about that particular moment, while he looked at the page of the diary, and we stood waiting, that frightened me more than anything that had happened that evening.

I dug my nails in my hands. I could not look at Maxim. Surely Colonel Julyan must hear my heart beating and thumping in my breast?

'Ah!' he said. His finger was in the middle of the page. Something is going to happen, I thought, something terrible is going to happen. 'Yes,' he said, 'yes, here it is. Hair at twelve, as Mrs Danvers said. And a cross beside it. She kept her appointment, then. Lunch at the club, and a cross beside that. What have we here, though? Baker, two o'clock. Who was Baker?' He looked at Maxim. Maxim shook his head. Then at Mrs Danvers.

'Baker?' repeated Mrs Danvers. 'She knew no one called Baker. I've never heard the name before.'

'Well, here it is,' said Colonel Julyan, handing her the diary. 'You can see for yourself, Baker. And she's put a great cross beside it as though she wanted to break the pencil. She evidently saw this Baker, whoever he may have been.'

Mrs Danvers was staring at the name written in the diary, and the black cross beside it. 'Baker,' she said. 'Baker.'

'I believe if we knew who Baker was we'd be getting to the bottom of the whole business,' said Colonel Julyan. 'She wasn't in the hands of money-lenders, was she?'

Mrs Danvers looked at him with scorn. 'Mrs de Winter?' she said.

'Well, blackmailers perhaps?' said Colonel Julyan, with a glance at Favell.

Mrs Danvers shook her head. 'Baker,' she repeated. 'Baker.'

'She had no enemy, no one who had ever threatened her, no one she was afraid of?'

'Mrs de Winter afraid?' said Mrs Danvers. 'She was afraid of nothing and no one. There was only one thing ever worried her, and that was the idea of getting old, of illness, of dying in her bed. She has said to me a score of times, "When I go, Danny, I want to go quickly, like the snuffing out of a candle." That used to be the only thing that consoled me, after she died. They say drowning is painless, don't they?'

She looked searchingly at Colonel Julyan. He did not answer. He hesitated, tugging at his moustache. I saw him throw another glance at Maxim.

'What the hell's the use of all this?' said Favell, coming forward. 'We're streaking away from the point the whole bloody time. Who cares about this Baker fellow? What's he got to do with it? It was probably some damn merchant who sold stockings, or face-cream. If he had been anyone important Danny here would know him. Rebecca had no secrets from Danny.'

But I was watching Mrs Danvers. She had the book in her

hands and was turning the leaves. Suddenly she gave an exclamation.

'There's something here,' she said, 'right at the back among the telephone numbers. Baker. And there's a number beside it: 0488. But there is no exchange.'

'Brilliant Danny,' said Favell: 'becoming quite a sleuth in your old age, aren't you? But you're just twelve months too late. If you'd done this a year ago there might have been some use in it.'

'That's his number all right,' said Colonel Julyan, '0488, and the name Baker beside it. Why didn't she put the exchange?'

'Try every exchange in London,' jeered Favell. 'It will take you through the night but we don't mind. Max doesn't care if his telephone bill is a hundred pounds, do you, Max? You want to play for time, and so should I, if I were in your shoes.'

'There is a mark beside the number but it might mean anything,' said Colonel Julyan; 'take a look at it, Mrs Danvers. Could it possibly be an M?'

Mrs Danvers took the diary in her hands again. 'It might be,' she said doubtfully. 'It's not like her usual M but she may have scribbled it in a hurry. Yes, it might be M.'

'Mayfair 0488,' said Favell; 'what a genius, what a brain!'

'Well?' said Maxim, lighting his first cigarette, 'something had better be done about it. Frank? Go through and ask the exchange for Mayfair 0488.'

The nagging pain was strong beneath my heart. I stood quite still, my hands by my side. Maxim did not look at me.

'Go on, Frank,' he said. 'What are you waiting for?'

Frank went through to the little room beyond. We waited while he called the exchange. In a moment he was back again. 'They're going to ring me,' he said quietly. Colonel Julyan clasped his hands behind his back and began walking up and down the room. No one said anything. After about four minutes the telephone rang shrill and insistent, that irritating, monotonous note of a long-distance call. Frank went through to answer it. 'Is that Mayfair 0488?' he said. 'Can you tell me if anyone of the name of Baker lives there? Oh, I see. I'm so sorry. Yes, I must have got the wrong number. Thank you very much.'

The little click as he replaced the receiver. Then he came back into the room. 'Someone called Lady Eastleigh lives at Mayfair 0488. It's an address in Grosvenor Street. They've never heard of Baker.'

Favell gave a great cackle of laughter. 'The butcher, the baker, the candlestick-maker, they all jumped out of a rotten potato,' he said. 'Carry on, detective Number One, what's the next exchange on the list?'

'Try Museum,' said Mrs Danvers.

Frank glanced at Maxim. 'Go ahead,' said Maxim.

The farce was repeated all over again. Colonel Julyan repeated his walk up and down the room. Another five minutes went by, and the telephone rang again. Frank went to answer it. He left the door wide open, I could see him lean down to the table where the telephone stood, and bend to the mouth-piece.

'Hullo? Is that Museum 0488? Can you tell me if anyone of the name of Baker lives there? Oh; who is that speaking? A night porter. Yes. Yes, I understand. Not offices. No, no of course. Can you give me the address? Yes, it's rather important.' He paused. He called to us over his shoulder. 'I think we've got him,' he said.

Oh, God, don't let it be true. Don't let Baker be found. Please God make Baker be dead. I knew who Baker was. I had known all along. I watched Frank through the door, I watched him lean forward suddenly, reach for a pencil and a piece of paper. 'Hullo? Yes, I'm still here. Could you spell it? Thank you. Thank you very much. Good night.' He came back into the room, the piece of paper in his hands. Frank who loved Maxim, who did not know that the piece of paper he held was the one shred of evidence that was worth a damn in the whole nightmare of our evening, and that by producing it he could destroy Maxim as well and truly as though he had a dagger in his hand and stabbed him in the back.

'It was the night porter from an address in Bloomsbury,' he

said. 'There are no residents there at all. The place is used during the day as a doctor's consulting rooms. Apparently Baker's given up practice, and left six months ago. But we can get hold of him all right. The night porter gave me his address. I wrote it down on this piece of paper.'

## 25

It was then that Maxim looked at me. He looked at me for the first time that evening. And in his eyes I read a message of farewell. It was as though he leant against the side of a ship, and I stood below him on the quay. There would be other people touching his shoulder, and touching mine, but we would not see them. Nor would we speak or call to one another, for the wind and the distance would carry away the sound of our voices. But I should see his eyes and he would see mine before the ship drew away from the side of the quay. Favell, Mrs Danvers, Colonel Julyan, Frank with the slip of paper in his hands, they were all forgotten at this moment. It was ours, inviolate, a fraction of time suspended between two seconds. And then he turned away and held out his hand to Frank.

'Well done,' he said. 'What's the address?'

'Somewhere near Barnet, north of London,' said Frank, giving him the paper. 'But it's not on the telephone. We can't ring him up.'

'Satisfactory work, Crawley,' said Colonel Julyan, 'and from you too, Mrs Danvers. Can you throw any light on the matter now?'

Mrs Danvers shook her head. 'Mrs de Winter never needed a doctor. Like all strong people she despised them. We only had Doctor Phillips from Kerrith here once, that time she sprained her wrist. I've never heard her speak of this Doctor Baker, she never mentioned his name to me.'

'I tell you the fellow was a face-cream mixer,' said Favell. 'What the hell does it matter who he was? If there was anything to it Danny would know. I tell you it's some fool fellow who had discovered a new way of bleaching the hair or whitening the skin, and Rebecca had probably got the address from her hairdresser that morning and went along after lunch out of curiosity.'

'No,' said Frank. 'I think you're wrong there. Baker wasn't a quack. The night porter at Museum 0488 told me he was a very well-known woman's specialist.'

'H'm,' said Colonel Julyan, pulling at his moustache, 'there must have been something wrong with her after all. It seems very curious that she did not say a word to anybody, not even to you, Mrs Danvers.'

'She was too thin,' said Favell. 'I told her about it, but she only laughed. Said it suited her. Banting I suppose, like all these women. Perhaps she went to this chap Baker for a diet sheet.'

'Do you think that's possible, Mrs Danvers?' asked Colonel Julyan.

Mrs Danvers shook her head slowly. She seemed dazed, bewildered by this sudden news about Baker. 'I can't understand it,' she said. 'I don't know what it means. Baker. A Doctor Baker. Why didn't she tell me? Why did she keep it from me? She told me everything.'

'Perhaps she didn't want to worry you,' said Colonel Julyan. 'No doubt she made an appointment with him, and saw him, and then when she came down that night she was going to have told you all about it.'

'And the note to Mr Jack,' said Mrs Danvers suddenly. 'That note to Mr Jack, "*I have something to tell you. I must see you*"; she was going to tell him too?'

'That's true,' said Favell slowly. 'We were forgetting the note.' Once more he pulled it out of his pocket and read it to us aloud. '"*I've got something to tell you, and I want to see you as soon as possible. Rebecca.*"'

'Of course, there's no doubt about it,' said Colonel Julyan, turning to Maxim. 'I wouldn't mind betting a thousand pounds on it. She was going to tell Favell the result of that interview with this Doctor Baker.'

'I believe you're right after all,' said Favell. 'The note and that appointment seem to hang together. But what the hell was it all about, that's what I want to know? What was the matter with her?'

The truth screamed in their faces and they did not see. They all stood there, staring at one another, and they did not understand. I dared not look at them. I dared not move lest I betray my knowledge. Maxim said nothing. He had gone back to the window and was looking out into the garden that was hushed and dark and still. The rain had ceased at last, but the spots fell from the dripping leaves and from the gutter above the window.

'It ought to be quite easy to verify,' said Frank. 'Here is the doctor's present address. I can write him a letter and ask him if he remembers an appointment last year with Mrs de Winter.'

'I don't know if he would take any notice of it,' said Colonel Julyan, 'there is so much of this etiquette in the medical profession. Every case is confidential, you know. The only way to get anything out of him would be to get de Winter to see him privately and explain the circumstances. What do you say, de Winter?'

Maxim turned round from the window. 'I'm ready to do whatever you care to suggest,' he said quietly.

'Anything for time, eh?' said Favell; 'a lot can be done in twenty-four hours, can't it? Trains can be caught, ships can sail, aeroplanes can fly.'

I saw Mrs Danvers look sharply from Favell to Maxim, and I realized then, for the first time, that Mrs Danvers had not known about Favell's accusation. At last she was beginning to understand. I could tell from the expression on her face. There was doubt written on it, then wonder and hatred mixed, and then conviction. Once again those lean long hands of hers clutched convulsively at her dress, and she passed her tongue over her lips. She went on staring at Maxim. She never took her eyes away from Maxim. It's too late, I thought, she can't do anything to us now, the harm is done. It does not matter what she says to us now, or what she does. The harm is done. She can't hurt us any more. Maxim did not notice her, or if he did he gave no sign. He was talking to Colonel Julyan.

'What do you suggest?' he said. 'Shall I go up in the morning, drive to this address at Barnet? I can wire Baker to expect me.'

'He's not going alone,' said Favell, with a short laugh. 'I have a right to insist on that, haven't I? Send him up with Inspector Welch and I won't object.'

If only Mrs Danvers would take her eyes away from Maxim. Frank had seen her now. He was watching her, puzzled, anxious. I saw him glance once more at the slip of paper in his hands, on which he had written Doctor Baker's address. Then he too glanced at Maxim. I believe then that some faint idea of the truth began to force itself to his conscience, for he went very white and put the paper down on the table.

'I don't think there is any necessity to bring Inspector Welch into the affair – yet,' said Colonel Julyan. His voice was different, harder. I did not like the way he used the word 'yet'. Why must he use it at all? I did not like it. 'If I go with de Winter, and stay with him the whole time, and bring him back, will that satisfy you?' he said.

Favell looked at Maxim, and then at Colonel Julyan. The expression on his face was ugly, calculating, and there was some-thing of triumph too in his light blue eyes. 'Yes,' he said slowly, 'yes, I suppose so. But for safety's sake do you mind if I come with you too?'

'No,' said Colonel Julyan, 'unfortunately I think you have the right to ask that. But if you do come, I have the right to insist on your being sober.'

'You needn't worry about that,' said Favell, beginning to smile; 'I'll be sober all right. Sober as the judge will be when he sentences Max in three months' time. I rather think this Doctor Baker is going to prove my case, after all.'

He looked around at each one of us and began to laugh. I think he too had understood at last the significance of that visit to the doctor.

'Well,' he said, 'what time are we going to start in the morning?'

Colonel Julyan looked at Maxim. 'How early can you be ready?'

'Any time you say,' said Maxim.

'Nine o'clock?'

'Nine o'clock,' said Maxim.

'How do we know he won't do a bolt in the night?' said Favell. 'He's only to cut round to the garage and get his car.'

'Is my word enough for you?' said Maxim, turning to Colonel Julyan. And for the first time Colonel Julyan hesitated. I saw him glance at Frank. And a flush came over Maxim's face. I saw the little pulse beating on his forehead. 'Mrs Danvers,' he said slowly, 'when Mrs de Winter and I go to bed tonight will you come up yourself and lock the door on the outside? And call us yourself, at seven in the morning?'

'Yes, sir,' said Mrs Danvers. Still she kept her eyes on him, still her hands clutched at her dress.

'Very well, then,' said Colonel Julyan brusquely. 'I don't think there is anything else we need discuss, tonight. I shall be here sharp at nine in the morning. You will have room for me in your car, de Winter?'

'Yes,' said Maxim.

'And Favell will follow us in his?'

'Right on your tail, my dear fellow, right on your tail,' said Favell.

Colonel Julyan came up to me and took my hand. 'Good night,' he said. 'You know how I feel for you in all this, there's no need for me to tell you. Get your husband to bed early, if you can. It's going to be a long day.' He held my hand a minute and then he turned away. It was curious how he avoided my eye. He looked at my chin. Frank held the door for him as he went out. Favell leant forward and filled his case with cigarettes from the box on the table.

'I suppose I'm not going to be asked to stop to dinner?' he said.

Nobody answered. He lit one of the cigarettes, and blew a cloud of smoke into the air. 'It means a quiet evening at the pub on the highroad then,' he said, 'and the barmaid has a squint. What a hell of a night I'm going to spend! Never mind, I'm looking forward to tomorrow. Good night, Danny old lady, don't forget to turn the key on Mr de Winter, will you?'

He came over to me and held out his hand.

Like a foolish child I put my hands behind my back. He laughed, and bowed.

'It's just too bad, isn't it?' he said. 'A nasty man like me coming and spoiling all your fun. Don't worry, it will be a great thrill for you when the yellow Press gets going with your life story, and you see the headlines "From Monte Carlo to Manderley. Experiences of murderer's girl-bride," written across the top. Better luck next time.'

He strolled across the room to the door, waving his hand to Maxim by the window. 'So long, old man,' he said, 'pleasant dreams. Make the most of your night behind that locked door.' He turned and laughed at me, and then he went out of the room. Mrs Danvers followed him. Maxim and I were alone. He went on standing by the window. He did not come to me. Jasper came trotting in from the hall. He had been shut outside all the evening. He came fussing up to me, biting the edge of my skirt.

'I'm coming with you in the morning,' I said to Maxim. 'I'm coming up to London with you in the car.'

He did not answer for a moment. He went on looking out of the window. Then 'Yes,' he said, his voice without expression. 'Yes, we must go on being together.'

Frank came back into the room. He stood in the entrance, his hand on the door. 'They've gone,' he said, 'Favell and Colonel Julyan, I watched them go.'

'All right, Frank,' said Maxim.

'Is there anything I can do?' said Frank, 'anything at all? Wire to anyone, arrange anything? I'll stay up all night if only there's anything I can do. I'll get that wire off to Baker of course.'

'Don't worry,' said Maxim, 'there's nothing for you to do — yet. There may be plenty — after tomorrow. We can go into all that when the time comes. Tonight we want to be together. You understand, don't you?'

'Yes,' said Frank. 'Yes, of course.'

He waited a moment, his hand on the door. 'Good night,' he said.

'Good night,' said Maxim.

When he had gone, and shut the door behind him, Maxim came over to me where I was standing by the fireplace. I held out my arms to him and he came to me like a child. I put my arms round him and held him. We did not say anything for a long time. I held him and comforted him as though he were Jasper. As though Jasper had hurt himself in some way and he had come to me to take his pain away.

'We can sit together,' he said, 'driving up in the car.'

'Yes,' I said.

'Julyan won't mind,' he said.

'No,' I said.

'We shall have tomorrow night too,' he said. 'They won't do anything at once, not for twenty-four hours perhaps.'

'No,' I said.

'They aren't so strict now,' he said. 'They let one see people. And it all takes such a long time. If I can I shall try and get hold of Hastings. He's the best. Hastings or Birkett. Hastings used to know my father.'

'Yes,' I said.

'I shall have to tell him the truth,' he said. 'It makes it easier for them. They know where they are.'

'Yes,' I said.

The door opened and Frith came into the room. I pushed Maxim away, I stood up straight and conventional, patting my hair into place.

'Will you be changing, Madam, or shall I serve dinner at once?'

'No, Frith, we won't be changing, not tonight,' I said.

'Very good, Madam,' he said.

He left the door open. Robert came in and began drawing

396

the curtains. He arranged the cushions, straightened the sofa, tidied the books and papers on the table. He took away the whisky and soda and the dirty ash-trays. I had seen him do these things as a ritual every evening I had spent at Manderley, but tonight they seemed to take on a special significance, as though the memory of them would last for ever and I would say, long after, in some other time, 'I remember this moment.'

Then Frith came in and told us that dinner was served.

I remember every detail of that evening. I remember the ice-cold consommé in the cups, and the fillets of sole, and the hot shoulder of lamb.

I remember the burnt sugar sweet, the sharp savoury that followed.

We had new candles in the silver candlesticks, they looked white and slim and very tall. The curtains had been drawn here too against the dull grey evening. It seemed strange to be sitting in the dining-room and not look out on to the lawns. It was like the beginning of autumn.

It was while we were drinking our coffee in the library that the telephone rang. This time it was I who answered it. I heard Beatrice speaking at the other end. 'Is that you?' she said, 'I've been trying to get through all the evening. Twice it was engaged.'

'I'm so sorry,' I said, 'so very sorry.'

'We had the evening papers about two hours ago,' she said, 'and the verdict was a frightful shock to both Giles and myself. What does Maxim say about it?'

'I think it was a shock to everybody,' I said.

'But, my dear, the thing is preposterous. Why on earth should Rebecca have committed suicide? The most unlikely person in the world. There must have been a blunder somewhere.'

'I don't know,' I said.

'What does Maxim say? Where is he?' she said.

'People have been here,' I said – 'Colonel Julyan, and others. Maxim is very tired. We're going up to London tomorrow.'

'What on earth for?'

'Something to do with the verdict. I can't very well explain.'

'You ought to get it quashed,' she said. 'It's ridiculous, quite ridiculous. And so bad for Maxim, all this frightful publicity. It's going to reflect on him.'

'Yes,' I said.

'Surely Colonel Julyan can do something?' she said. 'He's a magistrate. What are magistrates for? Old Horridge from Lanyon must have been off his head. What was her motive supposed to be? It's the most idiotic thing I've ever heard in my life. Someone ought to get hold of Tabb. How can he tell whether those holes in the boat were made deliberately or not? Giles said of course it must have been the rocks.'

'They seemed to think not,' I said.

'If only I could have been there,' she said. 'I should have insisted on speaking. No one seems to have made any effort. Is Maxim very upset?'

'He's tired,' I said, 'more tired than anything else.'

'I wish I could come up to London and join you,' she said, 'but I don't see how I can. Roger has a temperature of 103, poor old boy, and the nurse we've got in is a perfect idiot, he loathes her. I can't possibly leave him.'

'Of course not,' I said. 'You mustn't attempt it.'

'Whereabouts in London will you be?'

'I don't know,' I said. 'It's all rather vague.'

'Tell Maxim he must try and do something to get that verdict altered. It's so bad for the family. I'm telling everybody here it's absolutely wicked. Rebecca would never have killed herself, she wasn't the type. I've got a good mind to write to the Coroner myself.'

'It's too late,' I said. 'Much better leave it. It won't do any good.'

'The stupidity of it gets my goat,' she said. 'Giles and I think it much more likely that if those holes weren't done by the rocks they were done deliberately, by some tramp or other. A Communist perhaps. There are heaps of them about. Just the sort of thing a Communist would do.'

Maxim called to me from the library. 'Can't you get rid of her? What on earth is she talking about?'

'Beatrice,' I said desperately, 'I'll try and ring you up from London.'

'Is it any good my tackling Dick Godolphin?' she said. 'He's your M.P. I know him very well, much better than Maxim does. He was at Oxford with Giles. Ask Maxim whether he would like me to telephone Dick and see if he can do anything to quash the verdict? Ask Maxim what he thinks of this Communist idea.'

'It's no use,' I said. 'It can't do any good. Please, Beatrice, don't try and do anything. It will make it worse, much worse. Rebecca may have had some motive we don't know anything about. And I don't think Communists go ramming holes in boats, what would be the use? Please, Beatrice, leave it alone.'

Oh, thank God she had not been with us today. Thank God for that at least. Something was buzzing in the telephone. I heard Beatrice shouting, 'Hullo, hullo, don't cut us off, exchange,' and then there was a click, and silence.

I went back into the library, limp and exhausted. In a few minutes the telephone began ringing again. I did not do anything. I let it ring. I went and sat down at Maxim's feet. It went on ringing. I did not move. Presently it stopped, as though cut suddenly in exasperation. The clock on the mantelpiece struck ten o'clock. Maxim put his arms round me and lifted me against him. We began to kiss one another, feverishly, desperately, like guilty lovers who have not kissed before.

## 26

When I awoke the next morning, just after six o'clock, and got up and went to the window there was a foggy dew upon the grass like frost, and the trees were shrouded in a white mist. There was a chill in the air and a little, fresh wind, and the cold, quiet smell of autumn.

As I knelt by the window looking down on to the rose-garden where the flowers themselves drooped upon their stalks, the petals brown and dragging after last night's rain, the happenings of the day before seemed remote and unreal. Here at Manderley a new day was starting, the things of the garden were not concerned with our troubles. A blackbird ran across the rose-garden to the lawns in swift, short rushes, stopping now and again to stab at the earth with his yellow beak. A thrush, too, went about his business, and two stout little wagtails, following one another, and a little cluster of twittering sparrows. A gull poised himself high in the air, silent and alone, and then spread his wings wide and swooped beyond the lawns to the woods and the Happy Valley. These things continued, our worries and anxieties had no power to alter them. Soon the gardeners would be astir, brushing the first leaves from the lawns and the paths, raking the gravel in the drive. Pails would clank in the court-yard behind the house, the hose would be turned on the car, the little scullery maid would begin to chatter through the open door to the men in the yard. There would be the crisp, hot smell of bacon. The housemaids would open up the house, throw wide the windows, draw back the curtains.

The dogs would crawl from their baskets, yawn and stretch themselves, wander out on to the terrace and blink at the first struggles of the pale sun coming through the mist. Robert would lay the table for breakfast, bring in those piping scones, the clutch of eggs, the glass dishes of honey, jam, and marmalade, the bowl of peaches, the cluster of purple grapes with the bloom upon them still, hot from the greenhouses.

Maids sweeping in the morning-room, the drawing-room, the fresh clean air pouring into the long open windows. Smoke curling from the chimneys, and little by little the autumn mist fading away and the trees and the banks and the woods taking shape, the glimmer of the sea showing with the sun upon it below the valley, the beacon standing tall and straight upon the headland.

The peace of Manderley. The quietude and the grace. Whoever lived within its walls, whatever trouble there was and strife, however much uneasiness and pain, no matter what tears were shed, what sorrows borne, the peace of Manderley could not be broken or the loveliness destroyed. The flowers that died would bloom again another year, the same birds build their nests, the same trees blossom. The old quiet moss smell would linger in the air, and bees would come, and crickets, and herons build their nests in the deep dark woods. The butterflies would dance their merry jig across the lawns, and spiders spin foggy webs, and small startled rabbits who had no business to come trespassing poke their faces through the crowded shrubs. There would be lilac and honeysuckle still, and the white magnolia buds unfolding slow and tight beneath the dining-room window. No one would ever hurt Manderley. It would lie always in a hollow like an enchanted thing, guarded by the woods, safe, secure, while the sea broke and ran and came again in the little shingle bays below.

Maxim slept on and I did not wake him. The day ahead of us would be a weary thing and long. Highroads, and telegraph poles, and the monotony of passing traffic, the slow crawl into London. We did not know what we should find at the end of our journey. The future was unknown. Somewhere to the north of London lived a man called Baker who had never heard of us, but he held our future in the hollow of his hand. Soon he too

401

would be waking, stretching, yawning, going about the business of his day. I got up, and went into the bathroom, and began to run my bath. These actions held for me the same significance as Robert and his clearing of the library had the night before. I had done these things before mechanically, but now I was aware as I dropped my sponge into the water, as I spread my towel on the chair from the hot rail, as I lay back and let the water run over my body. Every moment was a precious thing, having in it the essence of finality. When I went back to the bedroom and began to dress I heard a soft footstep come and pause outside the door, and the key turn quietly in the lock. There was silence a moment, and then the footsteps went away. It was Mrs Danvers.

She had not forgotten. I had heard the same sound the night before after we had come up from the library. She had not knocked upon the door, she had not made herself known; there was just the sound of footsteps and the turning of the key in the lock. It brought me to reality and the facing of the immediate future.

I finished dressing, and went and turned on Maxim's bath. Presently Clarice came with our tea. I woke Maxim. He stared at me at first like a puzzled child, and then he held out his arms. We drank our tea. He got up and went to his bath and I began putting things methodically in my suit-case. It might be that we should have to stay in London.

I packed the brushes Maxim had given me, a nightdress, my dressing-gown and slippers, and another dress too and a pair of shoes. My dressing-case looked unfamiliar as I dragged it from the back of a wardrobe. It seemed so long since I had used it, and yet it was only four months ago. It still had the Customs mark upon it they had chalked at Calais. In one of the pockets was a concert ticket from the casino in Monte Carlo. I crumpled it and threw it into the waste-paper basket. It might have belonged to another age, another world. My bedroom began to take on the appearance of all rooms when the owner goes away. The dressing-table was bare without my brushes. There was tissue-paper lying on the floor, and an old label. The beds where we had slept had a terrible emptiness about them. The towels lay crumpled on the bathroom floor. The wardrobe doors gaped open. I put on my hat so that I should not have to come up again, and I took my bag and my gloves and my suit-case. I glanced round the room to see if there was anything I had forgotten. The mist was breaking, the sun was forcing its way through and throwing patterns on the carpet. When I was half-way down the passage I had a curious, inexplicable feeling that I must go back and look in my room again. I went without reason, and stood a moment looking at the gaping wardrobe and the empty bed, and the tray of tea upon the table. I stared at them, impressing them for ever on my mind, wondering why they had the power to touch me, to sadden me, as though they were children that did not want me to go away.

Then I turned and went downstairs to breakfast. It was cold in the dining-room, the sun not yet on the windows, and I was grateful for the scalding bitter coffee and heartening bacon. Maxim and I ate in silence. Now and again he glanced at the clock. I heard Robert put the suit-cases in the hall with the rug, and presently there was the sound of the car being brought to the door.

I went out and stood on the terrace. The rain had cleared the air, and the grass smelt fresh and sweet. When the sun was higher it would be a lovely day. I thought how we might have wandered in the valley before lunch, and then sat out afterwards under the chestnut tree with books and papers. I closed my eyes a minute and felt the warmth of the sun on my face and on my hands.

I heard Maxim calling to me from the house. I went back, and Frith helped me into my coat. I heard the sound of another car. It was Frank.

'Colonel Julyan is waiting at the lodge gates,' he said. 'He did not think it worth while to drive up to the house.'

'No,' said Maxim.

'I'll stand by in the office all day and wait for you to tele-phone,' said Frank. 'After you've seen Baker you may find you want me, up in London.'

'Yes,' said Maxim. 'Yes, perhaps.'

'It's just nine now,' said Frank. 'You're up to time. It's going to be fine too. You should have a good run.'

'Yes.'

'I hope you won't get over-tired, Mrs de Winter,' he said to me. 'It's going to be a long day for you.'

'I shall be all right,' I said. I looked at Jasper who was standing by my feet with ears drooping and sad reproachful eyes.

'Take Jasper back with you to the office,' I said. 'He looks so miserable.'

'Yes,' he said. 'Yes, I will.'

'We'd better be off,' said Maxim. 'Old Julyan will be getting impatient. All right, Frank.'

I climbed in the car beside Maxim. Frank slammed the door.

'You will telephone, won't you?' he said.

'Yes, of course,' said Maxim.

I looked back at the house. Frith was standing at the top of the steps, and Robert just behind. My eyes filled with tears for no reason. I turned away and groped with my bag on the floor of the car so that nobody should see. Then Maxim started up the car and we swept round and into the drive and the house was hidden.

We stopped at the lodge-gates and picked up Colonel Julyan. He got in at the back. He looked doubtful when he saw me.

'It's going to be a long day,' he said. 'I don't think you should have attempted it. I would have taken care of your husband you know.'

'I wanted to come,' I said.

He did not say any more about it. He settled himself in the corner. 'It's fine, that's one thing,' he said.

'Yes,' said Maxim.

'That fellow Favell said he would pick us up at the cross-roads. If he's not there don't attempt to wait, we'd do much better without him. I hope the damned fellow has overslept himself.'

When we came to the cross-roads though I saw the long

green body of his car, and my heart sank. I had thought he might not be on time. Favell was sitting at the wheel, hatless, a cigarette in his mouth. He grinned when he saw us, and waved us on. I settled down in my seat for the journey ahead, one hand on Maxim's knee. The hours passed, and the miles were covered. I watched the road ahead in a kind of stupor. Colonel Julyan slept at the back from time to time. I turned occasionally and saw his head loll against the cushions, and his mouth open. The green car kept close beside us. Sometimes it shot ahead, sometimes it dropped behind. But we never lost it. At one we stopped for lunch at one of those inevitable old-fashioned hotels in the main street of a county town. Colonel Julyan waded through the whole set lunch, starting with soup and fish, and going on to roast beef and Yorkshire pudding. Maxim and I had cold ham and coffee.

I half expected Favell to wander into the dining-room and join us, but when we came out to the car again I saw his car had been drawn up outside a café on the opposite side of the road. He must have seen us from the window, for three minutes after we had started he was on our tail again.

We came to the suburbs of London about three o'clock. It was then that I began to feel tired, the noise and the traffic blocks started a humming in my head. It was warm in London too. The streets had that worn dusty look of August, and the leaves hung listless on dull trees. Our storm must have been local, there had been no rain here.

People were walking about in cotton frocks and the men were hatless. There was a smell of waste-paper, and orange-peel, and feet, and burnt dried grass. Buses lumbered slowly, and taxis crawled. I felt as though my coat and skirt were sticking to me, and my stockings pricked my skin.

Colonel Julyan sat up and looked out through his window. 'They've had no rain here,' he said.

'No,' said Maxim.

'Looks as though the place needed it, too.'

'Yes.'

'We haven't succeeded in shaking Favell off. He's still on our tail.'

'Yes.'

Shopping centres on the outskirts seemed congested. Tired women with crying babies in prams stared into windows, hawkers shouted, small boys hung on to the backs of lorries. There were too many people, too much noise. The very air was irritable and exhausted and spent.

The drive through London seemed endless, and by the time we had drawn clear again and were out beyond Hampstead there was a sound in my head like the beating of a drum, and my eyes were burning.

I wondered how tired Maxim was. He was pale, and there were shadows under his eyes, but he did not say anything. Colonel Julyan kept yawning at the back. He opened his mouth very wide and yawned aloud, sighing heavily afterwards. He would do this every few minutes. I felt a senseless stupid irritation come over me, and I did not know how to prevent myself from turning round and screaming to him to stop.

Once we had passed Hampstead he drew out a large-scale map from his coat-pocket and began directing Maxim to Barnet. The way was clear and there were sign-posts to tell us, but he kept pointing out every turn and twist in the road, and if there was any hesitation on Maxim's part Colonel Julyan would turn down the window and call for information from a passer-by.

When we came to Barnet itself he made Maxim stop every few minutes. 'Can you tell us where a house called Roselands is? It belongs to a Doctor Baker, who's retired, and come to live there lately,' and the passer-by would stand frowning a moment, obviously at sea, ignorance written plain upon his face.

'Doctor Baker? I don't know a Doctor Baker. There used to be a house called Rose Cottage near the church, but a Mrs Wilson lives there.'

'No, it's Roselands we want, Doctor Baker's house,' said Colonel Julyan, and then we would go on and stop again in front of a nurse and a pram. 'Can you tell us where Roselands is?'

'I'm sorry. I'm afraid I've only just come to live here.'

'You don't know a Doctor Baker?'

'Doctor Davidson. I know Doctor Davidson.'

'No, it's Doctor Baker we want.'

I glanced up at Maxim. He was looking very tired. His mouth was set hard. Behind us crawled Favell, his green car covered in dust.

It was a postman who pointed out the house in the end. A square house, ivy covered, with no name on the gate, which we had already passed twice. Mechanically I reached for my bag and dabbed my face with the end of the powder puff. Maxim drew up outside at the side of the road. He did not take the car into the short drive. We sat silently for a few minutes.

'Well, here we are,' said Colonel Julyan, 'and it's exactly twelve minutes past five. We shall catch them in the middle of their tea. Better wait for a bit.'

Maxim lit a cigarette, and then stretched out his hand to me. He did not speak. I heard Colonel Julyan crinkling his map.

'We could have come right across without touching London,' he said, 'saved us forty minutes I dare say. We made good time the first two hundred miles. It was from Chiswick on we took the time.'

An errand-boy passed us whistling on his bicycle. A motor-coach stopped at the corner and two women got out. Somewhere a church clock chimed the quarter. I could see Favell leaning back in his car behind us and smoking a cigarette. I seemed to have no feeling in me at all. I just sat and watched the little things that did not matter. The two women from the bus walk along the road. The errand-boy disappears round the corner. A sparrow hops about in the middle of the road pecking at dirt.

'This fellow Baker can't be much of a gardener,' said Colonel Julyan. 'Look at those shrubs tumbling over his wall. They ought to have been pruned right back.' He folded up the map and put it back in his pocket. 'Funny sort of place to choose to retire in,' he said. 'Close to the main road and overlooked by other houses. Shouldn't care about it myself. I dare say it was quite pretty once before they started building. No doubt there's a good golf-course somewhere handy.'

He was silent for a while, then he opened the door and stood out in the road. 'Well, de Winter,' he said, 'what do you think about it?'

'I'm ready,' said Maxim.

We got out of the car. Favell strolled up to meet us.

'What were you all waiting for, cold feet?' he said.

Nobody answered him. We walked up the drive to the front door, a strange incongruous little party. I caught sight of a tennis lawn beyond the house, and I heard the thud of balls. A boy's voice shouted 'Forty-fifteen, not thirty all. Don't you remember hitting it out, you silly ass?'

'They must have finished tea,' said Colonel Julyan.

He hesitated a moment, glancing at Maxim. Then he rang the bell.

It tinkled somewhere in the back premises. There was a long pause. A very young maid opened the door to us. She looked startled at the sight of so many of us.

'Doctor Baker?' said Colonel Julyan.

'Yes, sir, will you come in?'

She opened the door on the left of the hall as we went in. It would be the drawing-room, not used much in the summer. There was a portrait of a very plain dark woman on the wall. I wondered if it was Mrs Baker. The chintz covers on the chairs and on the sofa were new and shiny. On the mantelpiece were photographs of two schoolboys with round, smiling faces. There was a very large wireless in the corner of the room by the window. Cords trailed from it, and bits of aerial. Favell examined the portrait on the wall. Colonel Julyan went and stood by the empty fireplace. Maxim and I looked out of the window. I could see a deck-chair under a tree, and the back of a woman's head. The tennis court must be round the corner. I could hear

408

the boys shouting to each other. A very old Scotch terrier was scratching himself in the middle of the path. We waited there for about five minutes. It was as though I was living the life of some other person and had come to this house to call for a subscription to a charity. It was unlike anything I had ever known. I had no feeling, no pain.

Then the door opened and a man came into the room. He was medium height, rather long in the face, with a keen chin. His hair was sandy, turning grey. He wore flannels, and a dark blue blazer.

'Forgive me for keeping you waiting,' he said, looking a little surprised, as the maid had done, to see so many of us. 'I had to run up and wash. I was playing tennis when the bell rang. Won't you sit down?' He turned to me. I sat down in the nearest chair and waited.

'You must think this a very unorthodox invasion, Doctor Baker,' said Colonel Julyan, 'and I apologize very humbly for disturbing you like this. My name is Julyan. This is Mr de Winter, Mrs de Winter, and Mr Favell. You may have seen Mr de Winter's name in the papers recently.'

'Oh,' said Doctor Baker, 'yes, yes, I suppose I have. Some inquest or other, wasn't it? My wife was reading all about it.'

'The jury brought in a verdict of suicide,' said Favell coming forward, 'which I say is absolutely out of the question. Mrs de Winter was my cousin, I knew her intimately. She would never have done such a thing, and what's more she had no motive. What we want to know is what the devil she came to see you about the very day she died?'

'You had better leave this to Julyan and myself,' said Maxim quietly. 'Doctor Baker has not the faintest idea what you are driving at.'

He turned to the doctor who was standing between them with a line between his brows, and his first polite smile frozen on his lips. 'My late wife's cousin is not satisfied with the verdict,' said Maxim, 'and we've driven up to see you today because we found your name, and the telephone number of your old consulting-rooms, in my wife's engagement diary. She seems to have made an appointment with you, and kept it, at two o'clock on the last day she ever spent in London. Could you possibly verify this for us?'

Doctor Baker was listening with great interest, but when Maxim had finished he shook his head. 'I'm most awfully sorry,' he said, 'but I think you've made a mistake. I should have remembered the name de Winter. I've never attended a Mrs de Winter in my life.'

Colonel Julyan brought out his note case and gave him the page he had torn from the engagement diary. 'Here it is, written down,' he said, 'Baker, two o'clock. And a big cross beside it, to show that the appointment was kept. And here is the telephone address. Museum 0488.'

Doctor Baker stared at the piece of paper. 'That's very odd, very odd indeed. Yes, the number is quite correct as you say.'

'Could she have come to see you and given a false name?' said Colonel Julyan.

'Why, yes, that's possible. She may have done that. It's rather unusual of course. I've never encouraged that sort of thing. It doesn't do us any good in the profession if people think they can treat us like that.'

'Would you have any record of the visit in your files?' said Colonel Julyan. 'I know it's not etiquette to ask, but the circumstances are very unusual. We do feel her appointment with you must have some bearing on the case and her subsequent – suicide.'

'Murder,' said Favell.

Doctor Baker raised his eyebrows, and looked inquiringly at Maxim. 'I'd no idea there was any question of that,' he said quietly. 'Of course I understand, and I'll do anything in my power to help you. If you will excuse me a few minutes I will go and look up my files. There should be a record of every appointment booked throughout the year, and a description of the case. Please help yourself to cigarettes. It's too early to offer you sherry, I suppose?'

Colonel Julyan and Maxim shook their heads. I thought Favell

410

was going to say something but Doctor Baker had left the room before he had a chance.

'Seems a decent sort of fellow,' said Colonel Julyan.

'Why didn't he offer us whisky and soda?' said Favell. 'Keeps it locked up, I suppose. I didn't think much of him. I don't believe he's going to help us now.'

Maxim did not say anything. I could hear the sound of the tennis balls from the court. The Scotch terrier was barking. A woman's voice shouted to him to be quiet. The summer holidays. Baker playing with his boys. We had interrupted their routine. A high-pitched, gold clock in a glass case ticked very fast on the mantelpiece. There was a postcard of the Lake of Geneva leaning against it. The Bakers had friends in Switzerland.

Doctor Baker came back into the room with a large book and a file-case in his hands. He carried them over to the table. 'I've brought the collection for last year,' he said. 'I haven't been through them yet since we moved. I only gave up practice six months ago you know.' He opened the book and began turning the pages. I watched him fascinated. He would find it of course. It was only a question of moments now, of seconds. 'The seventh, eighth, tenth,' he murmured, 'nothing here. The twelfth did you say? At two o'clock? Ah!'

We none of us moved. We all watched his face.

'I saw a Mrs Danvers on the twelfth at two o'clock,' he said.

'Danny? What on earth . . .' began Favell, but Maxim cut him short.

'She gave a wrong name, of course,' he said. 'That was obvious from the first. Do you remember the visit now, Doctor Baker?'

But Doctor Baker was already searching his files. I saw his fingers delve into the pocket marked with D. He found it almost at once. He glanced down rapidly at his handwriting. 'Yes,' he said slowly. 'Yes, Mrs Danvers. I remember now.'

'Tall, slim, dark, very handsome?' said Colonel Julyan quietly.

'Yes,' said Doctor Baker. 'Yes.'

He read through the files, and then replaced them in the case. 'Of course,' he said, glancing at Maxim, 'this is unprofessional you know? We treat patients as though they were in the confessional. But your wife is dead, and I quite understand the circumstances are exceptional. You want to know if I can suggest any motive why your wife should have taken her life? I think I can. The woman who called herself Mrs Danvers was very seriously ill.'

He paused. He looked at every one of us in turn.

'I remember her perfectly well,' he said, and he turned back to the files again. 'She came to me for the first time a week previously to the date you mentioned. She complained of certain symptoms, and I took some X-rays of her. The second visit was to find out the result of those X-rays. The photographs are not here, but I have the details written down. I remember her standing in my consulting-room and holding out her hand for the photographs. "I want to know the truth," she said; "I don't want soft words and a bedside manner. If I'm for it, you can tell me right away."' He paused, he glanced down at the files once again.

I waited, waited. Why couldn't he get done with it and finish and let us go? Why must we sit there, waiting, our eyes upon his face.

'Well,' he said, 'she asked for the truth, and I let her have it. Some patients are better for it. Shirking the point does them no good. This Mrs Danvers, or Mrs de Winter rather, was not the type to accept a lie. You must have known that. She stood it very well. She did not flinch. She said she had suspected it for some time. Then she paid my fee and went out. I never saw her again.'

He shut up the box with a snap, and closed the book. 'The pain was slight as yet, but the growth was deep-rooted,' he said, 'and in three or four months' time she would have been under morphia. An operation would have been no earthly use at all. I told her that. The thing had got too firm a hold. There is nothing anyone can do in a case like that, except give morphia, and wait.'

No one said a word. The little clock ticked on the mantelpiece, and the boys played tennis in the garden. An aeroplane hummed overhead.

'Outwardly of course she was a perfectly healthy woman,' he said – 'rather too thin, I remember, rather pale; but then that's the fashion nowadays, pity though it is. It's nothing to go upon with a patient. No, the pain would increase week by week, and as I told you, in four or five months' time she would have had to be kept under morphia. The X-rays showed a certain malformation of the uterus, I remember, which meant she could never have had a child; but that was quite apart, it had nothing to do with the disease.'

I remember hearing Colonel Julyan speak, saying something about Doctor Baker being very kind to have taken so much trouble. 'You have told us all we want to know,' he said, 'and if we could possibly have a copy of the memoranda in your file it might be very useful.'

'Of course,' said Doctor Baker. 'Of course.'

Everyone was standing up. I got up from my chair too, I shook hands with Doctor Baker. We all shook hands with him. We followed him out into the hall. A woman looked out of the room on the other side of the hall and darted back when she saw us. Someone was running a bath upstairs, the water ran loudly. The Scotch terrier came in from the garden and began sniffing at my heels.

'Shall I send the report to you or to Mr de Winter?' said Doctor Baker.

'We may not need it at all,' said Colonel Julyan. 'I rather think it won't be necessary. Either de Winter or I will write. Here is my card.'

'I'm so glad to have been of use,' said Doctor Baker; 'it never entered my head for a moment that Mrs de Winter and Mrs Danvers could be the same person.'

'No, naturally,' said Colonel Julyan.

'You'll be returning to London, I suppose?'

'Yes. Yes, I imagine so.'

'Your best way then is to turn sharp left by that pillar-box, and then right by the church. After that it's a straight road.'

'Thank you. Thank you very much.'

We came out on to the drive and went towards the cars. Doctor Baker pulled the Scotch terrier inside the house. I heard the door shut. A man with one leg and a barrel-organ began playing 'Roses in Picardy', at the end of the road.

# 27

We went and stood by the car. No one said anything for a few minutes. Colonel Julyan handed round his cigarette case. Favell looked grey, rather shaken. I noticed his hands were trembling as he held the match. The man with the barrel organ ceased playing for a moment and hobbled towards us, his cap in his hand. Maxim gave him two shillings. Then he went back to the barrel-organ and started another tune. The church clock struck six o'clock. Favell began to speak. His voice was diffident, careless, but his face was still grey. He did not look at any of us, he kept glancing down at his cigarette and turning it over in his fingers. 'This cancer business,' he said; 'does anybody know if it's contagious?'

No one answered him. Colonel Julyan shrugged his shoulders.

'I never had the remotest idea,' said Favell jerkily. 'She kept it a secret from everyone, even Danny. What a God-damned appalling thing, eh? Not the sort of thing one would ever connect with Rebecca. Do you fellows feel like a drink? I'm all out over this, and I don't mind admitting it. Cancer! Oh, my God!'

He leant up against the side of the car and shaded his eyes with his hands. 'Tell that bloody fellow with the barrel organ to clear out,' he said. 'I can't stand that God-damned row.'

'Wouldn't it be simpler if we went ourselves?' said Maxim. 'Can you manage your own car, or do you want Julyan to drive it for you?'

'Give me a minute,' muttered Favell. 'I'll be all right. You don't understand. This thing has been a damned unholy shock to me.'

'Pull yourself together, man, for heaven's sake,' said Colonel Julyan. 'If you want a drink go back to the house and ask Baker.

He knows how to treat for shock, I dare say. Don't make an exhibition of yourself in the street.'

'Oh, you're all right, you're fine,' said Favell, standing straight and looking at Colonel Julyan and Maxim. 'You've got nothing to worry about any more. Max is on a good wicket now, isn't he? You've got your motive, and Baker will supply it in black and white free of cost, whenever you send the word. You can dine at Manderley once a week on the strength of it and feel proud of yourself. No doubt Max will ask you to be godfather to his first child.'

'Shall we get into the car and go?' said Colonel Julyan to Maxim. 'We can make our plans going along.'

Maxim held open the door of the car, and Colonel Julyan climbed in. I sat down in my seat in the front. Favell still leant against the car and did not move. 'I should advise you to get straight back to your flat and go to bed,' said Colonel Julyan shortly, 'and drive slowly, or you will find yourself in jail for manslaughter. I may as well warn you now, as I shall not be seeing you again, that as a magistrate I have certain powers that will prove effective if you ever turn up in Kerrith or the district. Blackmail is not much of a profession, Mr Favell. And we know how to deal with it in our part of the world, strange though it may seem to you.'

Favell was watching Maxim. He had lost the grey colour now, and the old unpleasant smile was forming on his lips. 'Yes, it's been a stroke of luck for you, Max, hasn't it?' he said slowly; 'you think you've won, don't you? The law can get you yet, and so can I, in a different way . . .'

Maxim switched on the engine. 'Have you anything else you want to say?' he said; 'because if you have you had better say it now.'

'No,' said Favell. 'No, I won't keep you. You can go.' He stepped back on to the pavement, the smile still on his lips. The car slid forward. As we turned the corner I looked back and saw him standing there, watching us, and he waved his hand and he was laughing.

We drove on for a while in silence. Then Colonel Julyan spoke. 'He can't do anything,' he said. 'That smile and that wave were part of his bluff. They're all alike, those fellows. He hasn't a thread of a case to bring now. Baker's evidence would squash it.'

Maxim did not answer. I glanced sideways at his face but it told me nothing. 'I always felt the solution would lie in Baker,' said Colonel Julyan; 'the furtive business of that appointment, and the way she never even told Mrs Danvers. She had her suspicions, you see. She knew something was wrong. A dreadful thing, of course. Very dreadful. Enough to send a young and lovely woman right off her head.'

We drove on along the straight main road. Telegraph poles, motor coaches, open sports cars, little semi-detached villas with new gardens, they flashed past making patterns in my mind I should always remember.

'I suppose you never had any idea of this, de Winter?' said Colonel Julyan.

'No,' said Maxim. 'No.'

'Of course some people have a morbid dread of it,' said Colonel Julyan. 'Women especially. That must have been the case with your wife. She had courage for every other thing but that. She could not face pain. Well, she was spared that at any rate.'

'Yes,' said Maxim.

'I don't think it would do any harm if I quietly let it be known down in Kerrith and in the county that a London doctor has supplied us with a motive,' said Colonel Julyan. 'Just in case there should be any gossip. You never can tell, you know. People are odd, sometimes. If they knew about Mrs de Winter it might make it a lot easier for you.'

'Yes,' said Maxim, 'yes, I understand.'

'It's curious and very irritating,' said Colonel Julyan slowly, 'how long stories spread in country districts. I never know why they should, but unfortunately they do. Not that I anticipate any trouble over this, but it's as well to be prepared. People are inclined to say the wildest things if they are given half a chance.'

'Yes,' said Maxim.

'You and Crawley of course can squash any nonsense in Manderley or the estate, and I can deal with it effectively in Kerrith. I shall say a word to my girl too. She sees a lot of the younger people, who very often are the worst offenders in story-telling. I don't suppose the newspapers will worry you any more, that's one good thing. You'll find they will drop the whole affair in a day or two.'

'Yes,' said Maxim.

We drove on through the northern suburbs and came once more to Finchley and Hampstead.

'Half past six,' said Colonel Julyan; 'what do you propose doing? I've got a sister living in St John's Wood, and feel inclined to take her unawares and ask for dinner, and then catch the last train from Paddington. I know she doesn't go away for another week. I'm sure she would be delighted to see you both as well.'

Maxim hesitated, and glanced at me. 'It's very kind of you,' he said, 'but I think we had better be independent. I must ring up Frank, and one thing and another. I dare say we shall have a quiet meal somewhere and start off again afterwards, spending the night at a pub on the way, I rather think that's what we shall do.'

'Of course,' said Colonel Julyan, 'I quite understand. Could you throw me out at my sister's? It's one of those turnings off the Avenue Road.'

When we came to the house Maxim drew up a little way ahead of the gate. 'It's impossible to thank you,' he said, 'for all you've done today. You know what I feel about it without my telling you.'

'My dear fellow,' said Colonel Julyan, 'I've been only too glad. If only we'd known what Baker knew of course there would have been none of this at all. However, never mind about that now. You must put the whole thing behind you as a very unpleasant and unfortunate episode. I'm pretty sure you won't have any more trouble from Favell. If you do, I count on you

418

to tell me at once. I shall know how to deal with him.' He climbed out of the car, collecting his coat and his map. 'I should feel inclined,' he said, not looking directly at us, 'to get away for a bit. Take a short holiday. Go abroad, perhaps.'

We did not say anything. Colonel Julyan was fumbling with his map. 'Switzerland is very nice this time of year,' he said. 'I remember we went once for the girl's holidays, and thoroughly enjoyed ourselves. The walks are delightful.' He hesitated, cleared his throat. 'It is just faintly possible certain little difficulties might arise,' he said, 'not from Favell, but from one or two people in the district. One never knows quite what Tabb has been saying, and repeating, and so on. Absurd of course. But you know the old saying? Out of sight, out of mind. If people aren't there to be talked about the talk dies. It's the way of the world.'

He stood for a moment, counting his belongings. 'I've got everything, I think. Map, glasses, stick, coat. Everything complete. Well, good-bye, both of you. Don't get over-tired. It's been a long day.'

He turned in at the gate and went up the steps. I saw a woman come to the window and smile and wave her hand. We drove away down the road and turned the corner. I leant back in my seat and closed my eyes. Now that we were alone again and the strain was over, the sensation was one of almost unbearable relief. It was like the bursting of an abscess. Maxim did not speak. I felt his hand cover mine. We drove on through the traffic and I saw none of it. I heard the rumble of the buses, the hooting of taxis, that inevitable, tireless London roar, but I was not part of it. I rested in some other place that was cool and quiet and still. Nothing could touch us any more. We had come through our crisis.

When Maxim stopped the car I opened my eyes and sat up. We were opposite one of those numerous little restaurants in a narrow street in Soho. I looked about me, dazed and stupid.

'You're tired,' said Maxim briefly. 'Empty and tired and fit for nothing. You'll be better when you've had something to eat. So

419

shall I. We'll go in here and order dinner right away. I can telephone to Frank too.'

We got out of the car. There was no one in the restaurant
but the *maître d'hôtel* and a waiter and a girl behind a desk. It
was dark and cool. We went to a table right in the corner. Maxim
began ordering the food. 'Favell was right about wanting a drink,'
he said. 'I want one too and so do you. You're going to have
some brandy.'

The *maître d'hotel* was fat and smiling. He produced long thin
rolls in paper envelopes. They were very hard, very crisp. I began
to eat one ravenously. My brandy and soda was soft, warming,
curiously comforting.

'When we've had dinner we'll drive slowly, very quietly,' said
Maxim. 'It will be cool, too, in the evening. We'll find somewhere on the road we can put up for the night. Then we can
get along to Manderley in the morning.'

'Yes,' I said.

'You didn't want to dine with Julyan's sister and go down by
the late train?'

'No.'

Maxim finished his drink. His eyes looked large and they were
ringed with the shadows. They seemed very dark against the
pallor of his face.

'How much of the truth', he said, 'do you think Julyan
guessed?'

I watched him over the rim of my glass. I did not say anything.

'He knew,' said Maxim slowly, 'of course he knew.'

'If he did,' I said, 'he will never say anything. Never, never.'

'No,' said Maxim. 'No.'

He ordered another drink from the *maître d'hôtel*. We sat silent
and peaceful in our dark corner.

'I believe', said Maxim, 'that Rebecca lied to me on purpose.
The last supreme bluff. She wanted me to kill her. She foresaw
the whole thing. That's why she laughed. That's why she stood
there laughing when she died.'

I did not say anything. I went on drinking my brandy and

soda. It was all over. It was all settled. It did not matter any more. There was no need for Maxim to look white and troubled.

'It was her last practical joke,' said Maxim, 'the best of them all. And I'm not sure if she hasn't won, even now.'

'What do you mean? How can she have won?' I said.

'I don't know,' he said. 'I don't know.' He swallowed his second drink. Then he got up from the table. 'I'm going to ring up Frank,' he said.

I sat there in my corner, and presently the waiter brought me my fish. It was lobster. Very hot and good. I had another brandy and soda, too. It was pleasant and comfortable sitting there and nothing mattered very much. I smiled at the waiter. I asked for some more bread in French for no reason. It was quiet and happy and friendly in the restaurant. Maxim and I were together. Everything was over. Everything was settled. Rebecca was dead. Rebecca could not hurt us. She had played her last joke as Maxim had said. She could do no more to us now. In ten minutes Maxim came back again.

'Well,' I said, my own voice sounding far away, 'how was Frank?'

'Frank was all right,' said Maxim. 'He was at the office, been waiting there for me to telephone him ever since four o'clock. I told him what had happened. He sounded glad, relieved.'

'Yes,' I said.

'Something rather odd though,' said Maxim slowly, a line between his brows. 'He thinks Mrs Danvers has cleared out. She's gone, disappeared. She said nothing to anyone, but apparently she'd been packing up all day, stripping her room of things, and the fellow from the station came for her boxes at about four o'clock. Frith telephoned down to Frank about it, and Frank told Frith to ask Mrs Danvers to come down to him at the office. He waited, and she never came. About ten minutes before I rang up, Frith telephoned to Frank again and said there had been a long-distance call for Mrs Danvers which he had switched through to her room, and she had answered. This must have been about ten past six. At a quarter to seven he knocked on the door and found her room empty. Her bedroom too. They looked for her and could not find her. They think she's gone. She must have gone straight out of the house and through the woods. She never passed the lodge-gates.'

'Isn't it a good thing?' I said. 'It saves us a lot of trouble. We should have had to send her away, anyway. I believe she guessed, too. There was an expression on her face last night. I kept thinking of it, coming up in the car.'

'I don't like it,' said Maxim. 'I don't like it.'

'She can't do anything,' I argued. 'If she's gone, so much the better. It was Favell who telephoned of course. He must have told her about Baker. He would tell her what Colonel Julyan said. Colonel Julyan said if there was any attempt at blackmail we were to tell him. They won't dare do it. They can't. It's too dangerous.'

'I'm not thinking of blackmail,' said Maxim.

'What else can they do?' I said. 'We've got to do what Colonel Julyan said. We've got to forget it. We must not think about it any more. It's all over, darling, it's finished. We ought to go down on our knees and thank God that it's finished.'

Maxim did not answer. He was staring in front of him at nothing.

'Your lobster will be cold,' I said; 'eat it, darling. It will do you good, you want something inside you. You're tired.' I was using the words he had used to me. I felt better and stronger. It was I now who was taking care of him. He was tired, pale. I had got over my weakness and fatigue and now he was the one to suffer from reaction. It was just because he was empty, because he was tired. There was nothing to worry about at all. Mrs Danvers had gone. We should praise God for that, too. Everything had been made so easy for us, so very easy. 'Eat up your fish,' I said.

It was going to be very different in the future. I was not going to be nervous and shy with the servants any more. With Mrs Danvers gone I should learn bit by bit to control the house. I would go and interview the cook in the kitchen. They would like me, respect me. Soon it would be as though Mrs Danvers had never had command. I would learn more about the estate, too. I should ask Frank to explain things to me. I was sure Frank liked me. I liked him, too. I would go into things, and learn how they were managed. What they did at the farm. How the work in the grounds was planned. I might take to gardening myself, and in time have one or two things altered. That little square lawn outside the morning-room with the statue of the satyr. I did not like it. We would give the satyr away. There were heaps of things that I could do, little by little. People would come and stay and I should not mind. There would be the interest of seeing to their rooms, having flowers and books put, arranging the food. We would have children. Surely we would have children.

'Have you finished?' said Maxim suddenly. 'I don't think I want any more. Only coffee. Black, very strong, please, and the bill,' he added to the *maître d'hôtel*.

I wondered why we must go so soon. It was comfortable in the restaurant, and there was nothing to take us away. I liked sitting there, with my head against the sofa back, planning the future idly in a hazy pleasant way. I could have gone on sitting there for a long while.

I followed Maxim out of the restaurant, stumbling a little, and yawning. 'Listen,' he said, when we were on the pavement, 'do you think you could sleep in the car if I wrapped you up with the rug, and tucked you down in the back. There's the cushion there, and my coat as well.'

'I thought we were going to put up somewhere for the night?' I said blankly. 'One of those hotels one passes on the road.'

'I know,' he said, 'but I have this feeling I must get down tonight. Can't you possibly sleep in the back of the car?'

'Yes,' I said doubtfully. 'Yes, I suppose so.'

'If we start now, it's a quarter to eight, we ought to be there by half past two,' he said. 'There won't be much traffic on the road.'

'You'll be so tired,' I said. 'So terribly tired.'

'No,' he shook his head. 'I shall be all right. I want to get home. Something's wrong. I know it is. I want to get home.'

His face was anxious, strange. He pulled open the door and began arranging the rugs and the cushion at the back of the car.

'What can be wrong?' I said. 'It seems so odd to worry now, when everything's over. I can't understand you.'

He did not answer. I climbed into the back of the car and lay down with my legs tucked under me. He covered me with the rug. It was very comfortable. Much better than I imagined. I settled the pillow under my head.

'Are you all right?' he said; 'are you sure you don't mind?'

'No,' I said, smiling. 'I'm all right. I shall sleep. I don't want to stay anywhere on the road. It's much better to do this and get home. We'll be at Manderley long before sunrise.'

He got in in front and switched on the engine. I shut my eyes. The car drew away and I felt the slight jolting of the springs under my body. I pressed my face against the cushion. The motion of the car was rhythmic, steady, and the pulse of my mind beat with it. A hundred images came to me when I closed my eyes, things seen, things known, and things forgotten. They were jumbled together in a senseless pattern. The quill of Mrs Van Hopper's hat, the hard straight-backed chairs in Frank's dining-room, the wide window in the west wing at Manderley, the salmon-coloured frock of the smiling lady at the fancy-dress ball, a peasant-girl in a road near Monte Carlo.

Sometimes I saw Jasper chasing butterflies across the lawns; sometimes I saw Doctor Baker's Scotch terrier scratching his ear beside a deck-chair. There was the postman who had pointed out the house to us today, and there was Clarice's mother wiping a chair for me in the back parlour. Ben smiled at me, holding winkles in his hands, and the bishop's wife asked me if I would stay to tea. I could feel the cold comfort of my sheets in my own bed, and the gritty shingle in the cove. I could smell the bracken in the woods, the wet moss, and the dead azalea petals. I fell into a strange broken sleep, waking now and again to the reality of my narrow cramped position and the sight of Maxim's back in front of me. The dusk had turned to darkness. There were the lights of passing cars upon the road. There were villages with drawn curtains and little lights behind them. And I would move, and turn upon my back, and sleep again.

I saw the staircase at Manderley, and Mrs Danvers standing at the top in her black dress, waiting for me to go to her. As I climbed the stairs she backed under the archway and disappeared. I looked for her and I could not find her. Then her face looked at me through a hollow door and I cried out and she had gone again.

'What's the time?' I called. 'What's the time?'

Maxim turned round to me, his face pale and ghostly in the darkness of the car. 'It's half past eleven,' he said. 'We're over half-way already. Try and sleep again.'

'I'm thirsty,' I said.

He stopped at the next town. The man at the garage said his wife had not gone to bed and she would make us some tea. We got out of the car and stood inside the garage. I stamped up and down to bring the blood back to my hands and feet. Maxim smoked a cigarette. It was cold. A bitter wind blew in through the open garage door, and rattled the corrugated roof. I shivered, and buttoned up my coat.

'Yes, it's nippy tonight,' said the garage man, as he wound the petrol pump. 'The weather seemed to break this afternoon. It's the last of the heat waves for this summer. We shall be thinking of fires soon.'

'It was hot in London,' I said.

'Was it?' he said. 'Well, they always have the extremes up there, don't they? We get the first of the bad weather down here. It will blow hard on the coast before morning.'

His wife brought us the tea. It tasted of bitter wood, but it was hot. I drank it greedily, thankfully. Already Maxim was glancing at his watch.

'We ought to be going,' he said. 'It's ten minutes to twelve.'

I left the shelter of the garage reluctantly. The cold wind blew in my face. The stars raced across the sky. There were threads of cloud too. 'Yes,' said the garage man, 'summer's over for this year.'

We climbed back into the car. I settled myself once more under the rug. The car went on. I shut my eyes. There was the man with the wooden leg winding his barrel organ, and the tune of 'Roses in Picardy' hummed in my head against the jolting of the car. Frith and Robert carried the tea into the library. The woman at the lodge nodded to me abruptly, and called her child into the house. I saw the model boats in the cottage in the cove, and the feathery dust. I saw the cobwebs stretching from the little masts. I heard the rain upon the roof and the sound of the sea. I wanted to get to the Happy Valley and it was not there. There were woods about me, there was no Happy Valley. Only the dark trees and the young bracken. The owls hooted. The moon was shining in the windows of Manderley. There were nettles in the garden, ten foot, twenty foot high.

'Maxim!' I cried. 'Maxim!'

'Yes,' he said. 'It's all right, I'm here.'

'I had a dream,' I said. 'A dream.'

'What was it?' he said.

'I don't know. I don't know.'

Back again into the moving unquiet depths. I was writing letters in the morning-room. I was sending out invitations. I wrote them all myself with a thick black pen. But when I looked down to see what I had written it was not my small square handwriting at all, it was long, and slanting, with curious pointed strokes. I pushed the cards away from the blotter and hid them. I got up and went to the looking-glass. A face stared back at me that was not my own. It was very pale, very lovely, framed in a cloud of dark hair. The eyes narrowed and smiled. The lips parted. The face in the glass stared back at me and laughed. And I saw then that she was sitting on a chair before the dressing-table in her bedroom, and Maxim was brushing her hair. He held her hair in his hands, and as he brushed it he wound it slowly into a thick rope. It twisted like a snake, and he took hold of it with both hands and smiled at Rebecca and put it round his neck.

'No,' I screamed. 'No, no. We must go to Switzerland. Colonel Julyan said we must go to Switzerland.'

I felt Maxim's hand upon my face. 'What is it?' he said. 'What's the matter?'

I sat up and pushed my hair away from my face.

'I can't sleep,' I said. 'It's no use.'

'You've been sleeping,' he said. 'You've slept for two hours. It's quarter past two. We're four miles the other side of Lanyon.'

It was even colder than before. I shuddered in the darkness of the car.

'I'll come beside you,' I said. 'We shall be back by three.'

I climbed over and sat beside him, staring in front of me through the wind-screen. I put my hand on his knee. My teeth were chattering.

'You're cold,' he said.

'Yes,' I said.

The hills rose in front of us, and dipped, and rose again. It was quite dark. The stars had gone.

'What time did you say it was?' I asked.

'Twenty past two,' he said.

'It's funny,' I said. 'It looks almost as though the dawn was breaking over there, beyond those hills. It can't be though, it's too early.'

'It's the wrong direction,' he said, 'you're looking west.'

'I know,' I said. 'It's funny, isn't it?'

He did not answer and I went on watching the sky. It seemed to get lighter even as I stared. Like the first red streak of sunrise. Little by little it spread across the sky.

'It's in winter you see the northern lights, isn't it?' I said. 'Not in summer?'

'That's not the northern lights,' he said. 'That's Manderley.'

I glanced at him and saw his face. I saw his eyes.

'Maxim,' I said. 'Maxim, what is it?'

He drove faster, much faster. We topped the hill before us and saw Lanyon lying in a hollow at our feet. There to the left of us was the silver streak of the river, widening to the estuary at

427

Kerrith six miles away. The road to Manderley lay ahead. There was no moon. The sky above our heads was inky black. But the sky on the horizon was not dark at all. It was shot with crimson, like a splash of blood. And the ashes blew towards us with the salt wind from the sea.

# Afterword

Rebecca, first published in 1938, was Daphne du Maurier's fifth novel. It was to become the most famous of her many books; over sixty years later, it continues to haunt, fascinate and perplex a new generation of readers. Yet its enduring popularity has not been matched by critical acclaim: *Rebecca*, from the time of first publication, has been woefully and wilfully underestimated. It has been dismissed as a gothic romance, as 'women's fiction' – with such prejudicial terms, of course, giving clues as to why the novel has been so unthinkingly misinterpreted. Re-examination of this strange, angry and prescient novel is long overdue. A re-appraisal of it should begin, perhaps, with the circumstances under which it was written.

Du Maurier began planning it at a difficult point in her life: only a few years had passed since the death of her adored but dominating father, the actor-manager Gerald du Maurier. She was pregnant with her second child when at the planning stage of the book, and, by the time she actually began writing, at the age of thirty, she was in Egypt, where her husband, Frederick Browning, an officer in the Grenadier Guards, had been posted with his battalion. What many would regard as the quintessential Cornish novel was therefore begun, and much of it written, not in Cornwall, not even in England, but in the fierce heat of an Egyptian summer, in a city du Maurier came to loathe: Alexandria.

Du Maurier was desperately homesick; her longing for her home by the sea in Cornwall was, she wrote, 'like a pain under the heart continually'. She was also unhappy: this was the first time she had ever accompanied her husband on a posting, and she hated the role forced upon her in Egypt by her marriage.

Shy, and socially reclusive, she detested the small talk and the endless receptions she was expected to attend and give, in her capacity of commanding officer's wife. This homesickness and her resentment of wifely duties, together with a guilty sense of her own ineptitude when performing them, were to surface in *Rebecca*: they cluster around the two female antagonists of the novel, the living and obedient second wife, Mrs de Winter, and the dead, rebellious and indestructible first wife, Rebecca. Both women reflect aspects of du Maurier's own complex personality: she divided herself between them, and the splitting, doubling and mirroring devices she uses throughout the text destabilise it but give it resonance. With *Rebecca* we enter a world of dreams and daydreams, but they always threaten to tip over into nightmare.

At first, du Maurier struggled with her material. The novel had a false start, which she described as a 'literary miscarriage' – a revealing metaphor, given the centrality of pregnancy and childbirth to the plot and themes of *Rebecca*, and given the fact that du Maurier's second child, another daughter – she had hoped for a son – was born during the time she worked on it. She tore up the initial (fifteen-thousand-word-long) attempt at the book, the first time she had ever done this, and an indication, perhaps, of the difficulties she sensed in this material. She began again while still in Egypt, and finally completed it on her return to England.

She sent it off to her publisher, Victor Gollancz, in April 1938. He knew little about the novel at that stage: du Maurier had briefly described it to him as 'a sinister tale about a woman who marries a widower . . . Psychological and rather macabre'. Gollancz must have been somewhat nervous as he awaited that manuscript. Du Maurier's previous novel, *Jamaica Inn*, had sold more copies than any of her previous books, bringing her to the brink of bestsellerdom; but she was an unpredictable author, and difficult to categorise. Two of her earlier novels, *I'll Never Be Young Again* and *The Progress of Julius*, had sold much less well, and the sexual frankness of both books – especially the latter, which dealt with father–daughter incest – had been met with distaste from critics.

Gollancz's reaction to *Rebecca* was relief, and jubilation. A 'rollicking success' was forecast by him, by his senior editor, and by everyone to whom advance copies were sent. Prior to publication, du Maurier's was the lone dissenting voice in this chorus of approbation. She feared her novel was 'too gloomy' to be popular, and she believed the ending was 'too grim' to appeal to readers. Gollancz ignored such pessimism: *Rebecca* was touted to booksellers as an 'exquisite love story' with a 'brilliantly created atmosphere of suspense'. It was promoted and sold, in short, as a gothic romance.

On publication, some critics acknowledged the book's haunting power and its vice-like narrative grip, but – perhaps misled by the book's presentation, or prejudiced by the gender of the author – they delved no deeper. Most reviews dismissed the novel with that belittling diminutive only ever used for novels by women: it was just a 'novelette'. Readers ignored them: *Rebecca* became an immediate and overwhelming commercial success.

The novel went through twenty-eight printings in four years in Britain alone. It became a bestseller in America, and it sold in vast numbers throughout Europe. It continues to sell well to this day: in the sixty-four years since first publication, it has never been out of print. Its readership was swelled by the Oscar-winning success of Hitchcock's memorable expressionistic film version, and has been increased since by countless theatre, radio and television dramatisations. Like Margaret Mitchell's *Gone With the Wind* (1936, and another novel that concerns women and property), *Rebecca* has made a transition rare in popular fiction: it has passed from bestseller, to cult novel, to cultural classic status. Why is that? What is it about this novel that has *always* spoken to readers, if not to critics?

*Rebecca* is the story of two women, one man, and a house. Of the four, as Hitchcock once observed, the house, Manderley, is the dominant presence. Although never precisely located (the word 'Cornwall' is never actually used in the novel), its minutely detailed setting is clearly that of an actual house, Menabilly. Du Maurier discovered Menabilly, on its isolated headland near Fowey, as a young woman, when she first went to live in Cornwall; she wrote a magical account of the first time she saw it. Eventually, after the war, and after *Rebecca*, she was able to lease the house. She lived there for over twenty years, using it as the location for several other novels; it lit her imagination, and obsessed her, for much of her life. Du Maurier's own term for Menabilly was the 'House of Secrets', and when she placed it at the heart of *Rebecca*, she created an elliptical, shifting, and deeply secretive book. The plot hinges upon secrets; the novel's milieu is that of an era and social class that, in the name of good manners, rarely allowed the truth to be expressed; and suppression coupled with a fearful secretiveness are its female narrator's most marked characteristics.

By the time du Maurier wrote *Rebecca*, she had mastered the techniques of popular fiction. Her novel came well disguised as bestseller material: an intriguing story of love and murder – a 'page-turner' in modern parlance. But examine the subtext of *Rebecca* and you find a perturbing, darker construct, part Grimm's fairytale, part Freudian family romance. You also find a very interesting literary mirroring, of course, an early example of intertextuality – and that is rare in a 'popular' novel, certainly one this early. *Rebecca* reflects *Jane Eyre*, but the reflection is imperfect, and deliberately so, forcing us to re-examine our assumptions about both novels, and in particular, their treatment of insanity and women.

None of these aspects of *Rebecca* was noticed by critics at the time of publication – and few have paused to examine them since. Instead, Charlotte Brontë's gifts were used as a stick with which to beat an impious, hubristic du Maurier over the head: she was Brontë's inferior, how could she dare to annex a classic novel? The critics moved swiftly on, not pausing for thought, and shunted du Maurier into the category of 'romance' writer – a category she detested and resented, but from which she was never able to escape. Thus was du Maurier 'named' as a writer. The question of how we name and identify – and the ironies and inexactitudes inherent in that process – is, of course, of central importance in *Rebecca*. Both female characters – one dead, one alive – derive their surname, as they do their status, from their husband. The first wife, Rebecca, is vivid and vengeful and, though dead, indestructible: her name lives on in the book's title. The second wife, the drab shadowy creature who narrates this story, remains nameless. We learn that she has a 'lovely and unusual' name, and that it was her father who gave it her. The only other identity she has, was also bestowed by a man – she is a *wife*, she is Mrs de Winter.

That a narrator perceived as a heroine should be *nameless* was a source of continuing fascination to du Maurier's readers. It also fascinated other writers – Agatha Christie corresponded with du Maurier on the subject – and throughout her life, du Maurier was plagued with letters seeking an explanation. Her stock reply was that she found the device technically interesting. The question is not a trivial one, for it takes us straight to the core of *Rebecca* – and that may well be the reason why du Maurier, a secretive woman and a secretive artist, avoided answering it.

The unnamed narrator of *Rebecca* begins her story with a dream, with a first sentence that has become famous: *Last night I dreamt I went to Manderley again*. Almost all the brief first chapter is devoted to that dream, describing her progress up the long winding drive, by moonlight, to Manderley itself. The imagery, of entwined trees and encroaching undergrowth that have 'mated', is sexual; the style is slightly scented and overwritten, that of a schoolgirl, trying to speak poetically, and struggling to impress. Moving forward, with a sense of anticipation and revulsion, the dream narrator first sees Manderley as intact; then, coming closer, she realises her mistake: she is looking at a ruin, at the shell of a once-great house. With this realisation – one of key importance to the novel – the dreamer wakes. She confirms that Manderley has indeed been destroyed, and that the dream was a true one. ('Dreaming true' was a term invented by du Maurier's grandfather, George du Maurier, author of *Trilby*; it was a concept that fascinated her all her life. Daphne was aware of Freud and Jung: George was not.)

Du Maurier's narrator can now begin to tell her story – and she does so in cyclic way; she begins at the end, with herself and her husband Maxim de Winter living in exile in Europe, for reasons that as yet are unclear. Their activities, as they move from hotel to hotel, sound like those of two elderly ex-pats. They follow the cricket, take afternoon tea; the wife selects dull newspaper articles to read to her husband, since – again for reasons unexplained – both find dullness reassuring and safe. The narrator describes a routine of stifling monotony, but does so in terms that are relentlessly optimistic and trite. This may be a marriage but it is one carefully devoid of passion, and apparently without sex.

It therefore comes as a considerable shock to the reader to discover, as the story loops back to this couple's first meeting, that this narrator is *young*. The lapse of time between this present and the past she will now describe is unspecified, but it is clearly only a few years. This makes de Winter a man of about fifty, and his childless friendless wife around twenty-five. Their life in Europe is never mentioned again, but *this* is the 'grim ending' to which du Maurier referred. It is easy to forget, as the drama unfolds, that the aftermath for the de Winters will be exile, ennui, and putting a brave face on a living death.

The plot of *Rebecca* thereafter will be familiar: it has echoes of *Cinderella* and *Bluebeard* as well as *Jane Eyre*. The narrator, working as a paid companion to a monstrous and tyrannical American, and staying with her in a palatial hotel in Monte Carlo, meets Maxim de Winter, a widower twice her age, who is the owner of a legendary house, Manderley. She marries him after a few weeks' acquaintanceship, returns with him to Manderley, and there becomes obsessed with Rebecca, his first wife. Patching together a portrait of Rebecca in her mind, she creates a chimera – and an icon of womanhood. Rebecca, she

434

comes to believe, was everything she herself is not: she was a perfect hostess, a perfect sexual partner, a perfect chatelaine and a perfect wife. This image she later understands is false, but before she can grasp the truth about Rebecca's life, she has first to be told the truth about her death. Rebecca did not drown in a yachting accident, as everyone believes: she was killed by de Winter, who from the days of his honeymoon (also in Monte Carlo) loathed his wife.

Mrs de Winter, once enlightened, accepts without question her husband's version of her predecessor as a promiscuous (possibly bisexual) woman, who was pregnant with another man's child when he killed her, and who taunted him that she would pass off this child as his. De Winter's confession – and a very hollow melodramatic confession it is – is accompanied by a declaration of love – the first he has made, despite months of marriage. There is also the suggestion – very subtle but it is there – that their marriage is consummated, and for the first time, after this confession (note the references to single beds in the novel, and the heroine's embarrassment when there is speculation as to whether she is yet pregnant – something that recurs frequently. Modesty may explain that embarrassment, but in a du Maurier novel, it may well not).

Without hesitation, Mrs de Winter then gives her husband her full support – her one concern from then onwards is to conceal the truth and protect her husband. Thus, she becomes, in legal terms, an accessory after the fact: more importantly, she makes a moral choice. This is the crux of du Maurier's novel: de Winter has confessed, after all, to a *double* murder. He believes he has killed not only Rebecca, but also the child she was carrying – a heinous crime, by any standards. Here, du Maurier was taking a huge risk, particularly in a novel aimed at a popular market. To have an apparent 'hero' revealed as a double murderer, one prepared to perjure himself, moreover, to save his neck, could have shocked and alienated readers in their thousands. Hitchcock, when he came to film the novel two years later, ran a mile from this scenario, which he knew would be unacceptable. In his version, there *is* no murder, and Maxim's crime is at worst manslaughter since, during a quarrel, Rebecca falls, and (conveniently and mortally) injures herself.

How does du Maurier occlude this issue? She does it with immense cleverness: so involved have we, the readers, become in Mrs de Winter's predicament, and so sympathetic to her, that we conjoin with her. Because she loves her guilty husband, and he appears to love her, we too begin to hope that he will escape justice. If Mrs de Winter is culpable, therefore, so is the reader who endorses her actions – and that issue ticks away like a time bomb under the remaining chapters of the book.

This final section of the novel, which is brilliantly plotted, concerns de Winter's attempts to suppress the truth, and – with his loyal wife's assistance – escape the hangman. And so he does, but not without cost. Returning to Manderley from London, with information that gives Rebecca a motive for suicide and thus saves him, both partners are uneasy. De Winter senses impending disaster; in the back of the car, his wife is asleep, dreaming that she and Rebecca have become one, and that their hair, long and black, as Rebecca's was, is winding about de Winter's neck, like a noose.

Mrs de Winter dreams vividly twice in the novel, once at the beginning and once at the end: each time, the dream conveys a truth to her that her conscious mind cannot, or will not, accept. She prefers the sketchy and cliché-ridden visions she summons up when she daydreams – and she daydreams incessantly. The vision she has just had, of Rebecca and herself united, of first and second wives merged into one dangerous female avatar, she instantly rejects. Her husband halts the car on a crest near their home; the night sky beyond is lit with a red glow. (The colour red is linked with Rebecca throughout the novel.) His wife assumes it is the dawn, but de Winter understands at once: Manderley, his ancestral home, is burning. This destruction was prefigured in the dream with which the novel opened, and the literal agent of the destruction (possibly Mrs Danvers) is far less important than the poetic agent, which is Rebecca. Like some avenging angel, Rebecca has marshalled the elements: she has risen from the sea to wreak revenge by fire – thus echoing, and not for the first time, her literary ancestress, that madwoman in the attic, the first Mrs Rochester.

In this way, and very abruptly, the novel ends; it has come full circle. It is melodramatic in places, of course (even *Jane Eyre* cannot entirely escape that criticism). But it is remarkable, given the plot, how consistently and skilfully du Maurier skirts melodrama. What interested her as a novelist can be summarised by the distinction that Charlotte Brontë drew between writing that was 'real' and writing that was 'true'. There *is* realism in *Rebecca*; the mores, snobberies and speech patterns of the class and era du Maurier is describing are, for instance, sharply observed. The elements that give *Rebecca* its force, however, owe nothing to realism: its power lies in its imagery, its symmetry, its poetry – and that poetry is intensely female. The plot of *Rebecca* may be as unlikely as the plot of a fairytale, but that does not alter the novel's mythic resonance and psychological truth.

One way of reading *Rebecca* is as a convention-ridden love story, in which the good woman triumphs over the bad by winning a man's love: this version is the one our nameless narrator would have us accept, and it is undoubtedly the reading that made *Rebecca* a bestseller. Another approach is to see the novel's imaginative links, not just with the work of earlier female novelists, such as Charlotte Brontë, but also with later work, in particular Sylvia Plath's late poems. *Rebecca* is narrated by a masochistic woman, who is desperate for the validation provided by a man's love – a woman seeking an authoritarian father surrogate, or, as Plath expressed it, a 'man in black with a Meinkampf look'. Her search for this man involves both self-effacement and abnegation, as it does for any woman who 'adores a Fascist'. She duly finds her ideal in de Winter, whose last name indicates sterility, coldness, an unfruitful season, and whose Christian name – Maxim, as she always abbreviates it – is a synonym for a rule of conduct. It is also the name of a weapon – a machine gun.

This woman, not surprisingly, views Rebecca as a rival; what she refuses to perceive is that Rebecca is also her twin, and ultimately her alter ego. The two wives have actually suffered very similar fates. Both were taken as brides to Manderley – a male preserve, as the first syllable of its name (like Menabilly's) suggests. Both were marginalised within the confines of the house – Rebecca in the west wing with its view of her symbol, the sea, and the second wife in the east wing, overlooking the confines of a rose garden. The difference between them lies in their reactions: the second wife gladly submits, allowing her identity to be determined by her husband, and by the class attitudes and value systems he embraces. Rebecca has dared to be an unchaste wife; she has broken the 'rules of conduct' Maxim lives by. Her ultimate sin is to threaten the system of primogeniture. That sin, undermining the entire patriarchal edifice that is Manderley, cannot be forgiven – and Rebecca dies for it.

The response of Mrs de Winter to Rebecca's rebellion is deeply ambivalent, and it is this ambivalence that fuels the novel. Her apparent reaction is that of a conventional woman of her time: abhorrence. Yet there are indications throughout the text that the second Mrs de Winter would like to emulate Rebecca, even to be her – and these continue, even when she knows Rebecca has broken every male-determined rule as to a woman's behaviour. Although Rebecca is dead, is never seen, and has in theory been forever silenced, Mrs de Winter's obsession with her insures that Rebecca will triumph over anonymity and effacement. Even a bullet through the heart, and burial at sea cannot quench her vampiric power. Again, one is reminded of Plath's embodiment of amoral, anarchic female force – *I rise with my red hair/And I eat men like air.* Within the conventions of a story, Rebecca's pallid successor is able to do what she dare not do in life: celebrate her predecessor.

She does so with cunning and with power (du Maurier, of course, is pulling the strings here). Long after the book has been closed, which character reverberates in the memory? Rebecca. And which of the two women are readers drawn to, which of these polar opposites fascinates and attracts? Rebecca, again, I would say – certainly for modern readers. But I think that was probably true for readers in 1938 too: thanks to the cunning of du Maurier's narrative structure, they were able to condemn Rebecca (a promiscuous woman – what other option did they have?); but secretly respond to the anger, rebellion and vengefulness she embodies.

There is a final twist to *Rebecca* and it is a covert one. Maxim de Winter kills not one wife, but *two*. He murders the first with a gun, and the second by slower, more insidious methods. The second Mrs de Winter's fate, for which she prepares herself throughout the novel, is to be subsumed by her husband. Following him into that hellish exile glimpsed in the opening chapters, she becomes again what she was when she first met him – the paid companion to a petty tyrant. For humouring his whims, and obeying his every behest, her recompense is not money, but 'love' – and the cost is her identity. This is the final bitter irony of this novel, and the last of its many reversals. A story that ostensibly attempts to bury Rebecca, in fact resurrects her, and renders her unforgettable, whereas Mrs de Winter, our pale, ghostly and timid narrator, fades from our view; it is *she* who is the dying woman in this novel. By extension – and this is daring on du Maurier's part – her obedient beliefs, her unquestioning subservience to the male, are dying with her.

The themes of *Rebecca* – identity, doubling, the intimate linkage between love and murder – recur again and again in du Maurier's work. That the circumstances of her own life were the source of many of those themes is, I think, unquestionable. That she often chose to explore those themes within the confines of a story about love and marriage is perhaps not accidental either; there had always been duality in her life – her bisexuality ensured that; after her marriage, that sense of a dual identity deepened, and was to feed all her fiction.

Du Maurier had been born into a rich, privileged but unconventional and bohemian family. Her father, Gerald, was notorious for his affairs – and for running back to his wife after them. She and her sisters grew up surrounded by the writers, actors and artists who were their parents' close friends. Before du Maurier was twenty-one, she had had several affairs with men and at least one with a woman. Yet she chose to marry a career soldier in one of England's most elite regiments, a man who was a traditionalist to his fingertips, a stickler for correct dress and behaviour, a man who was deeply shocked when – prior to their marriage – she suggested they should sleep together. After a long and distinguished military career, 'Boy' Browning, as he was nicknamed, was to go on to become a courtier, spending much of his time in London, while his wife remained at Menabilly. There can be no question of their love and loyalty for each other: long after he died, du Maurier remained fiercely defensive of her husband. But the differences between them were marked, and their expectations of marriage perhaps very different. Eventually that caused problems: there were infidelities on both sides, and later in life, Browning began to drink heavily. Meanwhile, du Maurier had two identities: she was a Lieutenant General's wife, and later, Lady Browning: she was also an internationally celebrated writer, and finally a Dame of the British Empire. That she found it difficult to reconcile the demands of two *personae* is apparent in her fiction, above all in *Rebecca*, but also in her often bitter, and shocking, short stories.

Throughout her life, she was torn between the need to be a wife and the necessity of being a writer – and she seems to have regarded those roles as irreconcilable. Half accepting society's (and her husband's) interpretation of ideal womanhood, yet rebelling against it and rejecting it, she came to regard herself as a 'half-breed' who was 'unnatural'. To her, both her lesbianism and her art were a form of aberrance: they both sprang, she believed, from a force inside her that she referred to as the 'boy in the box'. Sometimes she fought against this incubus – and sometimes she gloried in him.

Given those beliefs, the dualism, the gender-blurring and the *splitting* that are so apparent in *Rebecca* become more understandable. Du Maurier was wrestling with her own demons here, and when she gave aspects of herself to the two women who

440

are the pillars of her narrative she was entering into an area of deeply personal psychological struggle. She gave her own shyness and social awkwardness to Mrs de Winter. She gave her independence, her love of the sea, her expertise as a sailor, her sexual fearlessness, and even her bisexuality (strongly hinted at in the novel, if not spelled out) to Rebecca. It is for readers to decide where their own sympathies lie – and du Maurier's.

I would say that ultimately it is with Rebecca, with the angry voice of female dissent, that du Maurier's instinctive sympathy lies. But it is possible to argue the opposite view – one of the factors that makes *Rebecca* such a rewarding novel to reread and re-examine. One thing is certain: *Rebecca* is a deeply subversive work, one that undermines the very genre to which critics consigned it. Far from being an 'exquisite' love story, *Rebecca* raises questions about women's acquiescence to male values that are as pertinent today as they were sixty-four years ago. We may have moved on from the subservience of Mrs de Winter, but our enfranchisement is scarcely complete. A glance at the current bestseller lists will only confirm that the sly suggestion underlying *Rebecca* remains valid after sixty-four years: both in life and in bookstores, women continue to buy romance.

*Sally Beauman*
*London 2002*

virago

To buy any of our books and to find out more
about Virago Press and Virago Modern Classics,
our authors and titles, as well as events and
book club forum, visit our websites

**www.virago.co.uk**
**www.littlebrown.co.uk**

and follow us on Twitter

**@ViragoBooks**

To order any Virago titles p & p free in the UK,
please contact our mail order supplier on:

**+ 44 (0)1832 737525**

Customers not based in the UK should contact
the same number for appropriate postage
and packing costs.

Daphne du maurier

Daphne du maurier

Daphne du maurier

Daphne du maurier

Daphne du maurier

Daphne du maurier

Daphne du maurier

Daphne du maurier

Daphne du maurier

Daphne du maurier

Daphne du maurier

Daphne du maurier

maurier

Daphne du maun

Daphne du maurier

maurier

Daphne du man

Daphne du maurier

maurier

Daphne du man